# A Capable Woman

Catherine Bridwell

This book is a work of fiction. Names, characters, places, and incidents are the product of the author's imagination or are used fictitiously. Any resemblance to actual events, locales, persons, living or dead, is coincidental.

A Capable Woman

Published by Catherine Bridwell
Jerome, Idaho 83338
catherinelbridwell@gmail.com

Edited by JoEllen Claypool
Cover Designed by Catherine Bridwell. All rights reserved.
Cover Photo by Wendy Carson. All rights reserved.

Printed in the United States of America by Kindle Direct Publishing
January 2021

ISBN: 978-1-7336218-0-9
LCCN: 2019903827

# DEDICATION

This book is dedicated to

Elizabeth, Hannah, and Mary Catherine

# CONTENTS

# ACKNOWLEDGMENTS

Special thanks to Mary Catherine Lakey and Jan Bellin, my beta readers who helped edit.

This book wouldn't have been possible without JoEllen Claypool, who took my story from a manuscript to a published novel.

"Who can find a capable wife?
She is far more precious than jewels.
The heart of her husband trusts in her,
and he will not lack anything good.

She rewards him with good, not evil,
all the days of her life. [...]

Strength and honor are her clothing,
and she can laugh at the time to come.
She opens her mouth with wisdom
and loving instruction is on her tongue.
She watches over the activities of her household
and is never idle.

Her sons rise up and call her blessed.
Her husband also praises her:
"Many women are capable,
but you surpass them all!"
Charm is deceptive and beauty is fleeting,
but a woman who fears the LORD will be praised.

Give her the reward of her labor,
and let her works praise her at the city gates."

–Proverbs 31:10-12, 25-31
Holman Christian Standard Bible (HCSB)

# CHAPTER 1

Maggie thinks silence is more than just absence of sound. It's a physical presence as well—a weight that sinks into her ears and then her head before slithering with a thump into her chest, causing her stomach to clench and burn and her heart to stammer. It's worse at night when the house stops creaking and popping from the loss of the sun's heat. Then the silence not only fills her body, but the house becomes the silence and the very walls lean closer with the weight of it.

Sleeping has become a futile effort. She lies awake night after night smothered by the silence, her eyes burning with fatigue, yet unable to give in to the dark and the silence. She thinks if she sleeps the silence might become so heavy it will bury her. She will be in the dark forever like Clark is, so she keeps her vigil against the quiet of the night.

Only when the birds start to sing in the pre-dawn light will she finally close her eyes and give in to her body's cry for rest for a few hours. She doesn't know how long she can do this. She has been told sleep deprivation can cause insanity, but when a person is already crazy with grief, how would she know the difference?

Once the day starts, she is better. A shower, a cup of tea, then off to school where it is never quiet even when it's supposed to be. In her classroom, she is still herself, still Mrs. Sullivan, her identity intact. Outside  those walls, she becomes someone she doesn't know—a victim of tragedy, a widow, someone who has suffered a loss, someone she doesn't know how to be.

The energy of the kids in her class keeps her going until the last bell rings. By the time she finishes tidying her room and

1

correcting the day's papers the school is empty and then silence begins its descent there too. She hurries to lay out the next day's lessons and materials and drives home to more silence.

A quick change of clothes and she is stretching for her daily run. She started running again in those first terrible days when she needed an outlet for the grief and anger coursing through her body. She has been running farther and farther each day, hoping to become so tired she won't hear the silence, but so far it's not working very well. Tonight, for instance, her body is desperately tired, but her brain is whirling, whirling, whirling, and waiting for the weight of the silence to break down her defenses. Then the memories come thick and fast, a storm of faces and emotions that floods her mind as she recalls again the events of that awful day.

*Six weeks ago . . .*

Maggie Sullivan was teaching school on a normal Wednesday when her world was set adrift by a knock at her classroom door. She opened the door. As she stepped out, she saw the principal, Mrs. Thompson, standing in the hallway with one of the local deputies. This was not that unusual since even sixth graders these days occasionally had a brush with the law. The look on the principal's face told her something more serious was going on.

"Maggie, would you please step outside and shut the door? Deputy Hill needs to talk to you," Mrs. Thompson said quietly.

The police officer cleared his throat. Looking her in the eye, he said, "Mrs. Sullivan, I have some bad news. Your husband was in an accident today, and I'm sorry to tell you he was killed."

Maggie heard the words he said, but at some point while he was speaking they ceased to make sense. She heard an odd roaring sound in her head and then the hallway was growing dark around the edges as she felt her knees buckle. Her vision went gray and the next thing she remembered was the police officer saying, "Just lie still and take some deep breaths." She was on the floor in the hallway with the officer and her principal leaning over her. Gradually her head cleared and she was able to sit up without fainting again.

Maggie said, "I thought I heard you say my husband was

killed in an accident." She looked at Deputy Hill.

He looked away before finally bringing his eyes back to hers.

That averted glance told her what she needed to know—this was real. She said, "I think I'm going to throw up," and then she did. While she was heaving up her lunch, she felt as if she was watching herself from a distance, and her mind kept a running commentary. *That's just great. Way to make a bad situation even worse. You know the hall will smell like puke for a week.*

Several minutes later, with her rebellious stomach in control momentarily, she got shakily to her feet with the help of Officer Hill and Mrs. Thompson and was led down the hall into the principal's office. Once Maggie was seated, she asked for the details of what had happened to Clark.

Officer Hill informed her that while Clark was driving to a job site a few minutes after one o'clock this afternoon, he was hit broadside by a pickup that ran a stop sign and was killed instantly. The driver of the pickup, a young farmer she knew slightly, was unhurt. Maggie thought vaguely she should probably cry at some point during this recital of her husband's last moments, but everything seemed so far away she didn't seem to be able to.

"Where is he?" she asked.

"They took him to the hospital," replied Deputy Hill.

Looking at him, Maggie remembered how he used to chew his pencils in her classroom when he was in sixth grade. Now this former student was saying her beloved husband was never coming home. The incongruity seemed obscene and her stomach took another lurch. With great effort, she fought off the impending nausea and dropped her face in her hands, hiding from the world, her mind spinning frantically. *Now what? Now what? Now what? Focus, focus, focus . . . Oh, God, please don't let this be real . . . Now what? Focus Oh God, oh God, oh God.* Still the tears refused to come. Raising her head, she choked out, "I want to see him."

"I'll drive you there," replied Tommy Hill, her former student turned bearer of bad news.

"Is there anyone you'd like me to call?" Mrs. Thompson asked.

At first, Maggie didn't know what she could possibly mean, and then it struck her; she would have to tell the children and Clark's family that Clark was dead. The enormity of this task froze her in her chair, her mouth agape. With an effort, she mentally shook herself.

"Yes, please call my sister Tracy. The other calls are something I have to do myself . . . after I see him." Rising, she made her way to the door on numb legs, barely managing to remain upright.

The ride to the hospital was endless and, at the same time, passed more quickly than Maggie thought possible. The warm April breeze, smelling of spring, caressed her face as she walked through the parking lot with Deputy Hill, making it seem implausible that she was headed to see her husband's lifeless body.

Sympathetic glances shot her direction by the hospital staff pierced through her feeling of distance and she quickly looked away, keeping her face down as they continued through the halls. She blindly followed Deputy Hill's hand on her elbow, not looking or caring where they were going. Finally, they passed through a door into a room with a stretcher in the middle of it and there he was. Clark—the man she had adored since she was a twenty-two-year-old college student—lying there looking like he was asleep with a sheet pulled up to his chin.

Father Murphy stood by his side praying quietly. Pushing the officer's fingers from her arm and ignoring the outstretched hands of the priest, Maggie strode to the stretcher and looked down at Clark. His handsome face looked much the same as always, but as she gazed at him, a terrible blankness in his features told her, as nothing else could, that he was gone. She pulled the sheet back and looked at his shattered and broken body—the body she had held for uncountable nights and had expected to hold for many more.

Taking his cold hand in hers, she fell to her knees beside the stretcher and a cry rose up from her, coming from her heart and tearing her throat with its shrillness. Again, she had the eerie sensation she was watching herself from afar and could hear the same voice in the back of her head. *Gee, that's so dramatic. And what a lot of noise! Everyone will hear you and know that you lost it.* But she couldn't seem to stop.

Officer Hill and Father Murphy both started toward her, but Dr. Schultz, coming through the door in response to Maggie's tortured cry, pulled them back. "She needs to grieve," he said softly. "Let's leave her alone for a while." Stepping into the hall, the three men pulled the door shut behind them.

Maggie continued to wail, astonished at the level of sound that was spilling from her mouth, but still unable to stop. The cry was spiked with nails and filled up her throat with pain as it burst out, pulling her guts along with it. She could feel the cold, smooth floor under her knees, the cool hand of her dead husband, the hardness of his wedding band digging into her fingers as she held to him, and tried to tell herself to stop, but the sound continued to echo off the walls. Finally, she gave in to it and the world faded away for a while to just her and Clark and the agony of losing him.

Eventually, she became aware she had stopped shrieking and her knees were hurting from kneeling on the floor. Letting go of Clark's hand, she pushed up from the tiles and gathered herself together. On numb legs, she walked stiffly across the room and opened the door to see Dr. Schultz and Deputy Hill standing in the hall.

Dr. Schultz asked kindly, "How are you feeling, dear?"

Maggie replied, "I think I'm going to vomit. Where's the nearest bathroom?" She was escorted quickly to the restroom, where she fell on her knees once again. She heaved until there was nothing left in her stomach and then heaved some more. This pain seemed to dull the pain in her heart. Once the spasm had passed, she rose to her feet and stumbled to the sink to rinse her mouth and splash cold water on her face. A stranger in the mirror stared back at her—a stranger with a dry, terrible gaze and a white, haggard face with bruised-looking circles under the eyes. *So fast. So fast to go from a normal human being to a ghost.*

Those few minutes in the hospital bathroom were the last time she was alone for days after. Deputy Hill drove her back to the school and from there, Mrs. Thompson followed them to Maggie's house in Maggie's car. Tracy and her husband Danny were waiting to enfold Maggie in a warm hug that she barely felt and couldn't return.

"Maggie, we're so sorry," Tracy said, pulling back to look at her sister as she tucked a stray lock of hair behind Maggie's ear. This simple gesture undid Maggie completely and she clung to her older sister with dry eyes, searching vainly for comfort.

"Thanks, sis," Maggie eventually pulled away. "I know you and Danny loved Clark, and I'm sorry I can't help you through this," she continued. "I'm still reeling myself."

Tracy nodded and wiped her tear-filled eyes as Danny looked out the window and sniffed, trying to conceal his own grief.

Maggie went into her room and picked up the phone to call her children: Kevin with his wife and two little ones, Emma and

Ethan, in Seattle, and Maura with her husband and new baby, Patrick, in Boise. Afterward she could never clearly remember exactly how she found the words or even what she told them. What she remembered most was the feeling of being outside herself.

Kevin, his voice shaking with emotion, promised to book the first flight out in the morning. Maura, crying steadily through the conversation, said she would be on the road as soon as Tom was home from work and they could get the baby's things packed in the car. Maggie worried vaguely about Maura being home alone with Patrick until Tom could get there, but it wasn't something she could control, so she put it from her mind.

Next was the difficult task of notifying Clark's elderly parents, who lived in a care center in Weiser, and his siblings. He had two brothers, one in Nampa and one in Pocatello, and a sister in Lewiston. His parents seemed confused by the news, and Maggie wasn't sure if they realized completely what she was trying to tell them. Clark's siblings all told Maggie they would come immediately, which surprised her momentarily out of her daze. Clark was the youngest by 10 years and, as a result, wasn't especially close to his brothers and sister. Robert, the brother who lived in Nampa and was closest in age to Clark, agreed to pick up Mr. and Mrs. Sullivan, since neither one was able to drive, and give them a ride to Maggie's.

Once the necessary phone calls were finished Maggie felt at loose ends, unable to settle enough to sit but not focused enough to accomplish anything. Tracy suggested they start a pot of coffee, so Maggie gratefully occupied her shaking hands with this mundane task. As the fragrant brew was perking, she looked around the kitchen for something else to do. Clark's cup from his morning coffee was on the counter along with his spoon and bowl from his daily dose of his Honey Nut Cheerios. The sight doubled her over in agony. With a violent swipe, she knocked them to the floor, shattered crockery flying everywhere. Covering her face with embarrassment at this shocking behavior, she stood in her bright, cheerful kitchen, knowing her world would never be the same.

She felt Tracy again wrap her in a hug and stiffly endured the comfort being offered. Then she got out the broom and dustpan and cleaned up the mess. This triggered an obsessive bout of cleaning. Refusing all Tracy's offers of help, Maggie thoroughly cleaned the kitchen counters, sink and floors, the bathrooms, and the utility room. Dusting and vacuuming the entire house took up about 45 minutes, but the rest of the evening stretched before her.

Tracy, in the meantime, had made some phone calls of her own, and neighbors began to appear with covered dishes and cakes. Maggie was unable to bring herself to acknowledge them and continued her bizarre attack of cleanliness. She knew it was irrational and she should stop, but as her world spiraled into unknown waters, she needed to establish control of something, even something as trivial as housework. Eventually, everything was spotless and she was forced to stop, sitting numbly in a chair at the kitchen table while Tracy and Danny chatted with the neighbors.

That night Clark's parents, his brothers and sister, and Maura and her family arrived, and getting them all settled gave Maggie something to do. Maura, Tom, and the baby took Maura's old room. Mr. and Mrs. Sullivan were in Kevin's room. Robert and his wife were in the guest room. Phil, a bachelor, said he would sleep on the couch, and Evelyn and her husband opted for the local motel.

Everyone but Maggie was tearful and kept hugging each other, but she could not seem to find a way to connect with them. Even the sight of Maura's distraught face wasn't enough to bring Maggie out of the strange separation she was feeling.

The family ate a late dinner consisting of kind offerings from friends and neighbors and sat up into the night drinking and reminiscing about Clark. Maggie crept off to bed, leaving them to it, and fell into a deep, dreamless sleep.

The next day, Kevin, his wife Didi, and the children drove up from the airport in Boise and left their luggage at Tracy's where they were staying. Once they arrived, plans for the funeral service began. Maggie must have made the appropriate responses to it all, but later the whole thing was foggy, and she couldn't remember much about it.

An appointment at the funeral home was scheduled, a wake was planned for Friday, and friends and family were invited. An obituary was written and hymns and pallbearers were chosen. The phone rang nonstop, people were in and out of the house all day, and Maggie floated in a bubble, processing only as much as she was forced to. She spent a lot of time playing with her grandchildren.

On Friday, she rode to the funeral home with Maura and Kevin and watched her children choose a casket for their father. The funeral director met with them, first in his office to make sure of all the details for the service and then took them to a room filled with shiny new caskets in every style and color. Maggie felt as though she were buying a new car, overwhelmed by the patter coming from the man as he described the advantages and disadvantages of each model. She was horrified when he showed them the burial vaults—large, gray and unavoidable—into which the casket would be placed at the cemetery. The bald fact of Clark's death coalesced in a vision of what would happen to him once he was in the ground.

By the time they were finished, Maggie was shaking violently and feeling sick to her stomach again. Her throat cramped from unshed tears, but she refused to let them fall. It still seemed as unreal as a nightmare from which she couldn't exit.

When they returned to the house, she was kept busy getting ready for the wake, and the evening flew by in a flurry of preparation. People started arriving around 8:00 that night and by 9:30, alcohol was flowing freely and the house was full of those who had come to pay their respects to the family.

Maggie drifted from group to group, listening to stories about Clark. She felt as if the ice around her heart was gradually melting as the evening progressed and was able to offer some memories of her own. At one point, a feeling of impending doom overwhelmed her. She quickly handed Patrick back to Maura, rushed into the house, and shut herself in her room. The tears she had been postponing ever since she got the news caught up to her, and she curled into a ball on their bed and cried. She cried for her husband who would never get to do the things he wanted to do, for her children who had lost their father, and for her grandchildren who would grow up without knowing their grandfather. Mostly, though, she cried for herself as the loneliness and emptiness of life without Clark loomed ahead of her.

The funeral Mass took place as planned and, mercifully, the bubble separating Maggie from the events around her came back and lasted most of the way through the bereavement dinner. A burst of laughter from a group of people broke into her cotton-wool world, and she couldn't stay at the church a second longer. Her son drove her home where she lay down for a short nap and woke up four hours later. This proved to be the last good sleep Maggie would have for a long time.

The next day, everyone went home. Maura and Tracy protested they could stay if Maggie needed them, and Maggie assured them she would be fine. Wandering through the house, fluffing a pillow here, taking a dirty cup to the kitchen there, Maggie felt a sense of unreality descend. Could this really be her? A widow? Spending the rest of her life alone? What about their dreams and plans for the future? How would she cope by herself?

Thinking it might settle her nerves, she decided to clean the house. This led to mowing the lawn and then weeding the flower beds and sweeping the deck and sidewalks. By then, she was dirty, hot and tired, and night was falling. She had showered and was in bed when she remembered she hadn't eaten dinner. That was the first night she started to learn about silence, finally falling asleep around 3:00 a.m.

The next morning began Maggie's new life as a widow. Days faded together in a blur of trying to remember how to be normal—working, cleaning obsessively, keeping the house and yard spotless, washing the car, and anything else she could think of—hoping to be tired enough to rest and not remember every painful moment whenever she stopped moving.

The chirping of birds and the gray flush of dawn bring her back to the present, and she drifts off to the liquid warble of a blackbird. Three hours later, she wakes with a pounding headache and a sore throat. The spray of the shower hurts her skin, and she is sure she has a fever. However, it is harder to prepare for a sub than to go to work sick, so she takes some Tylenol and goes to school.

By afternoon, her throat hurts so badly she can hardly swallow, her head is throbbing with every heartbeat, and her eyes are hot and grainy. The drive home seems to take forever, the road a tunnel into a strange and alien world. She goes straight to bed and falls asleep immediately. She is dreaming, and it's a great dream.

*Clark is there, and he didn't die after all. She just didn't remember where to look for him, and he has been here in the house all along. She is so relieved and so full of joy to see him. Maggie touches his dear face and throws herself into his arms. He holds her close against his warm, strong body; she feels his breath ruffling her hair, his hands sliding up and down her back in comfort. She pulls away to look at him again; he is smiling.*

*He says, "I hear you've been having trouble sleeping."* She *nods and he tells her, "You know I'm okay, don't you? You don't have to worry about me now."*

*She stares at him in disbelief. If he's not dead, why is he saying this? She is filled with confusion. "I don't understand," she says.*

*"Yes, you do," he answers. "I can't be here with you anymore, but in a way, I'm always here with you. You need to let go and start to heal."*

*"I can't!" she cries. "It hurts too much!"*

*"Yes, you can. You are stronger than you know. I expect more from you than this drifting, floating life you're living." He pulls her into his arms again for a brief, hard hug, and strides away. "Live your life!" he calls as he walks from sight.*

*She stands there alone, unable to accept that he was here and now he's gone again, and a feeling of deep loss brings tears to her eyes. Faintly, like an echo, she hears his voice, "Live your life!"*

*A light shines ahead of her, moving closer and getting brighter, and then it is all around her, spinning and glowing, enveloping her with its warmth. Peace and joy fills her as she realizes the light is him—it is Clark, and he is surrounding her. She knows then he will never leave her. Not really. Not where it matters—in her heart and in her memories. She can go on now. She can stop letting his loss define her and remember his presence instead of his absence.*

Maggie sits upright in bed, gasping, looking frantically around the room for Clark. Gradually, she remembers he is gone; she was sick and laid down to rest, and now it is night. Then the dream comes back to her. She can recall every detail—the crispness of Clark's shirt, the roughness of his beard against the top of her head, the smell of him, the rightness of being held in his arms. The feeling of light and sense of peace is still there and she feels strengthened by the memory. She gets a drink of water and goes back to bed, where she falls asleep again immediately and sleeps until her alarm goes off in the morning.

When Maggie wakes up, the dream is still with her. She feels completely well and REAL for the first time in weeks, infused with peace and energy. There is still a lingering sadness she knows will be with her for the rest of her life, but she knows now she will be all right; she will live her life.

# CHAPTER 2

Maggie has a busy summer. She settles into a routine of exercise, cleaning, yard work, and volunteer work that most days leaves her tired enough to sleep. The pile of unopened mail and the unanswered calls on the voicemail she found impossible to deal with during the weeks when she wasn't sleeping have been taken care of. Clark had good life insurance and a retirement plan through his work, and the insurance company of the driver who hit Clark paid a settlement, so money isn't a problem. She sends generous checks to Kevin and Didi and Maura and Tom; she sets up college funds for the grandchildren, and then she hires a financial advisor to invest the rest. Maggie is surprised to find she enjoys handling the money and the bills, although in the past it was Clark's job.

Clark's office, a place where he would retreat from the world to do paperwork, read, or watch television is full of his things. Maggie has trouble even going in the room, and staying in it for very long gives her a headache. A month after his death, Maggie decides if she is going to work in the office, she will have to make the space less overwhelmingly Clark's. Seeing his belongings throughout the house has been both a delight and agony for Maggie ever since he died. Every glimpse makes her think of Clark, but also reminds her he is gone. Maggie has been struggling with what to do about the problem for some time now, and the office might be a good place to start.

Working quickly before she can change her mind, Maggie carefully takes down and packs in boxes all the photos and memorabilia on the walls and shelves, leaving only books. She cleans his personal items out of the desk drawers, keeping just the things she intends to use.

Once the walls are bare, she covers the bookshelves, windows, and furniture with drop cloths and paints the room a soft, sage green, covering the tan that Clark had previously picked out. When the paint dries and Maggie uncovers and dusts the furniture, it feels like a different place. She experiences a stab of guilt and sadness at what seems an attempt to eradicate Clark's presence, but knows she is only trying to survive and go on.

After that, whenever seeing something of Clark's takes her breath away as if she has been punched in the stomach, she packs it in a box in the garage. The things that make her smile in memory she leaves where they are. The things she won't even consider parting with are his clothes, still hanging on his side of the closet and still in his dresser drawers. Occasionally, when she is very lonely, Maggie goes into the closet to pull a shirt from the hanger and press it against her face, inhaling the fading scent of her husband as she cries in the dark.

She mows the lawn now, something else Clark always did, and learns to adjust the automatic sprinkler system when it malfunctions. She replaces a dripping faucet in the guest bathroom by herself, something she would never have tried before. Maggie volunteers at the local museum on Mondays and at the thrift store on Tuesdays and swims daily at the community center pool. When Tom and Maura come to visit, she has Tom show her how to hitch the camp trailer to the pickup and practices towing it around the block.

On the 4th of July, she meets them at Brownlee Campground with it, feeling a real sense of accomplishment as she pulls in. Of course, Tom has to back it into the camping spot for her, but she unhooks and sets up by herself. Slowly, oh, so slowly, she is living her life.

Now it is late August and the start of school is almost here, so today she is going to Boise to get her hair done. Afterward she is going clothes shopping. Earlier in the week, she caught an unexpected glimpse of herself in the plate-glass window of the thrift store and almost didn't recognize the scrawny, dowdy gray-ponytailed woman in clothes so big for her they were practically falling off.

Her sister Tracy has been telling her for weeks she needs new clothes, and she finally accepts how much weight has come off since Clark died. Even though months have passed, she is still frequently nauseous and is only able to eat small amounts of food without being sick, a strange sort of malady most likely caused by grief. Nevertheless, she is thinner now than at any point in her adult life and nothing fits.

She knows if she gets new clothes she will need to cut and dye her hair as well, or she will still look like a crazy woman, albeit a well-dressed one. Maggie gathers all her courage, so hard-won over the last three months, and heads out the door. Unexpectedly, she feels a pleasant sense of anticipation and cranks the radio up as she drives out of town.

It's early enough in the day that traffic is light, and the trip goes quickly. Once in Boise, Maggie heads straight to the mall and the hair salon, where she is immediately seated and cloaked.

The stylist unfastens Maggie's ponytail, spreads the long, gray hair out on Maggie's shoulders, and asks, "What are we doing today?"

Maggie, ignoring the stylist, stares in fascination at the stranger looking back at her from the mirror. This is the first time since the hospital bathroom—the day she said goodbye to Clark— that she has really, truly, looked at her face in a mirror. *How is it possible I can wash my face, comb my hair, and put on mascara every day without actually looking at myself?* Her previously soft, round, pale face now is thin and tan with visible cheekbones, and her double chin and chubby throat have morphed into a delicate jawline and slender neck. Her green eyes look huge as she tries to find herself in this image.

The stylist clears her throat and asks again, "Do you know what you want for your hair today?"

Maggie mentally gives herself a shake and answers, "I would like the gray covered and it needs cut—probably a lot shorter than this." She has always worn her hair shoulder length to help make her face look thinner but now suspects this would overpower her new, smaller face.

The stylist nods in agreement, and the magic begins.

Two hours later, a chic, stylish woman with shiny, brown hair cut into a blunt A-line and still wearing clothes five sizes too large for her pays the hair salon with a credit card that reads "Maggie Sullivan." Maggie is still not sure this woman is her, but agrees mentally to go along with it for now as she walks through the mall to her favorite store.

After about twenty minutes, Maggie comes to the unhappy realization this store doesn't sell anything in the size she is now. For an instant, she mourns her lost curves. After a lifetime of being voluptuous, she has finally become slender, but the reason for it breaks her heart. The clerk recommends a store down the mall, one she used to take Maura to when Maura was in high school. Maggie walks in, feeling silly to be in a store for teenagers, but soon realizes they sell everything: shorts and tank tops, professional clothes, and cocktail dresses. If the colors and styles seem alien to her, it is more because they are modern rather than because they are too young for her.

The cheerful, helpful retail associate soon puts together a basic wardrobe for Maggie in styles that fit her new figure. She chooses several pairs of shoes, some pretty scarves and costume jewelry and plenty of ensembles for school. She even talks Maggie into wearing one of her new outfits out of the store, making a ceremony of throwing her old jeans and t-shirt in the trash.

Maggie leaves the store in denim shorts and a sleeveless button-up blouse in lavender and white plaid. She feels like somehow she left more behind than her old clothes; maybe she left part of her old self. Then she realizes she hasn't LEFT part of herself, but part of her has come back. It feels so good Maggie can't stop smiling.

She meets Maura and the baby for lunch in a nice restaurant and is pleased that Maura doesn't recognize her at first. Maura's compliments bring on a brief feeling of guilt, as if Maggie shouldn't be trying to look good again, but she is able to squash this ugly intruder at once.

"Mom! You look fantastic! What happened?" Maura exclaims, settling Patrick in the high chair, while trying to examine her mother's face at the same time.

"Well, I just decided it was time to stop looking like a bag-lady," Maggie tells her, blushing with embarrassment at the attention. "I listened to you all those times you nagged me to eat and take a shower over the past few months, but I couldn't seem to make myself do more than the basics. I was exercising a lot to try to keep my mind off things, and I seem to have lost weight, so I decided it was time to get my act together."

Maggie tells Maura about seeing herself in the window and not recognizing her own reflection, and they have a good laugh,

Patrick joining in good naturedly although he has no idea what they're talking about.

It feels good to laugh again, especially with her daughter. She and Maura have always been close, able to almost read each other's thoughts. They can share a look across the room that speaks volumes without saying a word. Maggie knows this connection is precious. She kept Maura at arm's length all summer in an attempt to protect herself and instead, she has robbed them both of healing time together.

After lunch, Maggie gives her daughter and grandson hugs and heads to Costco and Wal-Mart, noticing that people turn to look at her as she walks by, and everyone is smiling. She has gotten into the habit of not looking at people for fear she will see sympathy in their gaze she is not willing to acknowledge, but these people don't know her; they don't know of her loss. They are responding to her as an individual and not as Clark's widow. This is a novel and refreshing experience that carries her easily through her errands.

On the way home, Maggie stops at the care center in Weiser to visit Clark's parents, but they don't know who she is. After 20 minutes of one-sided conversation, Maggie has enough and hugs them goodbye before she leaves. Their disintegrating memories put a damper on the day, but she determinedly shakes it off on the way home and regains her positive attitude.

Maggie's good mood lasts until she walks in her door and realizes there is no one to show her treasures to. Deflated, she slumps on the sofa surrounded by bags. After a few minutes she decides there are two choices before her: sit and mope or get up and start putting her purchases away.

Her first task is to take all her old, too-large clothes out of her closet to make room for the new outfits. Her attention is caught by the sight of Clark's side of the closet, still filled with his clothes. Suddenly, she can't stand to have them in the house anymore and quickly pulls them from the hangers and stuffs them into garbage bags along with her old clothing. Two trips later, they are loaded in the car for a trip to the thrift store next week. Walking back into the empty closet exhilarates Maggie, and she begins to clip tags and hang all her pretty things.

Just then the phone rings. It's Maura checking to make sure her mother made it safely home. While Maggie is telling Maura how much she wishes she could show her all the new outfits, she thinks of the webcam on her laptop. She tells Maura to log on in order to video chat online and then does the same herself after changing to some new jeans and a black, lacy shirt. Maggie and her daughter have a long-distance fashion show over the internet with much laughter involved.

That night, Maggie goes to bed feeling like she did as a child the night before the first day of school—tired but excited, and ready to begin the new school year on Monday.

# CHAPTER 3

Now the September air is crisp in the evenings, football season has started, and on Friday nights, the lights of the field shine in her back yard during games. It has been almost four months since the accident, and life has settled into a satisfying routine for Maggie. She is still lonely, but it's okay; everyone is lonely in some way.

It is Tuesday night and she meets her sister for dinner at a downtown restaurant. They started the weekly practice shortly after Clark died, and it has become an iron-clad appointment, cancelled for nothing short of an emergency. She arrives first and is already seated when Tracy comes bustling in, her round, friendly face smiling as she approaches.

Flinging herself into her seat, she says, "Hiya, kiddo."

Even though Maggie is 51 years old, her big sister still calls her kiddo. It makes Maggie smile in return. They order their usual, the waitress not even bothering to write it down since they always order the same things. The two catch each other up on the week's happenings; chattering and laughing as sisters do while they eat their dinner.

Once the dishes have been cleared, Tracy leans across the table. "Kiddo, I have something I want to talk to you about."

"Uh, oh," Maggie answers, "that sounds serious."

"It's nothing bad, but it is serious—a serious proposal that I promised I'd ask you about," Tracy tells her. "Do you remember Danny's friend, Jack Hallas? He lives out north of town on a ranch, and he has two boys, Brad and Trent. I think you had Brad in school."

Maggie nods. She remembers Brad—a quiet, serious boy,

well-mannered and good at math. She also remembers his father Jack from parent-teacher conferences he attended with his wife.

"Well," Tracy continues, "Jack's boys are in trouble. They are flunking out of school and have started hanging out with a bad crowd. Jack is gone from sunup to sundown working on the ranch, and his wife left him a year and a half ago, so the boys are running wild. He kind of broke down the other night and talked to Danny about it for a couple of hours outside the feed store. He needs an older woman, someone capable who is good with kids, to stay with them after school and make sure they do their homework. She would also need to clean the house and fix dinner, and Danny and I both thought of you. We know you are trying to stay busy and that you're home alone most evenings, so we hoped you might consider it." Tracy sits back, watching Maggie and waiting for a reaction.

Maggie is thinking, thinking hard. Her first inclination is to say no, absolutely not, she couldn't possibly, but then she thinks about the children. She thinks about her own children and how hard it would have been to raise them alone, and her heart goes out to Jack Hallas. He is a few years older than she is, married later in life, and his kids are still in middle school while she is a grandmother. Maggie doesn't understand how a mother can leave her children but knows that some do. She looks back at her sister who is watching her with anticipation. *Yes! This could be good for everybody involved.*

Tracy carefully offers, "Just think about it for a few days, and then we can sit down with Jack and talk about it."

Maggie nods in agreement. She will think about it.

After Tracy talks to her about Jack Hallas and his sons, Maggie spends the next week thinking about their situation and trying to decide if she wants to get involved. She lets herself imagine what it might be like—helping the boys with their homework, fixing a meal big enough for growing boys and a man to eat, sitting around the table at dinner listening to the boys tease each other and talk about school, sports, and girls, picking up dirty socks and towels, doing a mountain of laundry every week, and cleaning up after teenage boys.

She compares this picture in her mind to life as she knows it: coming home alone, grading papers and writing lesson plans in the kitchen with only the radio for company, warming up leftovers for the third day in a row or cooking a solitary burger, eating alone in front of the television, tidying up the few dishes she has used in less than ten minutes and then realizing that it's still only 6:00 and she has HOURS to go before it will be late enough to sleep. Once the weather changes and there is no yard work, it will be too cold and icy to go running and she can't imagine what she will do to fill the time between school and sleep.

Maggie calls her children and asks their opinions, describing the Hallas family and what Tracy is asking her to consider.

Kevin says, "Mom, have you lost your mind! Why would you think you could take care of someone else's children when you're barely coping with your own life?"

Stung by his attitude, Maggie chokes out, "I think there's someone at the door. Goodbye," and hangs up the phone.

Maura is more sympathetic, but voices many reservations. In spite of her children's misgivings (or perhaps because of them), by her meeting with Jack on Wednesday evening, she makes up her mind to take the job.

Catherine Bridwell

# CHAPTER 4

Jack Hallas stands at his bathroom sink shaving. He is a tall man, six feet one inch, broad-shouldered and slim-hipped with the typical build of cowboys. His skin is the skin of a man who spends many hours outdoors—tanned, weathered, and with deep crow's feet around his faded blue eyes. The salt and pepper stubble on his face matches his hair, which is cut short. He has his shirt off and the mirror shows a typical farmer's tan—dark brown on his face, neck, and arms, and a stark white on his torso. As he shaves, he thinks about the reason he is home this early in the day, the reason he is shaving at all. He left the hired help, Parker and Morris, finishing the repairs to the barn roof on the Smokey Boulder place and drove the sixty miles back to his house so he could shower, shave, and change into clean clothes to meet a woman. Not just any woman, but a capable woman who could change his life and the lives of his sons in a deep and permanent way.

He knew when Caroline left, the boys would struggle. He has read some of the studies about boys who are abandoned by their mothers and has done everything he knows to help them, short of selling the ranch. The hours he works are part of the problem, but there is no way to change that right now.

The ranch barely stayed afloat during the recession, and it is only the crushingly long, hard hours he puts in now that are finally getting them into a good financial position. The ranch is the legacy he intends to leave to his sons, and he is determined to leave a viable, healthy business. He needs a solution, and soon. So, although the boys are too old for a nanny, he can afford to hire someone to supervise chores, help with homework, cook and keep the house clean. He just hopes Maggie Sullivan lives up to her billing.

Jack is a few minutes late getting to Danny's house, where he has agreed to meet with Mrs. Sullivan to discuss his job offer, so her car is already in the driveway. As he walks to the door, he is trying to remember what she looked like when she was Brad's sixth-grade teacher. He has a vague idea—she was short and kind of chubby with graying brown hair. He remembers a kind, competent presence that would be a perfect fit for what he has in mind.

Danny answers Jack's knock at the front door and ushers him into the kitchen, where Tracy and another woman are seated at the kitchen table. Jack nods to them and is looking around for Mrs. Sullivan, when he realizes the second woman *is* Mrs. Sullivan. She is not at all what Jack remembers. This woman is small and slender, with shiny brown hair and a lovely face dominated by big green eyes. In spite of the laugh lines at her eyes and around her mouth, she is solemn and has an air of fragility and sadness. He remembers her husband was killed earlier in the year and supposes that accounts for the sorrow in her face. She stands to shake his hand when Tracy introduces them, and as he clasps her small cool hand in his, he can't help but notice she is wearing a dress and has fantastic legs. Feeling slightly dazed, Jack sits down at the table and begins to tell his tale.

"Brad is a sophomore and Trent is an eighth grader. They are both good students but are currently in danger of failing this quarter, which is almost over. Neither boy has been doing nor turning in their assignments, and they are both on academic probation as well as ineligible for football. They are good athletes, so their coaches aren't happy about it and have offered to help, but the boys refuse to take advantage.

"Because I leave the house to begin work on the ranch before daylight, no one is there to make sure the boys get out of bed and go to school, so their attendance this fall has been spotty. Even the days they go to school, they don't always stay, cutting class a lot to hunt or hang out and play video games with some older boys who have dropped out. Quite often, on the days they go to school, they don't come home at a decent hour, and many times I have driven back to town after a long day of work to look for them and escort them home."

Clearing his throat, Jack continues, "I have tried giving them extra chores, withholding phone and television privileges, and taking away Brad's pickup keys. I have scolded them, grounded them, and reasoned with them, and nothing has made any difference. I think they are angry with me because their mother left and are choosing this behavior as a way to get back at me.

"A few weeks ago, the boys were caught vandalizing the local park, and now the law is involved and is talking to the school about the boys' attendance and grades. They told me to get control of my children or the county will do it for me."

Jack looks straight at Maggie. "I need a capable, responsible person to get the boys up in the mornings, drive them to and from school, supervise their chores, and help them with their homework. I need this person to cook breakfast and dinner and keep the house clean. Because the ranch is so far from town and on a dirt road, I think it would be in the housekeeper's best interest to stay at the house with the boys during the week, especially when the weather is bad, but you would have weekends off."

Jack can see the trepidation on Maggie's face when he mentions this, so he quickly adds, "I think your reputation can weather the gossip and besides, it's all for the good of the children." He goes on to explain, "I have an extra bedroom on the second story for you to use when you're there, and I'll buy your gas for driving Brad and Trent to school and pay you a monthly wage."

Feeling like he has just run five miles, Jack sits back in his chair and waits to see what Maggie's reaction will be. He forces himself to unclench his fists and tries to relax as his children's future hangs in the balance.

Maggie is studying her hands, and after what seems like a year, looks up at Jack. "When would you like me to start?" she asks.

His whole body sags in relief. They work out the details of her schedule: Sunday after Mass through Friday at noon each week. Because the school is on a four-day week, both Maggie and the boys will have this coming Friday off, so Jack and Maggie agree she will meet him at the turn-off to the ranch Friday morning, follow him home to meet the boys, then stay to clean the house.

Maggie tells him, "I'll have time on Saturday to pick up any groceries or other items you might need. Can I have your permission to speak to the boys' teachers about missing assignments and upcoming projects?"

"Sure," Jack answers. "So it's settled then. You'll drive back to the ranch after Mass every Sunday so you can fix dinner for the boys and help them get organized for school Monday morning, and you'll stay with them during the week. On Fridays I'll take them with me to help around the ranch, so you can clean the house with no one underfoot. When you finish, the rest of the weekend is yours until Sunday afternoon when you come back to the ranch."

Maggie nods her head in agreement.

After a few minutes of social chat, Jack says goodbye and walks out to his pickup. The drive home goes by quickly as Jack plans what he will say to his sons. He knows the house is a terrible mess, but that's why he hired Maggie, and besides, there is no time to clean it before Friday. He will need to come to town tomorrow and buy a new mattress for the bed in the guest room before she arrives since the old one has wires poking up through the cover.

He feels light, as if a huge weight has been lifted from his shoulders. His only misgiving is how pretty Maggie Sullivan looked tonight, but he will hardly ever see her, so it should be all right.

After Jack leaves, Maggie is left alone with Danny and Tracy, who are both looking at her with happy expressions on their faces.

"What?" she says defensively.

"Nothing!" they both say at the same time.

"We're just glad Jack is going to get some help, and you won't be home alone every night," Tracy adds. "I've been worried about both of you lately, and now I can let it go."

"I wish you wouldn't worry about me," Maggie tells her. "I'm okay and besides, I'm a grown woman."

"I know," Tracy answers, "but you're still my little sister."

Maggie gives both of them hugs and heads to her car. She is feeling a little buyer's regret now that the commitment has been made, but hopefully it will go away once she starts the job.

Earlier, when Maggie stood to shake Jack's hand, she realized he was quite tall, with big warm, callused hands. He looked a lot older and more careworn than he did four years ago. She had heard through the grapevine his wife left him for another man, but doesn't know if it's true. Her heart aches for him and his children as she thinks about the difficulties the little family is going through, and she resolves to try to heal these lost and broken souls.

She makes a list in her head, as she drives home, of the

cleaning supplies she will need to take with her on Friday. She doesn't trust a single dad to have much on hand in that department. Maggie falls asleep wondering what the house will look like. All she knows for sure is it has an upstairs with at least one bedroom in it.

# CHAPTER 5

At eight o'clock on Friday morning, Maggie pulls her car off the pavement onto a dirt road where Jack is waiting in his pickup and follows him to the ranch. The road is narrow and winding, rutted and full of potholes, and she has to hang back quite a ways to stay out of the choking dust raised by the pickup in front of her. It won't be much fun driving this twice a day, and Maggie is grateful her SUV has all-wheel drive. Maybe once Brad has earned back his pickup keys, he will drive occasionally.

After about twenty minutes, the trees surrounding the car thin, the road crests a hill, and she drives into a small beautiful, green valley with a big white, two-story house on the far side. There is a barn and several other buildings close to the house as well as other vehicles and farm equipment. As she gets closer, she realizes the house is old and not well-maintained—the paint is peeling, the windows are dirty, the yard is overgrown and littered with various farm debris, and the wrap-around porch is cluttered with all manner of items. She pulls in beside Jack's pickup, shuts off her car, and gets out.

*Here we go—now we'll find out if the boys are going to buy into this idea.* She hopes with all her heart Brad and Trent are receptive to their father's solution and to her presence in their home. Jack leads her through the yard and up the steps, winding his way through boots, tack, and baling twine to the front door.

After the bright sunlight, it takes a minute for Maggie's eyes to adjust. When they do, she realizes the house is just as dirty and cluttered inside as the yard and porch are outside. It smells stale to her, like wet dogs, garbage, and old sweat. She tries breathing just through her mouth until her nose can adjust to the odor.

The curtains are shut, making the large living room dim and cave-like, lit only by the television playing in the corner. Both boys are slumped on the couch, eyes glued to the television. They don't look up when Jack shuts the door behind her.

"Hey!" Jack says to them. "Turn that off and get over here."

Grumbling, the boys do as he asks and shuffle over to the adults.

"Brad, you remember Mrs. Sullivan," he says. "Trent, this is Mrs. Sullivan. Remember what we talked about—if this doesn't work out, you will both end up in juvy."

The boys politely shake Maggie's hand when she offers it, but they don't speak or meet her eyes.

"Good morning," Maggie tells them, in her best teacher voice. She hopes there is enough of a connection already established between her and Brad to make it easy to reach him, but she will be starting new with Trent. She reminds herself to be patient with them.

"Well," Jack says, "it's time for us to head out. Grab your coats, guys, and load up. Mrs. Sullivan, I hope you don't have too much trouble getting this place in shape."

"Is there anything that's off limits?" Maggie asks. Her question is greeted with blank stares. "I mean," she explains, "is there anything I shouldn't clean or touch?"

"Oh," Jacks says, frowning in consideration. "You don't need to clean my room. I can take care of it. Other than that, feel free to do whatever you want." Turning from her, he and the boys go out the door.

She watches them get in the pickup and drive away, and peers about her with a sinking heart at the smelly, dirty house. It reminds her of an old movie, *Seven Brides for Seven Brothers*, when the heroine, Millie, arrives at a bachelor pad in similar condition to this one. *At least I have running water,* she thinks, and marches outside to get her cleaning supplies.

Maggie has brought with her rubber gloves, a broom, dustpan, mop, mop bucket, cleaning rags, multiple cleaning solutions, paper towels, a scrub brush, dish detergent, laundry soap, fabric softener, trash bags, and furniture polish. She also packed a lunch in a cooler along with several water bottles and an iced tea with lemon. She wears a pair of old jeans pulled from the thrift store bag at the last minute and cinched them around her slim waist with one of her new belts, and a t-shirt of Clark's she kept out of sentiment. Maggie thinks she needs Clark's spirit around her today if she is to accomplish the task she has set for herself. Picking up the cooler and her purse in one hand, she grabs the box of cleaning supplies and heads back into the house. Somehow she thinks it might be a while before she is ready for the broom and mop.

First things first, Maggie thinks and walks through the house to see the layout. There is a utility room which is a combination mud/laundry room, kitchen, living room, bathroom, and master bedroom on the first floor. Upstairs are three bedrooms, one empty except for a bed with a brand new mattress and a tall bureau. The other two bedrooms obviously belong to the boys.

Maggie is appalled that children are living in such squalor, and her opinion of Jack Hallas goes down a notch or two. The whole house is filthy—cobwebs, dirt, hay, dirty dishes, dirty laundry, empty take-out containers (and even worse, NOT empty take-out containers full of moldy, dried food), papers, magazines, mail, and just plain garbage covering the floor and every surface. She isn't sure how the kitchen table is still standing under the weight of the clutter mounded on it or how the mound stays in place without crashing to the floor.

The bathroom and kitchen are the worst, mostly because of the smells. The shower is mangy with orange slime and black-spotted mildew, the curtain stiff with soap scum and calcium deposits. The sink is caked with dirty soap scum, whisker debris, and shaving cream. The vanity is covered with a detritus of male hygiene products, dirty washcloths, used cotton swabs, and magazines. The toilet is a putrid, black-looking nightmare of pee splashes and brown splotches. The floor is piled high with dirty clothes and towels, trash, empty soda cans, and even dirty dishes.

Maggie decides to begin with the worst and work her way to the easiest, so she starts in the bathroom. Putting on her rubber gloves and grabbing a trash bag, she quickly pitches everything that is on the floor and isn't trash out the door into the living room, trying not to breathe too deeply or look at what is in her hands, and fills the bag with the remaining debris.

When the floor is bare and the trash bag is full, she carries in her cleaning supplies and squirts the toilet liberally with the toilet cleaner. While the toilet is soaking, she takes the shampoo bottles, the slivers of soap, the dirty washcloths, the men's body wash, and whatever else is in the tub/shower enclosure out and sets it in the hall with the rest. She sprays the shower walls and tub with shower cleaner and moves on to the sink. Then it's back to the toilet, first flushing it, then re-applying toilet cleaner and scrubbing, which she does several times before it is clean enough for her satisfaction.

She makes a mental note to buy a pumice stone. It takes Maggie most of an hour to scrub the shower and sink. She leaves the shower curtain, adding the purchase of a new one to the growing list in her head. She washes the light fixture, wipes out the storage cupboards and medicine cabinet, cleans the splattered mirror with glass cleaner, and now the bathroom is clean enough to use. The last step is to re-position all the toiletries belonging to Jack and the boys in the now-sparkling room.

Next task—start some laundry. Maggie pulls enough towels from the pile on the floor outside the bathroom to make a load and goes into the utility room. The washer, a fairly new model, is empty so she fills it with towels, adds detergent from her supplies, and turns on the washer.

Then she takes another trash bag from her box of goodies and begins clearing a path to the kitchen sink. Maggie opens all the cupboards to see what Jack keeps where and isn't surprised to see that a majority of the cupboards are empty. Most of the dishes the family owns are dirty. *That makes it easy*, she thinks. *I can put things wherever I want.*

First though, she must clean out the sink, which is a stinking hole full of dishes with remnants of food clinging to them, half submerged in scummy, cold, moldy-smelling water. She gingerly pulls out the dishes and is able to find the drain, and once the sinks are empty, she scrubs them with cleanser and hot water. She then fills one side with steaming, soapy water and attacks the empty cupboards, scrubbing every shelf, cupboard door, and trim board with a scrub brush, stopping frequently to wipe the surfaces with clean rags. She uses grease-cutting spray and goes to work on the tougher spots. By the time she finishes the cupboards, her hands, arms, and shoulders are aching. She is hot and sweaty, and it is 10:00 already. She takes a restroom break and drinks a bottle of cold water from her cooler.

Maggie refills the sink with fresh, hot, soapy water, loads it full of dirty dishes and, while they are soaking, moves the clean towels to the dryer and starts a load of jeans in the washer. Then she starts washing dishes, beginning with the ones on the counter, then gathering them from the floor, the kitchen table, and other rooms in the house. She finds a dish rack under the sink and clears a spot on the counter for it. Maggie washes, rinses, dries, and puts away dishes until 11:30. Her hands are wrinkled and sweating inside the rubber gloves, her fingers sore from scrubbing, and her back hurts from standing so long. She has never seen so many dirty dishes at one time, or such nasty, dirty dishes. Some of the plastic containers smell so awful she doesn't even try to wash them. They go straight into a garbage bag.

Since her nose is already used to the stink, she decides to tackle the refrigerator next, taking out a fresh garbage bag. *Anything in a plastic container is going in the trash,* she vows to herself. The refrigerator turns out not to be as horrible as Maggie has anticipated, as there is hardly anything inside. Once she has emptied it, she washes the inside with hot soapy water and returns the lonely condiments to the shelves. All the other food goes in the trash. She checks the freezer, which is also mostly empty, so she takes out the few packages of frozen meat and washes the freezer as well. The dishes she removed from the refrigerator she quickly washes and puts away. Next is the stove. She scrubs the cooked-on, burned-on, dried-on food from the stove top, puts the burner pans and rings into the sink to soak, and turns on the self-cleaning oven.

Maggie has had enough for a while, so she takes her cooler into the yard and eats lunch in the shade of a large elm tree. The September sun is warm enough, even up here in the mountains, to make the cool shade welcome. Maggie looks around at the rugged countryside surrounding this beautiful little valley and feels peace flowing into her mind and heart. After she finishes eating, she relaxes in the shade for a few more minutes before going back into the house.

Before she can move the laundry, she needs a place to fold it, so she finds an empty cardboard box on the porch and clears the table for folding laundry in the utility room by sweeping everything off into the box, then washing the table thoroughly. She moves the laundry, folding and putting away the clean towels, starts another load and goes back to the kitchen, ready to conquer the countertops, which are old, stained Formica. Again, Maggie gets out the cleanser, and before long, the ancient surfaces shine with a surprisingly pleasant light yellow color. The papers on the kitchen table she sorts by who owns them, throwing away any garbage and putting away what she can of the assorted belongings left. Everything else goes into another cardboard box that she puts in the utility room. Moving the piles of papers onto the chairs, she is able to wipe off the table, which turns out to be a beautiful, antique, ranch oak table. When the table is dry, she neatly stacks the papers back on it.

The cobweb-covered light fixtures over the kitchen table and the sink go into hot water for a quick scrub before being re-attached. Maggie gets the broom from the car and makes short work of the cobwebs left on the ceiling and in the corners, and then does the kitchen windows. The screens she sprays off in the yard with a garden hose and leans them against the house to dry while she washes the windows inside and out.

Once the windows are clean and the screens reinserted, it's time for the floor which appears to be hardwood but is barely visible under layers of muck. Maggie goes back to the car and brings in the dust pan, mop and mop bucket and sweeps and mops the kitchen, bathroom, and utility room.

*What a change*, Maggie thinks, turning in a circle to survey her handiwork. The kitchen is bigger than she first thought, with warm pine paneling, tall old-fashioned, painted white cupboards, white enamel sink, and white appliances. The old hardwood floors, though obviously thoroughly lived on, are still beautiful and catch the sunshine streaming in through the sparkling windows. The oak table gleams in the afternoon light, which also brings a glow to the butter-colored countertops.

Leaving the floors to dry and with a good feeling of accomplishment in her heart, Maggie heads upstairs where, again, she starts with the messiest room, which she deduces is Trent's by way of reading the sign on the door which says, "Trent's Room – KEEP OUT!" Working quickly, Maggie strips the bedding and piles it in the hall along with all the clothing on the floor. She picks up what's left on the floor, throwing away the trash and putting books, papers, and belongings in logical places. She organizes and dusts the dresser top, bedside table, bookshelves and desk, takes off the light fixture and runs downstairs to wash it (starting a load of Trent's bedding while she's there), and finds a light bulb to replace the burnt out one.

Trent's one window overlooks the front of the wrap-around porch, so Maggie removes the bottom pane, takes out the screen, and steps gingerly out onto the porch roof so she can wash the outside of the top pane. From out here, she can see the other bedroom windows also open over the porch. Going back inside, she removes the bottom panes from all the bedroom windows, takes all the screens down to wash and sun-dry, then goes back up and out the window to wash the outsides of all the top panes. The slope of the porch roof isn't too steep, but Maggie is keenly aware of how high up she is and that no one is there to know or help if she falls. It is a relief to finish the outside windows and crawl back into the house. The inside of the top panes and both sides of the bottom panes are next. She then goes back downstairs to get the screens. Ten minutes of putting it all back together and the upstairs windows are finished. Maggie wipes the windowsills clean with a wet rag, then the bed frame, and it's time for the floor. After sweeping Trent's room, she mops her way out the door into the hall. One down, two to go!

Brad's room gets the same treatment, only faster since the windows are already clean, and then Maggie enters the room which is to be hers during the week. It still seems inconceivable to her that on Sunday night she will be sleeping in this room. She checks the closet for bedding, but doesn't find any, so adds that to the shopping list in her head. The only cleaning needed here is to wipe down the windowsills and Mission-style bed frame, dust the bureau, and sweep and mop the floor. Back in the hall, she makes several trips downstairs with dirty laundry, making sure to keep each boy's clothing piles separated so she knows where they belong when it's time to put them away. She also hauls down the full trash bags. Maggie sweeps and mops the hall and stairs, and the upstairs of the house is finished until the bedding is clean and dry.

In the living room, Maggie starts with the pile of stuff she cleared off the bathroom floor, sorting out the laundry from the rest of it. It doesn't take long to pick up the living room floor, also hardwood, and dust the furniture, stopping once to move the laundry. Next, Maggie brings out the vacuum cleaner she finds in the utility room and vacuums the area rug under the coffee table. All that is left is sweeping and mopping the floor. She empties the dirty mop water for the fifth time, rinses the mop under the faucet, and then carries it out to her car along with the broom and dust pan. Trent's bedding is dry, so she takes it upstairs and makes his bed. While she waits for Brad's blankets to come out of the dryer, she puts her cleaning supplies away under the sink, and then sits on the porch step with a bottle of water.

Evening shadows are creeping into the yard, the breeze is getting a bite to it, and the bird songs have changed to the sleepy chirp of dusk. Maggie shivers, thinking about the coming fall and winter, and is suddenly missing Clark with all her being.

She has spent the entire summer either consumed by thoughts of Clark and wallowing in sorrow and self-pity or deliberately NOT thinking about Clark, which means not really thinking at all. This is easiest when she is doing something physical such as running, swimming or cleaning, when all she allows in her mind is the thought of what her body is doing—each step/stroke, each breath, how far she has gone, how far she intends to go, how tired she is. Sitting here in this beautiful place, she realizes that all day her mind has been roaming freely while she cleaned, and not once until now has she thought about Clark, a fact which is both saddening and hopeful.

The buzz of the dryer startles Maggie from her reverie, and she hurries inside to make Brad's bed. She leaves the rest of the laundry on the floor in the utility room, worried that if she starts a load in the washer, no one will move it and by Sunday evening it will have soured. Taking one last look around the clean, fresh-smelling house, Maggie smiles, wishing she would have taken before and after pictures with her phone, and heads for her car.

On the drive home, she wonders what Jack's bedroom looks like and why he didn't want her to clean it. Several reasons occur to her: maybe it is so messy he is embarrassed for her to see it; or maybe he isn't comfortable with a stranger seeing his dirty underwear and his personal belongings; or maybe his room is a shrine to his runaway wife. *Or maybe,* she thinks hysterically, *he has an altar there where he cuts the heads off dead chickens and practices voodoo!* The absurdity of this idea brings laughter to Maggie's lips, and the sound makes her jump. So far, Jack and his boys are having a good effect on her mood.

She pulls into her garage and shuts off the car, groaning a little as she gets out. Her back has stiffened up on the way home, and she knows she will be sore tomorrow. Evidently, yoga, running and swimming are not adequate preparation for a day of extreme housework.

Twenty minutes later, flushed from standing under the hot spray of the shower, Maggie puts on her pajamas, throws a frozen dinner in the microwave, and sits down to eat in front of the television. She becomes engrossed in a movie, *Raiders of the Lost Ark*, which she has seen a dozen times, but which is still able to hold her interest. Her bobbing head wakens her. The movie is over, and she has fallen asleep in her chair. Maggie puts her dishes in the sink, turns out the lights, brushes her teeth, and tumbles into bed, falling asleep as soon as her head hits the pillow.

Maggie wakes in the morning before her alarm rings at 6:30, and although she showered last night, a shower is how she brings herself to life in the morning, so into the shower she goes. Once she is dressed, with her hair dried and styled and her makeup on, Maggie fixes a cup of tea and takes it out to the deck, along with a cold piece of leftover ham and some fruit. She breakfasts in the early morning light, listening to the liquid warble of the blackbirds. The birdsong reminds her of Jack's ranch, and that reminds her of all she needs to accomplish today. Taking her cup back to the kitchen for more tea, she grabs a notepad and pen and returns to the deck to make a list. Once she is satisfied with the list, she puts her cup in the dishwasher, fills a water bottle, grabs her purse, and heads out. Maggie drives 70 miles to the nearest superstore and goes shopping.

She buys lamps for the boys' bedside tables, bedding for her bed, a half-dozen bath towels, several hand towels, a dozen washcloths (many of Jack's that she laundered yesterday were thread-bare), kitchen towels, dishcloths, dish towels, more cleaning and laundry supplies, toilet paper, paper towels, some vintage-looking table cloths that will be perfect for the kitchen table, curtain rods and curtains for the kitchen and all the upstairs bedrooms, and also rugs to put beside the beds. The thought of putting her bare feet, warm from the bed, onto the cold, wood floor this winter makes her shiver. She also purchases a nightstand for her room, a full-length mirror so she can style her hair in her room and make sure her clothes are on right, a cart with drawers to hold all her hair products, hair appliances and cosmetics, and a lighted make-up mirror to hang over the bureau. With four people and only one bathroom, even if Jack leaves before the others get up, Maggie thinks it will be best if she can get ready each morning in her room. She buys a cork board to hang over Brad's desk along with a package of brightly colored push pins to help control the multitude of photographs he has lying around, and a display case for Trent's Indian artifact collection that she noticed residing on the floor of his closet.

Next on the list—groceries. Staples such as sugar, flour, salt, various spices, olive oil, and baking supplies go in the cart, followed by canned goods, dried pastas, cereal, and bread. Jack has let her know the Hallas family raises beef cattle, not dairy cattle, so Maggie stocks up on milk, butter, and cheese. Then she hits the produce section, loading up on fruit and vegetables. Jack has very little food in the house except for meat of which, judging by the freezer in the utility room, he has plenty. He told Maggie to get what she thought they needed and he will pay her back, so she does, mentally planning to cross off the items for her room from the receipt. Pushing one cart and towing another, Maggie gets in line to pay for her purchases, which takes quite a while considering the massive amount of shopping. It takes some doing, but eventually it all fits in the car.

From the superstore, Maggie drives to a ranch supply store. She suspects that supervising the boys' chores may require a more hands-on approach than simply watching from the kitchen window and waiting for them to return, and Maggie owns nothing that would be suitable to wear for such activity. In the store, Maggie buys three pairs of jeans, the kind that are comfortable for horseback, a pair of boots with a heel tall enough for riding but flat enough for ground work, and two pairs of soft leather work gloves. She has never worn such attire, and feels silly trying it on, but it is important the jeans and boots fit, so she perseveres.

In no time at all, she is back on the road. She stops on the way home for a quick bite of lunch and, after arriving at her house, brings in from the car the items that need refrigerated. Everything else she leaves where it is.

She changes clothes and mows the lawn, sweeps the sidewalks and deck, deadheads the flowers and pulls a few random weeds, then cleans the house thoroughly. Even though she is exhausted, she won't be back here again until next Friday, and she wants to leave it spotless. Finally, there is nothing left to do except rinse off the dirt, grass clippings, and sweat in her second shower of the day.

By now, Maggie is hungry, so she barbecues a steak, puts a potato in the microwave and fixes a nice green salad, then eats on the deck again. It is her favorite place in the summer. After tidying the kitchen and starting the dishwasher, she curls up on the couch with a new book she bought this morning and loses herself in other people's lives for a few hours.

When she notices her eyes are burning and her neck is getting a kink, she heads off to bed, but when she lies down, flashes of all the things she bought today whirl around and around in her head. After about an hour and a half of this, she gets up for a drink of water and tries to figure out why she can't sleep. She thinks it is probably nerves. After all, she is about to begin a new job; her car is full of stuff she bought for other people, people who may not be happy with the choices she has made for them; and she will be living in a house she has never lived in before with a man and two boys whom she doesn't know. That is plenty to be nervous about, she decides, but once she has identified the source of her insomnia, she knows how to combat it. Returning to bed, Maggie begins saying the rosary in her head, a kind of meditation that never fails to work, and finally she dozes off.

The next morning, Maggie wakens at her normal time, 6:30, but is able to convince herself to go back to sleep. She dreams again of Clark.

*They are making love, sweet and slow and good, and she is so happy to be in his arms. He kisses her as if he has never kissed her before, his mouth so wet and firm on hers, tasting of Clark.*

The shrill ringing of the phone rudely interrupts this wonderful dream, and Maggie groggily picks it up. It's her sister Tracy asking if she is coming to brunch. Maggie looks at the clock and it is 10:30. She hasn't slept this late in months! She tells Tracy yes, and then rolls out of bed. After a quick shower, Maggie puts on a pretty summer dress with a matching cardigan, slips into some sandals, fixes her hair, applies mascara, and hurries out the door.

On the drive over, the remnants of her dream linger, and she finds herself remembering having sex with her husband. Clark was a good lover, tender and considerate, with a great sense of adventure. He wasn't afraid to laugh at himself and was always able to get Maggie to laugh along with him. After years of practice, their coming together as husband and wife was comfortable and intimate, each knowing what the other needed without having to say it, and it was a major reason for the success of their marriage. For the first time since Clark died, Maggie misses sex.

After brunch with Tracy and Danny, Maggie hurries home to pack before it is time to go to the 3:00 Mass at St. Jude's. From there, she will swing by the house to pick up the groceries in the refrigerator, and then she will drive to her new job. She chooses work clothes for each day along with shoes, accessories, and appropriate undergarments, and adds jeans, shorts, tank tops, t-shirts, socks, and tennis shoes for evenings at the ranch.

While shopping yesterday, Maggie bought an extra hair dryer and straight iron, a new toothbrush, and duplicates of everything she uses in the shower and to get ready each day. She will leave these things at Jack's to avoid the necessity of taking them back and forth each week, and they are already in the car, still in the shopping bags.

She wheels her bulging suitcase to the front door, drapes a light jacket over it, and lays her new book and the papers she brought home to grade on top of the little pile. She hasn't had a chance to work on them yet, but hopes to after dinner tonight at Jack's. The thought causes a little trill of nerves to dance through her stomach. She hopes she is making the right choice by working for Jack Hallas.

By now, it is time to leave for church. All during the Mass, Maggie prays for the Hallas boys and asks God to help her be a good example and teacher for them. When church is over, Maggie drives back to her house, loads her suitcase, jacket, book, and papers in the car, grabs the bags from the refrigerator and, after checking the light switches and the burners on the kitchen stove, she locks the front door and begins a new chapter in her life.

# CHAPTER 6

Jack Hallas and his sons are watching Sunday football on television and waiting for Maggie Sullivan to arrive. Jack thinks back to the day before yesterday when Maggie first came into his house. He could tell she was shocked at the way the house looked and smelled, but she hid it well, and she was very friendly to the boys.

All that day, Jack wondered what she was doing and what the house would look like when they returned. He kept the boys busy helping repair the old barn Jack and the hired men had been working on all week, and by the time he judged enough progress had been made, it was getting dark. They stopped for dinner at the fast-food restaurant in New Meadows before continuing on home and walked in the door around 8:00.

Even before Jack turned on the lights, he could smell the clean drifting through the house on the evening air, but the sight that met his eyes was still a surprise. He expected Maggie would probably just tidy up and wash the dishes, but he underestimated his new housekeeper. As he and the amazed boys walked through their home, Jack could see Mrs. Sullivan had cleaned the old place down to its bones and left every surface sparkling. The only thing out of place was the piles of laundry on the utility room floor, and he suspected she had simply run out of time.

After seeing the kitchen and checking out the bathroom, the boys looked at each other and raced for the stairs. Jack heard their feet thumping overhead as they explored their rooms, then they thundered back down, interrupting each other in their eagerness to tell him what Maggie had done up there.

"That's great, boys," Jack told them. "Now let's try to keep it that way until Sunday, okay?"

Now it is Sunday, and inevitably the house has gotten messy again, but Jack is confident Maggie will set it to rights when she gets here. Just then, he hears Maggie's car pull up in the driveway and shut off, so he gets out of his chair and heads for the door. The boys, however, beat him to it and are to the car before Jack gets to the porch.

Maggie steps out of the car with her purse over her shoulder and her arms full of what looks like books and papers. She is wearing a pink summer dress with some sort of sweater over it, and Jack thinks she is lovely in the soft dusk with her tan legs and silky-looking, brown hair.

"Hi," she says softly to his children. "How was your weekend?"

Both Brad and Trent start talking to her at once, telling her everything they have done over the past three days. Jack watches from the doorway, astounded at his normally sulkily-silent teenagers and the burst of information flying from their mouths.

She gives Jack a wave and starts toward the house, the boys falling in behind her. Stopping, she turns back to them and says, "Don't come in empty-handed; everything in the car needs to go in the house."

The boys look at her, then at each other before going back to the vehicle and opening the rear passenger door. Brad hands Trent some grocery bags, then reaches in for his own burden.

Again, Jack is astonished. Usually it takes a threat of some dire punishment to get his offspring to help carry in groceries. He starts toward the car, passing Maggie and the boys on his way, and leans in the still-open passenger door. The SUV is packed from floor to ceiling with bags and boxes, and a large suitcase is crammed into the front passenger seat. It looks like Maggie has cleaned out the superstore and packed half her house as well. Jack grabs a load and heads back inside.

The boys have followed her into the kitchen with their armloads of bags, so she tells them to start a pile in the middle of the kitchen floor and goes back outside for another trip. Eventually, all the groceries, household items, and Maggie's suitcase are stacked in the kitchen.

Jack and the boys stand beside the pile and look at Maggie.

"It's not as much as it looks like," she says defensively.

Jack raises one eyebrow in disbelief, but then gives her a half-smile that tells her he isn't mad.

"Besides," she reminds him. "You were out of everything, and you told me to get whatever I thought you needed, so I did."

Jack nods in agreement. "What next?" he asks.

"Well," Maggie says hesitantly, "maybe I could start putting groceries away, and the three of you could put this together." She pulls the box containing the nightstand for her room from the pile and hands it to Jack.

He and his sons take it into the living room, open the box, and start pulling out pieces and parts. From the living room, while he and the boys work on the nightstand, Jack watches Maggie Sullivan in his kitchen putting away groceries. He finds her quick, neat manner fascinating. She reminds him of a honeybee, moving with purpose from place to place, suspended from graceful flight momentarily while she accomplishes each task.

He thinks again of the way the house looked on Friday night. It hadn't looked that good since Caroline was still here. In fact, he has to admit, it never looked that good even then. Caroline kept the dishes washed and the floor picked up, but tended to let the rest slide while she watched endless hours of real-life television drama. Jack wonders if Maggie was just trying to impress them, or if she always does such a thorough job. Watching her now, as she makes short work of stashing the quantities of food and supplies away, he suspects the latter of Mrs. Sullivan. He thinks he has made the right choice bringing her here.

Once Maggie puts the curtains and curtain rods in the utility room, he sees her take the sheets and blankets for her bed from their packaging and go back into the utility room. He hears the washing machine start and knows she must be washing them so she can make her bed later. She comes back into the kitchen and gets all the new kitchen and bathroom towels and adds them to the pile of laundry already on the floor. Gathering up the bags containing her duplicate toiletries and cosmetics, Maggie trots up the stairs. She makes several more trips, taking the long mirror, pillows for the bed, bags of hangers, and the cart that will hold her hair products and "girly stuff" up to her room.

When Maggie comes down from a trip to her room, Jack and the boys proudly show her the finished nightstand. It is Mission style to match the bed frame and is stained the same dark walnut.

"Looks great," she tells them. "Shall we take it up and put it where it belongs? Maybe, Jack, you could bring that screwdriver and hang my mirror."

Jack agrees, and they follow the boys, who carry the nightstand between them, up the stairs to her room. Brad and Trent ask which side it should go on and place it carefully beside the bed. The eager way they look to Maggie for approval touches Jack deeply, and she is quick to thank them profusely and praise their work. Jack asks where Maggie would like the mirror and then hangs it to her specification on the wall beside the closet.

They all troop back downstairs and look at the items remaining on the kitchen floor. Maggie shows the boys the lamps and rugs for their rooms, and sends Brad to the utility room for light bulbs. Taking her own lamp and rug, she accompanies them upstairs, where the three of them spend a pleasant few minutes situating their new belongings, going back and forth between each other's rooms to compare and give advice.

In the meantime, Jack carries Maggie's suitcase to her room while he listens to her interact with Brad and Trent and hears her say, "We will need to have a discussion about rules for knocking and respecting privacy, but it can wait until later."

The boys seem to really like her so far, and he is hopeful for the first time in months they will begin to heal from the emotional upheaval of their parents' divorce.

He sees the corkboard, push pins, and display case she bought and, assuming they are for the boys, brings them upstairs as well. He goes to Brad's door, where he can hear all three voices. Setting the display case on the floor in the hall and holding the corkboard and push pins in his hands, he asks, "Who does this belong to?"

Maggie turns to see what he is holding and then answers, "That is for Brad. I thought he might like it for pictures and other stuff he wants up. It will help keep his desk clear so he can use it."

Brad looks at her, and the look on his face breaks Jack's heart a little, for it is more than gratitude. His face shows the relief of a child who remembers, after a long, horrible time, that someone loves him, that someone cares enough to do something special for him. Jack feels like the worst dad in the world, yet he knows he is doing the best he can.

"Thank you!" Brad tells Maggie, meeting her eyes briefly

with his bright blue ones, then looks shyly away. "It's great."

Brad turns to Jack, saying "Dad, do you think you could help me hang it?" His tone is hesitant, as if he expects the answer to be no, and his face lights up when Jack agrees immediately.

Jack notices the eagerness in his son's expression, and he is saddened that Brad expects so little from his father.

"What's for me? What's for me?" Trent demands with the unselfconsciousness of a thirteen-year-old.

Jack and Maggie both laugh, and Jack shows Trent the display case.

"It's for your Indian collection," Maggie tells him.

"Wow!" Trent says. "That's so cool! We need to put it up, Dad!"

"As soon as I'm done helping Brad," Jack replies.

Trent carries the case to his room and holds it to the walls in various places, trying to find the perfect spot.

Jack knows it's childish, but he feels a little left out and jealous she didn't buy anything for him. He is trying to remember why he told Maggie not to clean his room. He hadn't planned it, but when she asked if there was anything off limits in the house, it just popped out. He supposes he is embarrassed the room is a mess, but forces himself to admit the truth. Jack doesn't want Maggie to see the bed where he sleeps, alone, night after night, for fear that she will guess how gut-wrenchingly lonely he is and feel sorry for him. He had enough pity from people after his wife left to last him a lifetime, and he doesn't want it from Maggie.

Maggie leaves them to their projects and goes to her room, shutting the door behind her. She is overwhelmed. The level of noise and energy accompanying teenage boys is something to which she has become a stranger. She treasures the easy conversation they had earlier and realizes this is precious bonding time, but the emotional need she senses from these three people is exhausting, and Maggie can only pray she is up to the job.

Maggie unpacks her suitcase, hanging her school clothes on new hangers, lining her shoes up neatly on the closet floor, and putting the rest of her clothes in the bureau. She opens all the new toiletries and organizes them in the cart, which she rolls over beside the long mirror.

Maggie gathers the trash from her purchases into a single bag to take downstairs and looks around her room. She is much more settled now that her things are put away and she has had a few minutes of peace and quiet. Peace and quiet in this house will be in short supply, but strangely, the thought of that doesn't make her unhappy. Maggie opens her door and heads for the stairs just as Jack comes out of Trent's room, so they walk down together.

"Thank you for everything," Jack says. "It was very thoughtful of you to get something special for the boys."

"You're welcome," she replies. "I was happy to do it. Is spaghetti for dinner okay?"

"Sure," Jack tells her as they reach the bottom of the staircase. "Sounds great to me."

As Jack goes back to his interrupted football game, Maggie heads to the freezer in the utility room for hamburger. She pops the meat in the microwave to thaw, fills a large pot with water and puts it on the stove to boil, then moves her bedding to the dryer and starts a load of new towels. When the water is boiling, she adds salt and puts in the pasta along with a dollop of olive oil, then crumbles the thawed hamburger into a skillet to brown. Maggie usually makes her own sauce, but since it is already 6:00, tonight the sauce will come from a jar.

While the pasta cooks, Maggie starts a pan of freshly snapped green beans cooking on another burner, makes a salad, and slices crusty French bread. She steps to the bottom of the stairs and calls up to see if the boys will set the table. After a brief silence, she hears doors close and feet thudding overhead, so she goes back into the kitchen.

The boys come ambling through the door and stand looking at her as if they don't know what to do. She opens a cupboard and says, "Plates—we need four." She opens a drawer and says, "Silverware—knife, fork, spoon—four of each set."

Silently, Brad gets the plates and Trent gets the silverware, and they set the table, moving the piles Maggie sorted on Friday to the coffee table in the living room.

Maggie puts the bread on the table along with the butter, the salad, salad dressing, the green beans, and salt and pepper. She adds the sauce to the meat so it can warm, drains the pasta, and then mixes it all together in a big bowl while the boys stand watching. "Go wash your hands," she directs, and they leave to do as she asks.

"Jack," Maggie calls. "Dinner is ready." Jack turns off the television and walks into the kitchen. As he finishes washing his hands at the kitchen sink, the boys tumble through the doorway, each trying to be the first at the table.

"Boys!" says Maggie, at the same time as Jack says, "Knock it off!"

Trent gives Brad a final push and sits down with a plop. The others find seats at the table. As Jack reaches for the spaghetti, Maggie asks, "Shall we pray?"

The boys look at Jack uncertainly, and Jack tells them to bow their heads.

Maggie makes the sign of the cross and then begins to pray. "Bless us, oh Lord, in these, Thy gifts, which we are about to receive from Thy bounty, through Christ our Lord. Amen." Again, she crosses herself, and as the Hallas men sit frozen, she smiles at them and says, "Dig in! I hope you're hungry."

The boys do indeed dig in, and Maggie has forgotten how much hungry teenage boys and men can eat. The food seems to magically disappear down their throats as they keep filling their plates until only a small helping of spaghetti remains. Maggie has long since finished the small portion she was able to make herself eat, as she is still suffering from the odd loss of appetite and nausea that began the day Clark died, and watches them in fascination.

Jack pushes back his chair and rises, gathering his dirty plate and silverware. He takes them to the sink, the boys following his example, as Maggie does the same. Working together, they clear the table while Maggie runs hot water into the sink and starts washing dishes.

Once the table is clear and wiped off, Jack tells the boys to bring in their homework. Maggie watches them lackadaisically pull crumpled papers and a few books from their backpacks as she finishes the dishes. She finds the list of missing assignments she gathered from the boys' teachers last week and brings it to the table. As she questions them to determine if they have Monday's homework completed, she realizes they really have no idea, so she decides to start at square one.

Sitting between them, she has Brad and Trent empty their backpacks onto the table and helps them sort and organize the contents. Completed assignments they didn't bother to turn in go in one pile, partially completed assignments and any printed worksheets go in another pile, books and notebooks in a third, and everything else goes in the trash.

Maggie finds it interesting that most of the completed assignments are Brad's math homework. He obviously enjoys math, or he wouldn't have done the work, but she is at a loss as to why he hasn't turned them in, and makes him promise to do so tomorrow. She will check with his math teacher after school to make sure.

Once they are organized, Maggie consults the list and reminds them of what homework is due tomorrow, then watches as they begin their lessons. When she is sure they are on the right track, Maggie moves the laundry and takes her warm, clean bedding up to make her bed. She comes back down in time to see Brad slug Trent, starting a brief scuffle that quickly subsides as she walks in.

"What's the problem?" she asks.

"He called me stupid," Brad mumbles, not looking at her.

"Trent," Maggie says, "that is not nice, and I don't want to hear it from you again. Are we clear?"

Trent nods and apologizes to his brother without prompting.

Turning to Brad, Maggie tells him, "You know you're not stupid, right?"

"With this I am!" Brad bursts out. "I hate English!"

"Well, you're in luck then," Maggie says. "English is my favorite subject, so we'll get through this in no time." She gives him an encouraging smile. As Brad shows her his assignment, Maggie is able to explain the concept in a way he understands, and a light of dawning comprehension shines in his eyes. She loves that light; it is why she became a teacher.

With Maggie's help, both boys soon finish their homework, and she shows them how to pack so the completed assignments don't get crumpled and are easy to find to turn in. The uncompleted ones she keeps on the table for another day, realizing the youngsters have had enough for tonight. A lot of changes have occurred in their lives over the past few days, with more to come as they adjust to attending school all day, every day, and she doesn't want to frustrate and alienate them.

She sends them off to get ready for bed, and sits at the table thinking about the day. What a long strange one—beginning with her erotic dream of Clark and ending with sophomore English and eighth grade math. Maggie is more than ready to call it a day, but then remembers she still has papers to grade.

Under the pretense of watching football, Jack is monitoring the academic battle in the dining room and thinking about dinner. Long before Maggie called him in to eat, his stomach was growling in response to the good smells wafting from within the kitchen. When he entered the room and saw the table set and laden with food, the kitchen neat and homey-feeling, and a pretty woman with a smile like an angel's turning from the sink asking him to wash up, it all seemed slightly unreal to Jack, as if his life had been turned into a movie with a happy ending.

Now he can hear Maggie's soft voice interspersed with those of his sons—Trent's still a boy's and Brad's dipping into the deeper register with occasional jumps to an upper octave. He can't remember Caroline ever sitting with them and helping with homework. If anyone did, it was usually Jack if he was home in time, and it usually ended with the boys frustrated and Jack losing his temper. Maggie has a gift, he realizes as he listens. She can explain the most confusing ideas and rules in a way that can be easily understood, and her cheerful demeanor and excitement for learning is contagious. The constant sadness that veils her eyes lifts while she is teaching, and her features become as animated as Jack has yet to see them.

As they finish and she sends them from the table, Jack hears her sigh and sees her slump in the chair for a moment. The sadness comes back to her face, and she looks tired. Jack is surprised to find her sorrow causes him pain. He looks away as she pushes in her chair and walks into the living room.

"Do you mind if I watch the game while I grade papers?" she asks.

Jack shrugs his assent, so Maggie settles on the couch with her pile of papers, a red pen, and a glass of ice water.

A pleasant silence falls between them with the chatter of the television sports announcers and the boys' noisy bedtime routine as background. Occasionally, one of them makes a comment about a play or a call by an official, but neither feels the need for conversation.

Eventually, the boys are finished in the bathroom and come in to say goodnight. Jack stands and hugs each one in turn as Maggie wishes them pleasant dreams from the couch, and the two go galumphing up the stairs. Quiet returns to the room, broken only by the crackle of paper and scratch of pen as Maggie continues to grade papers.

She finishes just as the game concludes, gathers her papers into their folders, and puts them on the table ready for morning while Jack gets ready for bed and locks the doors. He tells Maggie goodnight before he goes into his room, the only room in the house she hasn't seen, and closes the door.

Maggie goes upstairs to get the bag she is using to take her things back and forth to the bathroom, then comes back down to brush her teeth and wash her face. As she turns off the lights and heads back to her room, she realizes *Oh, shoot! I didn't bring pajamas. I don't even OWN pajamas!* Maggie has slept nude since she and Clark got married thirty years ago, and the need for pajamas didn't occur to her. She doesn't even have a robe or sweats with her to wear down in the morning. *Oops! I guess I'll just have to wear my dirty dress, and then I can stop by my house tomorrow and grab something.*

She locks her bedroom door behind her, switches off the light and walks in the dark to the bed, putting her cell phone on the nightstand by touch to serve as an alarm clock. Stripping to the skin and dropping her clothes to the floor at her feet, she slides under the covers, shivering at their coldness. The September night is chilly up here in the mountains. The blankets on the bed are heavy enough to warm her quickly, and she feels her body relax. It is very quiet here with no cars, no sirens, no cats fighting, and the birds have gone to bed hours ago. Tonight, however, the silence doesn't bother her. She has the warm glow of a job well-done to protect her from it. Maggie falls asleep.

Downstairs, Jack is not so lucky. He usually falls into an exhausted coma as soon as his head hits the pillow, but tonight he can't stop thinking about Maggie Sullivan. He likes everything about her. He likes having her in his house, seeing her with his children, and he worries he might like her too much. The situation with the boys is tricky enough without throwing an attraction to their housekeeper into the mix.

Finally, though, it is the thought of her helping the boys with their homework that comforts him. Keeping them in school and helping them be successful at their studies has been a huge stress for him, and now that Maggie is here, he can let this burden slip from his mind. Finally, Jack sleeps also.

Catherine Bridwell

# CHAPTER 7

When Maggie wakes Monday morning, she puts on her dress from yesterday, grabs her bathroom bag and clean clothes, and goes downstairs. It is still dark, but the dawn is close enough to allow her to navigate the stairs without turning on a light. Jack's door is open, and she can tell by the feel of the house he has already gone. Maggie slips into the bathroom to get ready for the day. Showered, moisturized, and dressed, she goes upstairs to do her hair and makeup before coming back down to the kitchen to start breakfast. She doesn't know how long it will take Brad and Trent to get ready, so she wakes them up on her way down. The boys take turns in the bathroom, grumbling at each other as brothers do, and then come in for a breakfast of hash browns, bacon, and eggs as Maggie puts it on the table.

While the boys eat, Maggie quickly washes the pots and pans, then their plates and silverware while they brush their teeth. She has never been much of a breakfast person, preferring fruit and protein leftovers mid-morning to a heavy meal right after awakening, so she grabs a banana, her jacket, purse, and school papers and is ready to go. The boys hook their backpacks over a shoulder, and the three of them go to the car for the trip to town.

Maggie parks at the elementary school as usual and watches the boys walk across the field to the junior-senior high. On the way to town, she told them she would be e-mailing their teachers every period today to make sure they were in class, and she hopes knowing she will be checking on them will ensure they don't skip. Once the boys enter the other building, Maggie goes inside as well and begins her day.

As promised, she contacts each of Brad and Trent's teachers

at the start of the period to check on the boys' attendance. When school is out, the kids walk back over to the elementary school and into her classroom. Maggie gathers her things and they drive out to the ranch.

On the way home, the boys tell Maggie about their day. Things seem to have gone well, and she senses they are happy to be back in class with their friends and happy to have some structure back in their lives, even if they don't exactly realize it. Once in the house, Maggie gives the teens a snack of fruit, cheese, and crackers, after which all three change into work clothes, and the boys show Maggie the various chores Jack has assigned them, which include watering the free-range chickens and gathering eggs, feeding the pigs, checking the water trough at the horse pasture and filling it if needed, chopping kindling, and filling the wood box against the chill of autumn evenings. The fresh air and sunshine are invigorating and fill Maggie with energy.

After chores, Maggie starts some round steak to sear for Swiss steak while the boys get out their homework. First on the agenda are the assignments due for tomorrow, then Maggie chooses one missing assignment from each of their stacks and starts them on these while she adds the tomato sauce and onions to the steak and starts peeling potatoes to fry. Homework is finished with very little issue, the boys quickly realizing that, while Maggie will help them and explain it as often as needed, she means business. The two put their books and papers in their backpacks and go off to watch television.

Maggie covers the steak and puts it in the oven to finish, slices the potatoes into the pan and seasons them, then gets out her own papers and starts to work. Dinner and grading are finished simultaneously, so she puts the folders on a shelf near the door and calls the boys to set the table. Tonight, they don't need to be told what to do or where things are. They even help put the food on the table and bow their heads for the blessing.

Trent asks Maggie what the sign of the cross means, and the three enjoy a discussion about the symbolism of the gesture and about faith in general. After dinner, Maggie makes a plate for Jack as the boys clear the table. She washes dishes while they relax in front of the television. Maggie vows to herself to change this habit; maybe she can find some books to interest them.

Just before it is time for the boys to get ready for bed, Jack comes in. He looks chilly and tired but takes time to sit down with his sons and talk to them about their day. Maggie is pleased to see Jack really listen and ask questions that elicit more conversation. He tries to be a good father, she thinks; he just doesn't spend enough time with them. She imagines Jack coming home to a cold, dark house, with only the light from the television showing, to boys resentful from being left alone, and still having to fix dinner as well as try to get them to do homework. Or, worse yet, coming home to find them gone, driving back to town, finding them, and driving back out to the ranch with dinner, homework, and chores still needing to be done. It must have been a nightmare for Jack as well as the children. She is increasingly sure coming here was the right decision.

She goes into the kitchen and puts Jack's dinner in the microwave to warm up while he washes his hands in the utility room sink. Maggie brings the plate to Jack's place at the table, pours him a glass of ice water, and goes into the utility room as he sits down. She is still behind on laundry and spends the time, while Jack is eating, folding the new bathroom and kitchen linens she washed last night. Maggie starts another load from the piles on the floor and then puts the folded laundry away. At some point, she becomes aware that Jack is watching her, but when she looks at him, he looks away.

The boys come in to say goodnight to their father and, as he did last night, Jack stands to hug them then takes his dirty dishes to the sink as Brad and Trent leave the room.

Maggie follows them to the stairs, where she praises their behavior and hard work today, and tells them goodnight. She goes back to the kitchen to finish the dishes and wipe off the table and kitchen counters. When the kitchen is tidy, she locks the back door, turns off the kitchen light and takes her lesson plan book to the living room to finish the week.

Jack is in the shower by then. He comes out shortly, his dark hair wetly combed down, wearing flannel pajama pants and a t-shirt. Maggie realizes this is the first time she has seen him in anything except jeans and a button-up, long-sleeved shirt. She catches herself staring at his tan, muscled arms and looks quickly away, hoping he didn't notice. It is getting more difficult to keep Jack in the parent category instead of in the man category in her head.

Jack sits down and turns the volume up on the Monday night football game, and Maggie works on lesson plans and listens to the game. Neither of them speak, but for some reason, it's not awkward at all. Finally, Maggie is finished and heads up for her bathroom bag and gets ready for bed. She tells Jack goodnight on the way by, and he wishes her the same. Up in her room, Maggie changes into the pajamas she borrowed from Tracy today at lunch, puts her phone on the nightstand, and goes to bed. The first full day is finished.

Jack stays up to watch the end of the football game. He had a long, hard day but knows he is still too wound up to sleep. He listens to Maggie moving around first in the bathroom, then upstairs. He can smell the sweet scent of the lotion she uses lingering in the air.

Coming home tonight to the lights of a warm, clean house, with dinner waiting for him and his sons there and glad to see him was an experience Jack was not emotionally prepared for. He found himself moved to the verge of tears by the time he finished talking to the boys. He doesn't think Maggie realizes what a change has already taken place in this home, thanks to her, but Jack knows how huge it really is.

The game is over and Jack is yawning, so he shuts off the living room light and goes to bed. Tonight he falls right to sleep.

# CHAPTER 8

The first week Maggie lives with the Hallas family is difficult. The boys aren't used to a regular schedule, they aren't used to having someone keep such close track of them, and they aren't used to doing so much schoolwork. There are moments of defiance, frustration, and even anger, but through it all, Maggie is consistent, firm, and kind. By the end of the week, things settle down.

All the work assigned to Trent and Brad for the week is turned in on time, completed to Maggie's satisfaction. Many of the missing assignments are also finished and turned in, and the principal, impressed by the turn-around in their grades and behavior, has given them permission to start football practice on Monday. Maggie is a little concerned that practice will put them behind again and tells them if they start having late work, no more football.

By Friday, however, she is ready to be in her own house again. Jack gets the boys up early and takes them with him for a day working on the ranch, so Maggie takes a leisurely shower after they leave. She changes the sheets on all the beds except Jack's, dusts upstairs and down, tidies the boys' rooms, and sweeps and mops the upstairs rooms, hall, and stairs. She puts a load of dirty sheets in to wash while she cleans the bathroom from top to bottom and moves on to the living room.

After she dusts and vacuums the living room, she finally has time to wash the windows in that room, taking down the curtains to wash once the bedding is finished. Maggie uses Jack's cordless power screwdriver to hang curtain rods in the kitchen. She unwraps the curtains she bought for the kitchen and irons them before putting them on the newly installed rods. She does the same with the curtains for the upstairs bedrooms. Even though no one lives near the ranch, she still feels better once there are curtains on the windows.

The kitchen is already clean, so until the laundry is done, the only thing left is to sweep and mop the downstairs floors. She empties the mop bucket over the fence and takes a moment to enjoy the view and the cool mountain morning. The first load of sheets is ready for the dryer, so she goes back in to move the laundry and start the next load.

While Maggie was outside, she noticed some tools and pieces of what looked like tack in the tall grass along the fence, so she goes back outside and picks them up. This turns into a thorough search of the yard for hidden objects, and she has a box full of them by the time she finishes. Putting the box on the porch, she moves the rest of the sheets to the dryer and starts the living room curtains in the washer.

Maggie takes a notepad and pen out to the porch step and makes a quick menu for the following week and a shopping list. She sits in the sunshine until the buzz of the dryer sounds and goes into the house to put the curtains in the dryer and fold the linen. When she has folded the sheets, she takes them to the upstairs linen closet and goes to her room to pack her dirty laundry for the trip home. She goes down with the suitcase thumping behind her and loads it into the car.

While she waits for the curtains to finish, she goes through some of the clutter on the porch, throwing away what is obviously garbage, and sorting the rest into somewhat organized piles. Most of it Jack or the boys will have to deal with, but some of it she puts away in the utility room.

The curtains are dry, so she quickly irons and re-hangs them. The house is clean from top to bottom (except for Jack's room—she really needs to speak to him about that), and Maggie goes home.

During the past week, Maggie went home every day for lunch, so she was able to make sure things were okay at her house, but she is very glad to be back. She unpacks her dirty clothes, starts more laundry, and puts her suitcase away. She meets Tracy for lunch and shares her week with her sister.

The weekend passes quickly, and by Sunday afternoon, Maggie is headed back to the ranch. She realizes on the drive that she misses the boys (and Jack) and is excited to see them.

They are happy to see her too and talk non-stop for the first twenty minutes she is there, even Jack contributing to the conversation. Maggie checks their homework which, to her surprise, they have already finished, and starts dinner, and the second week begins.

This week the boys are sore and tired from football practice, and after the first day, Maggie brings a snack for them to eat on the trip home. This takes care of the irritability issue they had the day before. Hungry boys are cranky boys! They quickly settle into a routine that shapes the following weeks. After school, the boys go to practice while Maggie stays in her classroom to grade papers, write lesson plans, and prepare materials for the next day. Trent's shorter junior high practice finishes before Brad's, so Trent comes to her room and does his homework or reads at a table in the back while he munches on the snack she gives him. When Brad finishes practice, he walks over and they go home, Brad eating his snack in the car.

At the house, they change into work clothes, and Maggie helps with the chores so they can finish faster now that they are getting home so much later. Most days, she starts dinner in the slow cooker before they leave in the mornings so it is ready when they get in from chores, and she puts it on the table while the boys wash their hands, then they say the blessing and eat.

They help her clear the table, and Trent now dries the dishes for her while she helps Brad with his homework. Once Brad is done, the boys read or watch television, and Maggie does laundry or other housekeeping until Jack comes home. He and the boys talk, and Brad and Trent get ready for bed while Jack eats. Maggie washes his dishes and Jack takes a shower, then they sit in companionable silence.

Since Maggie is doing her school work while the boys are at practice, she now has time to read and has also started knitting again, making socks and scarves and hats for Christmas gifts. Jack usually watches television, but he also sometimes reads. More often, as time goes by, he tells her about his day. Then it's off to bed for both of them.

On Friday mornings, Maggie cleans the house and changes the bed linens. She has gotten permission from Jack now to clean his room. Apparently, he was just nervous about a stranger seeing his private space, and now he knows her well enough to be okay with it. His room is bare except for the bed and dresser and an old steamer trunk he uses as a nightstand, so all there is to do is make the bed, dust, and clean the floor.

Since it takes less time for the house now, Maggie can clean the porch and mow the lawn. She finds flower beds under the overgrown grass and makes plans for spring to bring them back to life.

Every Thursday at 5:00, there is a junior high football game. If it's a home game, Jack meets her there to watch Trent play. Brad comes over to join them after his practice. Trent is big for a junior high athlete, quick and aggressive, so he gets plenty of playing time. They go out to eat after the game and get home very late, but it's okay, because they have Friday off. If the game is away, Jack goes alone to watch Trent. She waits at school for Brad, and they go home as usual. In September, the weather is warm at this time of day, but by the first week of October, Maggie is wearing her heavy coat.

Every Friday, there is a varsity football game. The home games are all at 7:00, and Brad has to be there by 5:30, so they all come to Maggie's house in town for an early dinner before going to the game. If the game is away, Jack brings Brad to school to catch the team bus, then he and Trent pick Maggie up and they drive to the game. If there is time, they eat on the way; if not, they get a burger at the game. Maggie has always liked football, and she and Clark went to all of Kevin's games, so it is fun to be attending again.

Maggie enjoys watching Jack at these games almost as much as watching Brad. Jack gets very involved in the game, but in a positive way. He doesn't yell at his son, the other players, or the officials, but shouts encouragement to everyone and praises good play regardless of the team. He paces the sidelines, which Maggie has never done. She is so short, it is hard for her to see, but Jack soon realizes the problem and makes sure to clear a spot for her at his side. Since the varsity games are played in the evening, it is much colder, and after the first game, Maggie packs extra blankets for her and Trent to put around their shoulders. Jack never seems to get cold, no matter what the weather does.

Brad, who is tall and fast with great hands, plays receiver on offense and corner on defense. Although just a sophomore, he starts every game and is one of the leading receivers on the team, scoring at least one touchdown each game. Every week, Maggie sees his confidence growing. He seems to bloom under Jack's commitment to watch him play.

Football shapes her life these days, but she still meets Tracy for lunch every Friday. Saturdays are for yard work, cleaning, and taking care of bills and paperwork. Sundays, she writes lesson plans, packs for the week to come, and goes to Mass before driving to the ranch. During these weeks, Maggie still mows the lawn every Saturday. Even though the grass isn't growing much this time of year, the bagger on the mower picks up the leaves that have begun to fall. She cuts off her peonies and iris for the winter, plants some crocus bulbs by the front gate, and mulches the roses.

Maggie calls Ed at Furnaces are Us, and he comes by to give the furnace its annual checkup and change the filters. One Friday, when there is a home game, Jack brings the boys to town early and spends the afternoon winterizing her camper and Clark's boat. She doesn't know why she kept the boat after Clark died; she can't drive it or put it in or out of the water, but she hasn't been able to make herself sell it. It makes Maggie a little sad seeing Jack in Clark's garage working on Clark's toys, but she knows if she doesn't winterize them, they will be ruined.

The last weekend in September, Maggie drives to Boise and spends the day with Maura and Tom and baby Patrick. She stops on the way home to stock up on groceries, hoping to keep up with the appetites of her teenage charges. In October, she flies to Seattle to spend the weekend for her granddaughter, Emma's, fourth birthday. She and Kevin have a heart-to-heart, and he seems to finally understand why she is working for Jack.

The weeks pass quickly, and Maggie is happy. She still misses and mourns Clark, but she is happy.

Catherine Bridwell

# CHAPTER 9

For Jack, fall is a race against time, a race against the coming of winter. When Jack's father fell in love with the Council area and first purchased the home place in Lost Valley, most of the land outside of town—that wasn't part of the Payette National Forest or BLM—was owned by a few long-established families. Jacob Hallas, knowing he needed more property if he was to develop the kind of ranch he dreamed of, made do with buying anything in a 150-mile area that would make good pasture or hay ground. By the time Jacob died and Jack took over the ranch, he owned a raggedy patchwork of land from Weiser to north of New Meadows along Highway 95 and even some land over near Cascade in Long Valley. The distances between Jack's holdings made it time-consuming to travel between them, and the number of barns, outbuildings, and equipment needed at each site added to Jack's workload.

All summer, Jack and his hired men, Richard Morris and Dan Parker, worked night and day trying to get enough hay put up to feed the cattle and horses through the winter. Jack also has grazing rights on the Forest, so part of the summer work is to check on the cattle, keep them pushed into the right areas, make sure they have water, and move them to other grazes as feed becomes scarce. Jack got lucky with the weather this year and his hay didn't get rained on, and it is all baled and in the barns and sheds at the various sites where he needs it.

Now the equipment must be cleaned and overhauled, broken, damaged or worn-out parts replaced, fluid levels checked, and wheel bearings packed. The big barn on the Smokey Boulder place, where Dan Parker lives, lost half the roof in a wind storm in July. Jack and the guys, with help from Brad and Trent, spent the first three weeks of September rebuilding the barn roof. The barns at the Hornet Creek place and the home place need inspected so loose tin and boards can be repaired. The buildings need to be weather-tight against the winter storms and also against marauding herds of hungry elk or the cattle won't have enough hay. The fences at all the winter feeding areas have to be checked and loose and broken wires fixed before the cattle come down from the Forest. Equipment for moving snow needs to be in good working order or no one will be able to get to town, and the tractors won't be able to get the hay to the cattle. All these things must be done by the end of October so the gathering of the herd from Forest land can begin.

Jack, Parker, Morris, and the boys when feasible, will be riding every day on the Forest to find the cattle. They will leave before daylight in the mornings when Parker brings the big cattle truck from Smokey Boulder and Jack drives the pickup and horse trailer full of horses and tack from the home place. Morris will join them at some corral central to one of their grazing areas, and they will saddle their horses and mount up for a day of searching for cattle. They will push the animals through the trees and brush toward, and eventually into, the corral after which Parker will back the truck up to the loading chute so the cattle can be herded up the ramp into the trailer of the big rig. All the cattle are taken to the home place, and once Jack is sure all of his animals are accounted for, they will be vaccinated and sorted.

About half the herd will go to Hornet Creek where Richard Morris will feed them. Morris lives there with his wife and a half-dozen or so little Morris'. He lost count after the fourth one. Jack can't pay a huge wage, but there is a house, all the meat they can eat, and the ranch buys the fuel for their vehicles. Richard seems content and always does his work with a smile.

The first-calf heifers will be hauled to Smokey Boulder, and Dan Parker will keep a close eye on them for the winter, feeding them and checking them at intervals day and night once they start to calve until their calves are all on the ground. Jack heard a rumor once that Parker's fiancé left him at the altar when he was a young man. While that would certainly explain Parker's bitter dislike of all women, he has no idea if it's true. All he knows is that there is nobody better at helping a cow through a difficult birth than Parker. Crotchety bachelor or not, the man has a magician's touch with flighty, scared heifers trying to deliver their first calf.

All the steers except for the ones they keep for meat and any cows that aren't bred will be hauled to the sale ring. The rest of the herd will spend the winter at the home place under Jack's care.

Jack is doing a balancing act between all he needs to accomplish by the middle of November and spending time with his sons. He gets up earlier in the mornings and pushes himself harder during the days so he can leave early for football games without feeling guilty for not pulling his weight. These dearly bought hours, when he watches Brad and Trent play ball, listens to them talk about the games on the way home, and gets an occasional sweaty hug on the sidelines are precious to him, and he regrets none of the cost.

He is more grateful every day for Maggie Sullivan. Knowing the boys are safe, fed, supervised, and doing well in school gives Jack the strength to keep going—to keep building his legacy for his sons. Maggie has brought sanity to Jack's life, and warmth and grace. He likes her more each day: her sense of humor, her gentle smile, her spunkiness, her ability to be tough but kind with the boys, and her calm air of competence.

Jack likes walking into the games with Maggie by his side, likes standing on the sidelines with her huddled next to him wrapped to the nose in a blanket, likes sitting with her and his boys in a restaurant replaying the game while they eat, likes driving home with her in the front seat and the boys asleep in the back seat, listening to the radio and not needing to talk. In fact, Jack thinks he likes her way more than he should. In fact, Jack thinks he is falling in love with Maggie Sullivan.

Catherine Bridwell

# CHAPTER 10

By the last week in October, Trent's football season is over, so now once his homework is finished, he sometimes goes home with a friend to hang out or play video games until Brad is done with practice and Maggie picks them up. Brad has earned back his pickup keys, and he and Maggie take turns driving to school each day, so two days a week, Brad picks them up.

The mornings are cold now, and it has rained quite a bit the past few weeks making the roads rutted and muddy. Brad's team has one game left, but they already know they won't qualify for state. Maggie has planned a special dinner at her house to celebrate the boys' seasons. As she drives to town to meet Tracy for lunch, she runs through her plans in her head, making sure she hasn't forgotten anything.

After lunch, she makes a quick trip to the grocery store and heads home to start cooking. She starts a batch of yeast rolls and puts them over the heat register to rise, then bakes a peach cobbler for an after-game dessert and grates cheese for lasagna. By 5:00, the lasagna is ready, the table is set, a green salad is prepared, and Maggie is brushing the tops of golden-brown rolls with melted butter. She hears a knock at the door and hurries to let in Jack and the boys.

After dinner, Brad drives to the school to get dressed down and stretch for his game. Jack and Trent help Maggie clean up the kitchen. They watch television for a while and then bundle up for the last game of the year.

The three of them walk through the ticket gate at the football field, and a woman steps forward and speaks to them. "Hello, Jack. Hi, Trent," she says.

Maggie recognizes her at once from pictures in Brad's room. It's Caroline—Jack's ex-wife and mother to his children. Maggie, who was walking slightly behind Jack when he stopped abruptly in her path, bumps up against him, so she can feel his body tense when Caroline speaks. Maggie steps around Jack into a weighted silence as Jack stares at Caroline without saying anything.

"Hi, Mom," Trent says in a small voice, breaking the silence. He steps toward his mother, and she enfolds him in a long hug.

Jack watches without expression.

When Caroline finally releases Trent, Maggie, seeing that Jack is not going to talk, holds out her hand and introduces herself as Jack's housekeeper.

"Oh," Caroline says disdainfully, not bothering to take Maggie's hand, "I heard you were his girlfriend."

Stung, Maggie drops her hand to her side and turns to continue to the sidelines, pulling Trent with her so Caroline and Jack can talk. *What a bitch*, she thinks and is instantly sorry. Caroline has committed her share of sins (lying, coveting, greed, lust, and adultery, to name a few) but by judging her, Maggie is doing her own sinning, and she sends a quick prayer asking God for forgiveness. Finding the same forgiveness in her heart for Caroline may take a little longer.

She looks back over her shoulder once at the couple having an intense conversation behind her. Caroline is tall and willowy, dressed very stylishly with her tight, skinny jeans tucked into knee-high boots and her long, blonde hair trailing down her back over her black wool pea coat. Maggie sees where Trent's blond hair and Brad's tall, slender build come from. She also has an unpleasant feeling in her stomach when she notices what a striking couple Jack and Caroline make. Up until now, Caroline has been a mythical figure in Maggie's picture of the Hallas family, but tonight she has become real. Maggie puts an arm around Trent's shoulders and asks if he is okay.

Trent shrugs and looks back at his parents. "Do you think they are fighting?" he asks her.

"I don't know," Maggie truthfully tells him. "I hope not. I hope they're just having a good talk about you and your brother." She gives him a one-armed hug. "Go find your friends and try not to worry about it."

Trent shoots her a grin and runs off.

Maggie continues to their normal spot on the sidelines. After a few minutes, Jack joins her.

Caroline walks to the stands and sits partway up the bleachers beside an older, gray-haired man in a heavy dress coat and scarf. At first, Jack is silent, then he tells her that Caroline is here to watch Brad play ball and doesn't intend to cause a problem or upset the boys. Maggie hopes this is true. Once the game begins, they become swept up in the action and forget momentarily about Caroline.

Afterward, however, her presence is brought front and center when she goes to Brad and attempts to hug him. Through the crowd of parents, fans, and sweaty boys in football jerseys, Maggie sees Brad stiffen and allow the hug, but he doesn't return it.

Jack starts toward his son with Trent in tow. Maggie tries to excuse herself to give the family some privacy, but Jack pulls her forward with a hand on her arm as they come close enough to hear the conversation between mother and son.

"What are you doing here, Mom?" Brad asks.

Caroline answers, "I just missed you and wanted to see you play."

"It took you long enough," Brad says sarcastically, staring her down.

Ashamed, Caroline looks away. "I'm sorry, sweetie, it's just that I've been really busy."

"Well, I'm busy now, so you can go back to wherever it is you came from," Brad tells her and pushes past her to walk to the locker room with his teammates.

Caroline stares sadly after him and then turns back to Jack. "Great attitude," she says accusingly.

"Mom, don't," Trent says. "It's not Dad's fault Brad is mad at you."

"You're right, Trent. I didn't come tonight to upset you or your brother, so maybe it's better if I just leave," Caroline says repentantly.

Jack finally speaks. "Caroline, the boys are just surprised to see you. Give them a minute to process. Next time, you should probably call first so they can be prepared. It's been months without a word, and then you show up out of the blue. What did you expect?"

Caroline acknowledges Jack's rebuke with a shrug. "You're right, I guess. Next time, I'll call ahead. Hey, Trent, it was really great to see you." With that, she turns and walks away, leaving them all staring after her.

"Wow," Jack sighs. "That was awkward."

Both Trent and Maggie burst out laughing, and the tension is broken. They link arms and walk to the car for the drive to Maggie's house where Brad will meet them for dessert. When Brad arrives, he is in a foul mood, but it doesn't take long in Maggie's warm, cozy house with a plate of peach cobbler and ice cream in front of him before he starts to lighten up.

By the time Jack leaves with them, the boys seem to have recovered from the shock of seeing their mother. Maggie lies awake that night wondering if Jack will bounce back as quickly.

# CHAPTER 11

Jack is wondering the same thing. It was unreal having Caroline turn up at Brad's game like that.

*She hasn't even called the boys since last March, and now she wants to be part of their lives again?* Jack is pretty sure that's not okay. He's pretty sure he's not okay either. Even though he knows he doesn't love Caroline anymore, she can still push his buttons, and since she will always be the boys' mother, she will always be in his life. He doesn't want her flitting in and out of the picture, upsetting their carefully constructed happiness at will. He can only hope she will be true to form and vanish again for a few months. Jack tosses and turns half the night worrying about it.

When Jack wakens, there are three inches of snow on the ground. He knows the snow will bring the cattle down from the mountains. When he does chores, he sees some cows with calves milling around down by the pasture gate, so he jumps on the four-wheeler and drives across the valley to open the gate and let them into the home place. By noon, the snow will have melted and there will be plenty of grass for them. Every day now, more will show up on their own while he and his cowboys will be out gathering the rest.

Back in the house after the chores are finished, Jack fixes breakfast and rousts the boys out of bed. He let them sleep in since it was late when they returned from the game; also, they were a little rattled over seeing their mom so unexpectedly, so he sat up talking with them until almost midnight letting them vent a little.

After breakfast, Jack talks to the boys about riding for him during the next two weeks. He will take each of them out of school one day each week, scheduled around tests and important assignments, and expects them to help on Fridays and Saturdays as well until the cattle are off the Forest and safely home for the winter. The boys are excited to do what they consider "real" ranch work, but Jack knows they will be cold, sore, and tired by the end of each day and happy to be at school afterward.

To help them get ready, he suggests they ride the perimeter of the home pasture every day after school since there's no football practice. This will let them keep an eye on the cattle already in the pasture, and they can also check the fences for weak spots and watch for wolves and other predators. He tells them to take Maggie with them so she can learn to ride in case he needs her help.

Trent and Brad laugh at this, trying to imagine Maggie on a horse. Jack makes them promise to give her a gentle horse and help her with the saddle, and they agree. He hopes they won't be too ornery to her. Of course, he will have to approach Maggie about it first, and she may not be agreeable to the idea, but Jack has a feeling she will be willing to try.

Maggie loves the way the snow reflects the light early in the morning and hopes the white blanket is here to stay. The flowers come through the winter better if they have a good layer of snow over them before the temperature drops below zero; but by noon the sun is out, and the snow has melted. It's too wet to mow up leaves, the house is already clean, and Maggie soon finds herself at loose ends.

More often now, her weekends at home feel like she is just killing time until she can go back to the ranch. Maggie is a little alarmed by this; she tries to keep in mind that the ranch, the boys, and Jack are just a job, but it doesn't really feel like that. Her former life in town with Clark seems like a dream to her sometimes. When she is at Jack's, the quiet beauty of the setting and the connection she has with the boys (and with Jack if she is being truthful) has a way of making everything seem sharper, more defined. This feeling of awareness only happens when she is around Jack and the kids, and this frightens Maggie in a way she can't explain.

Restless and bored, she decides to go for a run. She is only running now three days a week, and today her body craves action. Maybe the crisp, fresh air will wipe the cobwebs from her head.

That night, the sound of crying awakens Maggie. At first she can't tell what the sound is, and as she raises her head from the pillow to listen more closely, she realizes the pillow is cold and soaked, and her sleep-clouded mind is slow to come to the realization that the sound is crying, and she is the person who is crying. As she becomes more awake, she is able to control the sobs still issuing from her body and after a few moments, lies quietly in the dark, breathing deeply and trying to overcome the feeling of disorientation common to people who wake suddenly from a deep sleep. Gradually, she remembers the dream she was having.

*Maggie is in a forest. She is wearing a blue dress she used to wear to church quite often, a dress Clark likes her to wear, but now in spite of the belt around the waist, it hangs on her as if she is a child wearing grown-up clothes. Instead of the sensible low heels she usually wears with the dress, she has on her cowboy boots.*

*She knows somehow, as one does in a dream, that the forest is on Jack's ranch. In fact, Jack and the boys are here with her in the forest somewhere; she just can't see them because of the thickness of the trees and the heavy snow coming down from the sky. The four of them are walking through deep snow, with more snow falling, the wind bringing it stinging against her skin. She can feel the bite of the snow against her legs as she walks, the cold shock as it falls into her boots down her shins to her ankles and heels. The thin fabric of the dress billows in the storm, doing nothing to keep the cold from her body. The snow is so deep it makes walking difficult, and Maggie's legs are starting to ache from the unaccustomed strain. She knows, however, that she must keep going.*

*She is looking for Clark, who is also out here in this endless forest somewhere. She calls his name, over and over, searching frantically through the dark evergreens, looking under and around the bushes, but she can't find him. Faintly, she can hear Jack and the boys also calling for Clark. Maggie is grateful they are helping but feels herself starting to lose hope. Finding her husband in this storm seems impossible.*

*Just as she starts to turn back in defeat, Maggie sees Clark ahead—a gray outline against the curtain of snow. Screaming for him to wait, she runs through the snow as fast as she can make her tired legs move, but no matter how fast she runs, she doesn't get any closer. She can feel her legs shaking with fatigue, her breath burning in her throat and lungs as she strives to reach him, and starts to cry with frustration as the distance between them remains.*

*Then Clark waves to her, a slow, solemn farewell wave, and Maggie knows he won't wait any longer. She staggers to a stop, falling to her bare knees in the freezing, wet snow, and watches Clark walk into the white, watches until there is nothing around her but white. Maggie is filled with the deepest sorrow she has ever known in her life, deeper even than the sharp pain she felt when Clark first died. She kneels in the drifts, wrapping her arms over her head, rocking back and forth on the ground as sobs shake her body with a grief that seems unending, her tears freezing on her face as they fall.*

This sorrow is what Maggie feels when she wakes up. In fact, though she has stopped sobbing, tears are still streaming from her eyes as she lies in bed and thinks about what the dream might mean. Maggie realizes there are stages of grief. She knows that from the first day Clark was killed, she was in a form of denial, able to function on the outside, but completely panicked inside, unable to cope with thoughts of a world where Clark doesn't exist. The bubble she found herself in through his funeral service is evidence of more denial as she swallowed all her emotion and forced it back out around her as protection.

Maggie suspects this swallowing and forcing back in of grief is why her stomach has been so nervous ever since her husband died. Before that day, she had a healthy appetite, which never seemed to abate regardless of Maggie's emotional state, and her stomach was calm. Now, she is seldom hungry; she eats when she has to, in small amounts, and is apt to feel nauseous at odd moments throughout the day, her stomach registering everything she won't let her mind process.

She knows the weeks of sleeplessness, the frantic cleaning, and exercise were also a stage of grief—still some denial, but more anger, and some bargaining as well—and if the house is spotless, the lawn is perfect, and she runs far enough, perhaps God will relent and Clark won't really be dead. The dream she had that ended her insomnia was her subconscious telling her it was all right to let him go, to start to heal. Until tonight, Maggie thought she was doing a good job of getting over her husband's death, if such a thing is possible.

Now she sees the difference between healing and total acceptance. Tonight, her mind has manufactured this dream to show her what she refuses to see when she is awake. Clark is dead. Clark will be dead forever. Clark is never coming back. She will never see his dear face again, never hear his voice, never feel his touch. Never, never, never. This is why, after months of feeling pretty okay about things, Maggie is now drenched in sweat, crying her heart out alone in her house. This is the grief she put off, pushed to the back of her head because she didn't think she could survive feeling it, and now grief has come calling for its proper acknowledgment. Maggie gives it.

The clock says 3:30 a.m. when Maggie finally feels the crying weaken; when gasping, still sobbing occasionally, she manages to walk to the bathroom to blow her nose and rinse her burning eyes with cool water. She leans against the sink, naked, with a cool wash cloth pressed to her face, waiting for a semblance of self-control to return.

The wind has come up, and she can hear leaves and even small branches skittering across the roof and thumping into the side of the house. She feels the weight of the empty rooms around her, this house that was once full of life and laughter, and she is as empty inside as the house tonight. Her hair is damp from tears and sweat, and she is cold, cold inside and outside, as if she really were out in a snowstorm half the night.

The thought of going back to her lonely bed with its soggy pillow and twisted sheets makes her shiver even more, so she decides to take a bath to warm up. Adding lavender bath salts, she runs the bathwater as hot as she can tolerate until the tub is full, then turns the water off, steps in and slides beneath the water. It is a pleasant shock to her cold skin, and Maggie leans her head on the edge of the tub and relaxes. As horrible as the dream was, and as hard as it was to come to terms with her grief, Maggie feels better somehow, as if something like poison or infection has been drawn out of her, leaving her weak but whole.

She stays in the tub until the water cools, then steps onto the rug to dry off with a fluffy towel. She sees her body in the mirror on the back of the bathroom door, pink from the bath, slender now instead of plump, and thinks that it's not such a bad body. Running, swimming, and yoga have left her toned, and she can still see her tan lines, the outline of her swimsuit a white imprint on her body. Her skin has lost some elasticity, and her diminished breasts droop a little but, after all, she is 51 years old.

She thinks for the first time since Clark died about sharing this body with someone besides Clark, accepting a man into herself—an idea that once seemed unconceivable but now seems possible. Unbidden, an image of Jack Hallas flashes across her mind, and Maggie swats it away as if it were a fly. She needs to keep Jack in the box she has labeled <u>Parent</u>, she thinks, and then laughs to herself. *I made a pun—Jack-in-the-box!* Realizing she is still standing in the bathroom in her towel, Maggie turns off the bathroom light, crawls into bed on Clark's side and falls immediately to sleep.

Because of her interrupted night, Maggie sleeps until 9:00 Sunday morning, then jumps into the shower and dresses for brunch at Tracy's. Her nighttime adventure seems far away, as if it happened to someone else, but the sense of wellness, of wholeness, persists and grows stronger throughout the day.

When Maggie reaches the ranch and starts upstairs to change and unpack, Jack tells her to put on her jeans and boots. Brad and Trent, capering merrily around the kitchen, tell her they are going to teach her to ride today. As she ascends the stairs, Jack calls after her to hurry; they haven't got much daylight left.

Maggie quickly changes and goes right back downstairs. Unpacking can wait until after dinner. They are waiting for her in the utility room, where they all don coats and gloves.

Although the sun is shining, it is chilly outside. Together, they walk to the barn where earlier in the day the boys had penned four horses, and as they walk, Jack explains his idea about going on scouting rides around the home pasture. The boys had ridden almost daily all summer, but once school started and then football, they are only riding occasionally on weekends.

Once in the barn, the boys catch the horses and lead them into the corridor near the tack room, where they tie the horses' halter ropes to a hitching rail.

Maggie has ridden before. When she and Tracy were small, they had a horse and spent many hours riding double bareback around the neighborhood. However, it has been 40 years since then, so Maggie doesn't mention it but listens gravely and pays close attention as the boys explain to her how to act around the animals and show her how to saddle the mare they have chosen for her to ride.

*They are so serious!* She thinks it's very sweet but would never tell them that.

Her horse, for Trent tells her it is hers for the season, is a tall, sorrel mare named Cupcake. Maggie hopes she is named Cupcake because of the sweetness of her nature and cautiously approaches to introduce herself. The horse sniffs Maggie then snorts and bumps her head into Maggie's arm. Maggie strokes Cupcake's neck, enjoying the silky feel of warm horsehair under her hand. The horses are just starting to get their winter coats and aren't shaggy yet.

She saddles the mare with instruction and advice from the boys as Jack gets his own mount ready for riding and watches in silence. When all the horses are saddled and bridled, Maggie brings the reins over the horse's head, takes them in her left hand as per Brad's direction, reaches her booted left foot as high as she can, and is just able to get her toes in the stirrup. She uses the saddle horn to pull herself up and then swings her right leg over Cupcake's back and settles in the saddle. Cupcake dances sideways, and Maggie instinctively moves with her, using the reins to bring the horse back under control. The boys praise her efforts, and she smiles back at them in appreciation.

Jack knows from the moment he sees Maggie around the horses that she has ridden before or has at least been around animals. The calm, easy way she moves, the tone of her voice, the way she stands slightly to the side in front of Cupcake so the horse can see her tells him this as clearly as if she were speaking. Maggie cups her hand under the horse's nose, lets Cupcake get her scent, and strokes her neck. Jack watches, letting the boys do the talking and teaching. When Maggie swings aboard and quickly settles the horse down, Jack is sure of his deduction.

Jack walks to her side, leading his horse. He hands his reins to her and checks the length of her stirrups. "A little short," he tells her. Moving her foot from the stirrup with a hand on her calf, Jack adjusts the stirrup and ducks under Cupcake's neck to adjust the other one. "How does that feel?" he asks.

"Better," Maggie tells him.

Jack takes his reins back from Maggie and mounts, and the foursome ride out of the barn. As they ride, he observes Maggie carefully. He sees she has a good seat and balance, with soft hands, and is a quiet rider, keeping her upper body still and using her legs to cue the horse. Jack is relieved. If he needs her to ride, it appears she will be more help than bother.

Jack shows them the circuit he wants them to make every afternoon and explains what signs to watch for to know if wolves or other predators are hanging around the cattle. He also cautions them to watch for broken places in the fence and advises Brad to carry fencing supplies on his saddle during these excursions. The boys have heard it all before, but they listen attentively as does Maggie.

# CHAPTER 12

The ride around the home pasture takes a little over an hour. As Maggie listens to Jack explain what he expects from them, she can't help but remember the way Jack's touch on her calf when he adjusted her stirrup, though casual, sent a wave of warmth up her leg and started her pulse racing. Maggie is surprised at her response to him and determines to keep Jack safely off-limits in his *Parent* box.

By the time they head back to the barn, Maggie's butt is sore. She's been wearing her boots and jeans every day helping the boys do chores, so the boots are scuffed now and nicely broken in and the jeans have been washed enough to be soft and comfortable, but neither do much to keep her feet and legs warm.

In the barn, they unsaddle the horses, brush them down, and turn them back out to pasture, then it's time to clean the tack and put it away. The boys show Maggie how Jack likes it done and where everything belongs. Maggie is intrigued by how clean and organized the barn is, especially compared to the condition the house was in when she arrived.

Thirty minutes later, she is hobbling to the house to start dinner with Jack and the boys alongside teasing her and calling her "Gimp" and "Hop Along." Maggie can only hope the daily rides will make her less saddle sore and not more! Cupcake, however, is a great horse, and Maggie thoroughly enjoyed the outing.

The next morning, Maggie is so sore she can hardly climb out of bed. Evidently, running 5-6 miles a week is not good preparation for an hour of horseback riding. This day marks the beginning of a new routine for Maggie, Brad, and Trent.

Now the boys come straight to Maggie's classroom after school, and they hurry home to change so they can ride before dark.

As Maggie had feared, the first two days make her sorer than she already was. Her sitting bones feel as if they are raw, her inner thighs are in agony when she has to grip Cupcake's sides, and her abdomen twinges with every movement. However, by Wednesday, she is feeling better, and by Thursday, isn't sore at all.

The boys are also sore, but being boys, they refuse to admit it, and being young, they recover more quickly. After their daily ride, they unsaddle, brush the horses, clean the tack, and go inside to wash up.

Maggie starts dinner and while she cooks, the brothers do their homework and clear and set the table. After they eat, the tired boys go to bed, and Maggie sits down to do her grading while she waits for Jack.

She hears the cattle truck rumbling over the little hill and down to the corral followed by the lighter sound of Jack's crew cab, dual-axle pickup. There are bangs and clanks as Parker opens the back of the truck, and Maggie can hear the sound of the cattle's hoofs over the sound of their anxious mooing as they clatter from the truck, down the ramp, and out through the chute into the corral. She knows once all the cattle are in the corral, Parker will close the back of the truck and drive away while Jack opens the gate to allow the cattle to go into the pasture. Then he will unload, unsaddle and rub down the horses, and clean and put away the tack.

When Jack gets in the house, he goes straight upstairs to tell the boys goodnight then comes down for supper. Maggie sits at the table with him while he eats and they talk about the day. When he is finished, he takes a shower while Maggie does the dishes and tidies the kitchen, and then they both go to bed.

Jack works long hours during this two-week period, leaving earlier than usual and not getting in until after 9 or 9:30 at night, so he is exhausted. The additional time it takes to ride each evening is taking its toll on Maggie and the boys as well, but every day there are more cattle in the pasture and the gathering is almost done.

One day, they see some fresh bear dung, but no other signs of predators. The weather remains clear, sunny, and warm during the days and cold at nights.

The second week, on Thursday, the three riders discover a large branch has fallen on the fence, breaking some wires, and the cattle have wandered out of the pasture into the surrounding woods. They move the branch and Trent and Brad repair the fence with the supplies from Brad's saddle bag. The boys send Maggie to open the gate while they start rounding up the cattle. By the time all the strays are back in the pasture, the gate shut and the horses put away, it is full dark. Maggie decides to make tacos for dinner, and the boys offer to help, but they have barely started when they hear the cattle truck pull into the corral. Jack is home early.

Jack walks into the warm house, bone-deep tiredness his constant companion. As he washes his cold, chapped hands in the utility room sink, he listens to his sons talk to Maggie in the kitchen as they cook. The sound of their happy voices is music to Jack's ears.

When he enters the kitchen, he sees Maggie at the stove, Brad grating cheese at the counter, and Trent chopping lettuce on the cutting board. He steps behind Maggie, leaning over her shoulder to sniff the good smells emanating from the pan in front of her. He stands close enough he can feel the warmth of her body through his cold shirt, and inhales the sweet scent of her hair and skin along with the spicy odor of the meal she is preparing.

"Smells great," he tells her, his breath ruffling the fine hair at her temple.

"It's almost finished," Maggie answers. He is standing very close to her, his clothes still smelling of fresh air and horses, and Maggie finds her pulse racing and skin flushing. It even becomes difficult for her to breathe for a moment before he moves away.

*Get a grip,* she scolds herself. *You're as giddy as a school girl around him.* Maggie is finding it more difficult every day to continue to see Jack as just a parent and not as a man, but she clings stubbornly to this plan. Quickly, she moves to get dinner on the table, and they sit down to eat.

During dinner, Jack tells them a big storm is on the way and is supposed to hit tomorrow night. There are a quite a few cattle left on Council Mountain, enough to fill the truck, and they have one more day to get them out before it's too late. There is a lot of ground to cover in a day, and he needs all the help he can get. Jack asks Maggie and the boys to ride with him tomorrow.

The boys are excited and chatter about the coming day as they finish eating. Maggie is nervous. She worries that she will slow them down or not be of any real help to Jack, but she is determined to try. Everyone helps with the dishes and clean-up tonight so they can all get to bed early.

The next morning, Maggie's alarm goes off at 5:00 and she goes downstairs to the bathroom. Jack is already dressed and is starting the fire. She hears him heading out for chores as she gets in the shower. She dresses quickly, putting on long johns under her jeans and a tank top and long sleeved t-shirt under her fleece sweatshirt, and goes upstairs to dry her hair, waking the boys on the way. They are sleepy and reluctant to get up, but once they remember why they are being awakened so early, they start moving more quickly. When Maggie's hair is dry, she puts on heavy, wool socks and her boots and goes downstairs.

Jack is back in from doing chores and has started coffee. Maggie turns on the tea kettle and pulls some frozen hash browns from the freezer to start breakfast. They eat a quick meal of hash browns, fried ham, scrambled eggs and toast, and quickly load the dishwasher.

Minutes later, Maggie steps outside into a cold, frosty morning. It is still dark, and the stars in the clear, pre-dawn sky seem close enough to touch. She is bundled in her down coat, with a wool scarf around her neck and fleece-lined gloves on her hands. The boys and Jack, similarly dressed, join her on the way to the barn. They catch six horses and load them into the horse trailer, which is still hitched to the pickup.

Jack put his saddle back in the trailer last night after cleaning it, along with the saddles of Parker and Morris, so he helps Maggie get hers loaded and checks to make sure the boys have everything they need. They all get in the pickup and head to Council Mountain. At first, the boys are garrulous, but eventually fall quiet as they doze off in the warm cab.

Maggie removes her scarf, gloves, and coat. Jack asks why

she doesn't wear a hat, and she tells him she has never liked hats; even as a child, she only wore one when forced to. They talk quietly and soon arrive in town, where they meet Parker in the cattle truck and Morris in his farm pickup at the gas station. Morris leaves his pickup in the back parking lot and climbs in with Parker, and Jack follows the truck back through town and up the road to the forest.

When they arrive at the corral, Parker pulls the big truck off the road into a clearing, and Jack parks behind him. The cessation of motion wakes the boys, and they throw open the doors and jump out. Maggie is a little slower, stopping to bundle up again against the chilled early-morning air.

At 7:30 a.m., it is still dark, but there is enough light to see to unload the horses and get them saddled and bridled. Jack divides the group, putting Maggie with Richard Morris, Brad with Dan Parker, and keeping Trent with him and sends them out to cover different areas of the mountain. The ranch hands know the area and know how large a bunch to gather before heading them to the corral, and Jack is confident leaving Brad with Parker. He would like to keep a closer eye on Maggie but doesn't want Trent out of his sight either, so he sends Maggie with Morris. He likes to keep Trent close because the boy tends to be impulsive and daring, and he can quickly get into a bad situation without even realizing it.

The teams spend the morning combing the draws and hillsides for cattle, flushing them out of the brush and sending them down the mountain. When they have a large enough group, they bring them down to the corral. Once there are animals in the structure, the gate must be kept shut and opened only to herd in more cattle. They all meet back at the corral around noon and share a cold lunch of sandwiches, chips, cookies, and fruit before heading back out. The sun is still shining, but it has gotten steadily colder all day instead of warmer, and a haze is rising in the south. It looks like the storm Jack anticipated is on its way.

Maggie is already sore by noon, and getting back into the saddle after lunch without groaning takes all her willpower. She is warm except for her hands and feet and is glad she thought to put on long underwear. Jack sends them over to a hillside close to where he and Trent are working. They have been riding for several hours without a sign of more cattle. At some point, Maggie finds herself riding next to Trent. She has lost sight of Morris and can no longer hear his horse moving through the brush and is nervous about being in the forest alone, so she stays with the boy for the time being. She thinks maybe they will run into Jack or Richard in the next clearing.

They run into something in the next clearing, all right, but it's not Jack or Richard. Maggie has been hearing something in the brush, first on her right, then her left, and thinks it is probably the other riders. The horses start acting skittish, jumping at branches and rolling their eyes, and Maggie has her hands full with Cupcake's unusual behavior. As they ride into the clearing, she sees movement from the corner of her eye and turns, expecting to see one of the guys. Instead, she sees what she immediately knows is a wolf. Maggie has never seen a wolf except on television, but the identity of the animal is unmistakable. It is large, appearing to be as tall as the distance between the ground and her stirrup, and dark gray, its pink tongue lolling, eyes locked on hers as it sits on its haunches at the edge of the brush.

"Maggie," she hears Trent say in a low voice. When she turns to look at him, he is staring at the other side of the clearing.

Following his gaze, Maggie sees another large wolf, this one darker in color, standing in the shadows. Frantically, Maggie tries to remember what to do in such a situation, but her mind is not cooperating. Feeling her rider's panic, Cupcake acts up even more, dancing in a circle and flinging her head against Maggie's attempt to control her.

Trent's horse also is sidestepping and fighting his rider. Just then, Trent's frightened horse bolts, and Maggie sees three other gray shapes streak through the brush after him. The two wolves near her haven't moved, and Cupcake is getting more and more anxious. The wolf on the left stands up and steps toward them, and the horse has had enough. Rearing and whinnying, Cupcake tries to run, and Maggie screams as she is thrown from the saddle, twisting her knee painfully as her foot hangs in the stirrup for a split second.

The fall stuns her, and all thought of wolves is driven from her mind as her breath leaves her body in a whoosh. Fighting for air, Maggie is vaguely aware of flashing hoofs close to her body, and hears a yelp as one of those hoofs makes contact. Cupcake is standing, trembling, close to Maggie's fallen body, fighting the wolves. Maggie sees the wolf that was kicked get back up and spring at the horse and Cupcake flees from the clearing with the wolf at her heels.

Groggy from the impact of her head against the frozen ground, Maggie rolls to her knees and tries to get up. She hears a growl from behind. Turning, she sees the second wolf, the darker one, advancing toward her, its muzzle drawn back from its long fangs, snarling as it comes at her. Maggie falls over backward in fear, scrabbling on her hands and heels like a crab to get away. The wolf keeps coming, still growling savagely, and Maggie keeps retreating, not taking her eyes off the wolf's. Suddenly, her head bangs painfully into something hard, and Maggie realizes she has backed into a boulder. There is nowhere left to go. Her mouth fills with the bitter taste of adrenaline, and Maggie prepares to defend herself against the impending attack.

Everything seems to slow down and her vision sharpens. She can see every hair on the wolf's neck, the saliva dripping from the exposed fangs, every leaf in the trees around the clearing; she can hear the harsh gasp of her breath and crackle of leaves as the giant paws pace closer to her. She feels the roughness of the rock against her back, the cold dampness of the earth through her gloves, and can smell the wet-dog odor of the approaching predator.

A shot cracks close behind her. The wolf jumps into the air, spins around nipping at itself, and falls in a heap at her feet. Maggie stares at it in disbelief. She is still sitting on the ground looking at the dead wolf when Jack leaps from his horse, the gun in his hand, and pulls her to her feet and into his arms. He is holding her so hard she can't breathe for the second time in the last five minutes.

She pushes at his arms, and he loosens his grip just enough to allow her to draw a deep breath. Maggie clings to Jack, trembling, still not quite able to believe she is safe. She can smell Jack's unique scent, clean and spicy, and also the sweat of his fear mixed in with horse and dust. Her cheek rests against his chest, and even through his coat she can hear his heart. While they stand holding each other, his heartbeat slows, and she feels his body relax.

Jack pushes her from him, inspecting her face and body to make sure she is okay. "Are you hurt?" he asks urgently.

"Just scared," Maggie tells him. "Did you see Trent? We have to find Trent!"

"What do you mean?" Jack yells, gripping her shoulders.

"What about Trent?" She can see the fear in his eyes as he waits for Maggie's response.

"He was with me," she explains. "His horse ran, and there were wolves chasing him. There was one after Cupcake, too. She tried to fight them for me," Maggie ends in a whisper.

"Let's go," Jack says, pulling her toward his horse. The horse, though nervous, is still standing where Jack dismounted. Jack swings into the saddle, moving his foot so Maggie can mount, and pulls her up behind him.

She points the way, and they set off along the trail of the fleeing horse. Maggie has both arms wrapped around Jack's middle and leans her cheek into the shelter of his back as they ride. She can't stop shaking, her whole body shuddering in reaction to the close call. She won't let herself think about what would have happened if he hadn't come to her rescue.

Jack can feel Maggie shaking as she hangs on tightly to him, and marvels that she is still here. When he rode into the clearing and saw her on the ground with the wolf just feet away from her, he was scared to death. Pulling out his gun and shooting the animal was an automatic reflex, and he thanks God that his aim was true. Jack feels a little shaky himself, mostly with fear for his son, and pushes the horse to move faster.

He hears a shout from behind and stops to wait for Brad and Parker. With them is a white, scared Trent riding between the two on his lathered, still-spooked horse. When they get to Jack and Maggie, both dismount, and Jack grabs his son in a hug. After making sure Trent is okay, Jack listens to the story.

When Trent's horse bolted, the gelding started up the mountain and then turned downhill, circling back around and running almost literally into Brad and Dan. The wolves backed off at the sight of others with guns on their saddles, and Dan was able to stop the headlong dash of the terrified horse. Trent, who up to this point was just hanging on for dear life, took control of his mount and led the group back up the hill to find Maggie. They made faster time than Jack did riding double and caught the pair from behind.

Richard Morris rides up as Trent finishes his story, and Jack quickly fills him in. Now the only one missing is Maggie's horse, Cupcake.

Sticking together this time, the group remounts and resumes following the trail of trampled grass and broken branches where first Trent's horse and then Cupcake had run from the wolves. Soon, they start hearing the sounds of cattle in the brush, a moo here and there, and the sound of a big body moving around. Then, with a crash of brush, Cupcake appears on the hillside above, herding before her a cow and calf, the stirrups on the empty saddle swinging as she walks.

Jack has heard of a horse working cattle on its own but has never seen it himself until now. They watch as Cupcake brings the cattle to them, then stands nickering and bobbing her head as if to say, "Aren't you proud of me?"

Maggie slides off Jack's horse and goes to Cupcake, walking slowly and talking to the mare in order not to spook her. When she reaches her, the horse rests her head against Maggie and Maggie strokes her neck. The others sit patiently and watch horse and rider reunite. Maggie gets aboard and rides back to the group.

"What now?" she asks.

Jack has been looking around while Maggie talks to her horse, and it appears to him that the cattle they were missing are on this hillside. He tells the others this, and they fan out to circle above the cattle and bring them down. Once the animals are in a loose herd at the bottom of the draw, Jack is able to count them and ascertains this is, indeed the last group on the mountain.

By now, the setting sun obscured by clouds, they can see their breath, and the first flakes of snow are falling in the growing dusk. Telling the others to stay in sight at all times, Jack starts the herd toward the corral. Soon, the snow is falling thickly, and it is hard to see farther than a few feet. Jack starts calling to the other riders, asking them to answer back so he knows everyone is all right. For a while now, Jack has known the wolves are following them, but he doesn't want to say anything until he has to. The cattle sense the presence of the wolves and are unusually docile and cooperative, wanting to stay close to their human protectors. The horses are skittish, making a hard ride downhill in bad weather even more difficult.

Jack is extremely relieved when they reach the bench leading to the corral. He sends Morris and Parker ahead to open the gate and get the truck into loading position and he, Maggie, and the boys bring the herd in a wild rush as the stragglers see the open gate. Morris swings it shut behind the last calf, and the riders stop their blowing horses and dismount.

Jack sees the wolves behind fade back into the trees and expects they will circle the corral and wait for a chance for a kill. He tells Maggie and the boys to get their horses loaded and wait in the truck and hands Brad the reins for Parker's horse as well. He gets back on his horse and leads Morris' through the gate as Richard opens and closes it behind him. Then Morris mounts up as well and the two work the cattle into the chute, up the ramp, and into the truck, which Parker has backed up to the ramp with the door open.

When Maggie starts to walk toward the trailer, the knee she twisted when she was thrown from her horse gives way, and she almost falls. She knew it was sore, but the ride off the mountain in the snow has numbed her pretty much from the waist down, and she hasn't realized how stiff her knee is. She recovers her balance and forces herself not to limp as she and the boys lead the four horses to the trailer. Maggie starts to unsaddle, but Brad stops her.

"The horses are too hot," he tells her. "They'll get chilled in the trailer if we unsaddle them now."

Maggie nods her understanding and helps the boys load the horses and tether them in the horse trailer. A mournful howl ululating through the snowy, twilight evening makes Maggie jump, and every hair on her head and body stands up. The boys look at her with frightened faces, and the horses stamp and whicker in distress. The howl is answered from across the corral, and Maggie understands the wolves have followed them down and are gathering around them.

Finally, the noise dies away and Maggie, who was frozen in place, can move again. Stepping cautiously from the trailer, Maggie tries to see through the snow, which is falling harder and faster all the time, how far away the wolves might be. She can't see anything but a white curtain and is reminded eerily of her dream two weeks ago, when she was searching for Clark in just such a snowstorm. Brad and Trent step down behind her, and the three make their way to the pickup.

Maggie hears the big door on the back of the cattle truck slam shut and realizes the cattle are loaded. Jack appears through the storm, leading Morris' horse and his own. He calls to Brad to start the pickup, so the three of them get in and shut the doors, Brad and Maggie in the front and Trent in the back. Brad starts the pickup and turns on the headlights, and they both gasp at the sight that meets their eyes. The lights reflect in the eyes of a half-dozen wolves in a rough semi-circle in front of the vehicle. The wolves sit without moving, watching the people inside watching them.

When Maggie sees the wolves sitting around the truck, she flashes back to the clearing on the mountain, with the wolf about to attack, and for an instant almost screams aloud. With difficulty, she turns the scream into a gasp and realizes she is shaking again. Doing some deep breathing exercises helps her regain control, but in the back of her mind, she is picturing Jack being dragged down and torn apart behind the trailer.

Jack also sees the wolves as Brad turns on the lights and feels his heart thud in his chest as he brings the last two horses inside the trailer. He shuts the door behind him while he replaces the horses' bridles with halters and clips the short halter ropes to the hooks. He takes the gun from the holster on his saddle, opens the door and steps out into the night, for it is truly dark now. He shuts and latches the trailer door, keeping an eye on the wolves while he does it, and walks quickly to the door of the pickup.

When he opens it, he startles Brad who is still sitting in the driver's seat. Brad climbs from the cab, and Jack opens the back door for him, standing between his son and the wolves, which are slowly moving closer as if sensing this is their last chance at a meal. When Brad is safely inside with the door shut, Jack gets in behind the wheel and pushes the safety to on before stowing his gun in the door pocket. The cattle truck, with Parker driving and Morris in the other seat, has pulled away and started down the road, so Jack puts the pickup in gear and follows.

Catherine Bridwell

# CHAPTER 13

Maggie almost screams when Jack opens Brad's door, but by the time they switch places and Jack drives away, she tries to seem normal, though she is still shaking. Jack cranks up the heater, and by the time they reach the highway, she is warm enough to remove her coat, and she has stopped shaking. The heat, however, is making her knee swell, and it has begun to throb. She hopes it is not seriously injured.

The cattle truck has pulled into the parking lot of the family-style café in town, so Jack stops as well and they get out. Maggie's knee is not cooperating, but she doesn't want Jack to know. She stalls beside the pickup, zipping her coat and putting her gloves back on while bending her knee back and forth to loosen it up. Finally, she walks across the parking lot with the others. They have driven out of the snow, but it is still very cold, and Maggie knows the snow will follow them down the mountain before the night is over.

The heat, lights, and noise of the restaurant hit her like a slap in the face. The six of them are seated at a large table in the corner, and the smiling waitress takes their orders. After the ordeal on the mountain, Maggie doesn't expect to be hungry but, surprisingly, she is. The special is chicken-fried steak with cream gravy, and they all order it.

Maggie excuses herself to go to the restroom to wash her hands and wipe her face with a damp paper towel. Her eyes in the mirror are bright, her cheeks flushed, her hair still a little damp from snow, and she doesn't look like someone who was almost killed today. Smoothing her hair with her hands, she goes back out to eat.

Jack makes a quick call on his cell phone, talking to Idaho

Fish and Game to report the wolf he killed that afternoon. The men and boys are all talking about the wolves, comparing stories and relating other close calls. None, however, is as serious as what almost happened to Maggie today, and she moves closer to Jack as the talk continues. Jack notices and leans a little toward her, allowing his shoulder and knee to brush hers in wordless comfort. Maggie moves even closer, accepting the kindness he offers.

Jack can feel the slight tremor in her body where her shoulder touches his and gives her hand a quick squeeze under the table. She smiles back at him. Jack knows how lucky they were today. There could have been many different outcomes, none of them good. He is a little surprised that Maggie didn't cry afterward; most women would have. He assumes the jitters she has now are the aftershocks.

Their food comes, hot and good and plentiful, and quiet falls over the table as they eat. Parker and Morris finish first and leave with the cattle truck while Jack gets the check. When they go out the door, it is snowing. They haven't discussed leaving Maggie at her house, and Jack has an absurd urge to keep her with him, so he drives through town and heads toward the ranch.

Maggie expects to go to the ranch with Jack to help put the horses up and drive back to town in her car, so she doesn't notice Jack's dilemma. She is a little concerned about driving since it's her right knee that is hurting. After being in the warm restaurant, it has swollen so much her jeans are skin-tight around it. Warm and fed, the boys doze in the back seat on the way home, and Jack and Maggie listen to the radio without speaking.

When they stop in front of the barn, the boys get out, stretching and yawning. Maggie carefully swings her sore leg out of the way and steps out on her good one, catching her breath in pain when she tries to put weight on the other. Jack and the boys are already behind the trailer opening the gate so they can unload the horses. Using the side of the pickup to lean on, Maggie limps slowly to the trailer. Once in sight of Jack, she straightens up and tries to walk normally.

He backs Cupcake from the stall, down out of the trailer and hands the reins to Maggie. She leads the mare through the snow into the barn, walking very slowly. He follows her inside, leading two horses, to where the boys are unsaddling.

The four of them quickly unsaddle the weary horses, brush the dried sweat from the shiny coats, and turn them into the pasture where fresh water and hay are waiting. They can hear Parker and Morris unloading the lowing cattle outside.

While they are cleaning tack, Parker steps in the barn and tells Jack they are finished and will be going home. Jack thanks them and says he'll call them tomorrow and Parker leaves.

It takes a while to finish the tack with two extra sets, and Jack sends the tired kids to the house to get ready for bed while he and Maggie work, asking Brad to pull the horse trailer over by the shed and unhitch it from the pickup before he goes in.

Once everything is wiped down and back in its place, Jack flips off the barn light and turns to Maggie. "How bad is it?" he asks, helping her up from the bench.

She looks at him, startled, and says, "How did you know?"

Jack laughs. "You don't do a very good job hiding it. Hurts a lot?"

"Quite a bit," she admits with a wry grin, "but I don't think it's serious." With Jack helping her, Maggie limps slowly to the house, up the porch steps, and through the door. Once they get their coats off and put away, Maggie sits down on the chair in the utility room and tries to take off her boots, but can't bend her knee enough to reach the right one.

Jack kneels in front of her and slips it off. "Go change into something so I can look at it," he tells her.

Maggie goes up the stairs clinging to the rail and practically dragging her injured leg behind her. Once in her room, she grabs baggy sweat pants, a warm flannel pajama top, and some fuzzy socks before beginning her painful descent. She quickly changes in the bathroom, then opens the door and calls Jack in.

Leaving the door open, Jack hunkers on the floor at Maggie's feet, slides her sweats up over her knee, and inspects the damage while Brad and Trent watch curiously from the living room. The tan which Jack had admired in September has faded, but the slim, shapely calf is unchanged. Above it, however, Maggie's knee is glorious shades of black and purple and hideously swollen. Jack gently probes the joint, feeling for knots or obvious damage, and she winces at his touch.

"It feels like everything is in the right spot," Jack tells her, sliding her sweats back down her leg. "It's probably just bruised. Let's get some ice on it." He leads her from the bathroom to the couch, helping her to recline and putting a pillow under her knee, then goes into the kitchen to get ice. Jack brings the ice wrapped in a kitchen towel along with a glass of water and some pain reliever. He places the cold pack carefully on Maggie's raised knee. Noticing the worried looks on his sons' faces, Jack tells them he doesn't think it's a serious injury, and they relax.

Maggie says something about going home, but Jack talks her into staying. He cites her injury, the lateness of the hour, and the road conditions as reasons for her not to go, and she gives in without much of a fight.

"Let's watch a movie," Trent suggests.

Jack agrees, so the brothers decide on a popular action thriller and turn down the lights to watch. The boys have the two recliners, so Jack settles on the couch at Maggie's feet and tries to become absorbed in the movie.

Pictures of the day keep intruding, and he is unable to follow the plot. He sees Brad, serious in the early dawn light, determined to do a man's job. He sees Trent, his face white with shock when he realizes how close he came to being wolf food. Most of all, he sees Maggie, laughing at something one of the boys had said; Maggie, huddling in her coat as she eats a sandwich while sitting on a log by the corral; Maggie, cowering in fear on the ground with a wolf crouched before her; Maggie, trembling in his arms after he killed the wolf; Maggie, with snow in her hair riding down the mountain beside him. He can't get her out of his mind.

Looking over at the source of his obsession, he sees she has fallen asleep. When the movie finishes, he sends the boys to bed and stands, looking down at her drowsing form. He decides to leave her where she is for tonight. She is resting so peacefully, and it will be too painful for her to get back up the stairs anyway.

Jack is exhausted from the weeks of hard work and the stress of the day. His arms feel like lead weights, and his legs seem encased in concrete as he moves into the bathroom. He can also smell his own sweat and knows he won't sleep well without a shower, so he makes the effort. Standing under the hot spray, Jack lets it wash away his fatigue and his fear. The cattle are gathered, his children are safe, and Maggie Sullivan is sleeping on his couch.

Catherine Bridwell

# CHAPTER 14

A few hours later, something wakes Jack up. At first, he doesn't know what it is, but it seems to be coming from the living room. Remembering Maggie is asleep on the couch, Jack jumps out of bed and hurries in. The snow has stopped and the moon has risen, its white light shining in through the windows onto Maggie's sleeping form. Jack looks around, not seeing anything out of place, and the noise sounds again. It is coming from Maggie.

Jack goes to the couch and sees she is in the grip of a dream, thrashing and occasionally crying out. Her cry is what awakened Jack. Whatever she is dreaming about apparently has her terrified, judging by the expression on her face. Jack sits beside her sleeping body and, taking her by the shoulders, gently shakes her, trying to wake her up without frightening her more.

Maggie opens her eyes and sits up with a gasp, looking with terrified eyes around the living room. It takes her a minute to realize where she is, that she is safe, that Jack is sitting and holding her by the shoulders.

"I was dreaming," she tells him, clutching at his hands. "The wolves were here, they were everywhere trying to get in, and I couldn't get the doors shut . . ." she trails off, staring at Jack with tear-filled eyes.

Suddenly, she is in his arms. He is holding her tightly to his bare chest, and she shudders with relief as a feeling of total safety floods over her. Maggie is crying on Jack's shoulder, and it feels so right; it feels so wonderful, and then he is brushing the tears from her face, cradling it in his big, callused hands, tilting her mouth to his as he kisses her. He tastes like he smells, clean and spicy, a taste that is only Jack, and Maggie drinks it in. His mouth is firm and warm, his lips questioning against hers, then he deepens the kiss, her mouth opening under his demands. His hands are on her back now as his tongue dances against hers, and both of them are breathing fast.

Jack is astounded at the silkiness of Maggie's skin, the velvet texture of her cheek, the sweet moistness of her soft mouth. He didn't intend to kiss her, was only trying to comfort, but now he feels an urgent need to keep tasting her honeyed lips and plunges his tongue deep into her mouth. She responds fervently, and he holds her close. He can feel her heart racing as her softness is pressed against him, and he doesn't want to ever stop kissing this incredible woman.

As all good things do, this too comes to an end. Jack hears one of the boys' doors open with a creak, the sound of footsteps heading toward the stairs announcing one of them coming down to the bathroom. Jack ends the kiss, holds Maggie away from him, and presses her back down onto the couch, then quickly rises and goes back to his room.

He hears his son—Brad from the footsteps—close the bathroom door. Jack goes back to bed and listens for Brad to do the same. He is tempted to go back out to Maggie, but something stops him. He thinks Maggie is not the kind of woman a man makes love to on the couch; she is worth waiting for a better place and time. After what seems like hours, Jack's blood cools enough for him to sleep.

Maggie, too, lies awake. Between the wolf nightmare and the surprise of Jack's kiss, her mind is spinning. She wonders if he will come back out after Brad goes back to bed. Part of her wants him to, and part of her doesn't. It seems a little undignified for people their age to be making out on the couch, but at the same time, she craves his warm touch. Finally, she decides he isn't coming out. Her knee is throbbing, so she hobbles to the bathroom, taking some more pain reliever before returning to the couch.

Maggie prays the rosary in thanksgiving to God that everyone came safely home today and also to put herself back to sleep. Somewhere in the fourth decade, she falls asleep.

The next morning, Jack awakes at his usual early hour, then remembers it is Saturday, and the cattle are off the mountain. He rolls over and starts to drift off for a much-deserved sleep-in, then he remembers kissing Maggie. This brings him wide awake.

He kissed Maggie last night! Thinking back on it, the whole thing seems almost dream-like. Jack wonders what Maggie thinks about their kiss. Waking from a bad dream as she did, she might have been disoriented enough to imagine she was still dreaming. He hopes not. He hopes Maggie is as aware of it as he, that it is as special to her as it is to him. Not knowing is driving Jack crazy.

Now his brain fires off different scenarios of how he should act when he sees her today. Pull her into his arms and start kissing her like a love-starved maniac again? (His favorite option, but she might not be amenable, and one or both of the kids might walk in again.) Say good morning and give her a quick hug and peck on the lips? Pretend nothing happened? Dating is apparently as confusing now as it was when Jack was a teenager.

He finally decides he won't be able to go back to sleep, so he might as well get up. As he walks through the living room on his way to the bathroom, he peeks over at Maggie on the couch, but sees she is still asleep and continues on his way.

Maggie, however, is not asleep. The throbbing of her knee awakens her sometime before 6:00 and, at first, she has trouble figuring out where she is. Nothing seems right in the darkness around her. Then she remembers she is on Jack's couch; she fell asleep during the movie, had a bad dream, and Jack came out in the night, woke her from the nightmare, and comforted her while she cried. The memory of Jack kissing her leaps to the forefront of Maggie's mind. Jack kissed her! She worries for a second that the kiss was part of her dream—that she dreamed of waking up as people sometimes do, as Maggie has herself done before, but the memory of Jack's mouth on hers is too vivid to be a dream.

The thought of Jack's mouth does mysterious things to Maggie, sending a flush of heat down into her belly. She hasn't felt this rush, this tingle, in a very long time. This is the rush and tingle of first times—first touches, first kisses, first lingering looks. And for Maggie, first times were finished thirty-five years ago.

A flash of guilt strikes Maggie. A man who is not Clark kissed her, and she enjoyed it. In fact, she was thrilled to the core by it and hasn't thought of her dead husband until now. What can this mean? Is she betraying Clark's memory by letting Jack kiss her?

*It's too early for this!* Maggie thinks and in true Scarlett O'Hara style, *I'll think about it tomorrow!* Right now, she just wants to bask in the glow of the sensual memory, but she hears Jack's door open. Exhilarated, embarrassed, and confused, Maggie closes her eyes and pretends to be asleep. She hears Jack stop beside her, feels his gaze on her face like a caress, but keeps her eyes closed, and he moves away toward the bathroom. When the bathroom door shuts, she opens her eyes and sighs in relief.

She knows she will have to figure out what she wants to do next, what she wants from this man who seems to have wormed his way into her heart; but for now, she decides to wait and see what Jack does and let him set the pace. Maybe it's an old-fashioned way to look at it, but to Maggie, it seems the natural course.

Jack finishes in the bathroom, goes to his room to dress, and heads outside for chores. Maggie doesn't stir as he passes by her sleeping form. As soon as the back door shuts, Maggie gets up, limps to the bathroom, and begins her morning routine. She didn't bring clothes downstairs for today, so after her shower she puts on the sweats she slept in and goes to her room to dress and do her hair and makeup. Her knee is much better this morning, and some pain reliever and the heat of the shower improve it even more, so she is barely limping when she comes back down to make breakfast. She starts a pot of coffee for Jack, turns on the tea kettle, and gathers ingredients for the meal.

By the time Jack comes in, Maggie is flipping fluffy, golden pancakes on the griddle while fragrant bacon sizzles and homemade maple syrup simmers on the stove. The wonderful smells make his stomach growl hungrily.

"Good morning," he says.

Maggie looks over her shoulder, her quick, graceful hands not slowing as she smiles at him and returns the greeting.

Encouraged by her welcoming gaze, Jack crosses the kitchen, slips his arms around her waist, and turns her toward him. She comes willingly into his arms, tilting her head to look up at him. Jack ducks his head to hers and kisses her gently but firmly on the mouth. When he pulls away, Maggie sighs and opens her eyes.

"I was worried it was a dream," she confesses with a shy smile.

"So was I," Jack breathes in relief. They both laugh, and he hugs her tightly, stroking her back. "I'm glad it's not," he avers, and Maggie agrees.

"The pancakes!" Maggie exclaims and pulls from his arms to turn the tasty morsels before they can burn.

Jack steps away and snags a piece of bacon from the plate where Maggie has piled the ones that are already cooked.

"Hey, get out of that!" she tells him jokingly. "Make yourself useful."

Jack looks around to assess what he can do to help and gets plates and silverware out to set the table. He puts on the butter, syrup, milk, juice, and napkins, then goes to the stairs to wake the boys while Maggie takes the last of the bacon from the pan and quickly scrambles some eggs.

By the time the sleepy teenagers amble into the kitchen, breakfast is on the table. To Maggie's surprise, Jack offers to say the blessing. He says a short, heartfelt prayer for all the blessings in their lives and thanks God for bringing them all off the mountain safely the day before.

Maggie feels her eyes start to tear up, and as soon as the prayer is finished, uses the excuse of getting more pancakes started to pull herself together. She is deeply touched by Jack's simple sincerity. The boys, meanwhile, are digging in, and Maggie gets up two more times to make more pancakes before everyone is full.

Noticing Maggie beginning to limp again, Brad and Trent insist on washing the dishes, settling Maggie comfortably on the couch with a fresh ice pack, her grade book, and a pile of sixth grade homework, while Jack retreats to the desk in his room to open mail and pay bills.

Once the dishes are done and the kitchen tidied, the boys come into the living room and ask Maggie what she wants to do now. This is the first weekend Maggie has spent at the ranch, and she has considered going home this morning. Two things hold her there. One is the wonderful sense of intimacy she feels with Jack and his sons today, a feeling she misses now that her children are grown and her husband is gone. The other is the snow that started again sometime after Jack and Maggie's romantic encounter and continues to come down in a steady swirl of fat, white flakes. The thought of driving through the storm on bad roads with a sore knee is unpleasant enough to keep her on Jack's couch.

Since this is new for all of them, Maggie realizes the boys need some signal from her and Jack for the shape of the day. Thinking quickly, Maggie suggests "What about a board game? The one with the most money by lunch wins and the one with the least fixes lunch."

This idea is greeted with enthusiasm by the boys, who go to the upstairs closet to find the game. Jack comes out of his office and moves Maggie's papers aside to sit beside her on the couch. "That was a nice thing to do," he tells her softly. Leaning over, he kisses her quickly, then gets up and offers her a hand. "Shall we go kick their butts?" he asks with a smile.

"You betcha!" Maggie agrees, and they walk to the kitchen together.

The game is great fun. Brad offers to be the banker, and Maggie enjoys watching his quick mind at work adding the rents and penalties in his head and doling out paydays to everyone. He plays with the same quiet confidence he brings to his school work. Trent is quick and aggressive as always, which means he is in over his head immediately, but later in the game, his gamble starts to pay off.

Jack, on the other hand, is very cautious and holds on to every dollar he can, keeping his risk to a minimum. Maggie, who is usually very good at games, for some reason today has terrible luck. She knows she is distracted—every time Jack looks at her, her heart speeds up and she feels like she can't breathe—but distraction can't cause the dice to roll low numbers whenever Maggie spills them onto the board. It takes her twice as long as the other players to go around, and she lands on every square possible for pulling the maximum amount of cash from her swiftly dwindling pile.

Maggie thinks Jack may be distracting her on purpose. Each time she looks at him across the table, he is looking at her, his cool blue gaze boring into hers. Sometimes he stares at her mouth, and the heat in his eyes tells Maggie he is thinking about the kisses they shared. The word that keeps recurring when Maggie tries to analyze her state of mind is twitterpated. She now understands exactly what it means. As the game continues, Maggie plays so badly the boys take pity on her and loan her money so she can keep going. By 11:45, Maggie concedes defeat and she and Brad—the two with the least amount of money—start lunch while Jack and Trent fill the wood box and stoke the fire.

After a tasty lunch of homemade potato soup and grilled ham and cheese sandwiches, Jack and the boys don their coats and boots and head out to feed cows. Maggie has been informed that ranchers "feed cows" in the winter, the word cow meaning all the cattle regardless of gender. They will also feed the horses and make sure all the stock have water.

Maggie considers going with them, but by the time she fixes lunch and cleans the kitchen, her knee is throbbing again, so she remains inside. She hobbles up the stairs, strips the beds and throws the dirty linens to bottom of the staircase, and quickly makes the beds back up with clean sheets. Back downstairs, Maggie starts a load of laundry, takes more pain reliever, gets some ice from the freezer, and props her sore knee on pillows while she writes lesson plans for the week.

There are only two weeks of school before Thanksgiving, and Maggie's class will be putting on a play about the first Thanksgiving this coming Thursday evening. The children have been practicing their parts for several weeks, and some of this week's class time will be dedicated to finishing the set and rehearsing. Maggie is happy with their progress and excited to see the final product. She mentally makes plans to invite Jack and the boys to the performance and maybe to dinner following the play.

# CHAPTER 15

The afternoon passes swiftly with Maggie alternating between laundry, housework, resting her knee, and school work. By the time Trent, Brad, and Jack come in from feeding and chores, Maggie has the laundry mostly caught up, her regular Friday cleaning finished, and is ready for school Monday morning.

Jack insists Maggie remain on the couch while he cooks dinner with some assistance from his sons. He allows her to help clean up after the meal and steals a quick kiss when the boys go upstairs to look for another board game to play. All morning, Jack couldn't take his eyes off Maggie. He was obsessed with her mouth. Watching her bite her full lower lip in concentration reminded him of how her mouth felt under his when he kissed her last night, and it was all he could do to stay in his seat and not pull her across the game board into his arms. Now he has a chance to do just that, and he takes it.

Removing the dish towel from Maggie's hands and tossing it on the counter, Jack slides his hands around her waist and pulls her close, feeling her slim body curve to his. He lowers his mouth to hers, breathing in her sweet scent and capturing her soft lips in a deep kiss. They are both breathing hard by the time Jack reluctantly pulls away. Romancing a woman with two teenage boys in the house is proving to be difficult, but if stolen kisses are all Jack can have, he will gladly take them.

Another rowdy game keeps them occupied until the Boise State football game comes on, at which time the boys hurry to the living room for the kick-off while Maggie moves the last load of laundry to the dryer and Jack makes microwave popcorn. Again, the boys take the recliners, leaving Jack and Maggie the couch. Tonight, Maggie slides her feet to the far end of the couch and leans comfortably against Jack, who is sitting beside her, while they watch the game. The boys don't seem to notice the change or the fact their father is cuddling with their housekeeper.

By the time the game finishes, Maggie is yawning. The hard day yesterday, interrupted sleep last night, and early morning are taking a toll. Maggie brushes her teeth and goes upstairs to bed while Jack and his children enthusiastically discuss the football game.

Sunday morning, Maggie drives to town after breakfast, against the protests of Jack and the boys. She needs clean clothes for the week, the family needs groceries, and Maggie needs some time alone to think. Walking into her house is a little like trying to put on clothes that are too small—nothing seems to fit right. The house smells stale and feels closed in and empty to Maggie.

She quickly unpacks and starts her laundry, which she is still washing at home instead of at Jack's, then drives to Tracy's for their regular Sunday brunch. Catching her sister alone in the kitchen, Maggie fills her in on all that has happened over the weekend. She spills out her confusion, guilt, and growing attraction to Jack to her sister's sympathetic ear. Tracy listens in silence and pulls Maggie close for a quick hug.

"I couldn't be happier for you," she tells Maggie. "Jack is a great guy with wonderful children, and I think if you like him, you should go for it. Clark would want you to be happy, so stop worrying about betraying him. The biggest hurdle I can see is telling your kids, but once they have some time to adjust to the idea of you dating, I think they'll be fine with it."

"Am I dating?" Maggie asks. "It doesn't feel like dating. It feels more like coming home."

"Well," Tracy tells her, "dating is different when you're older and both of you have children. It's more a question of figuring out if you can merge your lives than the thrill of falling in love."

Maggie doesn't agree, since she has been feeling thrilled ever since Jack kissed her the first time, but keeps silent. She is glad to have someone to talk to, and some of the guilt slides away as she shares her feelings about Jack with her sister. "I just don't know the rules," she says finally. "What happens next?"

"What do you want to happen next?" Tracy asks her.

"I'm not sure," Maggie replies ruefully. "Part of me wants to jump into the sack with him, and part of me doesn't want things to change. I know we can't go back now to how it was before, but I don't see how to go forward either. Do we keep playing grab-ass whenever the boys aren't looking? Can I sleep with him in the house where his children are right upstairs? Do we tell our kids? What about in public? Do we pretend to be just friends or what? The more I think about it, the more questions I have."

"I think it's whatever you and Jack agree feels right," Tracy says. "Every relationship is different and only the two people in the relationship can make these decisions. I would advise you to be up-front with his kids and yours, or there might be a feeling you went behind their backs, but it's no one else's business unless you want to go public. Sit down with Jack and talk it out. I'll bet you find the answers are easier than you realize."

"Thanks, sis," Maggie tells her. "I feel better already."

"That's what sisters are for, kiddo," Tracy replies with a smile.

After brunch at Danny and Tracy's, Maggie stops by the grocery store to stock up on groceries and goes home to move the laundry and pack for the week before going to Mass. During the Mass, Maggie offers up her feelings of guilt and confusion over Jack, and gives thanks for all her blessings. She feels a deep sense of peace fill her mind and soul and leaves the little church strengthened and energized.

At the ranch, the men are still outside feeding, so Maggie carries in her suitcase and the groceries, puts everything away, and makes a chicken casserole to put in the oven for dinner. The boys and Jack come in from feeding, bringing a cold draft of snowy air smelling of hay and cow manure with them. Maggie greets them with a smile and tells the boys to get started on their homework.

With Brad and Trent bent studiously over their books at the kitchen table and dinner started, Maggie goes to find Jack. He is in his room doing paperwork at his desk, and Maggie puts her arms

around his neck from behind and kisses his cheek.
"Can I talk to you for a minute?" she asks.

This is the first time Maggie has taken the initiative and touched Jack of her own volition, and he thrills to the feel of her arms around him and her soft lips on his face. Her silky hair swings against his cheek as she leans over and her warm, sweet scent engulfs him. He pivots his chair and pulls her down to his lap for a proper kiss, cradling her face with one hand and settling the other in the curve of her waist. After a moment, Maggie pulls away and gazes into his eyes, a serious look on her face. Jack feels his stomach clench.

Whenever Caroline said they needed to talk, she usually meant she was going to talk and Jack better listen and agree or there would be big trouble. These "talks" always seemed to turn into a fight, with Caroline screaming insults and Jack stonily ignoring her until she ran from the room and slammed the door.

Jack reminds himself that Maggie is not Caroline and that Maggie will almost certainly listen as much as she talks, so Jack stands her up from his lap and leads her into the living room to the couch. He is thinking deeply about how to say what is in his heart without scaring Maggie off. Once they are seated, Maggie turns to Jack and begins to tell him some of her concerns about their growing attraction to each other, and as Jack listens to her soft voice, a feeling of great tenderness overcomes him. He will do whatever he can to make Maggie happy and hopes never to cause her pain. She has had enough pain.

"I like you, Jack. I like how I feel when I'm around you. I like it when you touch me, and I'm looking forward to seeing what we can be together. I don't need to label it, and I'm not asking for a commitment from you. I'm just not sure how fast we should go or what happens next or when we should tell the kids or if we want go public at some point. I was hoping you had some ideas." Maggie looks at Jack for answers.

Jack knows the depth of his feelings for Maggie; what he doesn't know is if Maggie returns those feelings. He worries it is too soon after her husband's death; he worries about his sons. He doesn't want to get their hopes up about Maggie becoming part of their family only to have them dashed if she changes her mind. He considers carefully before he speaks.

"I like you too, Maggie. I think we have a chance to make a future together, to be happy with each other. The thing I don't want is to move too fast. I want you to have time to be sure this is what you want; I don't want to put pressure on you. So, I think we should back off for a while. Not that I want to," he stresses, "but it might be best. Let's keep things as they are for now and give ourselves a chance to spend more time together, get to know each other better. Say, maybe, until after Christmas. If we still feel the same, then after Christmas we'll sit down with the boys and tell them we want to be more than friends. How does that sound?"

"It sounds okay," Maggie answers. "Do I have to wait until after Christmas to kiss you again?" she asks with a twinkle in her eyes.

"No," Jack tells her. "Please, please, don't wait until after Christmas to kiss me again! We'll just be discreet and try to keep our hands off each other until then. What do you say?"

"Until after Christmas, then," Maggie says. "I can do that."

# CHAPTER 16

The week passes quickly, and before Maggie knows it, the night of the play arrives. She stays after school to finish last minute preparations. Trent comes over to help while Brad is at basketball practice which started Monday. The play is scheduled to begin at 6:00 and by 5:30, all the students have arrived. Maggie is busy getting everybody organized, into their costumes, and to the right spot before the curtain goes up, so she doesn't notice Jack come in until he steps forward and says, "Break a leg! I hope it goes well."

Maggie's heart lightens at his presence. "Thanks!" she says brightly. "The kids have worked hard and they're ready. I'm sure they'll do fine. You better find a seat before they're all taken," she advises, squeezing his arm as she moves to guide a small 12-year-old girl to the correct staging area. "I'll talk to you after the play." Jack leaves to sit down. Maggie continues directing the students, and then it's time to begin.

Maggie is right—the students do a fine job, and the play proceeds without a mishap. Afterward, excited children and their proud parents swarm around Maggie. Jack and the boys watch from the edge of the crowd as she gives each child, in turn, her undivided attention and offers her sincere praise for their part in the production. Jack can see the children love her and their parents respect her, and his heart swells in appreciation of her generous spirit. Finally, the set is taken down and everyone is gone. Maggie shuts off the lights, locks the doors, and the four walk out to the parking lot.

The only vehicles remaining in the snow-packed area in front of the school are Jack's pickup and Maggie's car. Jack offers Brad the opportunity to drive his pickup, which Brad eagerly accepts, and the two boys pull out of the parking lot. Jack scrapes Maggie's windshield and she starts the car. Jack listens to Maggie chatter about the play on the way to her house.

When she falls silent, he tells her about the phone call he got right after the play. "Caroline called me tonight," he says. "She wants the boys for Thanksgiving."

"Oh, no!" Maggie says. "I was hoping all of you would come to my house for dinner! Although I'm sure the boys would love to spend some time with her," she quickly adds. "They must miss her a lot."

Jack says, "I know they do; and I want them to spend time with her. It's just that I'm afraid she'll flake and not show up or she'll call the night before and tell me she's changed her mind. It wouldn't be the first time. I hate it that she has the power to hurt them!"

"Maybe she's changed," Maggie offers hopefully. "People can change if they want to."

"Maybe," Jack answers. "I guess we'll find out next week. I think I'll see if she will wait until evening to take them so we can have dinner with you first. What do you think?"

"I think that sounds like a good compromise," Maggie says.

When they reach her place, the boys are waiting on the porch, and they all go inside for a late dinner before driving back to the ranch. Maggie stays at her house that night since the boys will go straight to bed, and there is no real reason for her to go with them. Wound up from the excitement of the play, Maggie lays awake thinking about the week.

Things with Jack are back to normal except for the looks they exchange occasionally that say, "I'm thinking about what it feels like to be in your arms." Every morning he kisses her in the kitchen before the boys get up, and every night he kisses her goodnight, but while the kisses are great and very thorough, Maggie senses they are both holding back. She thinks they are trying to keep the heat turned down while they still can, keeping things mellow until after Christmas. Maggie isn't sure what the latest development with Caroline will mean to their fragile, new bond buts hopes they will weather it together.

⁓

Jack tells the boys on the way home their mother wants them to visit over Thanksgiving break. Trent is excited and pelts Jack with questions about the details, which Jack answers as best he can. Brad is silent.

Finally, Jack asks, "What are you thinking, son?"

"I'm thinking I hate her!" Brad bursts out. "Why did she leave? And why did it take her so long to want to be with us?"

"I don't know, Brad," Jack answers. "I didn't know then why she left, and I don't know now. What I do know is it's not your fault. Sometimes people can't find a way to be happy with their lives, so they run away from their problems. It doesn't usually work because what they're really running away from is inside, and it goes wherever they go. I think your mom has realized how much she misses you, so she's trying to fix it. Maybe you should give her a break and visit, you know, see what it's like to spend some time with her."

Brad is quiet while he digests his father's words. "OK," he says. "I'll go. But if I don't like it, can I come home?"

"Sure, son," Jack tells him.

Trent, who has been listening anxiously from the back seat, whoops with delight. "Sorry, Dad," Trent mutters. "It's not that I don't like living with you; I just want to see Mom."

"I understand, buddy," Jack soothes. "You aren't hurting my feelings."

When they reach the house, Jack calls Caroline to tell her the boys will be visiting, and they arrange to meet in Weiser at 7:00 on Thanksgiving evening. Caroline asks to speak to the boys, and they each talk to her for a few minutes before getting off the telephone.

Jack tells them they will be going to Maggie's for Thanksgiving dinner and then to their mother's house in Meridian afterward. While they get ready for bed, the boys tease Jack about his cooking last year and talk about all the good things Maggie will make.

Jack is glad to hear their cheerful banter. He worries constantly about being a good father, and part of being a good father is letting his children know their mother, but Jack knows seeing Caroline can be as hazardous to his children's emotional health as not seeing her. He hopes he is making the right decision.

# CHAPTER 17

Thanksgiving morning dawns cold and clear. Maggie is up before daylight getting the turkey ready to put in the oven, peeling potatoes, chopping celery and onions for stuffing, slicing cheese and summer sausage for a pre-dinner snack, and putting the finishing touches on the table. She wants everything to be perfect for her family and Jack's and wants to be able to enjoy the day without feeling stressed over dinner. Kevin and his family are going to Didi's parents' for the holiday, but Maura, Tom, and Patrick drove up last night and are sleeping in Maura's old room.

Once Maggie's pre-dinner preparations are taken care of, she starts breakfast. Soon the smells of hot coffee and bacon bring Maura from bed, carrying a bright-eyed baby. Handing Patrick to Maggie, Maura pours a cup of coffee and perches on a stool at the island.

Maggie smiles at her daughter over her grandson's downy head. "Happy Thanksgiving, sweetheart," she says.

Maura smiles back and Patrick waves his tiny hands in happiness, making them both laugh. "It's weird without Dad," Maura muses. "I keep looking for him in every room I go into. How do you stand being here, Mom?"

Maggie thinks about what Maura has asked. "At first, it was hard. Like you, I kept expecting to see him. He was such a strong presence in this house. Eventually, I stopped looking for him, and now I'm not home much, just the weekends. I actually find it comforting picturing him sitting in his chair or standing by the window. I guess it's harder for you because you haven't had time here without him like I have."

Maura nods in agreement, sipping her coffee. Maggie hands

Patrick back to his mother so she can turn the bacon and asks Maura how things are in Boise and they begin to talk, passing Patrick back and forth as they prepare breakfast together. When the eggs are done, Maura wakes Tom up, and they eat in the kitchen. Then they load the dishwasher and wipe off the stove and counters. Maggie really misses her dishwasher when she's at the ranch; it's the one thing about Jack's house she would change if she could.

Maura disappears to take a shower, and Patrick plays on his father's lap in the living room while Maggie checks her list to see what she should be doing next. She puts the turkey neck and giblets in a pan of water to cook so she can add them to the stuffing and gravy later in the day and cuts up vegetables for a relish tray. By 10:30, Maggie has done all she can until it's time to start the rolls, so she goes to her room to change before Jack arrives with the boys.

Maggie is nervous about Jack meeting her family. She is worried that her feelings for Jack will be apparent to Maura and Tom, and she isn't sure Maura is ready for that revelation. Maggie decides Jack was wise by wanting to wait until after Christmas to announce their relationship.

She puts on a new dress she bought in Seattle in October—a dark red, wool blend, soft and warm, with long sleeves and a sweetheart neck. Maggie hopes the color isn't too dark for daytime, but she loves the way it plays up the sheen of her hair (recently cut and touched up), the way the fabric feels against her skin, and the way the dress follows her shape and makes her look almost curvy. Her face is flushed from her exertions in the kitchen, and her green eyes sparkle in anticipation. Maggie feels prettier than she has felt in a long time and hopes Jack and the boys are on time.

Jack also wakes before daylight on this Thanksgiving morning, but since daylight isn't arriving now until after 7:30 a.m., he rolls over to look at the clock. It is only 6:30, so he lies there for a few minutes remembering last Thanksgiving. It was the first holiday they had to manage on their own after Caroline left. The boys were moody and difficult and Jack was irritable; he accidentally cooked the turkey with the neck and the giblets, still in their paper bag, inside the cavity of the bird; and the oven didn't work properly, so they didn't eat until 7:00 that night. He hopes this year goes better and trusts Maggie to be sensitive to the boys' emotional state, especially with the impending visit to see their mother.

He rolls out of bed and goes to the bathroom, then wakes the boys before getting dressed. It will take all three of them to feed and do chores if they are to have time to shower and change and drive to town by 11:00.

Trent and Brad are grumpy from sleep, but soon the excitement of the holiday has them cheerfully helping their father, and the morning's work goes quickly. Back in the house, the three take turns in the shower and soon the house is filled with the aroma of aftershave and deodorant. At 10:30, Jack yells up the stairs and the boys thunder down, suitcases in hand for the trip to Meridian, dressed in new jeans and polo shirts, their hair combed and their faces shining. Soon, the bags are in the pickup, and they start the drive to Maggie's house.

Jack pulls up to Maggie's and parks on the street since a car with Ada County license plates is in the driveway. He assumes it belongs to Maggie's daughter, Maura, who is here with her family for Thanksgiving. Jack is nervous about meeting Maggie's family. He wants them to like him and his kids, and he wants the boys to like them. He is just worried the boys, who form attachments easily, will be hurt if things don't work out between him and Maggie. Quelling his anxiety, he strides confidently to the door and rings the doorbell.

When Maggie opens the door, Jack is dumbstruck by her loveliness. She is wearing a red dress that clings in all the right places and hints at her curves without revealing anything. Her face is beaming in welcome, her soft skin flushed, radiant in the late morning light. Jack swallows hard and manages to say hello and, still slightly dazed, steps into the house with the boys behind him.

Maggie takes their coats, and they slip out of their boots and walk in stocking feet into the living room, where she introduces them to Tom. Tom stands to shake their hands as Maura comes in from changing Patrick, the baby perched on her hip. Patrick waves his arms in delight and gurgles enthusiastically at the sight of Brad and Trent.

Maggie watches, her heart touched by the unselfconscious tenderness the older boys display to the smiling baby. Maura, never one to be standoffish, quickly has the baby playing on the floor with Trent while the men talk football and wait for the Cowboys game to start.

The women retreat to the kitchen to bring snacks in for the game, and soon the side table is filled with delectable appetizers. Jack watches Maggie going in and out of the room, her quick graceful steps making the red dress sway and swing around her. He can't keep his eyes off her, though he tries to mask his fascination from the others in the room.

The house is filled with the enticing smell of baking turkey and pumpkin and apple pie, and Jack's stomach growls. Neither he nor the boys had breakfast this morning in their hurry to get to town, so he walks to the snack table and fills a plate. Maggie comes back with a pan of chicken wings and brushes by Jack to put it down.

"Good morning," he murmurs, using the pretense of reaching for the fruit tray to lean close to her.

She turns to look at him, her amazing green eyes open and trusting. "Good morning to you too," she answers. "I'm so glad you're here."

"Me too," Jack replies. "You are so beautiful. You literally took my breath away when you opened the door."

Maggie blushes at the compliment. "Thank you. You look pretty good yourself," she says, looking at Jack, dressed in jeans and a snap-up western shirt. His clean-shaven, rugged face with its clear blue eyes staring into hers breaks into a smile, lighting his features like a small sun coming out after a storm.

The two stand gazing at each other without speaking for a breathless moment, then Maggie turns away to speak to Maura as her daughter comes in from the kitchen, and Jack returns to the couch with his plate of snacks.

Maura looks curiously at her mother. "What's up with you two, Mom?" she asks. "You look funny."

"Oh, just talking about the boys," Maggie says brightly. "No big deal."

She feels bad telling this little white lie to Maura, but doesn't think this is the time or place to say what's going through her mind. *I was just admiring Jack's hot body in those tight jeans and wondering when we can get a moment alone to swap tongues.* This is not the sort of thing one says to one's child when said child is still mourning her dead father.

The conflict between Maggie's feelings for Jack and what she thinks Maura can handle knowing about those feelings stresses Maggie, but she resolves not to worry about it. Maybe Maura will figure it out without Maggie having to tell her, and maybe she will be okay with it. With that thought, Maggie goes to sit on the couch beside Jack, playfully making a show of pushing Brad out of the way.

Maura settles in the rocking chair to nurse an increasingly fussy baby Patrick, considerately covering her exposed breast and the baby's head with a light blanket, while the two families settle in to watch the football game.

Jack is surprised but pleased when Maggie sits next to him on the couch. Her close presence is intoxicating to him and suddenly, Jack thinks it was ridiculous of him to ask Maggie to wait until after Christmas before moving forward with their relationship or telling their children about it. Maybe if the boys see physical affection between him and Maggie develop over time, they will figure it out on their own and it won't be a big deal.

He purposely shifts closer to her, letting his arm rest against the softness of her arm and chest, letting his hand brush her leg through the soft fabric of the red dress. He feels her body tense in response as she turns to look questioningly at him. Jack gives her a slight shrug and a smile, pressing even closer, and gradually Maggie relaxes against him.

As the game progresses, Maggie rises several times to go to the kitchen to check on dinner and refill drinks. On one of these trips,

Jack follows her with his empty glass in his hand. As soon as they're out of sight of the living room, Jack sets his glass near the sink, plucks Maggie's glass from her unresisting hand, and presses her against the counter with a hand on her abdomen. Sliding his other hand into her silky hair, he turns her face to his and tastes her soft lips, soft teasing touches at first, then searching the sweet depths of her mouth with his tongue. He slips his hand from her belly to the small of her back, pulling her hips against him, relishing in the feel of her in his arms, feeling the slide of her dress against some silky undergarment as his hands caress her back.

With a soft sound of regret, Maggie pulls away, holding him at arm's length. "Jack, what are you doing? I thought you wanted to keep things slow until after Christmas. Do you want us to get caught?"

"Maybe," Jack admits sheepishly. "I just got carried away, and it seemed like a good idea." He runs a thumb over her mouth, red and swollen from his kisses, and she turns her face into his hand, kissing his palm. "I'll try to behave."

Jack releases Maggie, picks his glass up, and fills it with water. Maggie silently hands him her glass, and he fills it up as well. The two go back into the other room. No one looks up or seems to notice they were even gone, Maggie notices with relief. It's one thing to decide to bring their relationship into the open, but she doesn't want it to be all at once by having someone walk in on them in a heated embrace.

Sitting next to Jack on her couch with her family and his gathered around, Maggie is truly thankful: thankful she is alive; thankful she has such a wonderful daughter and son-in-law; thankful for the baby sleeping in Maura's arms; thankful for Brad and Trent, who bring energy and laughter into her life; and thankful for Jack, this man who has reminded her what it feels like to be attractive and desirable, who is on his way to filling the hole in her heart.

Once the game is over, everyone streams to the kitchen and preparations for dinner accelerate. Tom lifts the roaster from the oven, and he and Jack remove the turkey to let it rest. Maggie turns the burner on under the potatoes and uses broth from the turkey to moisten the stuffing, which goes in a pan in the oven. Maura, who laid Patrick in his crib to finish his nap, slices apples and bananas for fruit salad while Brad and Trent open cans of olives and cranberry jelly to fill the crystal bowls Maggie hands them. She sets Jack and Tom to work peeling hard-boiled eggs, then slices them in half and pops the yolks into a bowl for deviled eggs. She mashes the yolks with a fork, mixes in mayonnaise, mustard, salt and pepper, puts the mixture back into the whites with a spoon, and sprinkles the tops with paprika.

Maggie is in her element, preparing delicious food for people she loves, her kitchen full of talk and laughter as everyone works together. When the men finish peeling the eggs, they set to work carving the turkey, laying the juicy slices of meat on Maggie's grandmother's white, stoneware platter. The potatoes are cooked, so Maggie drains them for Maura to mash, saving some of the potato water to stir into the gravy she makes in the big roaster pan. The rolls go in the oven and finally everything is done and on the table, and Maggie herds them all to their seats.

Looking around the table, Maggie's heart overflows. Hesitantly, she clears her throat, and all heads turn to look at her. Nervously, Maggie starts to talk. This is Clark's job, something he does every Thanksgiving, and now Maggie is continuing the tradition. "Thank you all for coming here for Thanksgiving," she begins, "and thanks for all your help with dinner. I couldn't have done it without you. Today is a day for giving thanks, for acknowledging our blessings, and I know I am blessed by your presence here. We have a tradition in this family, started by your dad, Maura," with a nod to her daughter, "and I intend to keep it. When we bow our heads for the blessing I'm asking all of you to take a moment and give thanks for what you have been given."

Making the sign of the cross, Maggie bows her head and closes her eyes to pray, silently sending all the love in her heart to God in gratitude. After a moment of quiet reflection, she begins to say the familiar prayer aloud, joined by Maura and Tom, and before the end, Jack, Brad, and Trent's voices chime in as well. "Bless us, oh Lord, for what we are about to receive from Thy bounty, through Christ our Lord, amen."

With a hearty amen from those seated around the table filled with a delicious feast, dishes of food are handed around, plates are mounded high, and voices fall silent as mouths fill. For a while, the only sounds are murmurs of appreciation and the occasional request for someone to please pass the butter, or the gravy. Eventually, one by one, they sit back in their chairs with sighs of repletion.

"Wow, Mom, that was even better than usual," Maura praises. The others join in with Maura in their appreciation.

Jack tells her, "I don't think I've ever had such a great meal, Maggie."

Flustered, Maggie stands to go to the kitchen, flapping a hand at those still seated at the table. "You helped cook it, so don't give me all the credit." She starts gathering dirty plates and silverware as the others join in to help.

Just then, Patrick begins to cry in the bedroom, and Maura leaves to tend to him. Jack and the boys finish clearing the table while Maggie puts food away and Tom loads the dishwasher. The kitchen is soon back to normal, the leftovers stored in the refrigerator for evening snacking, the pots and pans scrubbed and put away, the dishwasher humming softly, and the table and counters wiped clean. Looking around, Maggie can see nothing else to do, so now it's time to play games.

She gets the pinochle cards from the drawer and calls everyone to the table for a game of six-handed pinochle. Maggie, Maura, and Tom have played together many times. Jack knows how but is rusty, and Brad and Trent are rookies. Maggie explains the rules to the teenagers and they divide into teams and play a few hands for demonstration. Once real play begins, Maggie is pleased to see how quickly the two boys pick up the concepts, strategies and scoring of the complex game. It is Maggie, Tom, and Trent against Maura, Jack, and Brad, and Maggie is sitting next to Jack.

The teams are evenly matched, and the score remains close throughout the game. Finally, Maggie's team is victorious when she gets a double family in spades with two jacks of diamonds to go with it. Maura, Jack, and Brad demand a rematch and thoroughly trounce the other team. Everyone is having a great time, trash talking each other and crowing over good plays.

After the second game, they take a break and Maggie serves dessert—homemade pumpkin pie with real whipped cream, and apple pie ala mode made from Maggie's grandmother's recipe, the crust golden, tender and flaky, the filling a melt-in-your-mouth combination of tart apples, cinnamon, butter, and sugar. The boys try some of each, Maggie marveling at the amount of food they manage to put away. All too soon, Jack looks at the clock and says it's time for them to go.

"Ah, Dad, do we have to?" Trent asks. "I have a good feeling about the next game; I think we're going to win!"

"Sorry, son, but we don't want to keep your mother waiting," Jack answers.

The boys obediently put their dirty dessert plates in the kitchen sink while Maggie gets their coats from the coat closet. At the door, she wishes them a happy Thanksgiving and, to her surprise, Trent spontaneously grabs her in a bear hug.

Maggie hugs him back fiercely and when she lets him go, Brad steps forward and hugs her as well, not quite as enthusiastically as his brother, but Maggie's eyes fill with tears at the gesture. It is the first hug the boys have given her, and she hopes it's just the beginning.

Jack tosses the keys to Brad, saying, "Why don't you get the pickup started, Brad. I think I'm too full to drive."

"Shotgun!" Trent calls, and the two fling open the door, race down the driveway to Jack's pickup, and jump in.

Maggie and Jack are laughing from the doorway, but when Brad starts the vehicle, Jack pulls Maggie out onto the front deck and shuts the door behind them.

He puts his arms around Maggie, pulling her close and burying his face in her hair. "Thank you," he whispers. "This is the best Thanksgiving I've ever had."

"You're welcome," Maggie responds, her face pressed against Jack's firm, warm chest. "It was a pretty great one for me, too." In fact, from the moment she opened the front door and saw the look on Jack's face, the day has gotten better and better, and Maggie feels a wave of contentment flow over her. "You should get on the road," she says, tilting her face up to kiss him goodbye. "It could snow any minute and you don't want to be late."

Jack, mindful of the boys waiting in the pickup, turns Maggie so his broad shoulders block the view from the street and kisses her waiting lips. He intends just a quick farewell peck, but the velvety softness of her mouth fascinates his, and he tilts his head to slant across her mouth more deeply, slipping his tongue into the warm, wet cave. When he ends the kiss, they are both flushed and breathing hard. Jack has a strong urge to say, "Forget about Caroline, kids, we're staying here. I want you to go in the living room with Tom and Maura while I make love to Maggie for a few days, then we can play some more pinochle," but of course he doesn't. He steps away, still looking at her, then turns and walks quickly to his pickup, getting into the back seat where he has been relegated.

Maggie, shivering on the deck, watches them drive away.

When Maggie steps back into the house, she is greeted with her daughter's raised eyebrows. "Okay, Mom, spill it," Maura says firmly. "We can see you really like him, so why don't you tell us what's going on?"

Maggie answers by bursting into tears, something she rarely does, and sinks onto the couch, covering her face with her hands. Maura and Tom sit quietly and wait for the storm to pass.

When Maggie stops crying, Maura hands her a tissue and a glass of water and soon Maggie's composure returns. "I was afraid you would be angry with me," she begins. "Afraid you would think I was somehow betraying your father's memory." With halting words, she tells her family about her growing affection and attraction to Jack. As she talks, the telling becomes easier. Her daughter listens without speaking and, when Maggie is finished, walks over and envelopes her in a hug.

"Mom, we just want you to be happy. We know how much you loved Dad and how lonely you've been since the accident. If you feel ready to see someone, that's up to you, not us. We think Jack is great, and his kids are awesome, so please, please, don't live your life to please us," Maura tells her.

Tom nods in agreement.

"Okay, then, that's settled," Maggie says in relief. "Shall we play some three-handed pinochle now or watch a movie?"

The three decide to do both, stopping the card game for a late evening meal of leftover Thanksgiving feast before putting the movie on. Maura falls asleep before the movie is over, but Maggie feels wide awake.

The kids go to bed, where Patrick has been for several hours, and Maggie prowls around the house, picking up empty glasses and pop cans, emptying and reloading the dishwasher, and finally finds herself at the table looking out at the snowy night. She thinks Jack should be home by now and wonders how the transfer of kids worked out. She hopes the boys are enjoying their time with Caroline. Sunday evening suddenly seems a lifetime away.

# CHAPTER 18

Jack is home, also wide awake, memories from the day wheeling through his head. When he told Maggie this was the best Thanksgiving he ever had, it was the truth. Childhood holidays were usually more of an excuse for his parents to drink than to celebrate with family, and even when he and Caroline were together, he doesn't remember the feeling of warmth and love present at Maggie's today. He thinks the difference is Maggie who pours out a balm of trust, respect, and affection on everyone she touches, and Jack thanks God for bringing this extraordinary woman into his life.

For Jack, the next two days bring with them a sense of suspended animation. He gets up in the mornings, gets dressed, starts coffee, and does chores. When he comes in, he fixes breakfast and catches up on paperwork. After lunch, he feeds and waters the stock and spends the evenings staring at a television show he doesn't remember.

The house is eerily silent except for the creaks and groans old houses make, and Jack jumps every time the wind bangs a branch outside. He keeps waiting for the sound of galumphing feet coming down the stairs, the sound of boys arguing and laughing over a football game. Jack realizes this weekend is the first time he has spent at home without his sons since Caroline left, and he misses them terribly. By Sunday morning, he is more than ready to make the trip to Weiser to pick them up.

Jack gets to the gas station, where he is meeting them, a little early, and the whole time he waits, his imagination serves up pictures of everything bad that could happen to them on the way to Weiser. Finally, Caroline's car pulls in beside his. Breathing a sigh of relief, Jack gets out and helps the boys with their luggage. They give him a casual hello, wanting to look cool in public and in front of their mother, when all Jack wants is to sweep them both into a hug and hold them tightly. They tell Caroline goodbye, and Brad gets into the front passenger seat, leaving Trent to pile in the back seat with the suitcases.

All the way home, the boys talk non-stop about their weekend. Jack gets a clear idea of what his ex-wife's new life is like: engaged to a successful man who is an attorney, big house, nice car, the best of everything—all Jack couldn't give her. He supposes she must be happy now. Jack snaps from his musings in time to hear Brad say Caroline wants them to come again over Christmas break.

Jack's heart falls. While he wants them to see her, the weekend alone at the ranch makes him reluctant to let them go again, but he arranges a smile on his face. "Sure, son," he says. "We'll look at the calendar and your practice schedule when we get home."

Maggie spends Friday and Saturday enjoying her family. She gives Patrick his bath, plays peek-a-boo over the towel, rubs his butter-soft skin with lotion, bundles him into his diaper and pajamas, and holds his soft, sweet-smelling, sturdy, little body close, enjoying the feel of his little hands on her neck. She and Maura fall quickly into the easy companionship they have always known: cooking meals, taking care of the baby, and keeping the house tidied, doing what is needed without having to discuss it between them.

Tom shovels the walk, replaces the weather stripping around the back door and the light bulb in the garage Maggie can't reach without a ladder. They play games, read, and watch movies, a stress-free time of relaxation Maggie hasn't had in months.

By Sunday, she is rested and refreshed and ready to get back to her life. Maura, Tom, and Patrick go to brunch with her at Tracy's and then drive back to Boise. Maggie does her weekly grocery shopping and packs to go to the ranch. She feels a sense of anticipation so great that she can hardly sit through Mass and hardly stops to speak to anyone before getting in her car and going to Jack's.

On the drive, Maggie makes a mental list of all she needs to do when she gets home and laughs aloud in the car as she realizes what she just thought. She called Jack's place home—something that suddenly seems perfectly right. She is going home.

At the ranch, the boys come out as soon as she stops in front of the house, pulling their coats on as they walk, and Maggie smiles at their youthful exuberance. Talking non-stop, Brad and Trent carry in the groceries and her suitcase.

"Dad's feeding," Trent informs her. "We're supposed to help you get dinner started."

Maggie puts the groceries away, takes her suitcase to her room to hang her school clothes in the closet, and goes down to make dinner. She starts the boys peeling vegetables for a rich soup to go with the fresh French bread she bought at the market earlier and chops some sirloin to sauté with onions in the stock pot. Soon the kitchen is redolent with the smell of cooking food.

Maggie listens to the boys as they tell her about the weekend at Caroline's. They seem to have had a great time and are excited to go back over Christmas break. Maggie is happy for them and sad for Jack. She senses how conflicted Jack is about having Caroline back in their lives.

Maggie makes a green salad while the boys set the table and is setting the soup pot on a trivet in the center of the table as Jack comes in the back door. Her eyes jump to meet his, and it's all she can do to stand still and say a quiet hello instead of flying into his arms. Judging by the look on Jack's face, he feels the same way, but he also manages to contain his emotions as he takes off his coat and washes his hands in the utility room.

She and the boys sit down to wait for Jack, and as he comes by her chair, he gently squeezes her shoulder in greeting. Maggie smiles up at him, and he sits and they say the blessing. Another week has begun.

At breakfast on Friday of the first week after Thanksgiving, Jack announces today they will cut their Christmas tree. When the dishes are done and the kitchen clean, the four bundle up against the cold and head to Jack's pickup. Jack drives to the main road, turns toward the mountains and drives up into the forest. They drive for about thirty minutes before he pulls off the road in a turnout and stops.

Maggie gets out, the crisp, cold, evergreen-scented air refreshing on her face. Jack and the boys are milling around, getting an axe and a hand saw from the back of the pickup, along with a rope. When they are ready, Jack leads the way up the bank through the snow to the glistening hillside. Maggie follows, trying to stay in his tracks, her breath freezing in her nose and against the scarf wrapped around her neck.

The boys examine and reject half a dozen trees before selecting the perfect one, and Jack uses the hand saw to cut it down. Maggie and the boys stand out of the way and watch as the small tree crashes down, a flurry of snow flying up from the impact. Jack ties the rope around the base of the tree, hands the end to Brad, steps back and lets the boys start down the mountain first, pulling the tree behind them.

Taking Maggie's gloved hands in his, Jack leans over and kisses her, his mouth warm against her chilled lips.

Maggie steps closer, loses her footing in the snow, and seemingly in slow motion, drags Jack over with her as she falls.

Jack tries to cushion the fall as he lands right on top of her. He immediately rolls to his side, his arms still around her, looking anxiously into her face to see if she is hurt.

The deep snow is soft as a down comforter under Maggie; Jack's arms are strong around her, his handsome, worried face peering into hers. Maggie experiences a moment of absolute happiness. She is completely safe and cherished, held in the embrace of a man she thinks she is falling in love with. The sun is shining, the sky is blue, and Maggie bursts into laughter in pure joy.

Jack's blue eyes crinkle mischievously. "So that's how you want to play," he growls, and with one hand scoops up a handful of snow and dumps it right in Maggie's face. Gasping and laughing, she tries to get up, or at least roll away, but Jack holds on. They struggle briefly and Maggie gives in, allowing Jack to pin her with the weight of his body. Silence falls over them as they stare into each other's eyes, both totally aware of their bodies pressed tightly together.

"Jack," Maggie says, "how long are we going to dance around what's going on here? I mean, we're not teenagers. We know where this is headed. I get that you're trying to give me time, to make sure I'm ready after losing Clark, but at this rate, you won't even get to second base by spring!"

Jack considers her question with a serious expression. He is surprised and a little turned on she is the one voicing what he has been thinking. He thinks of Maggie as a classy lady. He has put her on a little bit of a pedestal in his mind, even when he imagines making love to her, and her saucy attitude shows him a different side of this complicated woman.

"What?" he asks, "You getting impatient, baby?"

"Maybe," she teases. "You are quite a temptation, you know."

"I'm not sure why I'm going so slowly," Jack replies. "I guess it's just awkward with the boys around. I want to be a good example to them, and sleeping with their housekeeper might not give them the right message. It's definitely not because I want to wait; the opportunity just hasn't presented itself."

Maggie nods in agreement. Although she also feels constrained by the boys' presence in the house and knows they are taking their cues from the behavior of the adults around them, she isn't a timid virgin. It has been months since she has had sex, and Jack has yet to do more than kiss her. She didn't plan to ask Jack about it but is glad the subject is in the open.

"I'm not trying to rush things," she tells him. "I just feel a little strange sneaking kisses like we're teenagers hiding a romance from our parents. Surely the boys are old enough to understand their father is still interested in sex."

"Very interested," Jack says in a suggestive tone. "You don't know the danger you're in, little lady. But right now, I'm getting snow down my neck and my left arm is going to sleep, so maybe we could continue this conversation another time."

He pulls his arm free and struggles to his feet, holding a hand out to help Maggie up. He brushes her off briskly, turns her by the shoulders, and gives her a gentle shove to start her down the trail.

When they get to the pickup, the boys have the tree loaded and tied down and are sitting on the tailgate waiting. "What took you guys so long?" Trent asks curiously. "We're getting cold, and I'm hungry; and why are you both covered in snow?"

Jack replies, "You're always hungry! We're covered in snow because Maggie knocked me down and tried to take advantage of me. I managed to escape, so now let's go home."

The boys consider this outrageous remark then look at each other and burst into laughter. Jack scoops some snow from the side rail of the pickup and throws it, hitting Trent in the side of the head.

"Oh, man, you're on!" Trent yells.

He and Brad leap from the pickup and run around the side to the far bank, where they begin making and throwing snowballs as quickly as they can. Jack pulls Maggie down in the shelter of the vehicle where they build their own arsenal. When the barrage from the boys slows, they stand and retaliate and a full-blown snowball fight ensues.

Finally, Maggie and Jack call a truce and the winded, laughing group pile into the pickup for the ride home. Maggie's gloves are soaked, she has snow down her neck and matted into her hair, but it is a small price to pay to see Jack playing with his children.

Back at the ranch, the boys grab a snack and head to the living room to help Jack set up the tree while Maggie gets started on the weekly cleaning. She gets the beds changed and the upstairs rooms dusted, swept and mopped, but progress slows when she comes downstairs.

Brad and Trent keep calling her into the living room where they are unpacking boxes of decorations and stringing lights on the tree, asking her opinion and showing her special ornaments. Finally, she gives up trying to clean and stays near the tree, mostly listening, occasionally helping, watching Jack and his sons decorate the fragrant fir.

When everything is hung to their satisfaction, the boys plug in the lights and stand back to see the effect. They are all silent, looking at the glowing tree. Jack reaches out and pulls both boys to him with an arm around their shoulders.

"Good job," he compliments. "It looks great."

He knows they are thinking of last year, when Caroline's absence was the biggest thing in their lives, when putting up a Christmas tree was beyond Jack's fragile capacity to function, when Christmas was only one more thing to try to get past. This year will be different, he vows; this year will be special.

Maggie is brought to tears by the scene—Jack standing with his almost grown sons in front of the Christmas tree—and she silently steps from the room to give them time alone. In the kitchen, she wipes her eyes, leans against the sink and looks out at the beautiful winter day. The wounds left on this family by Caroline are deep, and Maggie thinks they are just now starting to heal. She can only pray the scars fade eventually.

Catherine Bridwell

# CHAPTER 19

Maggie leaves Jack's at her normal time and drives to her house. She and Jack didn't have a chance to talk again before she left, so nothing has been resolved. After the hectic morning, her place is too quiet and empty, and Maggie gets a case of the blues. She thinks about putting up her own Christmas tree, but doesn't have the energy to mess with it. Sitting around and feeling that moping won't get anything done, on a whim, she decides to go Christmas shopping. She calls Maura and arranges to meet them for dinner and gets in her car to make the drive to Boise.

Buying clothes and toys for her grandchildren takes Maggie's mind off her Christmas blahs, and by the time she arrives at the restaurant they have chosen, she is cheerful again. Maura, Tom, Patrick, and Maggie have a good visit over dinner. Maura invites her to stay overnight, but Maggie didn't think to bring a change of clothes or her toiletries, so she declines and drives home in the starry night. She parks the car in the garage and carries in her packages, then gets ready for bed. It is late, and she is very tired; this morning's snowball fight seems like it was days ago.

The dream is vivid, so vivid she isn't sure it's really a dream.

*A man stands behind her, his chin scratching her bare shoulder as he leans around and gently bites the side of her neck. She shivers in response and leans her head back against his chest to give him better access to the sensitive skin. As his mouth moves down her neck, his hands slide up her belly to cup her breasts and she feels her nipples harden in response. His erect penis throbs urgently against her butt, and he moans as she reaches between their bodies to cup his testicles. He turns her around, lifting her against him with both hands under her hips, holding her against the wall and*

133

*spreading her legs as he plunges into her. Her breath stops at the sensation and she opens her eyes. It is Jack—Jack looking at her with those blue, blue eyes; Jack gripping her ass with his big callused hands; Jack claiming her mouth in one of his soul-searing kisses, and the realization sends her over the top into a wave of pleasure.*

Maggie wakes to the pulse of her orgasm, the dream still holding her in its sensual grasp. Heart pounding, she lies in the dark, her body already forgetting the sensations so recently coursing through it as she ponders the dream. Drowsily, she thinks the real thing will be even better than a dream and drops back into a deep sleep.

The next morning, Maggie feels the echoes of the erotic dream in her body as she showers. Her womb feels heavy, her breasts tingling at the touch of the wash cloth, and she hopes things with Jack don't drag out too long; she doesn't know if she can take much more deprivation. She and Clark had a healthy, active sex life, something she took for granted until it was gone, and she misses it incredibly.

She hopes she didn't shock Jack yesterday by bringing it up, but is still glad she did. It is important to Maggie to be open and honest with Jack, especially if they are to have anything lasting between them. Her shower over, she quickly dresses and does her hair and makeup. Suddenly, she is energized and ready to face the day.

By mid-afternoon, Maggie has cleaned the house, done her laundry, put up the Christmas tree and decorated the house. It proves harder than expected; the familiar traditions, always shared with Clark and with the children when they were at home, feel hollow and pointless alone. Several times, a particular ornament brings a memory so sharp it hurts, and Maggie's throat aches with unshed tears, but finally it is finished. She hauls the empty boxes back to the garage and vacuums up a few pieces of tinsel.

It is almost time for Jack and Trent to pick her up to go to Brad's junior varsity basketball game, which is at home tonight, so Maggie changes into nice jeans and a sheer black blouse over a red camisole. She gives her hair a quick comb and hears the doorbell ring as she freshens her mascara.

When Jack steps into the room, Maggie has a quick flashback to her dream and feels her face flush in reaction. Trying not to let

Jack see she is rattled, she turns quickly to grab her coat and the three leave for the game.

When they enter the gym, the team is warming up, and Brad gives them a quick wave from the floor. Maggie is surprised when Jack takes her hand, linking his fingers with hers and leading her around to the home section of the bleachers. Trent is ahead of them and doesn't notice, but Maggie is sure somebody in the crowd will. When they reach their seats, Jack doesn't let go of her hand, holding it casually by his knee as they watch the warm up. In fact, he holds her hand until the first score of the game when he lets go to clap. Maggie is sure by now Trent has seen, but he doesn't say anything.

Maggie spends the whole game in a haze—super-aware of Jack's warm body beside her, the scent of his aftershave heady and exhilarating, his knee grazing hers, occasionally taking her hand in his big one. She knows this is ridiculous; a woman of her mature age with years of marriage behind her shouldn't be this aroused by a man simply sitting beside her at a basketball game, and she blames her dream of the night before for her hypersexual state. Finally, the game is over, and she uses the excuse of the restroom to get some space from Jack and collect her composure.

They stay for the varsity game since the coach has asked Brad to dress for it and sit on the bench in case the team needs more substitutes. Maggie is more comfortable by now with Jack's new public demonstration of affection and is able to get into the game, which ends up being very close and exciting. Brad plays several minutes in the fourth quarter and is able to make a lay-up after stealing the ball. They all stand and cheer loudly, and Brad shoots them a wide grin in response.

Everyone is in a good mood after the game, and the boys talk non-stop all the way to the local café right up until the food arrives, replaying the key moments of the game. Jack and Maggie mostly listen, adding a comment now and then, enjoying the moment.

After dinner, they drive Maggie home and Jack gets out and walks her to the door. He kisses her goodbye with great fervor.

Maggie responds in kind, instantly aflame with the touch of his mouth.

Jack reaches under her coat and pulls her closely to his body during the kiss.

Maggie thinks her little talk with him might be responsible for this change and arches her hips into his. Jack makes a sound in his throat that sends heat flashing through Maggie's body. She wishes the boys weren't waiting in the pickup, and the thought cools her off enough to break the kiss and gently push Jack to arm's length.

"You should go," she says. "Your kids are getting impatient."

The honk of the horn emphasizes her words, and Jack sighs heavily. "Someday they won't be waiting," he replies.

"Promises, promises," Maggie teases.

Jack cups her face in his hands and gently kisses her once more before releasing her and walking away.

Maggie lets herself in and takes off her coat, wondering what she will dream tonight.

# CHAPTER 20

The four weeks between Thanksgiving and Christmas fly by in a whirlwind of school, homework, basketball practice, and games as Brad's season gets into full swing. Maggie, Jack, and Trent go to all Brad's games, near or far, coming home in the wee hours of the morning occasionally and dragging themselves out of bed the next day. Jack holds Maggie's hand frequently during these trips, and always kisses her goodbye at her door. Both she and the boys have grown accustomed to these changes. They have no time alone to talk, but, for now, both are content.

Maggie makes sure the boys are keeping up with their studies in spite of the hectic schedule, and this quiet time, whether in her room after school or around the kitchen table in the evening, becomes something Maggie treasures. They have such bright, quick minds, and she is privileged to be the one fanning the flames of their desire to learn.

Jack is busy on the ranch, plowing snow, tuning and repairing equipment, cleaning the barn, and always feeding cows. The weather, after a flurry of early storms, is clear and cold—the temperature sometimes below zero at night—but the sun shines every day, turning the snow to a sparkling vista of diamonds.

The second weekend in December, Maggie flies to Seattle for her grandson, Ethan's, second birthday. While she's there, she goes shopping with Kevin and Didi and is able to find gifts for Maura and Tom. She also buys Seattle Seahawks jerseys for Brad and Trent, and a hand-tooled leather belt for Jack. She would like to get them more; the boys are growing so quickly it's hard to keep them in clothes and shoes, but she doesn't want to overstep her boundaries and upset Jack.

Maggie gave up years ago trying to choose gifts for Kevin and Didi. Somehow her purchases never quite live up to Didi's standards, so she usually gets them gift cards for their favorite restaurants and department stores. She finds a beautiful crystal bowl for Tracy and a new pipe for Danny's collection. With her shopping complete, Maggie goes home content.

Somehow during the busy days following her trip, Maggie manages to wrap the gifts she purchased, make ornaments for her sixth graders, candy for the neighbors, and cookies for the staff party.

Two weekends before Christmas, Brad has a game at a charter school in the Treasure Valley in the middle of the day. Afterward, they have plans to go shopping at the mall. Caroline arrives at the game part way through the first quarter and comes over to sit by them on the bleachers.

Maggie sees Caroline looking curiously at her and Jack, and wonders what she thinks of Jack being with someone else. Maggie thinks turnabout is fair play, but who knows what is going through Jack's ex-wife's head.

After the game, the boys hug their mother goodbye. Jack and Maggie take them to the mall, where Maggie helps the boys pick out presents for their father while Jack goes off on his own to shop for them. They meet up a few hours later and go to a nearby restaurant for dinner before driving home.

The boys are bursting with secrets and can't resist teasing Jack about how much he will like the awesome gifts they got him. Maggie basks in the warmth and energy exuded by these young men and thinks what a good job Jack is doing raising them. She is a little surprised he still has her come to the ranch since the boys are doing so well and Jack is now home in the mornings and after school, but she enjoys being with them so much, she hasn't brought up the subject. Jack must have realized the same thing, but he hasn't said anything either.

There is one full week left of school before Christmas break with finals scheduled for the secondary students the Monday and Tuesday of the following week. Wednesday will be mostly spent on movies and parties before an early dismissal. The boys are studying for finals, and Brad is finishing his term paper for English. English is his hardest subject, and Maggie makes sure he keeps up with the schedule set by his teacher for completion of the paper. His English grade in September was a low D and now is a B+, and Maggie wants to keep it that way. If practice is early, he does his homework around the kitchen table after he eats a late dinner. If practice is late, he works in Maggie's room until she leaves with Trent then goes to a friend's until it's time to go to the gym. Maggie is pleased with the quality of his work, and even Brad admits it's getting easier.

Trent rarely has homework, so he and Maggie do the chores together when they reach the ranch, and often Trent helps prepare the evening meal. Maggie's sixth graders are finishing unit projects and preparing for end-of-course assessments, and she has piles of papers to grade as the semester comes to an end.

Today is the last rehearsal for the elementary music program scheduled to take place that evening in the high school gym. Maggie is at the high school for the last period with her class, watching the practice, when the high school principal comes in, heads straight for her, and asks her to come to his office. Maggie's mild curiosity at this summons changes to concern when she sees Trent sitting in the office, staring morosely at the floor. The principal shuts the door behind Maggie and asks her to take a seat. Maggie sits and looks at Trent for some clue as to what this is about. He won't look at her, even when she says his name, so Maggie looks at the principal for clarification.

"Trent got in a fight in shop class," the principal tells her. "He punched another boy in the face and had to be restrained from beating him further."

Maggie is speechless, waiting for Trent to explain, but the boy still refuses to look up, only hanging his head more at the principal's words. Finally, she asks the principal to give them a minute to talk, and he leaves the room.

Maggie scoots her chair close to Trent's and reaches out to take his hand in hers. His knuckles are bruised and swollen. He covers his face with his free hand and Maggie sees he is crying. She sits quietly until he regains control and looks out the window as he wipes his eyes.

Finally, she asks, "Trent, what happened? I know you wouldn't start a fight without a good reason, so tell me what it is."

Trent mumbles something, but too low and fast for her to understand him.

"Please slow down, and speak up. I need to know what happened so I can try to help you," Maggie probes.

With a huge sigh, Trent manages to look Maggie in the eye.

"He said you and Dad were doing it. I called him a liar, and he called you a bad name, so I punched him. I'm not sorry!" he says defiantly.

Maggie absorbs what Trent has told her and tries to sort out a response. She is angry at the uncalled-for accusation, disappointed at the immature boy who felt it necessary to taunt Trent with vicious gossip, proud of Trent for standing up for her, and sad that her relationship with Jack put his son in this situation.

"Trent, you know violence doesn't solve problems, but sometimes we feel a need to defend someone we care about, and it sounds like that's what happened to you today. Thank you for sticking up for me. I really appreciate it. Now, why don't we get Mr. Charles back in here and tell him the whole story." Maggie stands and opens the door, beckoning the principal to return.

Trent tells his story again. The principal listens carefully, and says he will need to confirm Trent's version by talking to other students. Trent and Maggie are ushered into the main office to wait while other students come in one at a time and speak to Mr. Charles. When the last one leaves, Mr. Charles comes out.

"Well, young man, your classmates support your story, so it's clear to me you were provoked. However, it's still against the rules to fight at school, so both you and the other boy are suspended for the rest of the day. When you come back tomorrow, I don't want to see or hear of any more issues between the two of you, understand?" Mr. Charles asks.

Trent nods as they get up to leave, and Maggie thanks the principal before sending Trent to get his backpack and come to the gym with her. By now, the rehearsal is winding down, the students restless and giggly, and Maggie tells Trent to sit on the bleachers while she takes control of her rowdy class, getting them lined up to go back to the elementary school. Trent follows, disconsolately dragging his feet through the snow on the walk over. He sits dejectedly in the back of the room waiting for Maggie to dismiss class.

Once the children leave for the day, Trent approaches Maggie tentatively. "Maggie, are you mad at me?" he asks.

"No, Trent," she tells him. "In fact, I'm a little mad at myself. I knew people might gossip when I started staying at the ranch with your family, but I didn't think about how it might affect you. I'm sorry you were caught up in something that isn't your fault."

"Can I ask you a question?" Trent says.

"Sure," Maggie answers. "You can ask me anything you want."

"Is it true?" he bursts out. "Are you and Dad having sex? I mean, I may be only 14, but I'm not stupid. I've seen the way you look at each other, and the way you hold hands, and I know he kisses you goodbye. I just never thought that you and Dad would do that, especially with us in the house." Trent looks miserably at Maggie.

"No, Trent," Maggie assures him. "We're not having sex. We like each other a lot, but we haven't done anything more than what you've seen, like holding hands and kissing once in a while." Inside, Maggie is fervently thanking God she can truthfully say this to Trent. The growing passion she feels for Jack can't be worth putting the boys through this; they will need to protect the boys and conduct their relationship with honor if she is to keep her conscience clean.

Trent's shoulders slump in relief. "That's what I told him," he says vehemently. "He should have believed me!"

"It's all over now," Maggie says. "Let's get this room ready for tomorrow so we can go home. We'll need to talk to your father about this before we go to the concert."

"Do we have to tell him?" the boy asks plaintively.

"Yes," Maggie says firmly and turns back to her desk to finish her afterschool tasks.

Catherine Bridwell

.

# CHAPTER 21

Jack feeds a little early this afternoon so he can be at Maggie's for dinner before the elementary concert. He hasn't been to one since Trent was a sixth grader, but when Maggie invited them, he couldn't say no. Feeding the cows is something Jack has done so often he could do it in his sleep, and his mind is free to roam where it will. Inevitably, it comes back around to Maggie Sullivan.

These weeks before Christmas have been magical for Jack and his family. The joy Maggie evokes from every occasion and every small holiday tradition brings back something they didn't know was lost until it was regained—a sense of unity, of family, of anticipation and even a sense of reverence. Maggie has been telling the boys the story of the baby Jesus born in a stable and laid in a manger. Although they are teenagers, Jack doesn't think they have ever really known the "reason behind the season." Neither he nor Caroline is religious, and the kids have simply never been exposed to Christian beliefs. Maggie has a way of talking about it that isn't pushy or self-righteous; she just tells the stories, her deep faith and awe making an impression on Brad and Trent and, Jack has to admit, on him. He is looking forward to Christmas with an eagerness he hasn't felt since childhood.

Jack finishes feeding, does his chores, showers, and dresses for the concert. He arrives at Maggie's, where she meets him at the door to take his coat. Once his snowy boots are removed, she leads him to sit on the couch and tells him about Trent's fight. Jack's first reaction is a fierce father's pride in his son for defending Maggie; his second reaction is dismay the comment was made at all. He worried about this when Maggie first came to work at the ranch, but as weeks went by with no reaction from the community, the concern disappeared. Now it has reared its ugly head as he suspected it might, and Trent is caught in the middle. He can see his own worry and regret reflected in Maggie's expression, and realizes they will have to find a way to either prevent such gossip or decide on a tactic to deal with the mean-spirited rumors. Jack pulls her close for a hug and stands to go deal with his son, who is waiting with trepidation in the kitchen.

After a heart-to-heart talk about fighting and violence and defense of those weaker than himself, Trent is absolved with a hug and an admonition to try to figure out a smarter way to solve problems. Brad comes in from basketball practice, and the four sit down to one of Maggie's delicious meals. The dishwasher is quickly loaded and the kitchen put to rights, and they hurry from the house to the school so Maggie can ride herd on her class until it's their turn to sing.

Jack and his boys take a program and sit toward the back of the gymnasium on the side closest to where the elementary students are waiting to perform. Jack watches Maggie with the children, marveling again at her seemingly effortless ability to keep her class quiet and engaged.

The program goes quickly, the children enthusiastic and only slightly off-key, the parents proud, and the teachers harried. Soon the last song ends, and people stand and begin to file out into the December night.

Jack is enjoying the holiday excitement in the air, nostalgically recalling other Christmas concerts when the boys were younger when someone grabs his arm from behind and pulls him around. Facing him is the father of the boy Trent slugged earlier in the day. Jack flinches, mentally preparing himself to get punched, but instead the man says, "Say, Hallas, what's the big idea? You should teach your kid better manners!"

Jack makes himself count to ten before responding, "Sorry about that. Sometimes youngsters react without thinking, even when they know better. Maybe you should teach your kid not to gossip."

The man steps closer, jabbing Jack in the chest with his finger. "If you weren't living in sin, there wouldn't be anything to gossip about. Next time, my boy will hit back, so just tell your son to stay away from him."

"Not a problem," Jack murmurs as the man strides furiously away. The crowd washes around Jack, some looking curiously at his glowering countenance. His Christmas spirit has leaked away, leaving Jack feeling melancholy, angry, and guilty. His mind frantically gropes for a solution, or at least a snappy comeback, but to no avail. He doesn't want Maggie's reputation besmirched or his boys caught up in the gossip, but the only way to stop it is to let Maggie go, and Jack's heart can't bear the thought.

Just then, Maggie steps to him through the crowd. "Did you like it?" she asks excitedly. "Didn't they do great?"

Jack pretends enthusiasm as he answers her questions and decides not to tell her about the ugly encounter. Knowing will only make her feel bad, and Jack feels bad enough for both of them. They gather up Brad and Trent and go back to Maggie's house for dessert before Jack takes the boys home. On the drive back to the ranch, Jack tells them about the rumors going around town and gives them some ideas for coping with the gossip. He assures them he and Maggie are doing nothing wrong.

Brad asks, "Will Maggie stop coming home with us?"

Jack says, "I hope not, son, but if things get bad enough, she might. We'll just have to hope it all dies down quickly." A gloomy silence falls in the pickup as the three contemplate life without Maggie.

Catherine Bridwell

# CHAPTER 22

Maggie has trouble falling asleep. She is always jazzed after a concert, and tonight she is also worrying about the incident Trent had today. She doesn't want him to have to stand up for her again and wishes people would just mind their own business, but she saw the father of the boy Trent fought with confront Jack after the concert. She doesn't know what was said, but could tell from Jack's face he was furious.

*What a mess,* she thinks. *I should probably just tell Jack I can't work for him anymore, but that wouldn't be fair to the boys.* Her heart tells her they need her, and her quitting would only make them feel abandoned again. She bristles at the thought of giving in to mean, nosy people's ideas of what is right and wrong.

Maggie tosses and turns for quite a while, finally dozing off around midnight. She dreams she is at the Christmas concert, naked, in front of the crowd, while Jack fights man after man in the audience.

When she wakes in the morning, the disturbing dream is clear in her memory, and resurfaces throughout the day, making Maggie feel upset and troubled. The students are still wound up from the previous night's performance, and the day drags by as Maggie struggles to maintain order and actually impart some knowledge.

By 4:00, she is exhausted, but Brad has a home game, so she goes straight from work to the gym, meeting Jack and Trent at the door. Her heart lifts at the sight of their handsome, smiling faces, and she smiles in return.

Jack gives her a one-armed hug, and they walk around the gym floor to their accustomed spot in the bleachers, Jack's big, warm hand possessively resting on the small of her back.

She can feel eyes on them, hear muttering as they pass, and her imagination tells her everyone is staring and talking about them. Once seated, she can see she was just being paranoid. The crowd around her behaves just as always, and soon the action of the game sweeps her up and takes her mind off things.

At half time, Maggie goes to the restroom and stops at the concession stand for a snack and a bottle of water. While she is in line, Mr. Sharper, the school board chairman, approaches and asks if he can have a word. Maggie follows him to the foyer and listens while he stutters and blushes and eventually gets to the point. He has heard a rumor Maggie is living "as man and wife" (here he nearly chokes on his words, turning beet-red) with Jack Hallas, with innocent children in the house during these sinful episodes. As chairman of the board, he feels it is his duty to remind Maggie she is a role model, and her behavior should be above reproach at all times.

"Teachers are held to a higher standard," he tells an astonished Maggie. "I won't say your job is in jeopardy, but I will say people are watching you, and people are starting to talk. Don't put the board in a position of having to make a difficult decision."

"Mr. Sharper, please stop," Maggie says firmly. "First of all, what Jack and I do is nobody else's business, and second of all, having a consensual sexual relationship with someone is not grounds for termination. However, because I appreciate your sincerity, I will tell you Jack and I are not having sex. Just because a man and woman like each other and sleep in the same house doesn't automatically mean something is going on. Perhaps instead of believing gossip, the board should believe in the morality of its staff."

Refusing to look her in the eye, Mr. Sharper replies, "Well, anyway, I felt it was my duty to say something to you."

"And now you have," Maggie answers pleasantly. "I hope you feel better for having done your duty." She turns and walks quickly away, her heart racing, her face burning. She is trying really hard not to cry, knowing if she does, the gossipers have won a small victory.

By the time she reaches her seat again, she has regained her composure, and decides not to worry Jack by telling him what Mr. Sharper said. He has enough to worry about, and there is nothing he can do about it anyway.

She tries to forget it herself, but the thought of losing her job makes it impossible. She has been a teacher for almost thirty years and can't imagine anything different. She doesn't think the board would fire her over a rumor, but stranger things have happened. The conversation keeps replaying in her mind, and she has trouble concentrating on the game. She is very aware of Jack's arm around her, and every time she looks at Mr. Sharper across the gym, he seems to be staring at them.

"You seem distracted," Jacks says during a lull in the game. "What's wrong?"

Maggie says she is fine, just tired, and he accepts the explanation. It feels to Maggie like circumstances are conspiring to drive the two of them apart, and the thought of losing Jack and the boys makes Maggie feel even worse.

Finally, the last game is over. Maggie waits with Trent and Jack for Brad to shower and dress before they take her home. After discussing it with Jack, she has decided not to return to the ranch tonight. She feels it would be best not to give the rumormongers any new fuel for the rumor mill.

While Brad is in the locker room, Jack and Maggie make plans to attend the game on Saturday in a nearby town and discuss the upcoming Christmas holiday. Maggie will spend the week at the ranch as usual, doing the deep cleaning on Wednesday afternoon, and will fix a special early dinner on Christmas Eve so they can go to Midnight Mass, which is held at 7:00 p.m. in consideration for the elderly.

Kevin and Didi and the little ones are flying in on December 25th and Tom, Maura, and Patrick will pick them up at the airport. They have rented a large van and will be driving up from Boise together for a late dinner on Christmas Day.

The boys are disappointed Maggie isn't coming home with them but readily believe her when she tells them she has a ton of papers to grade before Monday and lots of presents to wrap—all of it true. Jack walks her to her door and kisses her goodnight. She hugs him back especially hard tonight, wondering how much longer she will be able to hold him in her arms.

She is tired, her head hurts, her back is sore from sitting on the bleachers, and she is chilled to the bone from the cold, damp weather, so she takes some pain reliever and runs a hot bath. Maggie soaks in the steaming water until her skin is wrinkled and the water is cooling, trying not to think about rumors, or the school board, or giving up her job at Jack's. Finally, she steps from the tub and goes to bed, where her sleep is plagued with bad dreams.

*She is in the gym at the high school, but instead of a basketball game, it is a courtroom, and she is on trial for something horrible she is sure she hasn't done. The jury is the school board and the boys' basketball team. They all keep asking her why she did it, and all she can do is keep denying it. The judge, whose face has been mysteriously blank to her as sometimes happens in dreams, suddenly turns to Maggie, and she sees it is Clark. Her heart fills with joy, and she starts from her seat to go to him, but her attorney, a pimple-faced sophomore cheerleader, pulls her back down. Clark looks at her with the serious expression she remembers so well, and she is so happy he is here she forgets the reason for the trial. Then Clark bangs the gavel on the bench and says, "Guilty!"*

*"No!" Maggie screams at him. "It's not true, please, you have to believe me!"*

*Clark only stares at her sorrowfully, and the same officer who came to school to tell Maggie that Clark was dead approaches and takes her by the arm to lead her away.*

Maggie wakes up with a start, her heart pounding as she tries to orient herself. *Wow!* she thinks foggily. *What a crazy dream. Maybe I have a guilty conscience after all.* As she lies there in the dark, she realizes she does feel guilty—guilty for allowing herself to love Jack and his boys and be happy, when Clark is dead.

She sends out a prayer asking Clark to please forgive her, and then she prays for God to help her forgive herself, and while she's asking, she prays for God to change the hearts of those who are trying to cause trouble for her and Jack. Feeling better, she is able to go back to sleep and if she dreams again, she doesn't remember them in the morning.

The weekend flies by as Maggie finishes her grading and prepares the end-of-course assessments she will give on Monday and Tuesday. The new common core standards are pushing her students, and Maggie wants to make sure the tests reflect both the standards and what she has taught the sixth graders this semester.

She gives the house a thorough cleaning and airs the beds in the guest rooms in preparation for the kids' arrival.

On Saturday afternoon, taking a break from grading, she goes to the grocery store and makes a huge purchase of all the items she needs for both the dinner on Christmas Eve at Jack's, Christmas dinner at her house, plus enough food, snacks, and beverages to feed company for several days. She isn't sure how long Kevin and Maura and their families will stay and wants to have everything but the fresh produce already on hand.

At brunch on Sunday, she and Tracy exchange the small gifts they have for each other and enjoy a long visit before church. Tracy casually asks if Maggie has heard any interesting gossip, and Maggie stares at her sister with suspicion.

"Why?" she asks. "What have you heard?"

"Oh, only that you and Jack are doing the nasty in front of the kids," Tracy says airily.

Maggie buries her hot face in her hands. "How is this happening to me?" she moans. "I'm 51 years old; I shouldn't have to worry about romance rumors anymore!"

"Come on, kiddo," Tracy says anxiously. "It'll be okay. You know how people like to talk. I'm sure it's nothing serious and will all blow over soon. Besides, the people who really know you would never believe it."

Maggie straightens and drops her hands away, tears of frustration and anger shining in her eyes. "You know that, and I know that, but what about all the other people who hear it? Did you know Trent got in a fight at school because of it?"

"I did hear something about it," Tracy says. "What are you going to do?"

"I have been trying to figure that out for a week now, but I don't have any ideas," Maggie says mournfully. "I know I don't want to quit working there, or stop seeing Jack, so where does that leave me?"

Tracy gives her a hug and tells her again not to worry; it will all be okay; but Maggie isn't sure it will. Not sure at all. With a heavy heart, she tells Tracy goodbye and goes home to pack before church.

She knows Father Murphy is hearing confession before Mass today, and she decides to go. Maybe just talking about it will make her feel better. As soon as Maggie enters the quiet stillness of the little church, she feels her frayed spirit start to mend. She kneels to pray, asking God to help her make a good confession. When it's her turn, she enters the confessional and after the opening prayers, tells the listening priest the whole story. He knows Maggie and has known her since the children were still in high school. He also officiated Clark's funeral Mass, so she doesn't have to explain parts of it, but it still takes a while to tell him about her growing affection for and physical attraction to Jack. She tells him some of the ugly rumors floating around town and finally is silent, having run out of words.

"Father, what should I do?" she asks.

Father Murphy sits quietly, considering, and then he tells her, "Marry him."

Maggie gapes at him for a moment and snaps her mouth shut. "Marry him?" she repeats in disbelief.

"Yes," he says. "Marry him. Then your relationship will be sanctified and blessed, and no one can gossip about it. I can tell you love him, Maggie, and I really think this is the only solution you will be truly happy with."

"Do I deserve to be happy?" she asks in a small voice. "It hasn't even been a year since Clark died, and I'm already in love with someone else. Doesn't that make me a horrible person? Shouldn't I have to suffer more?"

Father Murphy responds, "Of course you deserve to be happy! You are a blessed child of God, and God wants all His children to be happy. You loved your husband, and you were a good wife, but now your husband is gone, and God has put this man, Jack, in your path. Don't turn aside from what He is offering you; seize it and give thanks for the blessing. All it takes to be happy is to allow yourself to be happy, so get out of your way and be happy!"

Maggie nods in understanding, dawning hope blossoming in her face. "I'll try, Father," she says earnestly, "but Jack has to want to get married before anything can change. Maybe I should pray for that, too!" Maggie bows her head to receive a prayer of absolution from Father Murphy forgiving her for her sins and leaves the little room to kneel in her regular pew.

She feels light, as if a heavy burden has been lifted from her shoulders, a singing sense of relief flowing through her. The solution, once voiced, seems so simple! They can just get married, and all the ugliness will stop. The feeling stays with her throughout the Mass, which is the fourth Sunday of Advent. Maggie loves the feeling of joyful anticipation resonating in the hymns and prayers; the Christ Child is coming; a Savior will be born. She reminds herself God has a plan for her and prays for understanding and a peaceful heart in this holy season.

Catherine Bridwell

# CHAPTER 23

Jack and the boys feed a little early on Sunday because he wants to make dinner for Maggie. She feeds them every night during the week and at her house during the week if there's a game, and she seemed so tired and down on Thursday that Jack wants to do something nice for her. With help from Brad and Trent, he has a simple meal of home-grown beef tenderloin, baked potatoes, green beans, and salad on the table as Maggie pulls into the driveway.

He hurries out to greet her, holding her off the ground while he kisses her to the boys' embarrassed delight, and the three help her carry in the groceries and her bags. Maggie stops dead inside the kitchen door, a look of surprised delight on her face. Jack loves making Maggie happy, so knowing he helped put the smile back on her face makes his day.

"How nice!" she beams. "Just let me put stuff in the fridge, and we can eat before it gets cold."

They all quickly stash the perishables and sit down for dinner. Maggie leads the blessing, pouring out her thanks for the food and this amazing family, and everyone digs in. Dinner is a cheerful time as the boys catch Maggie up on their weekend and quiz her about plans for Christmas.

Afterward, everyone pitches in to wash dishes and clean up the kitchen, and then Maggie settles at the table with the boys for one last study session before finals. Periods one, three, and five are tomorrow, with periods two, four, and six on Tuesday. Period seven will be Wednesday morning after which they will go to various rooms for movies and games until lunch time.

Brad really needs help with his grammar and literature review, so Maggie spends most of the time quizzing him and giving him tips on how to remember the various rules of the complicated world of English grammar. Trent needs practice on his state capitals for geography, and Brad patiently helps his younger brother. Jack loves watching the two of them interact in such a helpful way. Soon, it is time for bed, and the lights go out as the last week before break is ready to begin.

Jack finds Maggie in the kitchen the next morning when he comes in from chores and pulls her close for a kiss. The feel of her warm, slender body against his and the scent drifting from her silky hair makes him wish he could do more than just kiss her, but the memory of the fight Trent was in last week quickly squashes the thought. He steps away and helps her get breakfast ready for the boys, and then the three are off to school.

Jack washes the dishes and wipes off the table and stove and when he is finished, he brings out the gifts he bought for the boys and Maggie and wraps everything. He can't wait to see Maggie's face when she opens the necklace he had made for her. He has a friend, a silversmith, who designs western jewelry, and Jack commissioned a special piece for this special lady. He hopes she likes it but worries she will think it's too personal. Jack knows it has only been a few months since her husband died, and he doesn't want to rush her, but he also wants to let her know how he feels about her. From the way she responds when he kisses her, Jack thinks Maggie feels the same way about him, but saying the words has a way of changing things, and he wants to say those words to her. He just hopes he doesn't scare her away when he says them.

By the time Jack finishes feeding, Maggie and Trent are home from school. Jack walks into a warm kitchen fragrant with the smell of the casserole Maggie started in the morning and finds Trent at the table studying for his science final while Maggie makes a salad.

This is one of the best parts of his day. He remembers a time not that long ago when he would come home to a cold, dark, dirty house and have to fix dinner for two cranky teenagers who wouldn't do their homework.

Maggie has Christmas music playing on the computer and is

singing along while she chops lettuce and carrots. She has no idea how beautiful she is or how much it means to him to have her here in his house. Just then, she looks up and sees him in the doorway watching her and gives him a radiant smile. Jack grins in return and walks over to kiss her hello. She lifts her face to his and offers him her soft mouth, and Jack takes full advantage of the offering.

Fortunately, Trent is so involved in his studies he doesn't notice the two of them making out behind him. Finally, Jack reluctantly lets her go and moves over to sit with his son. Trent fills his father in on the results of the tests he took that day, and Jack tells Trent about the family of foxes he spotted in the pasture when he was feeding.

Maggie loves listening to Jack talk to his son and moves quietly around the kitchen finishing dinner preparations. Brad had early practice today and should be home in about thirty minutes, so Maggie will put the food on the table when he pulls into the driveway.

Her favorite Christmas carol, *O Holy Night,* is playing, and Maggie sings softly while she gets out dishes and silverware. This is one of those instances when she is completely in the moment and completely content. She thinks this could be her life if Jack wants to get married, and the thought makes her happy. Now if she can only find a way to bring up the subject without scaring Jack away, perhaps thought might become reality.

She glances over at Jack and sees he is watching her. Their eyes lock, and for a moment, Maggie feels as if time has stopped. With one look, he can turn her knees to jelly and send heat flashing through her body. Sometimes, she is almost afraid of what it might be like to actually make love to this man; she wonders if her whole body will simply burst into flames at his touch. Trent asks his father a question and Jack looks away to answer, and Maggie can breathe again.

Soon Brad arrives and the four sit down for dinner. Maggie encourages the boys and Jack to take turns leading the blessing, but usually they are reluctant. Tonight, Trent volunteers and offers thanks to God for the good grades he got on his finals today. Maggie hides a smile beneath her bowed head and folded hands.

The boys' complete lack of knowledge about God and Jesus Christ and faith in general has been a worry for Maggie. She wants to teach them, but doesn't want to push too hard and alienate them, and she is wary in case Jack has an issue. So far, he hasn't said anything to her about it and sometimes leads the prayer himself, and Maggie adds a quick silent prayer of her own asking God to lead Jack and the boys to the faith.

During dinner, Brads happily reports the results of his finals. He received a B+ on his English exam, and Maggie gets up from the table and gives him a big hug. Brad acts like he's embarrassed by the attention, but Maggie can tell he is pleased with her response.

"Hey," Trent says. "I got an A on my English final and I didn't get a hug!"

Laughing, Maggie gives him a quick hug as well before sitting back down. "I know how you feel," she tells him. "My sister struggled in school, so a B was a big deal for her. I got straight A's and never got the kind of attention for grades like she did, but getting good grades isn't about attention. It's about doing the best you can for the sake of self-satisfaction—knowing you tried your hardest. Since school is easy for you, you get the A without as much effort, so you don't get as much praise. I'll try to remember to make over you as much as I do Brad."

"Ok," Trent answers with a smile. "Maybe I could get cookies for every A I get," he suggests hopefully.

"Maybe that could be arranged," Maggie answers.

After dinner, Maggie cleans up the kitchen and helps Brad cram for his history final, the only one he has since his other classes scheduled for tomorrow are PE and shop, which have performance and hands-on tests.

Jack and Trent disappear upstairs on some mysterious errand involving much whispering and hiding of some object under a blanket. Maggie assumes it's a Christmas gift and smiles at their obvious attempt to be sneaky. She loves this time of year, when secrets abound and everyone is brimming with joyful anticipation.

*A Wonderful Life* comes on at 8:00, and they all settle in front of the television to watch, even though they've seen it a dozen times before. Maggie curls up on the couch and leans against Jack, inhaling his spicy scent mingled with fresh air and hay.

*This has been a wonderful evening*, she thinks drowsily.

*Thank you, God.*

Tuesday, Maggie gives the last of her end-of-course assessments to the sixth graders. She is pleased with the results, as every student showed growth in at least one subject area. She knows tomorrow will be a chaotic day full of interruptions and sugar-induced frenzy as the students finish their Christmas gifts for their parents and have a book exchange and class party.

Parents have volunteered to bring cookies and punch, and Maggie makes a batch of fudge after dinner for the party while the boys and Jack go out to the barn on another mysterious errand. They come in smelling of wood and varnish and that night is much the same as the one before as they watch *The Grinch Who Stole Christmas* and go to bed.

Wednesday morning, it is snowing hard when they leave for school. Maggie thinks if it continues like this all morning, it will be difficult getting home after lunch. The children are, as Maggie predicted, giggly and distracted, requiring much prodding from their teacher to complete the snowflake ornaments they are constructing for their parents before the party. This is a wasted day as far as teaching is concerned, so Maggie tries to go with the flow. Finally, the gifts are finished and put in decorated brown lunch bags.

After recess, the kids come in wet and cold, covered in fresh snow. Once they settle down, Maggie reads them an age-appropriate version of Dickens' *A Christmas Carol*, which they really seem to like. As she finishes the last page, parents begin to show up with refreshments and the party begins.

By the time the buses run at 11:45, Maggie is exhausted and welcomes the hush that falls over the room as the last straggler departs. It is still snowing outside, and the world is wrapped in a blanket of white. Maggie turns on her Christmas music station while she tidies the room for the long break.

Afterward, she stops by the store for some last minute groceries for Christmas Eve on her way to her house in town. Trent plays video games with a friend until Brad finishes basketball practice and then Brad picks up both Trent and Maggie for the drive to the ranch, allowing Maggie to leave her car in the garage for a day or two.

Once at the house, Trent and Brad disappear to the barn again, and Jack is feeding, so Maggie is able to give the house a thorough cleaning with no one underfoot. She makes a batch of snack mix, filling the house with the scent of toasted corn, nuts, and butter and stirs up a batch of sugar cookie dough to refrigerate while she cleans the kitchen.

By 5:00, the house is spotless, the laundry caught up and put away, the beds changed, meatloaf and scalloped potatoes in the oven for dinner, and Maggie curls up on the couch with her knitting in the light of the Christmas tree, listening to Christmas music. Soon, she hears the stamp of feet on the back steps as the men folk kick the snow from their boots, and she puts away the mostly-finished scarf she is making for Maura and goes into the kitchen.

"Oh, man, it smells good in here!" Trent exclaims. "What is that?"

Maggie laughs. "It's dinner and snack mix," she tells him. "We can eat in half an hour, so have a handful of it and help me set the table."

After a scrumptious dinner of Maggie's juicy meatloaf and creamy, cheesy potatoes, the boys do the dishes and then set up the table for a board game. They are in high spirits with school and basketball over for a few days and Christmas Eve tomorrow, and the evening is filled with laughter and teasing. Eventually, Maggie calls a halt to the festivities, pleading exhaustion, and the boys reluctantly put away the game, promising revenge at the next opportunity. Maggie lingers in the empty kitchen for a moment after they leave, savoring the quiet warmth as events from the busy day filter through her mind.

Jack, coming down from telling the boys goodnight, sees her standing at the counter and comes in. Turning Maggie to face him, Jack looks deep into her eyes, sending the usual thrill of heat flashing through her.

"Thank you," he tells her simply. "This night would not have happened without your help." Jack pulls her close for a hug, and Maggie relaxes in his arms.

*This,* she thinks, *is right. This,* she thinks, *is what life is about—loving and being loved in return.* She almost says the words aloud, but catches them back before they can leave her mouth.

"I think I'm the one who should say thanks," Maggie replies, pulling away to look at Jack. "You took me into your family, trusted me with your children, and helped me find a way to be joyful again. That's quite a bit, don't you think?"

Jack shrugs, as if he doesn't know quite what to say. "I think it's mutual; we both helped each other in a time of need. I guess that's what Christmas is about, right? That means we've had Christmas since September."

Maggie laughs, agreeing with Jack. It has felt like Christmas since September to Maggie, for the most part. "Well, anyway, we both have a lot to be grateful for, and now I think we should say goodnight."

She stands on tiptoe to gently kiss Jack's mouth and pulls away to get ready for bed, leaving Jack gazing after her. If she looks back, she will see the naked look of longing and love on his face, but she doesn't turn.

# CHAPTER 24

Everyone sleeps late the next morning except Jack who wakes at his usual time and can't go back to sleep, so he gets up to do chores. When he returns to the house, Maggie has showered and done her hair and is wearing a pretty, dark green sweater and black slacks. The sweater makes her green eyes look even greener, and Jack thinks again how beautiful she is. She is flitting around the kitchen, setting the table, stirring something on the stove, getting things from the refrigerator, and Jack assumes his favorite post— standing in the door, enjoying watching her in the morning light.

Maggie catches sight of him and whirls to give him a quick hug before darting back to the stove. "Good morning!" she exclaims. "Merry Christmas Eve! I hope you're hungry, because I'm making a huge breakfast. Get washed up, and you can help."

Jack laughs at her energy and enthusiasm and goes to wash his hands so he can assist the cook.

Maggie, with Jack's help, makes a hearty meal of hash brown potatoes, ham and cheese omelets, and biscuits and gravy. By the time they finish, the good smells bring the teenagers from their beds, and breakfast is quickly under way. Maggie is still amazed by how much these boys can eat as the mounds of food quickly disappear.

Eventually, even Brad and Trent are full, and Maggie sends them to get dressed while she cleans the kitchen and begins preparations for the Christmas Eve feast. She is roasting a honey-glazed ham and serving it with twice-baked potatoes and baby carrots, so she wants to get the potatoes started now so she can get the ham in the oven. Maggie cranks up the Christmas music and quickly gets to work. Her goal is to have dinner under control so she can relax and enjoy the day with Jack and the boys. Soon, the potatoes are in the oven, the dishes are washed, and the ham is soaking up the glaze.

The boys have come back down, now fully dressed, to watch television, so Maggie goes in and challenges them to another board game. Jack is out at the barn fixing a broken part on the tractor, so she and the boys play until the potatoes are baked.

Maggie takes a break from the game to remove the potatoes from the oven and put in the ham. When Jack comes back in an hour later, she calls an end to the marathon competition so she can finish the potatoes. She cooks bacon, and while green onions sauté in butter, she cuts the baked potatoes in half and scoops out the insides. She adds sour cream as she whips the potatoes and then stirs in the butter/onion mixture along with grated cheese, salt, and pepper. She spoons it all back into the potato skins and crumbles bacon over each. Maggie puts the potatoes on a baking sheet, covers them with plastic wrap, and puts them in the refrigerator until it is time to reheat them.

The ham is filling the house with its sweet, salty pork smell and even after the huge breakfast she ate, Maggie is starting to get hungry. One of the worst parts of cooking is cleaning up, and Maggie decides to make the salad now while the kitchen is still a mess from the twice-baked potatoes, and then does the dishes again and wipes off the counters.

With order restored, she goes to the living room with the others. They have found a football game to watch and are deeply involved, celebrating scores with high fives and groaning at bad calls. Maggie pulls out her knitting and settles in to see if she can finish Maura's scarf in time to wrap it tonight.

At half-time, Jack goes to feed, and all too quickly, it is time to trade the ham for the potatoes in the oven and steam the baby carrots. She puts a new red tablecloth on the table and sets it with care, adding tall, white candles in brass candlesticks, wanting everything to be perfect.

Maggie can't explain her need to make this one dinner so special but knows it has something to do with making up to this family for the neglect and hurt visited upon them by Caroline.

Christmas can be a time of great emotional upheaval and stress, but it is also a time of great healing, and Maggie is determined to be a tool in the process, hoping God's love will flow through her to Jack, Brad, and Trent.

When the ham is sliced, the potatoes cooked, and the carrots tender, Maggie calls the Hallas family in and is gratified to see the looks of wonder and delight on their faces when they see the elegant, bounteous meal she has prepared. The glow of candlelight flickers against a backdrop of red, reflecting in the white plates and sparkling in the silver utensils. Maggie has folded real cloth napkins into fan shapes and used Jack's crystal wine glasses and is quite pleased with the effect.

When everyone is seated, Maggie asks Jack to say the blessing. He reaches for her hand on one side and Trent's on the other, and the brothers join hands as well, as Brad takes Maggie's other one. Maggie bows her head and listens to Jack's deep, pleasant voice give thanks for the food, for each other, and for the birth of the baby Jesus. She says a quick, silent prayer of her own for the repose of Clark's soul, and wishes him Merry Christmas. By the time they say amen, Maggie is on the verge of tears, deeply moved by the love she feels at this table. With a squeeze of hands, the prayer is over, and Maggie feels the wave of emotion ebb as food is quickly passed around the table.

Everything turned out exactly as Maggie hoped, and Jack and his sons are effusive in their praise of the food and the atmosphere she has created. Maggie basks in the glow of accomplishment and drinks in the happy looks on young faces. She hopes this is a celebration they will never forget.

When no one can eat another bite, Maggie tidies the kitchen for the final time that day, helped by Jack and the boys, and then they go back to the living room for presents. Jack and the kids will have their own gift exchange in the morning, so the boys find the packages to and from Maggie under the tree and hand them around. Maggie has three packages; one is large, about two feet across both directions and about 10 inches deep, and is fairly heavy. One is the size of a child's shoebox and is also heavy. It makes a muffled clinking noise when she shakes it. The last is a small, narrow box of the type jewelry usually comes in.

"Maggie first! Maggie first!" the boys urge excitedly.

"Okay," Jack agrees, "Maggie first."

"Which one shall I start with?" Maggie teases, holding the smaller gifts in either hand.

"The big one!" Trent yells.

With a smile, Maggie puts down the other presents and pulls the large box onto her lap. When she pulls aside the paper and opens the box, she sees a small set of shelves inside. They are made of white fir, finished with a clear varnish, and each of the three shelves has a design of vines and leaves burned into the narrow front edge. It is beautiful, and Maggie wastes no time letting the boys know how she feels.

"It's for your room here," Brad tells her. "So you have a place for pictures and stuff." The two go on to tell her the details. Trent made the shelves in shop and brought them home to finish sanding so Brad could do the woodburning. Once that was finished, they worked together to varnish it.

"Did you trace it or is this free-hand?" Maggie asks Brad, running her fingertips lovingly over the delicate design.

"It's free-hand," Brad replies.

Maggie can see, when she looks closely, each shelf is unique. The quality of the work is amazing. She thanks them both and stands to give them each a hug.

"Now it's your turn," she tells them, and they waste no time ripping open the larger of the two packages from Maggie. They seem to really like the football jerseys, and Maggie is glad Kevin gave her the idea.

Next, Jack opens a present. He chooses the smaller box. Inside is a hat Maggie knitted him from soft, dark blue wool. He tries it on, and it fits perfectly.

"Thanks," Jack says. "Now you again, Maggie."

Maggie decides to save the smallest box for last and opens the shoebox-size present. Inside is a pair of spurs, just right to fit her boots. When she pulls them from the box, the rowels make the clinking sound she heard earlier. A silver plate is riveted on the top leather strap of each spur, and on it is engraved the life-like image of a tiny wolf. Maggie's eyes leap to Jack's in recognition, remembering the day on the mountain when Jack killed the wolf and the first time he kissed her later that night, and he nods an unspoken confirmation of her thoughts.

"They're for you to wear next time you ride on the mountain with us," Jack says. "I thought about asking for the wolf skin back and having it made into a coat or a rug for you, but I wasn't sure you'd like it."

"You made the right choice," Maggie replies with a shudder. "The only wolf I want to see on the mountain again is the one on this spur!" She has tried to forget the frightening experience, and now Jack has made something positive and fun from it. "It's the perfect gift, Jack. Thank you. It's beautiful and useful. Okay, boys, your turn again."

Brad and Trent open the other present from Maggie, revealing knitted hats and a bag of Maggie's homemade almond butter toffee coated in rich chocolate and sprinkled with more roasted almonds. Brad's hat is black with a red stripe and Trent's is red with a black stripe. They put on the hats immediately and then try the candy, making sounds of pure delight at the taste.

"Where's my candy?" Jack complains, looking in the empty box in case he missed something.

"Just open your other gift," Maggie tells him, laughing at his woeful expression. Of course, the box contains a bag of toffee for Jack as well as the belt she bought in Seattle. Jack seems really pleased with the belt, turning it over in his hands. He tells her he plans to put a buckle on it and wear it to church tonight, and Maggie is happy he likes it.

Now there is only one gift unopened and Maggie carefully unwraps the tiny, rectangular box. When she sees what is inside, she sits without speaking, her eyes brimming with unshed tears.

"Don't cry!" Jack says in concern, hastily getting up to go to her. "Maggie, it's supposed to make you happy, not sad!"

"I am happy," she answers, wiping away the tears and taking the necklace from the box. It is made of silver, a delicate chain holding a tiny, perfect spur. The miniature rowel even turns, Maggie sees, gazing with awe at the craftsmanship. "It's amazing, Jack. I can't believe you did this." With trembling fingers, she holds out the beautiful trinket.

Jack carefully places it around her neck, stepping back to observe the effect. "I have connections," Jack says, downplaying the emotion in the room. "They help me out once in a while."

"Well, they did you proud tonight," she tells him, giving him a quick hug. "Oh, man, look at the time! We need to hurry and get ready for church!"

She quickly picks up the torn wrapping paper and empty

boxes and piles them by the wood stove to burn in the morning, and goes upstairs to change while the men do the same. In her room, she changes into a black pencil skirt and a white, v-neck sweater scattered with dark red sunbursts. She pulls on tights and her knee-high black boots to help keep her feet and legs warm and checks her appearance in the mirror. A quick touch with the comb makes her brown hair lay nicely. Her eyes sparkle with happiness, her cheeks are flushed, and the little spur nestles in the hollow at the base of her throat. For some reason, she flashes back to the day Clark died when she went to see his body at the hospital and how horrible she looked in the mirror then. She looks and feels like a completely different person now, and that day, she thought she would never be happy again. Maggie is amazed at the gift of healing God has brought her.

Glancing at the clock, she hurries down to brush her teeth and get her coat and gloves. When she leaves the bathroom, Jack and the boys are waiting in the living room, looking very handsome and only a little uncomfortable in new Wrangler jeans and button-up western shirts. Their boots are polished to a shine, their hair is combed, and Jack is wearing his new belt.

"You look great!" she tells them. "Come on, we don't want to be late."

On the drive to town, they listen to Christmas music on the radio and talk softly now and then, Maggie describing what to expect during church. She invites them to go to the front of the church with her during communion to receive a blessing and explains how crossing their arms across their chests will let Father Murphy know they aren't Catholic.

When they arrive at the church thirty minutes before Mass, the parking lot is already half full. Christmas is one of the most well-attended Masses of the year, when families come home and go to church with their loved ones, and most know to arrive early if they want to get a good seat. Maggie's regular pew is still empty, so she leads them to it, dropping to one knee and making the sign of the cross to genuflect before entering the seat. This is the first time she hasn't been in church alone since Clark died, and Maggie enjoys the feeling of family as she walks up the aisle. Maybe, if God wills it, she might someday be a real member of this family she brings with her. Once in the pew, she pulls down the kneeler and kneels to pray while the boys and their father look around.

The small church is mostly dark, the only lights coming from the foyer and the candles burning on the altar, at the podium, and in the window ledges on both sides of the church. The organist softly plays Christmas hymns as the congregation trickles in. Maggie's heart is full, and she gives thanks for the many blessings she has received. She opens her mind, heart, and soul to the voice and the wishes of the Savior for whom this holiday is being celebrated. After a moment, she feels a sense of peace come over her, and the lingering sadness of Christmas without Clark lifts away. Maggie makes the sign of the cross again and settles into the pew. She whispers to the boys and Jack, "Sit when I sit, stand when I stand, and when I kneel, you can kneel too, or you can sit, whichever you feel like."

The four sit quietly and watch those around them, waiting for the service to begin. Finally, a man walks to the front, preceded by two women carrying candles, and reads, by candlelight, the proclamation about the first Christmas from a scroll. When he is finished, the three walk to the back of the church, and the priest asks the congregation to please rise for the opening hymn. The sound of the organ fills the little church with joyful praise as everyone joins in singing *O Come, O Come, Emmanuel*. As the priest walks to the altar, the lights are turned on, bringing the place to life in a blaze of color. Father Murphy carries an incense burner on a long chain and when he reaches the front, he paces around the altar, stopping several times to swing the burner in the sign of the cross, as he purifies the sacred communion table. The sweet, spicy, musty scent filling the air brings back memories of past Christmases for Maggie.

She sees Trent wrinkle his nose and wonders if the boys have ever smelled incense before. The hymn comes to an end and the Mass begins with the people standing throughout the opening prayers and the *Gloria*, which is sung to give praise to God. Everyone settles into the pews with a rustle and commotion for the readings from the Old Testament, and rises again for the Gospel reading from the New Testament. The boys at first seem puzzled, but as the story Maggie told them is read aloud, dawning looks of comprehension fill their faces, as if something has just clicked into place. The familiar rhythm of the liturgy soothes Maggie and pulls her into a place both exhilarating and calming.

Finally, it is time for communion, and the Hallas family rises to walk to the front for a blessing with Maggie. The boys and Jack seem to take it seriously and wait patiently in line until their turn comes, then stand with crossed arms and bowed heads under Father Murphy's kind hand while he asks for God to touch their lives. Maggie thinks maybe God already has.

The closing song is *Joy to the World*, and Maggie is surprised to hear not only Brad and Trent sing along but also Jack, who has a pleasant baritone. With a full heart, Maggie joins in, feeling that joy is truly in the world tonight.

After Mass ends, Maggie visits with those around her, introducing Jack and his sons and wishing everyone a merry Christmas. She sees many speculative looks directed at the two of them and hopes the thoughts behind the looks are charitable. Finally, they are able to make their way to the door, where Maggie shakes Father Murphy's hand and thanks him for the service, and they are out into the frozen night.

A quick drive to Maggie's house brings them back to the warmth of her cozy kitchen for dessert. Earlier in the week, she made an ice cream cake to store in the freezer for tonight, and the boys quickly devour it. By now, it is after 9:00 p.m., and Jack is yawning behind his hand as he prods the boys back into their coats. Maggie hugs each of them in turn and thanks them again for the gifts, and they are gone.

Silence falls over the house as she watches Jack drive away, and for a moment Maggie finds it hard to breathe as she struggles to control her emotions. She doesn't want to spend this time away from Jack, but she knows it's important for him to uphold the fragile traditions the three have established since Caroline left. She closes her eyes and prays for strength and eventually feels better, so she washes the dessert dishes and does a few last-minute finishing touches on the house before calling it a night. To her surprise, she falls asleep quickly and doesn't dream.

# CHAPTER 25

The sound of a phone ringing pulls Maggie from a deep sleep. At first, she can't identify what has awakened her, but eventually manages to find the phone and answer it. The bedside clock says 8:00, and she is amazed she slept so late.

It is Maura on the phone. "Merry Christmas, Mom!" she says exuberantly. Maggie can hear Tom echoing the sentiment in the background and Patrick chortling away as well.

"Merry Christmas, sweetheart," she answers. "What's going on?"

"Nothing," Maura tells her. "We just miss you and wanted to say hi. Kevin will be here at 11:00, and we're heading straight to you, so we should be there around 1:30 or 2:00 if everything goes well."

"Great!" Maggie says. "I'll have dinner ready to go on the table at 2:30 then. What's the weather like?" Lying in bed with the drapes pulled, she has no idea what it's doing outside.

"I don't know; we have an inversion," Maura answers. "Maybe it will be sunny up your way."

"I hope so. What did Santa bring Patrick?" Maggie asks.

"He got a bouncy horse. Of course, he's too little to ride it, but soon I think he'll have a great time!" Maura cheerfully announces. "I have to go now. Someone thinks he needs breakfast!"

"Okay, hon. Drive carefully, and I'll see you in a few hours. Love you," Maggie says and then hangs up the phone. For a few minutes, she stays in bed, thinking about the kids and other Christmases, then the realization of everything she needs to get done in the next few hours sends her flying to the bathroom for a shower.

The morning passes in a flurry of preparation as Maggie bakes pies, puts the turkey in the oven, and gets all the trimmings ready to cook later in the day. She takes a break at 12:30 for a light lunch. By the time her children and grandchildren arrive, dinner is almost ready.

The van barely comes to a stop before Emma is out and racing to the house. Maggie meets her granddaughter on the front step and swoops her into a hug as Emma covers her face with little girl kisses.

"I missed you, Gramma," Emma says, looking deep into Maggie's eyes.

"I missed you too, sweetie," Maggie answers. "Let's get you in where it's warm. She puts Emma down and leads her into the house. Emma's eyes widen when she spies the tree in the living room heaped high with presents.

"Are some for me?" she asks.

"A whole bunch are for you," Maggie tells her, kneeling down to help Emma off with her coat. Didi is next in the door, carrying a struggling Ethan.

"Want down, Mama, want down!" he shrieks.

Didi puts him down and straightens to remove her coat. "I don't know how you stand living out here in the middle of nowhere in all this snow," she complains waspishly. "Will you watch him while I go to the bathroom?" With that, she stalks away toward the bathroom.

"Merry Christmas to you too," Maggie mutters under her breath to Didi's back. Still on her knees, she turns to her grandson. "How are you, Ethan?" she asks.

Ethan stops crying and looks back at her, tucking a thumb in his mouth. She reaches out and unzips his coat, pulling him closer to tug the sleeves from his chubby arms. He surveys her with suspicion, but when Emma takes Maggie's hand to help her to her feet, he willingly takes the other hand, and she walks them into the living room. Maura comes through the door with Patrick, and Maggie leaves Ethan and Emma staring at the tree and goes to help.

Maura greets her with a strong hug and a kiss on the cheek. "Merry Christmas, Mom!"

"Merry Christmas to you too, Maura," she tells her daughter as she returns the hug. "You look fantastic!" The baby weight has come off and Maura is stunning in jeans and a blue sweater, her blond hair shining and her blue eyes sparkling.

"Thanks, Mama; so do you!" Maura looks her mother up and down, noticing her new dress and slender figure, but most of all noticing the shadows around Maggie's eyes have been replaced with a look of happiness.

Tom comes in behind Maura carrying the diaper bag and suitcases, which he drops in a heap by the door before sweeping Maggie into a bear hug. Kevin follows, also laden with luggage, and trips over what Tom has dropped, almost falling. Tom catches his arm to keep him upright and the four standing at the open door burst into laughter.

Didi, coming from the bathroom, doesn't think it's so funny. "Shut the door, will you? It's freezing outside!" she admonishes.

Everyone stops laughing, and Kevin obediently swings the door shut, pushing luggage out of the way with his foot. He, too, sweeps Maggie up in a hug, which she returns just as vigorously. It seems her children have missed her as much as she has missed them.

The men and Maura stomp snow from their boots and haul the luggage to the appropriate bedrooms and go back out to bring in the presents while Didi picks up the remote and sits in Maggie's chair with her boots dripping on the carpet.

Maggie keeps the children busy while their parents unload the van. Once everything is in the house, and boots and coats are stored away, Maggie hands Patrick back to Maura and checks on dinner.

"You have time for a drink before dinner," she announces. "Is anyone interested?" A chorus of assent greets her, so Maggie and Maura take drink orders and go into the kitchen to prepare the beverages.

Didi starts to follow but turns away to scold Ethan for getting too close to the tree.

Maura rolls her eyes at Maggie, and the two burst out laughing again. They are both used to Didi's critical, cranky behavior, and laughing about it helps to prevent her mood from ruining the day.

Maggie mixes whiskey and Coke for the men while Maura opens a bottle of wine and pours a glass for each of them. Didi has asked for sparkling water, a request Maggie anticipated, so she grabs a bottle from the refrigerator and fills a crystal glass.

As Maggie reaches to pick up drinks to take to the living room, Maura notices the necklace she is wearing and stops her with a hand, reaching out to gently finger the delicate silver. "Mom, this is beautiful! Where did you get it?" Maura asks wonderingly.

"Jack gave it to me for Christmas. A friend of his made it," Maggie answers.

"Wow, Mom, he must really like you!" Maura states with a grin and steps away to pick up her glass.

"I hope so," Maggie says, smiling back, "because I really like him." She carries her wine, Kevin's drink, and Didi's water, and the two return to the living room, handing the drinks around.

"Let's make a toast," she announces. "Here's to Christmas and families and loving each other." Maggie raises her glass and the others follow suit, clinking their glasses to hers with a "Cheers." After everyone has taken a drink, Kevin raises his glass again.

"I want to make a toast," he says. "Here's to Mom, for always being there for us and for being so strong and embracing life when she could have given up after Dad died. And here's to Dad, may he rest in peace and always look out for us."

"Hear, hear," the others chime in. With tears in her eyes, Maggie taps her glass to her son's. "Thank you, Kevin," she whispers.

"You're welcome, Mom," he answers, giving her a one-armed hug.

"If you're finished spouting off," Didi says sarcastically, "maybe you could see what your son is getting into."

Kevin turns away to pull Ethan out from under the tree.

"Presents, Daddy," the youngster chortles, pointing at the tree. Laughter again covers the awkwardness brought on by Didi's unpleasantness, and Maura and Tom settle on the couch with Patrick while Didi takes Emma to the restroom.

Maggie bustles off to check on dinner again, taking her glass with her. Everything is ready, so Maggie starts putting the food on the table. Tom steps in to help, and Maura brings out the high chair for Patrick and boosters for Ethan and Emma from one of the bedrooms where Maggie stores them. As everyone is seated, Maggie looks around the table at their dear, familiar faces. It has been months since they were all together, and she has missed them terribly.

Kevin looks back at her, Clark's crooked smile sitting well on his handsome, young face. Sometimes, her son's resemblance to his father is uncanny, and in the past has been painful for Maggie to see, but this afternoon she finds it comforting.

"Will you say the blessing, son?" she asks.

"Sure, Mom." He bows his head and says the old, familiar mealtime blessing.

So begins their first Christmas dinner without Clark, but it is far from sad and dreary. Three children under the age of five make for a hectic time, all of them demanding attention and eating their food with varying degrees of success and enjoyment.

Didi launches a diatribe aimed at Kevin about the table manners of "his" children, blaming him for their shortcomings.

Maggie tactfully changes the subject and tells her family about Jack and his boys and the gifts they gave her yesterday. She shows them the necklace Jack had made for her and explains the spur signifies the ride on the mountain on the day Jack killed the wolf and saved her life. Maggie hasn't told them much detail about the event, worrying they won't want her to ride with Jack anymore, but today she uses the story to entertain during dinner and to keep Didi from nagging Kevin. Maggie knows Didi loves Kevin, but sometimes she has a strange way of showing it, often picking a fight with him in front of his family.

Emma listens intently to her grandmother tell about the wolf ready to spring, a worried look on her small face, then smiles in satisfaction when Maggie describes Jack riding in and shooting the attacking wolf.

"I like Jack," she says solemnly. "He got that bad wolf!"

"Yes, he did," Maggie confirms. "That bad wolf won't bother anybody ever again."

By now, everyone but Didi has finished eating. Didi picks at her food with her fork, turning it over but not eating it. Maggie knows better than to call attention to the fact that Didi isn't eating. It will either turn into a criticism of Maggie's cooking with an inferred condemnation of her inadequate knowledge of nutrition and fine cuisine or a lecture about dieting and body fat, neither of which Maggie wants to hear, so she ignores her daughter-in-law and rises to start carrying dirty dishes and food back to the kitchen.

Emma is whining to begin opening presents, so Kevin takes her into the living room for a game to pass the time. Maura hands Patrick to Tom for a diaper change and begins helping Maggie clear the table. Didi has disappeared into the other bedroom with Ethan, presumably for the same chore, but conveniently stays out of sight until most of the work is done. When she comes into the kitchen, she leans against the counter and complains about the flight from Seattle and the drive from Boise while the other two women silently load the dishwasher, put the leftovers in the refrigerator, and wash the pots and pans. Soon, the kitchen is spick and span, and they head to the living room for presents.

Both little boys have dozed off on their father's laps, and Maggie smiles to see the men cuddling their sons. Maggie enlists Emma, Maura, and Didi to hand out packages and sits down to watch the fun. Finally, all the presents are divided into piles at each person's chair, and the opening begins. It is their family tradition to start with the youngest child and take turns based on age, going around until all the presents are open. Since the little boys are asleep, they start with Emma. She is so excited she can hardly stand it but manages to tear the paper and ribbon off in record time. Inside is a doll from her Aunt Maura and Uncle Tom, and even Didi smiles to see the little girl's delight in her new "baby."

"Auntie Maura, I wanted this dolly my whole life," she tells Maura earnestly, and cradles the doll to her chest, hugging it tightly. She doesn't understand the laughter that follows her avowal, but laughs along anyway. Patrick and Ethan wake up partway through the presents and bring everyone to laughter time and again with their antics.

After about two hours, all the packages are open and empty boxes and garbage bags of balled up wrapping paper are piled around the room. Maggie receives a beautiful cashmere sweater in shades of green from Maura and Tom, and tickets to a play in Seattle in the spring from Kevin and Didi, plus various other small, thoughtful gifts. Maura loves the scarf Maggie knitted, and the others all like the things she gave them, even Didi.

By now, the children are cranky from being overly-excited, so their fathers bundle them up and take them out to play in the snow before dark while Maura, Didi, and Maggie take their gifts to their rooms and pick up the boxes and trash from the living room. By the time the men and kids come back in, pink-cheeked and smelling of snow and fresh air, the house is back to normal and Maggie is cutting the pies for dessert.

After dessert, they settle the children on the floor to play with their new toys and start a game of Hearts at the kitchen table. Maggie thinks it isn't coincidence that Didi ends up with the Queen of Spades more frequently than anyone else. Soon, Didi has had enough and goes into the living room with the kids to watch television. The other four spend a fun evening playing cards, stopping for a late supper of leftovers before bathing the little ones and putting them to bed.

Once Maggie's grandchildren are asleep, the adults sit and talk late into the night, catching up on each other's lives. Face-to-face is much better than the telephone or internet, and Maggie thoroughly enjoys spending time with her children and their spouses.

At some point, the subject of Jack comes up, and Maggie is frank with them, telling them of her increasing fondness for Jack and the hope of something more than friendship in the future. Both Kevin and Maura are supportive, and Maggie's worries of their acceptance of her being with another man disappear under their loving approval. Eventually, the yawns outnumber the talk, so they say goodnight and go to bed.

# CHAPTER 26

Maggie is up early the next morning, fixing a big breakfast while the others sleep in. Ethan toddles in while she is cooking, his diaper sagging, so Maggie changes him with a diaper from the bag in the living room and settles him at the table with a plate of hash browns, scrambled eggs, and biscuits and gravy. He digs in with gusto, chattering away between bites. Maggie only understands a small portion of what he says, but it is enough to make him nod and smile and keep talking. She cherishes this time with her grandson, coming to know him a little better as he grows up.

Soon, Emma comes in, rubbing her eyes and looking for her grandma. Maggie gets her a plate, and as she puts it on the table, Maura comes in carrying Patrick who is soon settled in his high chair, his little fists full of eggs and gravy. Maura gets herself and Maggie a plate while Maggie interacts with the children, and the two eat breakfast in between fetching more for the kids.

The sound of voices and the smell of food eventually is enough to bring Tom and Kevin to the table, and then Didi meanders in, wandering from the stove to the refrigerator, turning up her nose at Maggie's cooking.

"Don't you have any fruit in this house?" she whines. Maggie sighs, and gets up to find Didi some fruit in the crowded refrigerator. When everyone has eaten and the kids and dishes are cleaned up, it is time for showers and clothes and then the games begin. The adults take turns keeping an eye on the toddlers while the others play cards. The day is spent in a leisurely fashion, games, movies, naps, leftovers and snacks keeping everyone occupied.

Once again, Kevin and Tom take the kids outside to play in

the snow, taking advantage of the sunny day to give them an experience they don't normally have where they live. Maggie and Maura go for a walk in the brisk air, talking the whole time, while Didi takes a nap.

To Maggie, it is a magical day, a day she will never forget, and she revels in having them all here at home, even if it's only for a few days. As the family grows, these times together will get fewer, and Maggie vows to herself to keep up the effort to make them happen.

The next day they all go skiing at Brundage except for Patrick, who is too little, and Maggie, who stays behind to watch him. Maggie plays with Patrick and uses naptime to catch up on the laundry and tidy the house, which has gotten a little out of control with the number of people staying there. She takes Patrick for a walk, pulling him behind her in the little sled that used to be his mother's. He loves it, babbling and laughing the whole way.

Maggie knows the kids will come home worn out and hungry, so when Kevin calls to tell her they are on the way, she orders take-out pizza and salad from the pizza parlor downtown, timing the call to coincide with their arrival. When they walk in the door, dinner is on the table, and the delicious smell of fresh pizza fills the air. Even Didi eats heartily without complaining and helps clear the table afterward.

Emma and Ethan barely stay awake through dinner and are immediately bathed and put to bed, and Patrick follows soon after. Maggie and the kids start a movie, but by 8:00, all but Maggie are asleep in their chairs, so she turns off the television and wakes them up to go to bed. She sits in the living room after they leave, soaking in the feeling of having the house full of sleeping family, and stares out the window into the night.

It has started to snow, first lightly, then heavily, all but masking the streetlight at the corner. Maggie wonders what Jack is doing right now. He was supposed to meet Caroline with the boys on Christmas day so they could spend part of the holiday with her, and she thought he might call or stop by, but he hasn't. She misses him, even with the kids here, and contemplates calling him, but it is late enough she thinks he is probably asleep, so she contents herself with thinking about him instead. She remembers how his blue eyes sparkled when she opened the tiny spur necklace, and she relives every moment in the kitchen with Jack the day before Christmas Eve.

Eventually, her mind circles around to the dilemma confronting them and the cruel gossip being perpetrated about their relationship. She thinks about the solution offered by Father Murphy—marriage—and dares to imagine being married to Jack. Maggie thinks it won't be much different from the time they spend together now at the ranch, and she also thinks it will be completely different, sharing a bed with Jack. It has been eight months now since Clark died, the longest stretch of celibacy in her adult life, and she is more than ready for it to come to an end. Now that she has her children's blessing, the path to marriage seems a little less bumpy if only Jack will come to the same conclusion. Closing the curtains against the storm, Maggie goes to bed.

Sunday is the last day the kids will be here, and Tracy and Danny have invited them all to their house for brunch. Maggie gives the little ones a snack when they get up to tide them over and helps her children pack the van for the trip back to Boise. She checks the bathroom and bedrooms for stray toys and socks, looks under the couch and the coffee table and finally finds the bottle for Emma's doll, and snags Ethan's blanket from under one of the beds. Maura rides to Tracy's with Maggie, knowing they will leave from there and wanting this last time alone with her mother.

"So, Mom," Maura begins. "You're really okay? You trust Jack, right? I mean, Kevin and Tom and I are worried you might get hurt, and we've only met Jack the one time, so we don't really know him well enough to know how he might treat you." She breaks off uncertainly, looking anxiously at Maggie.

"Honey, you don't need to worry about me," Maggie reassures her. "I know things with Jack kind of took off quickly, but I've been around him almost daily for four months now, and I've seen him with his kids and with his animals, and I trust him completely. He doesn't drink or do drugs, he hasn't slept around after his divorce, he takes care of his money and his property, so there aren't any danger signs I've been able to see." She is referring to a talk she and Clark had with Maura when Maura went off to college and began seriously dating, a talk where they gave Maura examples of some of the kinds of behavior to be watchful of when choosing a husband.

"There isn't a day that goes by that I don't think of your dad. I still miss him all the time, but he's gone, and he isn't coming back. Jack is the only man I've met in years I would consider having a relationship with, so I want to move forward if Jack wants to."

"Okay, Mom. My gut says he's a good guy, so between it and you, I guess I give Jack a pass. Just be careful, and if things get weird or you have any misgivings, kick him to the curb!" Maura tells her.

"Thanks for the advice, sweetie," Maggie responds wryly. "I think I can handle it. Let Kevin know, will you? Since you and he discuss me behind my back."

"Mom, you know it's just because we love you."

Maggie nods in assent. They do love her, and she is touched at their concern, even though she feels it is completely misplaced. If anyone is in a toxic relationship, it's Kevin, but Maggie has attempted to talk to him about it before and was shut down, so she no longer brings it up.

She pulls the car into the driveway beside the rental van and helps get the children out of their car seats and into Tracy's house. Once the hubbub of greetings and shunting of coats and boots is accomplished, the family troops into Tracy's large kitchen for brunch. Brunch at Tracy's is a lively affair with the extra family members and small children, but everyone gets fed and conversation abounds. Tracy, who is childless, dotes on her great niece and nephews and is in her element bossing everyone around and playing with the little ones.

All too soon, Kevin announces it is time for them to get on the road so they can make the airport in time for their flight. Fortunately, the weather is clear and sunny, the snow from last night's storm cleared from the roadways, and they should make a safe and easy trip to Boise. Danny and Tracy say their goodbyes and tactfully retreat to the house so Maggie can bid farewell to her children and grandchildren. Emma cries and Ethan joins in just to be helpful, which sets Patrick off, so with all three wailing, their parents hand them to Maggie for kisses and hugs and strap them in their car seats. Didi gives her a quick peck on the cheek and disappears into the van with the children, leaving Maura, Tom, and Kevin standing on the snowy sidewalk with Maggie.

"Take care, Mom," Tom tells her as he gives her a rib-cracking hug. "Thanks for the great food; I think I've gained ten pounds this weekend!"

Maura is next, holding Maggie tightly and letting her go with tears in her eyes. "Merry Christmas, Mom. I love you."

"Me, too," says Kevin stepping up for his turn to hug his

mother. "Thanks for all you do for us. Come see us soon."

The doors close, and the van pulls away. Maggie turns to watch, waving until it disappears around the corner and hurries back in, shivering. She walks to the kitchen, and Tracy steps up to hug her younger sister. "It's hard letting them go, huh, kiddo?" she asks.

"Yes, especially since the little ones are getting old enough to remember me from visit to visit. I hate it when they cry," Maggie answers, a little tearful, as she pulls away from her sister's hug. "Thanks, Tracy. I feel better; and thank you for having them here for brunch. I know it's a bit of a hassle."

"No, no, it's not a hassle at all," Tracy replies. "I love seeing them. Thank you for sharing them on your last morning."

The sisters settle at the kitchen table for a last cup of tea and a good talk before Maggie leaves. As she drives away, Maggie thinks how blessed she is to have a sister like Tracy in her life. After their parents were killed in a car accident when Maggie was small, Tracy became both mother and sister, helping to raise Maggie when an elderly aunt took in the two orphans, and they are exceptionally close now, the only family they have besides Maggie's kids and grandkids. Maggie considers how their relationship might change if she marries Jack eventually and hopes she is able to continue her weekly visits. She knows Jack and Danny are friends, so it shouldn't be a problem since Maggie will need to drive to town for church anyway.

Maggie laughs at herself, already planning a weekend schedule as if marrying Jack was a sure thing. For now, she decides to put it out of her mind and enjoy the rest of her Christmas break, knowing it will go way too fast and she will be back to writing lesson plans and grading papers.

When Maggie gets home, the silence of the empty house wipes away her ambition and all thoughts of cleaning up fly right into the winter day. She gets a glass of ice water and plops into her recliner with the remote in hand and spends the time until church watching football and dozing. All the late nights, the unaccustomed strain of having company and helping take care of toddlers have caught up with her and she is exhausted, physically and emotionally. She rouses to attend Mass and then settles back in front of the television. Around 7:00, she snacks on leftovers and starts a load of laundry, but even that small chore makes her tired, so she goes back to the chair for the Sunday night game, going to bed as soon as it is over. Her first Christmas as a widow is officially over.

Catherine Bridwell

# CHAPTER 27

While Maggie is enjoying an action-packed holiday weekend with her children and grandchildren, Jack is alone at the ranch. Christmas morning, after opening presents and breakfast, he took the boys up into the woods to shoot the new guns he got them for Christmas. Then it was time to leave to meet Caroline in Weiser so Brad and Trent could spend the weekend with her. They arrived in time to eat lunch and then Caroline and her boyfriend Harold drove up. Jack hugged his sons goodbye and watched them vanish into the cold winter afternoon.

He went home and fed the cows and now is trying to fill all the hours empty of Trent, Brad, and Maggie. He cooks, he eats, he does dishes and chores, he feeds cows, he showers, he watches television, and then he goes to bed to start all over the next morning. Jack has the same feeling of suspended time he experienced on Thanksgiving when the boys were with their mother. Somehow this is different from the days when he is at work and the boys are at school, and he worries he will feel this way every time she takes them. Jack thinks he won't be able to stand it unless Maggie is here to keep him company.

By Monday morning, Jack has had enough and heads to town for breakfast before making the trip to Weiser to collect the children. By the enthusiasm with which he is greeted and the relieved chatter from the boys on the way home, Jack gets the impression they are as ready to be home as he is to have them back. It seems the novelty of spending time with Caroline has worn off and the reality of dealing with her whims and selfish behavior has reinserted itself in the relationship. From what Brad and Trent say, and even more from what they don't say, Jack thinks they spent the weekend playing video games and watching sports and movies while Caroline slept and watched reality shows in her room. Apparently, Harold, Caroline's boyfriend, worked most of Saturday and part of Sunday, so Caroline had plenty of opportunity to spend quality time with her sons and didn't care to take advantage of it. This makes Jack angry for the boys' sake and for the time he spent alone while she wasted their presence in her home. His only solace is the boys are old enough to tell her they don't want to go if she doesn't spend more time with them.

They arrive at home for a quick lunch before it's time for Brad to go to practice. Trent asks to go to his friend's house to hang out, and even though Jack doesn't want them both to leave again so soon, he doesn't have the heart to say no. Instead, he offers to drive them both to town and gives Maggie a call to see if she wants company for a while. Maggie seems happy to hear from him and quickly agrees to spend the afternoon together. It was only Jack's reluctance to interfere with Maggie's family plans that kept him from calling or visiting while the boys were at Caroline's.

Jack is anxious to see her again, so with a light heart he gets back in the pickup with the boys and stops to check the mail on the way to town. There is a large manila envelope from Caroline and a small white one with no return address, his name and address printed in block letters in handwriting Jack doesn't recognize, and his happy mood immediately disintegrates. The two coming together can't be good. Jack doesn't let his anxiety show but merely puts the envelopes face down on the seat between him and Brad and continues down the road. All the way to town he worries about what Caroline might be up to while trying to make normal conversation with his kids, and as soon as Brad is dropped off at the school and Trent disappears into his friend's house, he opens the smaller, white envelope.

The contents confirm his trepidation. Inside is an anonymous hate-letter about him and Maggie, filled with misspelled accusations of immorality, citing Jack's relationship with Maggie and Maggie's presence in his home as an unhealthy and immoral influence on Jack's sons. The writer threatened to go to child protective services about the situation and start a petition to get the school board to fire Maggie, saying a woman living in sin with a man shouldn't be around young children. Jack is wild with anger and a deep sense of injustice as he reads through the pages. The idea of Maggie being an immoral influence on anyone is ludicrous as all who know her can testify, and Jack knows she will be very hurt at the content of the letter. Jack's first impulse is to shield her from it, but he knows she will have to be told, and part of him is relieved he will be able to share this with Maggie. He has come to rely on her calm, kind demeanor and her practical advice in times of stress and is glad she is expecting him today. Jack puts the paper back in the envelope and drives to her house. Maggie Sullivan will know what to do.

Catherine Bridwell

# CHAPTER 28

After a busy morning spent cleaning and reorganizing the house, Maggie is thrilled to get a phone call from Jack asking if he can visit this afternoon. She is a little hurt he hasn't called before now but tells herself she is being silly. After all, they are both adults, and she knows how to use a phone as well as he does and could have been the one who made the call, but she is absurdly pleased he called, and hums as she fixes chicken salad and soup for lunch. She eats in the breakfast nook, watching the chickadees and quail out the window. As much as she enjoys her house and her pretty yard, she has come to love the quiet, wild country in the mountains around Jack's ranch, and is looking forward to going back after the holidays.

When she finishes her meal, she loads the dishwasher, wipes the counters and hurries in to fix her hair and put on some makeup before Jack arrives. She feels a pleasant sense of anticipation, almost a giddy sensation, wrapped up in memories of Jack's face, his strong, warm hands, and the smell of his neck when he holds her. When Maggie finishes primping, she puts on a pot of coffee and gets out cookies left over from the weekend. Jack is always looking for a sweet snack, and she enjoys seeing his face when he bites into something she has baked. Cooking for people she loves is one of Maggie's favorite activities.

When everything is arranged to her satisfaction, she pulls on a sweater and hurries to the mailbox to get the mail. Back in the warmth of the kitchen, she sorts through the assortment, throwing away flyers and advertisements and stacking the bills on the counter.

At the bottom of the pile is a small white envelope, her name and address handwritten in small block letters, and there is no return address. For some unknown reason, Maggie's stomach drops, and she doesn't want to open the envelope.

*Stop being silly*, she chides herself, and rips open the missive. After seeing the contents, she wishes she had listened to her intuition and just thrown it away unopened. The accusations leap off the page: "immoral behavior," "sinful situation," "bad influence on children," "unfit to teach," "petition to the school board," "fired from teaching;" Maggie's mind reels as she reads to the end. Of course, it's unsigned. People who judge others rarely admit to what they are doing.

Shakily, she sinks into a chair in her sunny kitchen and reads through the hateful letter again. She realizes, unhappily, these people won't stop the harassment until they get their way. Maggie will either have to quit working for Jack or quit teaching, and neither option is okay with her.

The ringing of the doorbell startles her from her doleful contemplations. Maggie quickly slides the awful letter underneath her stack of bills before answering the door. Jack is standing on the porch.

She thinks again how handsome he is, tall and lean in his jeans and cowboy hat. She waves him into the house and stands on tiptoe for his kiss, reveling in the feel of him against her—cold against her warmth, hard against her softness, and smelling of snow and fresh air. He holds her tightly, keeping her snuggled into his arms after the kiss, rocking them both back and forth and stroking her back.

She tips her head back to look at him, and he stares back with a grave, sorrowful expression on his face. Startled, Maggie pulls away. "What's wrong? Are the boys okay?" she asks anxiously.

"They're fine, but we have a big problem," Jack tells her. "Let's sit down so we can talk."

Maggie takes his coat and leads him into the kitchen, pouring them both a cup of coffee while he settles at the table. She puts the coffee in front of him along with the plate of cookies, a sinking feeling in her stomach at the look on Jack's face.

Apparently, Jack has the same feeling and shakes his head at the offering of food. Jack lays two envelopes on the table print-side down and slides them over to Maggie without speaking.

She looks questioningly at him, but he just shakes his head and points at the envelopes. Maggie opens the thick manila one first. It is still sealed, so she knows Jack hasn't looked at it yet. She sees

Caroline's name in the return address, the writing loopy and childish. Inside are some official-looking pages and a note on pink paper in the same girlish print as the return address.

> *Dear Jack:*
>
> *I wanted to let you know before you hear it from someone else. I am getting married. Harold asked me several months ago, but since he is Catholic and I'm divorced, we had to apply to have the marriage annulled. Mine and yours, that is! The papers were approved and came in the mail right before Christmas, so the wedding will be on Valentine's Day.*
>
> *Since you weren't very good at it, I don't know if you ever plan to get married again, but in case you do, you might need a copy of the annulment papers, so here they are. Good luck.*
>
> *Caroline*

"Wow! She doesn't think much of your chances, does she?" Maggie asks.

Jack shakes his head in confusion, reaching for the note. Maggie hands him the pink paper and pulls the other pages from the envelope. As promised, it is a copy of the annulment of the marriage of Jack and Caroline Hallas, on official letterhead from the Roman Catholic Diocese of Idaho, properly signed and sealed.

Jack has finished reading the note, so she gives him the rest of the papers and picks up the second envelope. This one is opened, and must be the reason for Jack's silent gloom. As Maggie turns it over to open it, she recognizes the block printing on the outside. It is the same as the anonymous letter she just received.

Carefully putting the envelope down as if it might blow up, she walks to the counter and retrieves her own letter, laying them side by side on the table as she sits back down with Jack. The two of them stare at each other, realizing the seriousness of their predicament. The concern and sympathy in Jack's gaze is Maggie's undoing, and her eyes fill with tears.

"Why!" she asks angrily, her voice shaking with shock and outrage. "Why would someone do this?"

"They are hateful people who have nothing better to do. They probably have no intention of actually going through with any of it," Jack reassures Maggie, taking her hand in his and gently pulling the offending document away. "Don't cry. We'll figure it out."

Maggie sits quietly for a few minutes, absorbing the situation and trying to come to terms with it. Her mind is racing, thinking of solutions and discarding them just as quickly. The answer provided by Father Murphy is on the tip of her tongue, but she can't bring herself to say it aloud. Finally, she squares her shoulders and takes a deep breath. "I have to quit," she announces. "I can't stay at your house anymore or be around you and the boys until things settle down. When do they say they are going to the school board?" She reaches for the letters, but Jack pulls them away with a frown.

"Quit? What are you talking about? That won't help! It will only make all of us miserable, and they can still claim we're having an affair and hiding it," Jack argues. He has already played this scenario through in his head and is waiting for Maggie to follow his logic.

She reconsiders, chewing her lip in thought. This little habit of hers drives Jack crazy. It makes him want to kiss her every time she does it, but he knows thoughts like this helped get them in the fix they are in and tries to focus on the problem at hand.

All at once, a solution flashes into Jack's mind, taking his breath away. It is so simple and obvious, yet brilliant, and he marvels he didn't think of it sooner. "Maggie," Jack says. "I know what we can do." He slides out of his chair onto one knee, still holding her hand. "Marry me. I was going to ask you anyway when I thought you were ready, so let's get married because we love each other and want to be together, and let's do it now so we can be together without anyone pointing fingers at us. I love you, Maggie. Marry me."

Maggie sits speechless, unable to process the sudden change of events. She has thought about being married to Jack, but only in a dreamy, abstract way, and has never considered the when, where, and how of an actual proposal. Now Jack is looking at her with those crystal blue eyes, his face filled with love and longing, and Maggie needs to answer. Thoughts of Clark suddenly fill her mind, guilt and sorrow and anger mingled together in a wave of pain, and then she remembers her dream and knows what to say.

"Yes, Jack, my answer to you is yes, yes, yes!" Maggie tells him, starting to cry again. "I love you, Jack, and I will marry you whenever you want me to."

Jack stands, pulling her into his arms and kissing her over and over, her mouth, her face, her mouth again. He is laughing and Maggie is laughing through her tears, kissing him back just as feverishly. After a moment, they are silent, just looking at each other, the reality of what they have agreed to sinking in. "You're sure?" Jack asks her quietly. "We can wait if you need to."

"I'm sure," Maggie says. "Today, tomorrow, next week, I still say yes, yes, yes! Are *you* sure? I know you're not very good at it," she teases him, her green eyes sparkling.

"I'm way better at some parts of it," Jack teases back, wiggling his eyebrows suggestively and winking at her. "Let's set a date. The sooner we get married, the sooner I can show you how good I am at it."

Maggie bursts out laughing. "Okay, cowboy. How soon are you thinking?" She pulls him over to the calendar beside the kitchen telephone. "Today is Monday, New Year's Eve is Wednesday, New Year's Day is Thursday, so I say all three of those days are out. How's Friday or Saturday?" she asks, partly joking and partly serious. Now that they have decided to get married, she agrees with Jack's idea of the sooner the better, the white envelopes sitting side by side on her kitchen table a mute testament to the need to solve the problem.

He looks at the calendar and then back at Maggie. "Don't you want your kids there? If you do, Saturday would probably be the quickest they could make it. Why don't you call them and see what their schedules look like?"

Touched by his thoughtfulness, Maggie gives him a hug. "I think first I should call Father Murphy and see if he's available on Saturday. Are you okay with getting married in the Catholic Church? Since your first marriage is annulled and I'm a widow, there shouldn't be any delay." She looks questioningly at Jack, waiting for an answer to this very important question. They haven't had a chance to discuss any of the things couples usually talk about before getting engaged, and there are many things they don't yet know about each other when it comes to weddings.

Ever since he realized he wanted to marry Maggie, Jack has assumed she would want a church wedding. Her deep faith is one of the things he loves about her, and Jack is perfectly willing to get married wherever and whenever Maggie wants. "Of course, we can get married there," he assures her. "Call Father Murphy and find out."

Maggie looks at him intently, assessing him with her eyes. "You know it's forever, right?" she asks.

"Wouldn't have it any other way, sweetheart," Jack vows. "Call the priest!"

Smiling, Maggie picks up the phone and dials the rectory from the number tacked to her bulletin board beside the phone. While the phone is ringing, she wonders distractedly if every Catholic home has the priest's phone number on their bulletin board, and thinks they probably do. Father Murphy picks up on the second ring.

"St. Jude's, Father Murphy speaking," he says cheerily.

"Hello, Father, it's Maggie Sullivan," Maggie answers. "Do you have a minute to talk?"

"Sure, Maggie. What can I do for you?"

"Father, do you remember the other day in confession when you told me you thought I should marry Jack? Well, he just asked me to marry him and we were wondering if you might be able to do a wedding at the church on Saturday," Maggie says, watching Jack's face as he hears for the first time the priest's advice. He looks surprised and pleased, and she is filled with love for this wonderful man.

"Ah, Maggie! God certainly works in mysterious ways, doesn't He?" Father Murphy chuckles. "Let me check my calendar."

Maggie hears a clunk as he puts down the phone, followed by a riffle of papers, then he is back on the line.

"Saturday looks good to me. I'll let the ladies know so they can decorate. What time were you thinking?"

Maggie looks frantically at Jack and puts her hand over the phone to ask, "What time on Saturday?"

"Five o'clock," Jack answers randomly. "Just in time to eat and go to bed!" Again, he wiggles his eyebrows and winks, and Maggie stifles a giggle as she gets back on the phone.

"How does five o'clock sound?" she asks.

"Just fine! I'll see you on Saturday then. And Maggie, I think you're doing the right thing, and you and Jack will be very happy together. Bye!" With these parting words, Father Murphy hangs up and Maggie does the same on her end.

"Wow," she says softly. "We just scheduled our wedding." She and Jack look at each other for a long moment, both of them thinking about all the ramifications of the coming union—her kids, his kids, his ex-wife, the school board, anonymous letters, the church ladies, her house, his house. Deciding to get married seems to be the easiest decision they will have to make in the near future. Taking a deep breath, Maggie dials the phone again and calls Kevin at work.

Jack sits at the table, eating cookies and drinking coffee while she tells her son the news and invites him and his family to her wedding. *What a bizarre thing to be doing*, she thinks, *inviting your child to your wedding. It's not supposed to work this way.*

"Congratulations, Mom. I'm really happy for you, but I doubt we'll be able to get a flight at this short notice, and it's too far to drive with the little ones just for the afternoon, so I'll talk to Didi and call you tonight with a final decision," Kevin says, genuine warmth and love in his voice.

"I love you, son," Maggie tells him. "I hope you can make it, but I understand if you can't. I'll talk to you later."

"I love you, too, Mom," Kevin says. "Thanks for calling, and I'll call back tonight."

When Maggie hangs up, she finds herself on the verge of tears again. She isn't sure if it's because Kevin might not be at the wedding or if it's sadness at the finality of marrying someone else and saying it out loud to Clark's child. She blows her nose and gets a glass of water before calling Maura.

"I knew it!" Maura crows delightedly when Maggie tells her about the wedding. "I'm so happy for you, Mom. Of course we'll be there. Do you need me to do anything to help get ready? Do you have a dress? Do you need flowers? What about a reception?"

Taken aback at the barrage of questions, Maggie finally breaks in. "Whoa, there, little girl. Slow down! I haven't had time to think about any of that or talk to Jack about it. We just wanted to make sure you could come before we finalize the plans. I'm sure I'll need a dress and a bouquet, but it's going to be very small, mostly family, so there won't be a big hubbub." She looks at Jack for confirmation as she talks, but he shakes his head at her words. "Wait a sec, honey." Maggie covers the phone again and looks at Jack. "What don't you agree with?"

"I don't agree with a very small wedding," Jack says. "I want the whole town to know we're married and not just shacking up! How can we get them all invited by Saturday?"

"Hey, Maura, can I call you back?" Maggie asks. "Jack and I need to work some things out, and then I'll know what I need help with."

"Sure, Mom. I'll be home all evening. Congratulations! I love you!" Maura fades away in a wave of enthusiastic goodbyes, echoed by Patrick's happy hoots in the background.

Suddenly, Maggie is exhausted, the emotional toll of telling her children she is getting married catching up with her, and she sinks into a chair with a sigh. Jack takes her hands in his.

"You know the rest is just details, right?" he questions.

"Yes, but the devil is in the details," Maggie worries. "How are we going to pull this together by Saturday?"

"Well, we have another hour to talk about it before I have to pick up the boys, so let's make some decisions," Jack says determinedly.

He reaches past Maggie to grab a notepad and pen off the counter. A few phone calls and an hour later, a wedding has taken shape on the tablet. The ceremony will be at the Catholic Church at 5:00 p.m. with Kevin, Maura, Brad, and Trent standing up with their parents as witnesses, assuming Kevin can make it. Tracy will put invitations out on social media and get the event sent to the local newspaper today, Jack will call his friends, and Maggie will send emails to everyone at work, including the school board. After the wedding Mass, they will have a brief reception in the church basement with a cake and punch, and then family members will go to Tracy's for dinner. Jack will wear jeans and a new white shirt with a tie, and Maggie will go to Boise tomorrow and get a dress of a color yet to be decided. Tracy knows someone in town who can make a simple wedding cake, and she volunteers to make punch for the reception in addition to fixing dinner for the family if Maggie will buy the paper plates, plastic silverware, cups, and napkins.

They will go to the courthouse Wednesday and get a marriage license. Jack has a family heirloom wedding ring for Maggie, and she will get one for him when she goes to Boise. Maggie is amazed at how easily the arrangements are made and thinks it will be a classy, simple affair. They decide not to take any kind of a honeymoon since it would mean leaving the boys home and Maggie missing school, and she doesn't want to give the school board any reason to doubt her capability.

Finally, Jack stands to leave and Maggie walks him to the door. "I don't want you to go," she says. "I really missed you over Christmas. I missed the boys too. Why don't you bring them back here, and I'll make dinner or we'll get pizza? We could tell them about the wedding together," she suggests.

Jack quickly agrees and soon is on his way to pick up Brad and Trent.

While he is gone, Maggie looks in the freezer for ideas for dinner but soon decides pizza is the best answer. Knowing the kids will be starving when they arrive, she calls and places an order for their favorite kinds of pizza and a salad. She then calls Jack on his cell phone and asks him to stop and pick it up on his way back.

While she waits alone in her kitchen, Maggie thinks back over the events of the afternoon and finds it hard to believe she will be married to Jack in less than a week. She paces the kitchen, trailing her fingers over the shiny countertops, wondering if they will keep her house or sell it, something they haven't had a chance to discuss yet, trying to wrap her mind around the changes coming in her life. She is happy, sad, excited, scared, impatient, and incredulous at the ability of her heart to open to love again. Maggie knows how rare it is in life to find a man to share one's heart, and she has found such a man, not once, but twice. She doesn't know why God has chosen to bless her in this way, but she gratefully acknowledges the gift.

# CHAPTER 29

Jack and the kids blow into the house like a hurricane, bringing a blast of icy chill with them. The wind has picked up from the north, blowing a storm across the valley, and Maggie knows it will snow again before morning.

The pizza and salad are deposited on the counter beside the plates and silverware Maggie sets out, and she pours large glasses of milk for the thirsty boys while they help themselves to pizza and sit at the table. She opens a bottle of wine and gets down the good glasses, thinking this is an occasion for celebration. When all is ready, she sits as well and says the blessing and everyone eats amid a chatter of voices as Brad and Trent catch Maggie up on their weekend.

When it becomes obvious they are getting full and they start to run out of stories, Jack catches Maggie's eye then clears his throat to get his sons' attention. "Maggie and I have something to tell you," he announces.

The boys stop in mid-bite and look at him with wide eyes.

"This afternoon, I asked Maggie to marry me and she said yes, so we're getting married on Saturday," he finishes in a rush.

Trent lets out a whoop of joy so loud it hurts Maggie's ears, and a slow smile spreads across Brad's handsome face.

"Way to go, Dad," Brad says, playfully punching his father on the shoulder. "Took you long enough!"

Trent is around the table to give Maggie a hug and Brad stands up to do the same, and somehow the four of them are all hugging each other.

Maggie looks up at Jack and catches him wiping a tear from

the corner of his eye. She smiles and pats him on the back gently as she holds this family who are now truly going to be her family, more than a little choked up herself.

Finally, they separate and go back to their chairs and abandoned pizza as the boys ask questions about the wedding and what life after the wedding will be like. They talk through the remainder of the meal, then the boys turn on Monday night football while Jack helps Maggie clear up in the kitchen.

"I think that went well," he ventures. "Don't you?"

"Yes," Maggie responds. "They seem excited about it. Really, not much in their lives will change except where I sleep at your house and me spending the weekends there from now on."

"Let's talk about where you'll sleep," Jack says, dropping the dish towel he is holding to pull Maggie against him. "I have a queen-size bed that's been calling your name for months, and I can't wait to get you in it." He slides his hands around her waist and down to her hips as he kisses her deeply, the first real kiss they have shared since before Christmas.

Maggie answers with a hunger she didn't realize existed until the touch of Jack's mouth awakens it, twining her arms around his neck and her fingers into his hair to help her reach up to his height.

Sometimes with Jack, she feels like a teenager again, lusty and curious, only she knows exactly what the prize at the end is now, and how to reach it. Soon, they are both breathless with desire, wrapped up in each other, oblivious to the world outside. The ringing of the telephone startles them apart, and Maggie wipes her lips with a trembling hand as she goes to answer it.

Kevin is on the other end. He is coming to the wedding but Didi and the children will stay home. While Maggie is sad Emma and Ethan won't be there, she is thrilled to hear Kevin is coming, and relieved to find out Didi is not. She knows it's not nice to feel that way about Didi, but she just can't help it. Kevin plans to fly in to Boise Saturday morning and drive to Council with Maura and Tom, which sounds fantastic to Maggie. She hasn't realized how much she wants Kevin at her wedding until now, when she knows for sure he is coming. A warm feeling of joy spreads through her heart at his words, and she gives Jack the thumbs-up sign. Kevin says goodbye and puts Emma on the phone to talk to her grandmother. Maggie spends a few minutes chatting with the vivacious little girl before telling her goodnight and hanging up the phone.

"He's coming!" she exults. "I'm so glad. I was worried Didi would talk him out of it."

"Good," Jack says. "I'm happy if you're happy. Now, where were we?"

But somehow, the amorous mood is broken, and both Maggie and Jack recognize the moment is over. Maggie calls Maura to give her the details of the wedding plans while Jack heads to the living room to join the boys for the football game. When Maggie gets off the phone, they spend the remainder of the evening cheering on the Cowboys. Much to the boys' disgust, the bad guys win, and they leave for home grumbling and replaying the turnovers as they walk to Jack's truck.

Maggie stands shivering on the porch, watching them drive away, still feeling Jack's goodbye kiss on her lips. The storm is close, the smell of snow on the wind, errant flakes beginning to flutter past, skittering on the roof and flicking off the streetlights. Maggie is glad to go back inside her warm house and close the door against the weather.

She shuts off the lights and gets ready for bed, but the rising wind makes it difficult for her to sleep. She can't stop thinking about the wedding, especially the wedding night; the kisses in the kitchen with Jack have started a train of thought Maggie has difficulty stopping.

At some point, she realizes in the excitement of Jack's proposal and plans for the wedding, the horrible letters had been forgotten. Maggie remembers seeing the envelopes on the counter while she was on the phone with Maura the first time but not later in the evening and thinks Jack must have taken them when he went to pick up the boys.

Maggie's good mood and excitement evaporate as she thinks about the possibility of Jack losing custody of his boys or her losing her job. Even after the wedding, people could still try to get her fired, and Maggie can't help worrying about it.

After an hour of restless tossing and turning, she finally gets up to get a drink of water, listening to the storm shrieking outside. The house creaks and pops in the growing cold, and Maggie can feel the chill creeping in around the edges as she moves about. It seems to match the chill in her heart, and she gives up the thought of sleep for a while, choosing instead to take her book to the recliner in the living room and read. Forty minutes later, she realizes she has read the same paragraph three times and her head is drooping over the pages, so she shuts off the lamp and goes back to bed, this time falling asleep immediately.

Due to her late night, Maggie oversleeps in the morning and starts her trip to Boise later than planned. The roads are a mess, so she doesn't even get to Maura's house until almost noon. Maura has a sitter scheduled for Patrick, so they are able to leave for the mall shortly after Maggie arrives. They eat lunch at the food court and then look for a dress for Maggie.

Shopping is much easier now that Maggie isn't overweight, but she isn't quite sure what a fifty-something widow is supposed to wear to her wedding and is quickly frustrated at the lack of choices this time of year. Finally, she finds a long-sleeved, knee-length, wool dress in a soft cream color with gold embroidery around the curved neckline and a belt in the same gold. The dress fits like it was made for Maggie, flattering yet classy, the color a striking contrast to her shiny brown hair and green eyes, and Maggie actually feels like a bride when she wears it out of the dressing room to show Maura.

"Oh, Mom, you look beautiful!" Maura exclaims in delight. "I love it! It's so soft and elegant."

Maggie flushes with pleasure at her daughter's compliments and twirls in front of the mirror like a child. "What color of shoes should I wear?" she asks. "I don't think I can find any this time of year to match. So, maybe some gold ones, but that might be overkill. What do you think?"

"I think red, like Dorothy wore in Oz," Maura answers.

"Red?" Maggie questions doubtfully. "Really?"

"Really. Trust me on this, Mom. They don't have to be sparkly; I was teasing about that, but a dark red would be really pretty and seasonal."

Maura goes to look for red pumps in Maggie's size while she waits at the dressing room, looking at her reflection in the mirror. She almost doesn't recognize herself, this time in a good way, and it takes her back to the day last summer when she caught a glimpse of herself in a window and wondered who that dowdy old woman was. Maggie's life has changed so much since then; she feels like a different person.

Soon, her daughter returns carrying a pair of shiny, dark red pumps with a rounded toe and medium-length spike heels. Maggie isn't sure this combination of dress and shoes will work, but she puts the shoes on anyway to please Maura and parades again in front of the mirror. To her surprise, the shoes actually look good with the dress—just a touch of color in a sexy kind of way that makes the dress look even more conservative. Maggie, with Maura's enthusiastic approval, decides to purchase both the dress and the shoes.

Next, Maura wants to look at lingerie for the wedding night, but here Maggie draws the line. What she wears (or doesn't wear) on that special night is between Maggie and Jack. Maura reluctantly agrees, and the two look for a new dress for Maura to wear. Since it's so close to Christmas, they have no problem finding a beautiful, warm, red sweater dress for Maura.

They go to the men's store to get a white shirt and a red tie that matches Maggie's shoes for Jack, and white shirts for Brad and Trent. Kevin is bringing a white shirt and black pants, and Jack and the boys will wear new jeans they got for Christmas. Maggie thinks they will be quite an elegant-looking wedding party, especially on such short notice.

She wants to wear the tiny spur necklace Jack gave her for Christmas, but it's silver and won't match her outfit, so she decides to wear an antique pearl pendant on a gold chain that belonged to her grandmother. It is the only thing she has of her grandmother's, and it will qualify as something old.

Satisfied with their ensembles, the women go to the nearest jewelry store, and Maggie picks out a wedding band for Jack. When she sees the silver titanium one with the barbed wire pattern, she knows he will like it and the purchase is quickly made. Gathering their bags and putting on their coats against the freezing wind, they leave the mall for Costco, where Maggie buys paper plates, cups, napkins, and cutlery for the reception and dinner at Tracy's. Maggie asked to help with the food as well, but Tracy refused, saying she wanted to make dinner as a gift to her little sister so Maggie concedes to her wishes.

By the time they are finished shopping, it is already dark on this wintery, Idaho evening, and although Maura begs her to stay for dinner, Maggie knows the roads will be treacherous, and she still has to stop at the grocery store on the way home, so she contents herself with playing with Patrick for a half-hour and then says goodbye and drives away, happy with what they have accomplished today. The traffic is heavy as she leaves town, but thins out quickly the farther she gets from Boise, so when Jack calls, Maggie is able to talk while she drives.

He wants to finalize plans for getting the marriage license tomorrow and suggests he pick her up at 11:30 in the morning and then take her to lunch after they finish at the courthouse. Maggie tells him it sounds fun, and they talk briefly about how the shopping trip went and how the cows are doing in this nasty weather before saying goodbye and hanging up.

Maggie is still startled whenever Jack says he loves her and the words still feel strange in her mouth, but she is definitely happy to keep trying them out. She smiles as she drives, thinking about Jack and how much she loves him. Despite all the preparations underway, the wedding doesn't seem quite real to Maggie yet.

By the time she reaches Ontario, the sky is spitting tiny, hard flakes of snow, and Maggie makes a hurried stop at the store to get punch supplies and at a boutique for some pretty new underwear. She might not want Maura to help her choose lingerie, but she wants to look pretty for Jack, and her old "granny panties" just won't make the grade.

All the way home, Maggie drives on the edge of the storm but makes it there before the snow builds up on the highway, and pulls into the garage with a sigh of relief. She unloads the car, trades her coat and wet shoes for sweats and slippers, and unpacks her purchases while she warms up some soup for supper. The beautiful dress and shoes go in her closet to await Saturday afternoon, Jack's ring goes in her jewelry box, the new panties she tosses in the laundry basket to wash before she wears them, and she piles the supplies for the reception by the back door to take to Tracy's later in the week. Once her soup is hot, she curls up in her chair with a blanket, her cup of soup, and the remote, and lets the stress of the drive melt away. The only thing that would make the evening better would be if Jack and the boys were there. *Soon,* she tells herself, *just a few more days.*

# CHAPTER 30

Maggie sits in the passenger seat of Jack's pickup as they drive to the courthouse to get their marriage license. For some silly reason, she is nervous, and she thinks Jack is as well. Today, this piece of paper will be tangible proof they are really getting married on Saturday, and both of them are sobered at the thought of the commitment they are undertaking. Neither are young anymore, and both have been married before, so they understand the hard work it takes to make a successful union and they don't take it lightly.

At the same time, Maggie is giddy with excitement and can't stop sneaking glances at Jack, thinking again how handsome he is and how much she likes his smile and his blue eyes. It's a strange roller coaster of emotions and Maggie feels off-balance.

Jack catches her looking at him and gives her a grin; the flash of his white teeth against his winter-weathered skin takes her breath away. She gives herself a mental shake and smiles back, comforted by his presence, and then they are pulling into the parking lot.

Jack opens the door for Maggie and takes her hand to help her out of the pickup, keeping it in his as they walk to the door. The weak sun glints off her shiny, brown hair, which swings as she walks, making him want to run his fingers through the sleek strands. He feels as if Saturday will never come, as if he is a rutting teenage boy looking forward to his first time. Jack leads Maggie through the halls to the clerk's office and tells the woman who comes to the counter they want to buy a marriage license.

It turns out she is an old friend of Maggie's who offers heartfelt congratulations and quickly processes the necessary paperwork. Jack pays with cash, and the couple leaves with Maggie carrying the license safely in her purse. He drives to a local restaurant and again opens the pickup door and escorts Maggie through the door, where they choose a booth by the window.

At first, they are awkward with each other, both a little overcome by the seriousness of the occasion, but soon their natural camaraderie reasserts itself and they are chatting away. This is, in effect, their first date—the first time they have been out together without Brad and Trent—and as much as Jack loves his kids, he is thoroughly enjoying this time alone with Maggie.

She is different with him when the boys aren't around, more outspoken, more flirtatious, and Jack is captivated. Everything she does fascinates him. He can't remember ever feeling this way about Caroline. Part of Maggie's charm is she doesn't know how beautiful and sensuous she is; she is so down-to-earth and natural in every situation, never vain or arrogant. Jack is still amazed she is part of his life. The wedding can't come soon enough.

After lunch, Jack has to get back to the ranch to feed, so he drives Maggie home and walks her to the door, strangely formal now, and kisses her goodbye. It's funny to her how careful they are being with each other since they decided to get married, as if the prospect of being physically intimate has caused them to create an artificial distance between them. It seems like Jack is courting her, and Maggie is enjoying every moment.

Before Jack leaves, he asks her if she will go out with him tonight to the New Year's Eve dance, and they make a date for dinner and drinks before the dance starts. Maggie is excited at the thought of going to the dance and immediately starts planning what she will wear.

She calls her sister and finds out Tracy and Danny are going as well, so Maggie looks forward to a pleasant evening. The sisters have a nice chat on the phone finalizing the menu for the wedding supper, talking about the dress Maggie bought yesterday, and sharing Patrick's most recent adorable moment. Maggie knows Tracy loves

Maura's baby almost as much as she does and is always eager to hear what he's been up to.

When she finishes talking to Tracy, Maggie feels as if she should be doing something, but everything is done, and she is at loose ends until it is time to get ready for the dance. She decides to start packing. After all, she will be living at the ranch all the time now and there is a lot to be done before Saturday.

She starts in the kitchen, going through each cupboard and deciding what should go to Jack's and what should stay here. Jack's kitchen, though adequate, is still a bachelor's kitchen without many of the things Maggie considers necessary for daily living. She has made do at the ranch, but is glad she will have her own things to use there. The empty boxes she stored in the garage after Maura got married come in handy, and Maggie works quickly, wrapping glassware in newspaper, choosing her favorite cook books and kitchen gadgets, and stacking the filled boxes by the back door.

Finally, the kitchen is finished except for the things she needs to get through the week, and Maggie takes a break to consider what to pack next. She decides to box up her books, a task that fills the rest of the afternoon and before she knows it, she needs to stop and get ready for her date with Jack.

Jack is running late. The tractor won't start, and by the time he finds and fixes the problem and feeds the cows, he should be on his way to pick up Maggie. He hurries into the house to shave and take a quick shower, puts on a clean pair of jeans, a good snap-up cowboy shirt, and the belt Maggie gave him for Christmas.

He yells at Brad and Trent to get in the pickup while he pulls on his boots at the door, and they come thundering down the stairs, grab their coats, and rush out, followed by Jack. They are going to a well-chaperoned New Year's Eve party at the school sponsored by the PTA, so when they reach town, Jack drops them off there where they will be fed and allowed to play basketball and video games to their heart's delight until 12:30.

He pulls up in front of Maggie's house. As he is walking to the door, he realizes he is as nervous tonight as he was the night he met her for the first time at Tracy's. He tells himself he's being ridiculous; this is Maggie, his Maggie, and she loves him. This nervy feeling has been happening ever since he asked her to marry him, and Jack is trying to figure out why. He thinks the answer is sex. Before, there was the *idea* of sex with Maggie, shimmery in the distance like a mirage, not quite real, but tantalizing, underlying their glances, conversations, flirtations, and kisses like an unspoken possibility. Now, sex isn't just possible, it's inevitable. In fact, they have set a date for it. Jack thinks it's knowing they are going to make love on Saturday night that has him feeling skittish.

When Maggie opens the door, a smile on her face, and invites him in while she puts on her coat, the feeling intensifies until Jack feels like his stomach is full of butterflies. She is beautiful in her jeans and clingy, black sweater, her body slender as a girl's but curvy in all the right places, and she smells like apples and cinnamon when he pulls her close for a hello kiss.

She kisses him back eagerly, soft and yielding against him, and Jack has to force himself to hold back, to just kiss her instead of pushing her against the closed door and letting her know exactly how much he wants her. His head spinning from her nearness and sweet scent, Jack gently puts some distance between them.

"Sorry I'm late, mechanical breakdown," he apologizes.

"It's okay, I was running behind myself. I got caught up in packing and forgot the time," Maggie tells him.

"Packing?" Jack asks.

"Yes, packing," Maggie says with a grin. "Did you think I was going to move in with you and not bring my stuff?"

"Well, I guess I hadn't thought about it," Jack admits sheepishly. "Of course, you'll bring whatever you want to. We're not talking furniture too, are we?"

"Not unless you want something I have here. I assumed until we decide what to do with this house, we would leave the furniture in place. It's all stuff Clark and I bought, none of it is family heirlooms or antiques, and none of it is valuable," Maggie offers.

"Sounds like a plan," Jack answers. "We can work out the details after we're married. Right now, let's get some dinner. I'm starving!"

The local café is offering a special of prime rib, and Maggie and Jack eat a hearty meal accompanied by a glass or two of wine, and then head to the New Year's Eve dance for cocktail hour before the band starts. They meet Danny and Tracy there, and the four get a table together and order a round of drinks, talking and greeting friends as the crowd grows. Finally, the band finishes their sound check and starts the first song, and the rest of the evening Maggie barely sits down except when the band is on a break.

It turns out Jack is a fantastic dancer, doing the complicated Western Swing dance steps effortlessly, cueing Maggie on the turns and spins, and keeping her on the dance floor for song after song. Slow dancing with Jack is sweet torture for Maggie. He holds her tightly against him, one big hand splayed low across the small of her back and the other cupping her hand against his solid chest. His hips are firmly pressed against hers, his knee between hers with his muscular thigh snugly centered at the joining of hers, causing frissons of desire to skid through her every time they move to the beat of the music. Her cheek rests against his chest, and she can feel him breathe, hear his heart beat, and smell his spicy, musky scent. Maggie wants the dance to never end, and at the same time wants to do more than dance. She is flushed and warm by the time the song ends, looking up into his eyes as he pulls her into a hug and kisses her lightly on the mouth.

"Thanks for the dance, baby," he says, his lips close against her ear, his warm breath tickling her neck.

"You're welcome," Maggie says, twining her arms around his neck to keep him close to her. They stand in the middle of the dance floor, lost in each other, oblivious to those around them. Finally, the next song starts, breaking the spell and they move apart into a two-step position. Maggie can't decide if it's a good thing or a bad thing that the slow songs are few and far between. When the band breaks, she and Tracy head for the restroom together.

"Wow, sis, you two are dancing up a storm," Tracy comments while they wash their hands. "Looking good, Maggie. You guys are hot together! Good thing the wedding is soon."

"Thanks," Maggie answers. "The way I feel tonight, I wish it was already over!"

"Seriously, kiddo, I'm happy for you," Tracy tells her. "You make a great couple."

The sisters smile at each other and return to their table to get something to drink before the band starts back up. For Maggie, the night flies by, and all too soon, the countdown to midnight begins. She is standing with Jack in the middle of the dance floor, arms around each other, chanting with the crowd when the cheer goes up. "Happy New Year!" rings out around the room. Jack turns to Maggie, cupping her face in his callused palms and looking deep into her eyes.

"I love you, Maggie Sullivan," Jack says tenderly.

"I love you, Jack Hallas," Maggie responds, and then he kisses her, chastely enough for a public place, but deeply enough to make her toes curl. One last slow, swaying dance, one last kiss on Maggie's porch, and Jack drives away to pick up the boys. The next time they see each other will be at their wedding.

# CHAPTER 31

Maggie sits on her bed in her underwear and slip waiting for the polish on her toenails to dry. She has bathed, shaved, pumiced, moisturized, polished, and perfumed all the pertinent body parts. Now there is nothing left to do but put on her dress.

Maura, who arrived in time for lunch, helped Maggie with her makeup and her hair, arranging soft curls to frame her mother's radiant face. Maggie thought she would be nervous or anxious, but instead, she feels a peaceful sense of rightness and joy. Her mind is clear and calm, taking in every detail of this special day. Maura and Kevin are both getting ready while Tom keeps Patrick occupied. Maggie can hear the sweet sound of his baby chatter in the living room. Soon, Maura knocks softly at the door and comes in, closing it behind her.

"Ready to get dressed, Mom?" she asks cheerfully. "It's almost time to go."

"I think this nail polish is dry enough," Maggie answers, rising and picking up the dress laid carefully across the foot of the bed. With Maura's help, she pulls the dress over her head without mussing her hair and settles the soft folds, craning her neck in front of the mirror to get the total effect. Satisfied with the dress, she slips on the red shoes and turns to her daughter.

"Mom, you're gorgeous!" Maura exclaims, holding her clasped hands to her chest in delight. "In fact, I think I might cry a little."

"Don't cry, sweetheart, because then I might, and it will ruin all your hard work on my makeup," Maggie warns. "Do I really look all right?" she asks worriedly.

"Yes, you look perfect," Maura assures her. "Where's your

necklace?"

Maggie goes to her dresser and removes the pearl pendant from her jewel box and Maura fastens it around her mother's neck.

"I think you're ready," Maura says.

"Yes, I think I am," Maggie answers with a smile. "Let's go."

Together they open the door and walk to the living room where Kevin, Tom, and Patrick wait. They turn to look, and Maggie is gratified at the expressions on their faces as they see her in the doorway, luminous in her wedding dress, her eyes shining with expectation as she awaits their judgment.

"Mom. Wow!" Kevin says gruffly, clearing his throat as if he is speaking around a lump. He walks to her, taking her hands in his. "I think you're the most beautiful mom in the world, and Jack better appreciate you," he tells her.

Her green eyes glisten with sudden tears, but she manages to not let them spill over as Kevin pulls her close in a gingerly hug.

"Thank you, son," Maggie says sincerely. "You know your opinion means the world to me. I love you very much."

"I love you too, Mom," Kevin answers. "Now, let's go before we all start bawling." He glances over at Maura and Tom, who are both trying not to cry, and walks down the hall to pick up Maggie's suitcase from her bedroom and carries it to the door. The family dons coats and gloves and follows Kevin to the car with their belongings. Maggie turns down the thermostat and shuts off the lights and television.

She stops at the door to the garage and looks around her beloved house, this place where she and Clark raised their children and shared the daily ups and downs of life, this place filled with memories and love, realizing this is the last time it is truly her home. After today's ceremony, her home will be with Jack.

She thinks about Jack's house out on the ranch and how it feels to be there with Jack and the boys and resolutely shuts and locks the door behind her. This part of her life is finished now, and a new part is beginning. Maggie opens the garage door onto the snowy, cold, late afternoon, dusk creeping around the edges even at 4:30. She backs the car out, shuts the door with the remote and drives to the church where soon she will cease to be Mrs. Sullivan and will become Mrs. Hallas.

Mr. Hallas, in the meantime, is again running late, this time for his wedding. He got stuck while feeding and had to shovel the tractor out of a snow-hidden hole in the pasture, which put him behind, and he is rushing to finish getting ready.

Jack watches himself in the mirror while he carefully shaves and is reminded of the first night he met Maggie, when he cleaned up to drive to town to interview her for the job of nanny and housekeeper. He is eternally grateful for the decision to meet with her since it led to finding love again when he had given up. He rinses his face, dries it with the towel, and steps to the door to shout up the stairs.

"You two better be ready because we're late, and I don't have time to wait on you!"

"We're gonna be ready before you are," Trent yells back playfully. "Just hold your horses."

Jack goes to his room where he dons new black jeans and the white shirt and red tie Maggie bought him. He wears the new belt she gave him for Christmas which seems like it was months ago instead of just a week earlier. So much in his life has changed since then. As he bends to pull on his boots, he hears the boys thumping down the stairs in their normal thunderous descent.

"Dad, let's go," Brad says, peering around the half-open door. "You look fine. I'm going to start the pickup."

"Wait, son," Jack tells him. "I want to see you two before we go out the door."

Dutifully, Brad retreats to the living room, where Trent is already waiting, and Jack steps out to face his sons. The two stand straight and tall, looking very grown-up and handsome in black jeans and white shirts, their hair slicked down and their clean faces shining. Jack smiles at them, his heart full of joy and pride.

"Thank you, boys," Jack tells them sincerely. "If it weren't for you, I would never have met Maggie. I am so proud of you—first for the way you changed your behavior and your grades and second for the way you treat Maggie. I love you very much." His eyes burn with unshed tears as he swallows back his emotions, unused to voicing them.

"Gee, Dad, are you gonna cry or something?" Trent asks.

"No, Trent. I just thought you should know how I feel. Now, let's get out of here. We have a wedding to go to."

The three traipse through to the utility room to pull on their coats before going out to the pickup. Jack drives, lapsing into silence as he thinks about the upcoming ceremony and what it will mean to him and his family. The boys chatter and sing along with the radio, and Jack is grateful for their preoccupation. He isn't in the mood for conversation right now.

He is starting to feel extremely nervous, although he doesn't know why. This marriage is what he wants more than anything, and he knows they will be very happy together, so there is nothing to be nervous about. Thinking about Maggie has a calming effect and by the time they reach the church, Jack feels much better.

Maggie's car is already in the parking lot along with Tom and Maura's. Jack is surprised at how many other vehicles are there, with more arriving all the time. They walk down the snowy sidewalk to the church doors and step into the warm, quiet air of the little church. Jack sees Tom sitting in the front pew with Patrick. Danny and Tracy are there as well helping Tom keep the baby occupied. There is no sign of Maggie or her children.

Father Murphy appears and joins Jack, Brad, and Trent in the back of the church. "I think we're almost ready," the priest tells them. "We have about five minutes. Is there anything else we need to do or talk about?"

"Not that I know of," Jack replies.

Brad and Trent nod in agreement.

"Well, then, let's say a little prayer and we'll get on with it." Father Murphy leads the little group in prayer and nods to the organist, who starts playing softly, and then he goes to alert Maggie. Those five minutes seem to crawl by, and Jack feels as if an hour has passed before Father Murphy brushes by him and steps to the aisle of the church.

"Please stand," he announces, and the crowded pews rustle as everyone rises to their feet. The organ music changes to a joyful hymn as Father Murphy directs traffic.

Jack, flanked by his sons, follows the altar server to the front of the church, stepping to the right as they reach the altar. Kevin and Maura, who appeared from somewhere in the back of the church, follow them, stepping to the left, and last comes Father Murphy, who stops when he reaches the front and genuflects. He walks around behind the altar, beckoning Jack to step to the center, and the music changes once more to something soft and slow.

The confessional door opens, and Maggie Sullivan walks out. Jack doesn't think he has ever seen a more beautiful woman, and for the second time in the past hour, he swallows a lump in his throat and blinks away unwanted tears. She looks like an angel in cream and gold, the dress chaste yet showing off her curves. As she rounds the back pew and starts up the aisle, he sees she is wearing a wicked, sexy pair of red high heels, and he swallows hard again, this time in anticipation. He finds it difficult to breathe as his fiancé comes to him in front of the congregation, her green eyes glowing like lamps in the candlelit church. Maggie stops in front of him and, on trembling legs, Jack steps up to take her hands in his, and the couple turns to face the priest.

For Maggie, the time spent waiting in the confessional for the ceremony to begin flies by. From the time she enters the familiar little church, feelings of warmth and love wash over her, and she feels completely calm. Surrounded by her children, she sits in silence, letting the atmosphere soak into her soul, random thoughts and memories of Clark and their life together surging through her mind. Occasionally, she hears a raised voice outside and immediately recognizes Jack's pleasant baritone when he arrives. Her heart leaps in joy and anticipation, and suddenly she can't wait any longer. She stands as if to leave, but Maura stops her.

"Mom, where are you going? It's not time yet."

"I know," Maggie replies ruefully. "I just can't sit still anymore."

Maura gently puts an arm around her mother, giving her a loving squeeze. "I'm sure it's hard to wait, but it's only for a few more minutes." She leads Maggie back to her chair and sits beside her again. Suddenly, the door opens, and Father Murphy steps in.

"We're starting," he announces. "Kevin, you and Maura stand in the door, and once Jack and the boys reach the front, you start. Maggie, you can watch through the window and come out when everyone is in position. See you soon!" With that, he turns to go in a whirl of robes, and Maggie looks at her kids.

"I love you both so much," she tells them. "Thank you for being here for me today." They have a quick group hug and then Kevin and Maura step out and shut the door behind them. Maggie takes a deep breath to calm her sudden case of nerves, and then she feels it. A hand, warm and familiar, caresses her shoulder, and Clark's voice sounds in her ear. She feels his breath on her neck as he speaks, and she shivers in reaction.

"I love you, Maggie. I'll always love you, and I want you to be happy. You chose a wonderful man to share your life with, and you'll have many years to enjoy each other. I won't be coming to visit anymore, and I don't want you to be sad because I'm in a wonderful place," Clark tells her.

Maggie spins around, expecting to see him, but the room is empty. She shakes her head in bewilderment, on the verge of tears, unable to comprehend what just happened. Was it real, or did she imagine it? Shakily, she turns back to the tiny window in the door of the confessional and looks out in time to see Jack face the back of the church, waiting for her.

At the sight of him, she realizes anew how much she loves him and how right this marriage is, and Clark's farewell makes perfect sense. "I love you too, Clark," she whispers, "but I have to say goodbye now." She waits with bated breath, but nothing stirs, and as she watches her children walk to the altar, she feels a withdrawing sensation and knows Clark's spirit is gone.

With a heart brimming over with love and joy, Maggie opens the door and starts up the aisle, never taking her eyes from Jack's. She sees his eyes fill with tears when he sees her and also sees the desire in them, causing a bolt of heat to shoot through her body. She sees his pant legs tremble and knows his knees are shaking, but she still feels calm.

They reach out to each other and join hands, facing the altar together. Maggie loves the feel of Jack's hands in hers—big and rough and warm, a little sweaty with nerves tonight. She squeezes them gently in reassurance.

Jack gives her a brilliant smile, stopping her breath. Everything around her fades away and she knows only that Jack is looking at her, that Jack wants her and loves her, and her world is complete.

The music stops, and Father Murphy begins the ceremony, welcoming everyone and saying an opening prayer. He asks everyone to be seated, and Jack and Maggie sit in chairs provided for them in the aisle while Tracy walks to the front for the reading. They chose First Corinthians, a typical wedding reading, but it still is meaningful no matter how many times they hear it. Maggie imagines different situations with Jack as the familiar words ring through the church. She hears stealthy rustling and clearing of throats behind her but can't remember if she even looked at the standing crowd as she walked to Jack. She has no idea who is in attendance, but she knows the church is packed.

When the reading is finished and Tracy sits back down, another hymn is sung and then everyone stands while Father Murphy approaches the podium for the gospel reading. Again, they sit when the reading is finished, and Maggie is reminded of the first time she took the boys to church. Afterward, they commented on how much up and down there is in a Catholic Mass. Next, Father Murphy delivers a short but sincere homily on marriage and love and second chances, and Maggie feels blessed to have such a wonderful, compassionate priest.

After the homily, Father Murphy comes around the altar and asks Jack and Maggie to rise. They stand before him with clasped hands, eyes only for each other, as he charges them with the responsibilities and sacrament of marriage. They repeat the vows as he gives them, Jack's voice deep and shaky and Maggie's soft and sure.

Next, the rings are blessed and Jack gently slides the dainty, antique, gold, filigree ring that belonged to his great-grandmother on Maggie's slender finger, and she looks at it in awe then back at Jack's beaming face. Maggie's hands are steady as she takes Jack's ring and places it on his hand. Jack has to help her when the ring sticks briefly on his big-knuckled finger, but finally it slips into place, and they smile at each other in relief. At last, it is time for the final blessing, and Father Murphy gives Jack the go-ahead to kiss his bride.

Jack and Maggie feel a similar rush of anticipation and nerves as Jack solemnly lowers his mouth to hers. Jack's kiss is fiercely exultant. "She's mine!" it declares, while Maggie's response is giving, bending to his strength and answering, "I'm his!" They keep it short and proper, but the message to each other is so potent, even the audience picks up on the vibe, and applause and laughter break out as the couple parts.

"For the first time, I introduce to you Mr. and Mrs. Jack Hallas!" Father Murphy announces. The applause gets louder, Jack and Maggie beam at each other and at the crowd, and the organist plays *Ode to Joy,* filling the church with the stirring melody.

The newlyweds stride down the aisle, followed by their children and Father Murphy. They quickly descend the stairs to the basement, where hugs, kisses, and handshakes are exchanged in a flurry of excitement and happiness. As the crowd begins to filter down, the group forms a rough receiving line to accept the congratulations and well-wishes of their families, friends, and community members.

Both Jack and Maggie are amazed at how many people came to the wedding, especially with such short notice. All the teachers and school board members are there and many of her students and their parents, most of the area ranchers and many of the townspeople Jack does business with, as well as some of the boys' friends and fellow athletes with their families. Most of the town has come to witness this joyful event. Maggie wonders briefly how many came just to make sure they actually got married so the wedding could become the new subject of gossip but quickly dismisses the uncharitable thought. She won't let pettiness mar this perfect day, so she hugs and shakes hands with a will, no matter who is on the other end.

Once the line is through, Jack and Maggie move to the cake table and cut the cake, giving each other a quick taste, quite civilly, to the disappointment of the crowd. Then Tracy takes over, serving cake and punch until everyone is satisfied. Jack finishes his cake and stands, clearing his throat to signify he wishes to speak.

"Thank you, everyone, for coming today," he begins. "Maggie and I really appreciate you taking the time to celebrate with us. Falling in love with Maggie Sullivan has been the best thing that ever happened to me and to my boys, and we're grateful for your presence here today." Jack sits to hearty applause as Maggie stands.

She looks around the room, taking a moment to collect her thoughts. They had previously decided to forgo the traditional toasts, since this in many ways isn't a traditional wedding, but both agreed they should say a few words. Maggie reveres the sacrament of marriage but is determined to keep the tone of her wedding light and happy. There has been too much sadness in all of their lives over the past few years, and today is not the day to be reminded of it, so she picks her words with care.

"I second what Jack said. Thank you for coming today." She looks around, making eye contact with Tracy, Danny, and many of her friends. "Today is proof that people get second chances, and if ever two people, no, make that four people, needed a second chance, it's Jack, me, Trent, and Brad. God helped us find each other, with Tracy's help." Here, laughter bubbles through the crowd as many of them are acquainted with Tracy's knack for match-making. "And with more help from Above and from all of you, we hope for a great marriage and a happy family." With that, she sits beside her new husband, who pulls her close for a kiss and hug.

"That was really good," Jack whispers in her ear. "When can we get out of here?"

Maggie laughs and tells him to be patient, but with the speeches over and everyone full of cake, it is apparent the party is breaking up. Soon, only the family is left and some of the church ladies, who offer to stay and clean up. Maggie gratefully accepts their help, and they head up the stairs and out into the cold evening. It is completely dark now, but the mostly full moon shimmers off the snow and lights up the winter night.

Trent and Brad drive Maggie's car to Tracy's, leaving the newlyweds alone in Jack's pickup. Jack carefully hands Maggie up into the passenger seat and walks around to the driver's side to find she has scooted over into the middle, where she quickly snuggles in beside him, seeking warmth in the frosty cab. Jack thoroughly enjoys the short drive, with Maggie's soft hair brushing his cheek and sending sweet fragrance wafting by his nose. Visions of the night to come tantalize his mind, making it difficult to breathe. When they pull into Danny and Tracy's driveway, he can't help but pull his wife into a deep, hot kiss before opening the door and helping her down onto the icy ground.

Maggie walks into Tracy's bright, warm house still in a daze from Jack's kiss. Sitting so close to him in the pickup after months of riding in the passenger seat was enough to get her heart beating faster, and then that kiss! *Who needs a fire when Jack is here to kiss me*, she thinks happily.

They are quickly surrounded by the boys and baby Patrick who isn't happy at the lack of attention from his grandmother. Maggie picks him up and snuggles him into her neck, breathing in clean baby skin and getting a genuine hug from the toddler, while Brad and Trent jabber excitedly about the wedding and reception. Apparently, everyone had a very good time, and the house is full of laughter as the family gathers around Tracy's big table for the blessing before sitting down to the wedding feast.

Tracy has outdone herself, serving a scrumptious dinner of sautéed pork medallions covered in a sweet apricot reduction, garlic mashed potatoes, fresh asparagus spears, Caesar salad, and homemade rolls. Wedding cake before dinner hasn't dulled anyone's appetite, and they make quick work of the food.

Jack and Maggie both feel as if they are in a warm cocoon, surrounded by but not touched by anything but each other. Jack keeps his knee pressed against Maggie's under the table, constantly brushing his arm against hers as they eat. Soon, dinner is finished and Tracy laughingly refuses Maggie's offer to help with the dishes.

"You get on home before Jack picks you up and carries you out the door!" Tracy jokes as Maggie blushes and Jack nods in agreement. The new family gather their coats to leave, stopping to hug Tracy and Danny and thank them for the wonderful dinner. Both Tracy and Maggie tear up as they hold tight to each other, and Maggie whispers, "Thanks, sis. We wouldn't be together if not for you."

Tracy nods, too emotional to speak as her little sister heads out into the night with her new husband and sons.

# CHAPTER 32

On the way home, Jack lets Brad drive his pickup with Trent as a passenger. He and Maggie follow in her car, which is stacked as full as it can get with boxes from Maggie's house containing the rest of her clothes and toiletries, extra towels and bedding, and all the kitchen stuff she packed on New Year's Eve. School starts again on Tuesday, and Maggie doesn't want to worry about moving in the evenings after work when the weather is nasty and the night comes so early. She and Jack talk quietly on the drive home, discussing the wedding ceremony and the various guests who were there, and soon they are parking in the driveway next to Jack's pickup.

Now it is their ranch, not just Jack's, Maggie realizes, and the thought makes her happy. She has come to love this beautiful, isolated valley almost as much as she loves Jack and the boys, and she is glad to call it home.

The boys help Jack carry in boxes while Maggie watches from the porch in her dress and high heels, and the three of them quickly empty her car. They hurry in the house with the last boxes, ducking their chins against the freezing air, but Maggie lingers for a moment on the porch, looking back at the moon before Jack pulls her inside the warm mud room.

"What are you staring at?" he asks, turning her as he helps her off with her coat.

"Just the moon," Maggie answers. "It's beautiful tonight, and it's so light outside! Maybe we should go sledding."

"Yeah!" both boys shout enthusiastically. "That sounds great!"

"Oh, no," Jack groans. "I can see I'm outvoted on this one! Get changed and put on your snow pants. We'll meet you back here in ten minutes." He ushers Maggie before him through the house and into his room, the second time they have ever been in it at the same time, and closes the door behind them.

Maggie turns and looks at Jack as he walks to her, her breath aching in her throat as he pulls her close and covers her mouth with his. Rational thought flees as his lips and tongue stroke hers, firm and hot, claiming her for his own, and all she knows and all she feels is Jack—her husband, her man, her rock.

Maggie gives back the kiss with fervor, twining her arms around Jack's neck and trying to get closer to him. She craves his touch, his skin, and wishes they were alone so she could peel off his shirt and explore his body with her hands, but with a sigh, she pulls back and breaks the embrace.

"The boys are going to wonder what happened to us," she murmurs against his mouth as Jack tries to pull her back in.

"Let them wonder," Jack replies, but he knows Maggie is right and even though every fiber of his being longs to lay her down and make love to her, the parent in him makes its presence felt and he reluctantly lets her go so they can change into warmer clothes.

Maggie looks around the room and realizes that sometime between the last time she was here on Christmas Eve and today, Jack has hung the shelves the boys gave her for Christmas on the wall and moved her dresser down to their bedroom. When she opens the closet, all the clothing she left upstairs at the ranch is hanging next to Jack's clothes, and she is touched anew by his thoughtfulness. Maggie opens drawers to find her long johns, jeans, wool socks and heavy sweater while Jack lays his out on the bed.

Shyly, Maggie turns her back to him and asks if he will unzip her dress. Jack seems happy to comply, sliding his warm thumb down her spine in the wake of the zipper and causing shivers to tumble through her body. She feels his breath on the back of her neck a fraction of a second before his lips sear a kiss onto the tender skin, the light nip of his teeth making her gasp as she leans back into him.

Jack slides his hands up her shoulders and gently pulls the dress down, sliding the sleeves off Maggie's slender arms and stroking her soft skin while he continues to taste her neck with his mouth. He can feel her tremble and hear her breathing change as her desire grows, and the power of what he can do to her surges through him. At the edge of losing himself in her sweet softness, Jack remembers the boys are waiting to go sledding; he hears the thump of their feet down the stairs and knows they will soon be demanding the appearance of their father and new stepmother. With a sigh, he rocks Maggie in a quick hug and steps away.

"You better get some clothes on before I lose control," he tells her gruffly, turning away and beginning to unbutton his shirt. Not hearing any movement, he looks up to see Maggie watching him undress and is almost undone by the hunger in her eyes. He feels completely exposed to her gaze, the feeling as erotic as anything he has experienced before. If Maggie can do this to him without even touching him, he can't wait to see what happens when they are skin to skin with no more interruptions. He strips down to his underwear, watching Maggie watch him, growing more aroused by the minute. She continues to watch as he pulls on long underwear, blue jeans, a t-shirt, and heavy flannel shirt, her gaze never leaving him, the top of her dress down around her waist, her creamy skin spilling from a lacy bra and her lips still swollen from his kisses. Jack thinks, again, she is the most beautiful woman he has ever seen. Finally, he is dressed, and she meets his eyes and shrugs.

"Oh, well. I guess all good things must end," she says ruefully. "Good thing I'll have lots of other chances to watch you dress and undress." Her green eyes twinkle with humor as she pulls the dress the rest of the way off and steps out as it puddles around her feet, standing before him in her bra, half-slip, and red high heels.

Now it is Jack's turn to stare, and he feels his mouth go dry at the sight of his wife half-dressed. The slip quickly goes on the floor with the dress, only her lacy panties coming between Jack's eyes and her naked body. Maggie's delicate skin flushes with heat in response to his stare. The mood is broken, however, by a young male voice.

"Dad! Maggie! What the heck is taking you guys so long?"

Trent bellows. This is followed by a smack and a thud. "Ouch, Brad! What was that for?" the youngster complains.

Jack and Maggie stifle their laughter as Brad explains in a not-so-quiet voice that their father and new mother are probably "making out." There is a stealthy scuffle as Trent attempts to get even with his big brother, and the adults in the bedroom laugh harder, the strain of trying to keep quiet bringing tears to their eyes.

"We'll be right out," Jack finally is able to call, wiping his eyes, his face red with the effort of trying to make his voice laughter-free. Maggie quickly dresses, watched by Jack, both of them still chuckling occasionally, and soon they open the door to go into the living room, where the boys are waiting, trying to look nonchalant. "Ready?" Jack asks, trying not to make eye contact for fear he will burst out laughing.

"Yep! Let's go!" Trent exclaims enthusiastically. "You guys were really slow!"

Brad rolls his eyes at his little brother's naiveté, playing the role of the cool high-schooler to the hilt, and Jack's face reddens again as he chokes back laughter. Maggie jabs him in the side with her elbow, and he manages to breathe again.

"All right, last one out has to pull the sleds up the hill," he tells his sons, causing a stampede to the mud room, where coats, boots, hats, and gloves are hurriedly pulled on while the adults follow at a more leisurely pace, enjoying the youthful energy of the two boys.

Finally, everyone is ready, and Maggie ends up being the last one out. The night is breathtaking both in its beauty and its icy coldness, the moon lighting up the snowy valley, making Maggie think of the children's poem *The Night Before Christmas*:

> *The moon on the breast of the new fallen snow*
> *Gave a luster of midday to objects below.*

Maggie can see clearly across the barn lot to the corrals beyond and the pasture, where the cattle huddle against the freezing night. The evergreen trees are black on the foothills surrounding the valley, pooling shadows at their feet, inky against a blanket of white. The stars glitter overhead, remote and as icy as the frozen ground. Only the laughing company of Jack and his boys turn the winter darkness from something bitter and cruel into a magical white playground.

The four hurry to the barn, where Jack finds the sleds and hands them out the door to the boys. There are only three sleds, and Jack tells Maggie they have to share, somehow managing to sound both excited and disappointed about it at the same time, and soon has Brad and Trent in stitches with his antics. There is a fairly steep hill behind and to the right of the big barn, and they quickly walk toward it, pulling the sleds. By the time they slog through the deep snow to the top of the hill, all four are breathless and panting, even Brad who is in the best shape.

Maggie slips and falls more than once, and Jack hauls her back to her feet, brushing the snow from her bottom with gusto. At the crest, they have a short discussion on strategy and decide to send Trent down first, then Brad, and then Jack and Maggie, hoping gradually increasing the weight will pack down the runway so the sleds don't break through.

With a whoop of delight, Trent takes a running start and flings himself onto the sled, which goes about four feet and sinks, burying him in the snow. He digs himself up and out, staggering to the side and wiping snow from his face while the others shriek with laughter. Trent bends over and pulls the sled out of the hole and climbs back up the hill.

"Wait here, Maggie," Jack tells her, so she watches the three of them as they walk down the hill, stomping and packing a pathway as they go, then doing the same thing as they trudge back to the top. "Try again, Trent. I think this time you'll go all the way," Jack encourages.

Somewhat more gingerly, Trent pushes the sled a few feet down the slope and jumps on, and Maggie holds her breath to see if the trip is a success. The sleds sticks at first but, with Trent pushing with his hands on both sides, continues slowly down, picking up speed as it goes until boy and vessel are flying in the moonlight, a spume of white following their flight like jet wash. At the bottom, it slowly glides to a stop part way across the meadow, and Trent bails off, jumping around and shouting with delight.

Not to be outdone, Brad picks up his sled, places it in Trent's tracks, and takes his own rocket ride to the foot of the hill, where Trent is already climbing back up beside the track.

"Ready, Maggie?" Jack asks, and all at once Maggie realizes he means for her to get on this sled, which now looks about the size of a dustpan, with him and ride it into the white void. Suddenly, the bottom looks a million miles away. She swallows hard, trying to remember why she thought this was a good idea, and nods at Jack. He puts the sled in position and helps her sit on it, sliding her to the front and showing her where to put her feet. Then she feels the runners shift beneath her as Jack pushes it, running behind for several steps before plopping down behind her and stretching his legs alongside hers to guide the sleigh. She can feel his strong arms around her and leans against his solid frame, the air rushing by making her eyes sting and water, filling her lungs with ice, and she is laughing, laughing, laughing, loving the thrill and the speed, and the night, and this man, going down, and down, and down. The ride slows abruptly as the hill flattens into the meadow, and they are stopping.

"Again!" she shouts as eager as a child for another turn. Jack laughs and leans down to kiss her. Just then, Trent shouts from above, and they get out of the way barely in time to avoid the sled barreling into them. Brad isn't far behind, and they both pass Jack and Maggie on the way up for another round. The four spend the next thirty minutes sledding down the hill and walking back up, the cold not really bothering them due to the exercise of climbing the hill.

There are crashes and bombing runs as the boys try to push each other's sleds off the track, and all of them spend a great deal of time laughing. Once, Jack and Maggie tip over close to the bottom, spilling them out into the cold, crisp snow. Maggie lies there trying to get her breath back and then realizes part of why she can't breathe is because Jack is lying on top of her. She brushes the snow from her eyes and off her face and looks up at her husband, who is gazing intently back at her, his solid weight warm against the front of her body. Slowly, he drops his mouth to hers. His lips are cold on the outside, as are hers, with little crystals of snow caught between their mouths, melting as the heat builds and Jack's tongue gently caresses hers.

"I love you, Mrs. Hallas," he murmurs against her mouth. Maggie is about to answer him when a volley of snowballs rains down on their prone forms. The boys have taken advantage of Jack and Maggie's distraction to build an arsenal and are now pelting the adults furiously. Jack struggles to his feet in the deep snow, reaching down to help Maggie up from the ground, all the while trying to dodge snowballs. The boys run out of ammunition about the same time Jack focuses his full attention on them.

"Sorry, Dad," Trent yells, hiding behind his brother. "It was Brad's idea! Truce, okay?"

"I don't think so," Jack replies, stalking toward his sons and rolling a snow ball of his own on the way. Just then, an eerie, lonesome howl rings across the valley, pulsating through the trees and echoing off the snow-covered hills.

The four humans freeze as they listen, Maggie's eyes wide with remembered fear. She runs to Jack through the snow and holds on to him tightly, and Jack can feel her trembling.

"Was that a wolf, Dad?" Trent asks softly.

"Yes, son, it was," Jack somberly replies. "I don't think it's close, but where there's one, there's usually another. I wish I had my gun with me. Let's head back to the house."

He rights the overturned sled and pulls it behind him, leading Maggie by the hand as they retrace their path through the pasture to the barn. Brad and Trent follow behind, all of them walking quickly and looking over their shoulders often.

Maggie heaves a sigh of relief when they reach the barn. Jack makes all of them come inside while he puts the sleds away, and then they hurry to the house. The four of them crowd together in the mud room to take off their snowy boots and coats and then carry their wet gloves in to lay them by the woodstove in the living room. Brad and Trent go upstairs to change into warm pajamas, and Jack and Maggie do the same, not talking or flirting this time but dressing quickly in order to get back to the children.

Maggie and the boys go to the kitchen, and the teens raid the fridge while she makes microwave popcorn and finds some leftover snack mix in a container on the counter. They carry their booty and some cold drinks back to the living room, Jack starts an old movie, and soon the wolf is forgotten in the pleasure of being together, safe, and warm, and full. After about an hour, the boys' yawns are so loud Jack finally tells them to go to bed, and Maggie knows they must be tired because they go without arguing.

"Maybe sledding wasn't such a crazy idea after all," he

whispers to Maggie. "They went to bed early, and they'll sleep like rocks." He kisses her, softly at first and then more deeply, pressing her back into the old couch where she slept the night after the wolf almost attacked her, the night Jack kissed her the very first time, and Maggie is filled with sudden lust for this man. Jack, the one who kept her safe then and will keep her safe for the rest of their lives; Jack, with his handsome face and piercing blue eyes, his strong cowboy build, and gentle nature. She wants to do more with him now than kiss on the sofa, so she gently pushes him away.

"Let's get ready for bed, Jack," she says in a low voice. "You can have the bathroom first."

Jack looks confused but shrugs and does as Maggie suggests while she puts the dirty dishes in the sink and locks the back door. She knows it's silly, but she feels safer with the door locked even though wolves don't know anything about doors and locks. She shuts off the lights as she goes toward the bedroom to get her nightgown. Maggie doesn't plan on wearing it long but thinks she should at least make the attempt.

Jack is banking the fire when she walks past him to the bathroom to brush her teeth and wash off her makeup. She changes into the soft nightgown, padding barefoot through the dark, silent house to the doorway of their room, now lit only by the moon. She stops at the edge of the bed, watching Jack watch her, the silver glow from the window painting his face with shadows. He lifts the blankets for her in silent invitation and Maggie quickly slides under them and scoots to his side. She can feel the warmth of his bare skin through the delicate fabric of the nightgown.

"I wanted to see you in your nightgown and watch you take it off," Jack tells her softly, turning on his side to face her in the bed, "but I was worried you might get cold. Now this way I get to take it off for you, and you get to stay warm. Smart, right? I told you I was good at being married."

Maggie bursts into laughter at this ironic reminder of Caroline's opinion. "Stop bragging and kiss me," she answers him, pulling his face down to hers. "I'm hoping you're good at a lot of things," she whispers into his mouth as he complies with her request. This time there is no hurry, no fear of being caught or interrupted. They have all night, and the night after, and all the nights of the rest of their lives.

Jack's kisses are slow and gentle, light and teasing, first on her mouth and then along her jaw and down her neck, hitting all the sensitive places and causing Maggie to catch her breath in reaction, shivers running along her spine. He raises his head from kissing her neck and looks down at her, his face silver in the moonlight, tracing his finger gently across her cheek and down to her mouth, rubbing his thumb across the full bottom lip. Maggie nips his thumb lightly with her teeth, causing him to draw in his breath, and she delights in his reaction, reveling in her ability to arouse him.

"I love you, Maggie Hallas," Jack says softly. He runs his hand down her throat to the softness of her breast, claiming his right to touch her, and she arches into his big warm hand.

"I love you too," Maggie answers breathlessly. His nearness, his scent, the heat of his naked body against hers all serve to create in her a fierce longing to be closer to this new husband of hers, to experience all the first times she thought were long since in the past.

Jack's light kisses are driving her crazy, building anticipation for the taste of his mouth, his silky lips and tongue caressing hers, but he refuses to give her what she wants, instead holding both her seeking hands in one of his and continuing the butterfly assault on her senses. Only when she is almost sobbing with frustration does he finally release her hands, sliding his down to grip her waist and capturing her mouth in the way she has been longing for, taking control of the moment and of her senses in one motion. The kiss is everything she is anticipating, deep, sensual, quintessentially Jack, and Maggie feels it in every molecule.

She responds with fervor, running her hands across his skin, learning the contours of his body, the hard planes of his chest, the ropes of muscle in his back and buttocks, the soft fur of hair across his chest and down his belly, the swell of him hard against her abdomen as he pulls her beneath him, all the while continuing his assault on her mouth. This is what she wants—this heavy warm weight against her, the force of his thigh between hers, the answer to the need swelling inside her—her husband, Jack. Moaning with desire, Maggie runs her hands through his soft, dark hair, pulling his face even closer to hers, kissing him back with every ounce of her being, curving into the force of his body, telling him without words she is his for the taking.

Jack is doing everything in his power to hold off the desire coursing through him, to make the moment last, to make Maggie want him as much as he wants her. The soft nightgown she wears is infuriating, keeping him from touching what he needs to touch. As he is kissing her the way he has been dreaming of kissing her, he slowly slides one hand down to the lacy hem and starts pulling the gown up Maggie's thigh to her waist. To his delighted amazement, she pulls away and sits up, shedding the silky barrier in one quick pull over her head and tosses it over the edge of the bed, baring her body to him.

She sits still, the moonlight bathing her in liquid silver, letting him look his fill. He can see the fading outline of her summer tan, the shadows of her delicate collar bones and below, the creamy satin of skin no sun has ever touched. Jack drinks in the sight, and when he can stand it no more, he pulls her back down into the bed, almost rough in his haste to possess this woman, this angel, this wife he had the good fortune to find.

Now they are skin to skin for the first time, Jack's warm and firm against Maggie's silky coolness, and neither can get enough of the other. All the love they feel for each other and all the pent-up desire from the past four months find their expression in the sacred joining of husband and wife. Both have known the love between a man and woman before, but tonight everything is new. Jack has never been with someone as honest and generous as Maggie.

She welcomes him into her body and lets him see all she is feeling, making it easy for him to know how to please her. The more excited Maggie becomes, the better it is for Jack until finally the pleasure becomes overwhelming, and he loses himself in waves of sensation. Maggie's climax at the same time turns an already amazing experience into something neither one has known before—a complete melding of mind, heart, and body, a living testament of their love.

Maggie is completely unprepared for Jack's intensity. He makes love as if nothing else in the world exists but her, his powerful body and knowing hands and mouth bringing her quickly to the brink of ecstasy and then keeping her suspended there for what seems forever. For mindless moments, Maggie loses herself in Jack. The feel of him inside her, the weight of him over her body, his unique scent, spicy and musky and now sharp with the sweat of his desire, the strength of his arms around her, the tickle of his chest hair against her cheek are all parts of this man she loves that she is experiencing for the first time.

Slowly, the flush of making love fades, and the world around them comes back into focus. She must have moved involuntarily because Jack raises his head and shifts his weight from her, rolling both of them onto their sides.

Bending his head to kiss her, Jack says, "I love you, Maggie."

"I love you too, Jack," Maggie answers, lifting her hand to stroke his cheek. He turns to catch her fingers in his mouth, giving them a soft nip before releasing them again.

"I don't know about you, but that was the most erotic thing I've ever experienced," he tells her softly. "You are an amazing woman."

"You're pretty amazing yourself," Maggie says earnestly. "Maybe you are good at being married after all."

Jack laughs aloud at this and pulls her close, holding her tightly against him. Maggie snuggles into his embrace, loving the way it feels to be held in a man's arms again, not just a man's arms, but Jack's arms. Reluctantly, she pulls away and slides out of the warm bed, shrugging into her robe as she makes her way through the dark house to the bathroom.

Her reflection in the mirror startles her as she flips on the light switch. Who is this woman with her glowing eyes, flushed cheeks, kiss-swollen lips and disheveled hair? This woman who looks happy and well-loved shows no resemblance to the haunted, grief-stricken one Maggie remembers from earlier this year, and she finds herself thinking of the day Clark was killed, something she tries never to do. Tonight—her wedding night, the night she and Jack have just consummated the love they feel for each other—it seems wrong somehow to be holding onto these thoughts and memories of loss and grief.

Mentally shrugging away the sadness, Maggie gets a drink of water before making her way back to bed. She slips under the covers next to her husband, putting her icy feet against his warm ones and laughing at his shocked gasp.

Jack holds her close and kisses her again. "Goodnight, Maggie, sleep tight," he whispers in her ear.

"Goodnight back," Maggie says softly. She lies quietly in Jack's embrace, feeling him relax against her and hearing his breathing slow and deepen as he drifts off to sleep. Maggie feels both sleepy and wide-awake, scenes from the long day drifting through her tired mind. Jack mumbles something in his sleep and rolls away from her, and Maggie curls herself around his large, warm form, trying to quiet her racing thoughts.

Just as she feels herself slipping into sleep, a mournful howl jerks her back to consciousness. The wolf sounds as if it is very close to the house, and Maggie lies there wide-eyed, tensely listening for another howl. When nothing more comes, she eventually relaxes and soon falls asleep, the waning moonlight sliding over their slumbering forms and gilding them in its glow.

# CHAPTER 33

Maggie rises from sleep as if floating through a cloud, layers drifting away into the shadow of dreams, as she awakens into the dark of early morning winter. At first, she simply is—not really thinking, only being—not feeling the bed beneath her nor the blankets over her. Gradually, she becomes aware of heavy warmth across her mid-section and realizes it is Jack's arm. Suddenly, her brain recalls the events of the night before.

Wide awake now, she lies quietly, thinking about the wedding, and Jack, and her wedding night. Cocooned in the arms of her new husband, held closely to his solid form, Maggie feels totally safe and loved, a sensation she hasn't felt in almost a year. Reveling in the moment, she snuggles her chin into the covers and starts to drift back to sleep, only to be startled by the ring of the alarm beside the bed.

With a muffled oath, Jack reaches out a long arm and turns it off, half smashing Maggie in the process. Falling back onto his side of the bed, Jack faces Maggie, and the newlyweds stare at each other in the light of the digital alarm clock.

"Good morning, Mrs. Hallas," he whispers softly.

"Good morning, Jack," Maggie answers, pulling her hand from the blankets to tenderly stroke his rugged face. "Did you sleep well?" she asks considerately.

"Yes, until that darned clock went off," Jack says. "For some reason, I don't want to get out of this bed today. Remind me again why we didn't take a honeymoon? If we had, we'd be able to stay in bed as long as we wanted."

"Responsibilities," Maggie says with a sigh. "We can't

escape them."

"That's a dirty word this morning," Jack grumbles, "but I know you're right. Any rancher will agree that I might as well be married to the land and the livestock!"

"Don't forget the kids. They need us too," Maggie reminds him meaningfully, capturing his roving hand in hers. "We don't have time this morning for what you're trying to start, so let's just save our energy for tonight."

"As usual, you're right," Jack says, flopping dramatically on his back and throwing the offending hand across his side of the bed. "I just wish we had more time to ourselves."

Maggie leans over and kisses him briskly and then flinging the covers off, she jumps out of bed before she can change her mind. She reaches for her robe and pulls it on as quickly as she can. "Brrrr! It must be really cold outside," she says, hugging the robe to her and shivering. "This floor is like ice!"

She hurries to the dresser and pulls some heavy wool socks from a drawer to protect her bare feet from the cold and then heads to the bathroom for her morning routine. She is brushing her teeth in front of the wall heater when the bathroom door softly opens and Jack steps in, startling her. Eyes wide and toothpaste smearing her chin, she looks at her husband.

"It's okay," Jack reminds her. "We're married, Maggie."

Maggie steps to the sink to spit and rinse her mouth before turning to look at Jack and then realizes he is urinating. Face red, she turns back to the sink and waits for him to finish. This is one of the parts of married life she hasn't thought about resuming, and now with the reality, large and naked, standing in the bathroom with her, she realizes how many changes are about to take place in her life.

"I know we're married. I just forgot husbands and wives share the bathroom," Maggie says, still blushing. Making love to Jack in the half-dark of their moonlit bedroom is a far cry from seeing him naked under the bright lights of the bathroom, and his body is still new to her. She can't help but stare as he steps to the sink beside her and grabs his own toothbrush. His skin is very pale except for his arms and the back of his neck. *Farmer's tan,* Maggie thinks. *Jack's body,* she muses, *could be a model for a sculpture with its flat planes and angles and ropes of muscle.*

Jack, amused by her shy interest, turns to her and waits patiently while she looks her fill. "Well?" he asks. "Do I pass?"

"Yes," Maggie answers, still blushing pinkly. "I think you're beautiful."

"Beautiful!" Jack echoes. "You're supposed to say I'm rugged, or handsome, or hot! Not beautiful! You're the one who's beautiful."

"Me?" Maggie says doubtfully, looking into the mirror. "My hair is standing up, and I don't have any makeup on. I look awful!"

"Not to me," Jack tells her, turning serious for a moment. "You are the most beautiful person I've ever known, inside and outside." He pulls her to him, holding her closely and kissing the top of her head. "In fact, I think I better go out and leave you to it or we'll be doing more than just talking." Jack cracks the door open and sticks his head out, listening for the boys, and when the coast is clear, he slips out and goes to get dressed, leaving Maggie to continue her toilette alone.

After a quick shower, she dresses warmly in long johns, jeans, and a sweatshirt, and puts on socks and shoes to combat the arctic chill on the old floors. She is blow-drying her hair in their bedroom when she hears the back door shut and knows Jack is on his way out to do chores. Soon, Maggie is ready for the day and goes to the kitchen to start breakfast. By the time Jack returns to the house, she has prepared a wedding morning feast of scrambled eggs with ham and cheese, grapefruit, and toast. While Jack washes his hands, she goes to the foot of the stairs to call Brad and Trent down to eat and finishes putting the food on the table to the sound of their feet thundering down the stairs.

"Good morning," she tells them, giving each a quick hug before shooing them into their chairs. Jack comes in from the utility room and sits down, and Maggie says the blessing.

"How cold is it, Dad?" Trent asks as he passes the eggs. "My room was freezing! My windows have ice halfway up on them."

"It's about 25 degrees below zero," Jack answers. "It's supposed to stay like this all week, so get used to it and dress warm."

Listening to the conversation, Maggie eats her meal and soaks in the realization that this is now her life. She will be waking up and eating breakfast with Jack and his sons every day. Love fills her heart, and she sends up a quick prayer of thanks as she looks around the warm, cheery kitchen filled with her new family.

# CHAPTER 34

So begins the first day of Jack and Maggie's married life, and the days after continue in much the same pattern. Jack was right—the cold snap lasts all that week, and the next week, and the week after that with the temperature going as low as 20 degrees below zero at night and rarely getting to 10 degrees in the daytime. The cold is severe—the kind that freezes the breath coming from your nose before it can quite get out; the kind that burns in your lungs if you dare to breathe too deeply and then freezes onto your scarf in damp, chilly frost; the kind that brings instant tears to your eyes and then turns the tears to drops of ice; and the kind that makes your bones hurt if you're out in it too long. To make matters worse, a temperature inversion sets in, creeping up from the flatland to the south of town and blanketing the valley in a thick layer of gray, cotton-wool fog. Every day, driving into town from the ranch is like diving head-first into a pool of damp, dark gloom as they hit the leading edge of the inversion, and driving back up is bursting into the sunlight of the crystal clear, snowy mountains.

Jack is up before daylight doing chores while Maggie fixes breakfast, and she and the boys get ready for school. After they leave, Jack feeds the cows, a process usually accompanied by a mechanical breakdown of some sort caused by the extreme cold weather, which has to be repaired before he can finish the task. The cattle do fine in the sub-zero temperatures, but the horses and chickens need some extra TLC, which keeps Jack busy making sure their water isn't frozen and giving them additional feed when necessary.

Twice a day he chops a hole in the ice over the creek for the cows to get to fresh water. He comes in the house, stiff in every joint with his muscles sore from tensing against the cold, his eyebrows and scarf covered in frost from his breath, and his hands and feet numb no matter how heavy his socks and gloves are. Once he peels off his outerwear, he stokes the fire and then stands in front of it, waiting for the heat to soak into his freezing body and feeling his face and hands tingle as the blood rushes back into them. At night, he can barely keep his eyes open after dinner long enough to visit with the boys, the arctic air sapping his energy during the day.

Maggie starts her car and then rushes back in to stand by the stove while she waits for it to warm up, and then she and Brad and Trent go back out and huddle in their seats on the drive to town. Her classroom is chilly around the edges and sometimes the children wear their coats in the mornings. Maggie feels like her feet and hands are always cold, and her fingers crack and bleed in the dry air after a day spent handling papers. Many of the children have colds and several miss school, so she is always playing catch-up with assignments. People get cranky and tempers grow short as the cold snap lingers.

Trent's basketball team has started practice, although no games are scheduled until early March, so the only bright spots are Brad's basketball games. The Hallas family goes to every game, home and away, to cheer Brad and the team on. The boys are playing really well and are drawing large crowds, partly because of the level of play and partly because folks have nothing else to do. The noisy, warm gym filled with people is a nice change of pace, and Maggie relishes the time spent with her husband and step-sons.

Now she doesn't have to worry about people whispering behind their hands. They come right up and congratulate her and Jack on their marriage and ask how everything is going with the newlyweds. Maggie doesn't really feel like a newlywed. Being with Jack seems so natural it is hard to remember a time when they weren't together. Although the cold is wearing them down, they still find time and energy enough to make love every night, enjoying the pleasure they give each other and developing the intimacy every couple needs to be happy.

Finally, one day toward the end of January, the wind starts to blow, clearing away the fog that is so dampening to everyone's spirits, bringing with it a snowstorm that lasts three days, and warmer temperatures. That weekend, Jack takes Maggie and the boys out feeding with him, and afterward, they hike back to the hill where they went sledding on their wedding night and try it again in the bright sunshine.

Part of Jack's reason for the outing is to look for signs that the wolf they heard that night is still around. He has heard it again several times over the past few weeks, and since the cows are getting ready to calve, he needs to know what he is up against. As he suspects, the area along the edge of the pasture is full of tracks and scat with prints from several different wolves obvious in the fresh snow.

Jack shows the tracks to Maggie, Brad, and Trent and cautions them about being away from the house without a gun. They all know how to shoot, although Maggie has never shot anything but a target. Jack is worried about calving season, but there is nothing he can really do about it short of tracking the animals and trying to shoot them before they kill a calf or a cow or both, and he doesn't have the time right now as basketball season is in full swing. Although the cows aren't high risk for calving, they are at risk of being dinner for a wolf pack, and Jack realizes he will need to be very vigilant in the nights to come.

Groundhog Day dawns bright and clear, although the significance is lost on those living in the Idaho mountains, where winter almost always lasts into the middle of March. It is, however, an opportunity for Maggie to teach her sixth graders a short history lesson on the origins of the holiday, which also turns into a geography lesson when most of the class doesn't know where Puxatawney Phil lives. The children are engaged and excited, which pleases Maggie, but by the end of the afternoon, she is exhausted and feels as if she is coming down with a cold. She drives home alone, leaving the boys in town for basketball practice, and the whole way there, all she can think about is how good it is going to feel to curl up on the couch in her robe in front of the wood stove and drink a hot cup of tea. Her head is pounding, her eyes feel hot and grainy, she is congested, and her throat is definitely sore.

She is so engrossed in imagining the comforts waiting at home that she almost doesn't see the strange car parked in front of the house blocking the front sidewalk and forcing Maggie to park in a rutted part of the driveway where Jack's plowing has ended. When she steps out of the car, with her arms full of ungraded papers, she steps right into a pocket of snow deep enough to spill over the tops of her boots and send icy cold crystals onto her already chilled feet. Gritting her teeth, she struggles through the snow in front of the strange vehicle and hurries up the sidewalk, feeling her feet getting colder and wetter with every step.

The warmth of the utility room is a welcome relief, and by the time Maggie lays down her papers, kicks off her wet boots, and hangs up her coat, she is starting to feel somewhat better and is curious about who might be visiting them. Stooping to peel off her wet socks, she hears Jack's voice, low, answered even lower by a woman's voice. Now she is really curious, so she pads quickly on bare feet through the kitchen and into the living room, where she is brought to a sudden stop, staring with shocked gaze at her husband embracing another woman.

"Jack?" she finally gets out weakly.

Jack, startled, turns quickly, dropping his arms from around the blonde woman who continues to cling to him.

"Hi, Maggie," Jack answers. "I didn't hear you come in. Caroline is here—she's having a crisis." Jack pulls Caroline's arms from around his neck and turns her to face Maggie. Caroline's face is flushed and tear-streaked, her eyes red and swollen from crying, but Maggie thinks she still looks beautiful and a hot wave of jealousy sweeps through her body, adding to her already burning skin and pounding head.

"What happened?" Maggie asks politely, although the only thing she really wants to know is when Caroline is leaving. "Do you want to talk about it?" she continues, realizing some sort of interaction is going to be required of her and wanting to get it over with as quickly as possible. "Maybe we should all sit down, and I'll make us some tea."

"That's a good idea," Jack says, shooting Maggie a grateful

look. He escorts Caroline to the couch and sits beside her as Maggie goes to the kitchen.

Alone in the cheerful room, Maggie gives herself a stern, mental lecture on tolerance and forgiveness while she waits for the kettle to boil, hugging her arms around her shivering body, her feet feeling like chunks of ice on the drafty floor. Try as she might, all she can feel in her heart is annoyance at Caroline for invading their life and annoyance at Jack for comforting her.

Finally, the tea kettle whistles and Maggie prepares a pot of fragrant herbal tea, placing it on a tray with three cups and the honey and lemon juice. She carefully carries it back to the living room and sets it down on the coffee table in front of Jack and Caroline. Looking at the two of them side by side on the couch makes Maggie think of what they must have been like together when they were married. Her stomach gives an uneasy twinge to go with her stuffed-up nose and sore throat when she realizes the only place for her to sit is across from them in an arm chair.

Feeling like an unwanted third wheel and completely physically miserable, Maggie pours herself a cup of tea and doctors it with honey and lemon, sipping the hot liquid carefully. Once the others have their cups in hand, Maggie sits forward in her chair. "Now, what seems to be the problem?" Maggie asks in her most authoritative school-teacher tone.

Caroline starts to speak and then bursts into tears, covering her face with her hands as she sobs.

Jack speaks to her quietly, encouraging her to tell Maggie what happened.

"He died!" Caroline says, choking back her sobs enough to talk. "That son of a bitch died! Two weeks before we were supposed to get married! How could he do that to me?" she moans, once again burying her face in her hands.

Maggie, shocked at the news which resonates in her heart, gets up to find a box of tissue and give herself time to regain her composure. Returning to the living room, she takes her seat across from the grieving woman and hands her some tissues.

"When did it happen?" Maggie asks quietly, now with sympathy in her tone.

Responding to Maggie's change in manner, Caroline is able to summon her composure, blowing her nose, and carefully blotting around her tear-swollen eyes. "Yesterday. Last night, really. We were making love, and he just collapsed, and I couldn't wake him up, so I got dressed and called 911. The paramedics said he was already dead before they came, and there was nothing I could have done."

Maggie, picturing in her mind Caroline callously putting on her clothes and checking her hair and makeup before calling for help, is both saddened and shocked by the shallowness of this woman who used to be married to Maggie's beloved Jack. Remembering her own reaction to Clark's death, she can't imagine taking the time to get dressed before dialing 911 or trying CPR even if there was no chance to save a life. Her dislike of Caroline warring with her natural kindness, Maggie struggles to find words of comfort. Before she can think of anything to say, Caroline continues her story.

"I called Harold's partner in the law firm to find out what to do, and he called Harold's kids and that's when all the trouble started. They showed up early this morning and kicked me out of my own house! I was Harold's fiancé, and they treated me as if I was some nobody! They said horrible things to me—called me a money-grubbing gold digger, practically accused me of killing Harold, and told me I had to be out by noon. They watched me pack as if I might steal something, and I had to leave all the nice things Harold bought me. The only thing besides my clothes they let me take was my engagement ring. It's not worth a fraction of what those stupid, miserly brats of his are going to inherit." Caroline's lovely face is dark with anger, her eyes narrowed at the memory of her treatment at the hands of Harold's children.

Hands clenched into fists, Caroline pounds them against her thighs in frustration. "Harold told me he was going to change his will and make me his sole heir just as soon as we were married. He didn't like his kids because they never came to see him, so he was planning on cutting them out of his will. Why couldn't he have waited two more weeks to go and die?" she wails, starting to cry again. "Now I have nothing! All he had to do was stay alive until after six o'clock on Valentine's Day, and I would have been his wife, and then I would have been the one kicking them out of my house!" Exhausted from her outburst, Caroline leans limply against Jack, closing her eyes to Maggie's incredulous gaze.

Maggie is stunned. The woman has yet to say anything about how sad she is to lose the man she supposedly loves; her concern seems primarily to be about her loss of Harold's possessions and the chance to inherit his wealth. Maggie has no idea of how to respond to the circumstances but knows she has to say something. She doesn't care at all for the way Caroline seems to be snuggling up to Jack.

Finally, she is able to think of something to say. "Jack and I are so sorry for your loss, Caroline. I'm sure you must miss Harold and that you're very sad right now. Is there anything we can do to help you? Do you have a place to stay tonight?" Maggie asks, knowing in the back of her mind that Caroline would never have come here if she had anywhere better to go.

"No, I don't have anywhere to go," Caroline whispers in a pitiful voice. "My own mother doesn't even want me. All I could think of was my boys and how much I wanted to see them, so I came here. Where are they, by the way?"

Jack stands abruptly, almost toppling Caroline off the couch. "They are at basketball practice; they should be home around 8:00," he tells her, stalking over to stand behind Maggie's chair and resting his hand on Maggie's shoulder. She reaches up to gently squeeze his large, warm fingers. "Of course, for their sake we will help you if we can, but don't even think about using this to make them feel sorry for you," he continues.

"Jack," Caroline says reproachfully, "I would never do that, but thanks for offering your help. It would be really great if I could stay here for a few days until after the funeral and while I look for somewhere to live. I think I'd like to stay in the area so I can see the boys more. Without Harold, I'll have to get a job, and I don't know if there's anything open around here. I have some money saved that Harold's kids don't know about, so I'll be able to afford rent if I can find a place that's not a dump."

Jack and Maggie share a long look, Jack asking and Maggie answering without saying a word, and then Jack says, "Okay. You can stay here for a few days—but only a few days."

"Thank you, Jack!" Caroline exclaims tremulously, rising from the couch and throwing her arms around her ex-husband. "You don't know what this means to me! Oh, and you too, Maggie," she adds as an afterthought. Stepping away from Jack, she looks at Maggie as if she just now realizes that Maggie exists. "You look terrible," she comments. "Are you feeling okay?"

"Actually, I think I'm coming down with a cold," Maggie answers, also standing. "I'm going to take some medicine and go straight to bed, if you don't mind."

"Oh, no, go ahead and do whatever you need to," Caroline

says in an understanding way. "Jack and I and the boys will be just fine." She gives Maggie a smile that seems to both mock her and challenge her at the same time. Right now, Maggie isn't up to a battle, so she just nods in agreement and heads toward the bathroom.

"Dinner's in the slow cooker," she tells Jack over her shoulder, "and there's a salad in the fridge." Shutting the bathroom door behind her, she leans against it in sudden exhaustion, her head pounding in rhythm with her heartbeat. *Who does she think she is!* Maggie thinks angrily. *She shows up here as if it's her right after what she put them all through—hanging on Jack and treating me as if I'm still the hired help, and then she wants to stay for a few days. I'll bet it turns into a few weeks.* She closes her eyes against the thought of putting up with Caroline for more than a few days and tries to pray for patience and understanding, but she feels so ill, she can't formulate her thoughts.

Giving up, she goes to the medicine cabinet and takes some cold medicine and pain reliever, then washes her hands and face. She thinks about brushing her teeth but decides she might wake up in an hour or so and want some dinner, so she turns out the light and walks back through the living room to the bedroom she and Jack share.

Caroline is sitting on the couch again watching television, and Jack is nowhere to be seen. She watches Maggie cross the room and open the bedroom door. Maggie, realizing Caroline is staring, stops and asks, "What? Is there something you needed?"

"No," Caroline says, tossing her hair over one shoulder. "It just seems odd to me to see you going into our bedroom. I hadn't really thought about it before. You haven't changed things here much," she continues, gesturing around at the house. "It looks like it always did." She wrinkles her nose in disdain, looking at Maggie the whole time.

Maggie, remembering the way the house looked the first time she saw it, just laughs a little. "Well, Caroline, the house may look the same, but you don't live here anymore, and this hasn't been your bedroom for a long time. You forfeited your right to it when you left Jack," Maggie retorts brusquely. "There are sheets and blankets for the spare bed in the upstairs linen closet."

Without a backward glance to see how Caroline takes her statement, Maggie shuts the door firmly behind her. She puts on her warmest pajamas and climbs, shivering, under the heavy blankets. She slides over to Jack's side, wanting to feel closer to him and pulls his pillow to her face, inhaling the scent of him that lingers on the pillowcase. Thinking about Jack and how much she loves him, Maggie falls into a deep sleep.

When she wakes again, Jack is sliding her over so he can climb into bed. Maggie snuggles close to his long frame, and he holds her tightly to him, both of them reveling in the chance to touch each other.

"How are you feeling?" Jack asks quietly.

"I don't know," Maggie answers sleepily. "Better, I think. My head and throat don't hurt as badly."

"You feel like you still have a fever," Jack responds, laying his hand across her forehead.

Maggie turns her face into his palm and kisses it. She feels strange—half asleep and woozy from medicine and fever but filled with desire for her husband. She has an absurd urge to claim him in the way a woman claims a man, but she doesn't want to give him her cold, so she turns her head when Jack tries to kiss her. "You might get sick," she whispers, cupping her hands on the back of his neck and looking into his eyes in the moonlight.

"I don't care," Jack whispers back. "I've been waiting all day to kiss you." And he does, and they make love, slowly and carefully, Jack undressing Maggie as if she is made of delicate china, and touching her with reverence.

The fever makes her super sensitive, and every touch of Jack's hands on her skin feels like fire and causes her to shiver, until finally they both reach the pinnacle of sensation and tumble together down the slope into drowsy fulfillment.

Afterward, Maggie pulls on her robe to go to the bathroom and makes her way through the darkened living room, shivering with cold and fever. On the way back to bed, she hears something unfamiliar, and it takes her a moment to place the sound. She has forgotten Caroline is sleeping upstairs, and the sound is of her snoring. It gives Maggie a snide sense of accomplishment knowing what she and Jack have just done while Caroline snores her way through her selfish dreams. Maggie knows the thought isn't very kind, and she tries to squash it, but it still makes her feel better to know Caroline snores. Maggie walks quickly back to bed and climbs in naked beside her husband, curled up to his broad, warm back and waiting for sleep to claim her again.

# CHAPTER 35

When Maggie's alarm jolts her awake at 6:00 a.m., she knows she is too sick to go to work, so she leaves a message on the school's answering machine asking for a substitute and goes back to sleep. She is aware of Jack getting up and dressed and of the back door opening and shutting several times and once she hears the rattle of wood as Jack fills the wood box, but other than that, she is oblivious until about 10:30 when her full bladder brings her awake. As she rises from bed to go the bathroom, she realizes she feels better. Her throat still hurts quite badly, but the fever seems to be gone and her congestion and headache have mostly disappeared. Encouraged by the lack of symptoms, Maggie decides to shower and get dressed, but by the time she is finished, she is regretting her decision.

Feeling weak and sick, she makes her way slowly into the kitchen and puts on the kettle to boil, waiting in a chair at the table and looking out the window at the mountains. It is another beautiful, sunshiny day with the sun glinting off the deep snow and making blue shadows around the evergreen trees on the slopes above the valley. Drifting on the breeze with the hawk she sees in the bright sky, Maggie is startled back to Earth by the whistle of the tea kettle. While she is making her cup of tea, Jack comes in the back door, stomping his snowy boots on the rug and hanging up his heavy chore coat before walking into the kitchen.

"Good morning, sleepyhead," he teases, enveloping Maggie in a strong hug smelling of hay, horses, and Jack's spicy scent.

"Good morning yourself," Maggie answers, resting her cheek on Jack's chest. The sound of his heartbeat against her ear makes her feel so safe and calm, and it is a comfort to her poor aching, floaty-feeling head and body to be held in his arms.

Eventually, Jack releases her and steps back to look closely at her face. "You still look kind of pale, sweetheart. How do you feel?" he asks considerately.

"Not very good but better than last night," Maggie replies. "My throat is killing me."

"Let's have a look," Jack suggests, opening a nearby drawer to grab a flashlight. "Say ah," he instructs, bending down and aiming the flashlight beam at Maggie's mouth.

Obediently, she opens wide and says, "Aaaah," even though it hurts to talk.

"Just as I suspected," Jack announces, "I think you have strep throat. We better get you in to see the doctor."

"Really?" Maggie asks with dismay. "I haven't had that in years, and I don't want to go the doctor."

"Sorry," says Jack. "I really think it's the right thing to do."

"Okay," Maggie concedes with a sigh. "Whatever you think. I'm too miserable to argue." With that, she sinks back into the chair and wraps her hands around the hot cup of tea, sipping cautiously at the fragrant brew. She watches Jack pick up the telephone and make the call to get her an appointment with the doctor later that afternoon, thinking that she can't remember the last time someone took care of her when she was sick. Certainly not Clark. He couldn't tolerate being around sick people and would avoid the house as much as possible when one of them was ill. Jack simply takes charge and makes her feel comforted and cared for. She isn't too sick to notice how handsome he is in the strong morning light, his chiseled face creased in concern for his wife, and remembers with fondness the activities of last night.

"You see the doctor at 3:00," Jack tells her, hanging up the phone. "That will give me time to feed and you time to have a nap after lunch. What's Caroline doing this morning?" he asks, changing the subject.

Maggie, having lost the memory of Caroline staying with them in the mists of her high temperature, is immediately brought down from her pleasant sense of well-being in Jack's competent care by the thought of the woman who is the mother of Jack's children.

"I haven't seen or heard her all morning," Maggie answers. "I think she's still asleep. It's probably good for her; I'm sure she is exhausted from grief." Maggie isn't sure if Caroline is grieving for

Harold or for the loss of her lifestyle with Harold, but either way it is still grief, and having gone through it herself less than a year ago, Maggie realizes all too well how debilitating grief can be. "How did it go with the boys last night? Were they okay with her being here?"

"Well, it was kind of weird, mostly because you weren't out here with us, but I think they're fine with it, at least in the short term. Having her living in town will be a different story, as that could change a lot about how they interact with her," Jack explains. "I'm very worried about the effect this visit is having on the kids. Eating dinner last night with just the four of us gathered around the kitchen table kind of gave them the illusion that we are still a family. I really hope the boys are old enough to see through her flimsy attempt at reconstructing the past. Offering her hospitality is one thing, but it can't come at the expense of my sons' peace of mind."

Maggie can see Jack is worried about the situation, but she can't think of any way to make it better short of asking Caroline to leave, and for now, that isn't really an option. She sips her tea and watches her husband, vaguely admiring his vivid, blue gaze as he is lost in thought. "Well, anyway, she's here for now, so we'll just have to make the best of it," Jack says, coming out of his brief reverie. "Let's get you settled on the couch with a blanket, and we'll watch that movie we got for Christmas that we haven't had a chance to see yet." He helps Maggie up and walks her into the living room with his arm around her, Maggie's head leaning against his shoulder. "I hate seeing you sick, but it is a novel feeling having you need me like this when you're usually so strong and independent," he tells her.

Maggie spends the rest of the day on the couch watching television and drifting in and out of sleep. Caroline finally comes down about 11:30, yawning widely and slouching into the bathroom, where she stays for almost an hour, emerging in a cloud of fragrant steam. Wrapped only in a towel, she parades through the living room, stopping to say good morning and making sure Jack notices her before going back upstairs. When she comes down again, Jack and Maggie are just finishing lunch at the dining room table.

"That smells good," she remarks, leaning over Jack's shoulder to look at his empty plate. "What was it?"

"Left over pot roast," Jack answers, moving away from her to take the dishes into the kitchen. Caroline trails behind him, shooting Maggie a look over her shoulder that Maggie is unable to decipher. Deciding that she trusts Jack and that Caroline isn't worth the worry,

Maggie goes back to the couch and is quickly asleep.

Jack is left to deal with his ex-wife on his own, and after he shows her where Maggie keeps the plates and helps her operate the microwave, he uses the excuse of feeding to get out of the house and away from her. Of course, he really does have to feed; it is just a little earlier than normal. Also, he knows he has to take Maggie to the doctor later that afternoon and wants to be sure he is finished in time for the trip.

While he is feeding, he watches for wolf signs. The pack seems to have moved on over the past few weeks, but early this morning, when he checked the cows, he thought he saw one in the dim light flashing through the timber at the foot of the hills, and now he finds fresh tracks at the edge of the clean snow along the path of scattered hay. Jack sighs in exasperation. He knows it is only a matter of time before he loses a calf or a cow or both, as calving season is in full swing. Every night for the past week, there were at least three calves born, and the majority of the herd will calve in the next two weeks. Jack knows he won't get much sleep for a while since he will be patrolling the pasture with a gun for most of every night. He finishes his chores and then finds something to keep him out of the house until it is time to leave for town.

Maggie is awake when Jack comes back in. She goes to comb her hair and brush her teeth, then puts on her boots and coat. As they are going out the door, Caroline follows them into the utility room. "Do you mind if I come along?" she asks, a catch in her voice. "I just don't think I want to be alone way out here right now."

The thought of putting up with Caroline all the way to town and back, plus while they are waiting to see the doctor makes Maggie's already aching head pound, but she doesn't say anything. She can tell Jack wants to tell Caroline no, but he also says nothing, just looks at her.

"Great!" she beams. "I'll go get ready!"

Jack and Maggie exchange a look, and then Maggie takes off

her coat and walks back in to wait at the kitchen table while Jack goes outside to warm up the car. Neither of them know what Caroline needs to do to get ready since she was already showered and dressed and had her hair styled and her make up on. Ten minutes later, she reappears in the doorway, not looking any different, and announces she is ready to go just as Jack comes slamming in the door, muttering under his breath.

"Well, let's go then," he grouses. "We're going to be late if you dawdle around any longer."

Taking Maggie's hand, he leads her to her car and helps her into the front seat, leaving Caroline to fend for herself. All the way to town, Caroline keeps up a steady stream of chatter, talking about Harold's children, the unfairness of her situation, how boring she thinks their small town is, the likelihood of finding work in such a miserable place, and on and on. Maggie is too polite and too sick to interrupt her or point out the inaccuracies in her statements, and Jack is too irritated, so they ride in silence to the local clinic.

Again, Jack opens Maggie's door and helps her out and then walks her to the door with his arm around her, leaving Caroline to do as she wishes. She follows them inside and, sniffing with distaste at the antiseptic-tinged air of the clinic, picks up a fashion magazine and settles into a chair. Maggie checks in at the counter, and then she and Jack also sit down near Caroline. Maggie thinks this is an extremely awkward situation but doesn't have a clue how to ease it. She comes to the conclusion that Caroline is just an awkward person who seems determined to insert herself into their lives, and Maggie will just have to live with it for a few more days.

Eventually, the nurse calls Maggie back to the exam room, and to Maggie's surprise, Jack accompanies her without any urging from her. Dr. Meade quickly confirms Jack's previous diagnosis of strep throat, and Maggie has to laugh at his smug, cocky demeanor when he is proved correct. The doctor prescribes an antibiotic and tells Maggie to rest for several days, which means no going to school, so she calls the principal from her cell phone to give her the bad news while the nurse writes up the check-out paperwork and Jack pays the co-pay.

They collect Caroline from the waiting room on their way out and drive to the drug store, a small, family-run business on the main street in town which sells household goods, gift items, and fine jewelry in addition to being the town's pharmacy. This time, Maggie stays in the warm car and waits while Jack and Caroline go inside.

◦◦◦◦◦

The pharmacist, Ben Sanders, who is a friend of Jack's and has also known Maggie for years, drops what he was doing to fill the prescription, which Jack points out to Caroline is an advantage to living in a small town. She merely looks down her nose at him and walks away to browse the jewelry counter. Jack is reminded that Ben was one of the few men in town who turned Caroline away when she came around flirting and trying to start an affair. *No wonder she doesn't want to hear good things about the man.* Jack can't help himself from rubbing it in by mentioning to Caroline that Ben will be a good source for her to find out about housing and employment since he knows everyone in town and often listens to their troubles while they wait for medication in his pleasant store.

She is not impressed with this information, as Jack guesses, and gives him one of her famous dirty looks meant to make him cringe and beg her forgiveness, but Jack is past that now and just smirks back at her. Caroline, visibly irritated, turns her back on him with an exasperated sigh and ignores him, which suits Jack just fine.

Knowing how sick Maggie is, Jack purchases a bottle of water when he pays for the medication so Maggie can take it right away, and he and Caroline go back out to the car. Maggie has dozed off in the winter sunshine pouring in through the windshield, and Jack has to wake her up to take the first dose.

By the time they reach the ranch again, it is almost 5:00 and the sun is setting, painting the snowy ridges scarlet against the black of the trees. Maggie goes straight to the couch for another nap while Jack retrieves some steak from the freezer to thaw for dinner and starts peeling potatoes. As he suspects she will, Caroline avoids the kitchen and watches television instead of offering to help. By the time Maggie awakes, the boys are home from basketball practice and Jack is putting dinner on the table.

◦◦◦◦◦

Maggie stumbles to the bathroom, feeling disoriented and odd after sleeping so late in the day. When she enters the kitchen, Caroline is just sitting down in Maggie's place at the table next to

Jack, even though there is an empty chair between Trent and Brad. Seeing the four of them seated around her table increases Maggie's feeling of being out of place, and she looks helplessly at Jack for some clue of what to do.

"Mom, you're in Maggie's chair," Brad says, breaking the suddenly taut silence in the kitchen. "Come sit by me and Trent," he invites.

For a moment, Maggie thinks Caroline isn't going to move, but then she does, and Maggie shoots Brad a look of thanks before sitting down in the seat Caroline has just vacated.

Trent starts telling his parents about his day at school, and conversation swirls around Maggie, who is content to just listen, picking at the food Jack has prepared with little appetite. Maggie does notice that for every story the boys tell, Caroline has one of her own instead of leading her sons back into discussion of their events and behavior as Maggie is wont to do. Maggie thinks the woman is missing a great opportunity to connect with the boys and understands much about the relationship between mother and sons by watching this one episode of interaction.

Finally, Trent notices that Maggie isn't talking. "What's the matter Maggie?" he asks with concern. "Are you still sick?"

"Yes, Trent, I'm still sick," Maggie answers. "But I'm feeling better, and by Friday I should be fine."

"Oh, good, because Brad has a game, and you always go with us to watch him play. I wouldn't want you to miss it," he says sincerely.

"I can come too," Caroline interrupts. "I'm very excited to see the game. I think you're the best player on the team!"

"Mom," Brad says dryly. "I'm definitely not the best player, but we play pretty well as a team, which you would know if you ever came to watch."

Chastened, Caroline apologizes for not coming to more games, but Brad turns a deaf ear to his mother and begins a discussion with his father about the cattle.

Jack uses this opening to let his family know the wolves are back and reminds them not to go out on the ranch without a gun. This is the first Caroline has heard about the wolf pack, and she quickly becomes almost hysterical, railing at Jack about endangering the children and for encouraging the boys to use weapons which then starts to turn into a rant about Jack's abilities as a father.

Maggie, who has been listening to the whole scene in astonishment, has had enough by this point. Standing, she quickly brings Caroline's monologue to a stop by asking, "Jack, would you please help me back to the living room, sweetheart? I'm feeling a little weak." She flashes Jack her brightest smile, letting him know she believes in him and isn't about to let Caroline tear him down in front of the boys.

Gratefully, Jack returns the smile and rises to escort his wife from the room, leaving Caroline staring after them resentfully.

In the other room, Maggie clings to Jack, both arms around his solid form, while he strokes her back and runs one hand through her silky hair, cupping her fragile skull in his strong fingers.

"Thanks, Maggie," he whispers. "That was headed south in a hurry, and I wasn't sure what to do to head her off. I guess I'm out of practice at fighting with her."

"I'm glad you're out of practice," Maggie whispers back. "You just leave her to me. She's hurt you enough."

Standing in the dimly-lit room in each other's arms, husband and wife look into each other's eyes as the sound of Caroline and the boys clearing the table comes from the kitchen. Maggie smiles at Jack and stretches up to kiss him briefly. "I think your sons have put her to work," she chuckles.

Jack nods in agreement and helps her settle back on the couch, pulling the blanket up around her shoulders.

"Shall I leave them to it or go help?" Jack asks, standing beside the couch.

"Leave them to it," Maggie answers. "You've had a long, difficult day. Sit down with me and relax for a while."

Jack does as she suggests, moving her legs to sit at the end of the couch and then pulling her feet into his lap as he leans back with a sigh. Maggie listens while Jack gives her an update on the goings-on of the ranch and the livestock. He shares his fears about what might happen if he isn't able to keep the wolves from the cattle, and they discuss the laws on wolf depredation in Idaho and try to figure out what his options are for protecting his property.

All too soon, Trent, Brad, and Caroline join them in the living room, putting an end to their quiet talk. Maggie asks the boys about homework, and they lie down on the floor with their backpacks in front of the stove. Brad does math while Trent studies for a social studies test. Usually, Maggie or Jack will quiz him, but tonight, since

Caroline is there, Maggie suggests she help her son. This lasts about ten minutes before Caroline is bored, so Jack takes over.

When their books and papers are put away, the boys watch television for a few minutes before getting ready for bed, and as soon as she tells them goodnight, Maggie goes to wash her face, brush her teeth, and take her medication before going to bed as well. Tonight, the cold sheets feel good to her and, although she has slept much of the day, she drifts off almost immediately.

Catherine Bridwell

# CHAPTER 36

Over the course of the next few days, Maggie quickly recovers from her illness and is soon her usual self. By Friday, she is finding it extremely hard to rest, especially with Caroline in the house. The woman does nothing but watch television, never offering to help cook or clean and leaving her belongings scattered throughout the house.

Jack makes breakfast and lunch for everyone on Thursday and helps Maggie make a chicken casserole for dinner. On Friday, Maggie is back to doing the cooking while Jack helps clear up afterward. That night, they go to town early and have dinner at the local restaurant before Brad's game. Maggie still finds it odd to have Jack's ex-wife with them everywhere they go, but Caroline has made no further mention of Harold's funeral service or of finding a place of her own, so Maggie determines to make the best of the situation and hopes it doesn't last too long.

The game is a close one, and Brad doesn't play as well as he normally does (both Jack and Maggie think it is because his mother is there), but he does manage to hit all four of his free throws late in the fourth quarter to put the team over the top and secure the win, so he is happy. Their normal routine after a home game since Maggie moved out to the ranch permanently is to stop by Tracy and Dan's for dessert, but with Caroline there, Maggie isn't sure her sister will appreciate the visit. She takes a moment as the crowd is filing out to explain what is going on and ask Tracy if she minds an extra guest.

Tracy just laughs and says, "Sure, the more the merrier. Besides, you know I like drama!"

*Leave it to Tracy*, Maggie thinks, *to see the humor in the situation.* The thought lifts her spirits and, although she is feeling very tired, the whole group goes to Tracy's for dessert. Trent and Brad are wound up as usual after a game, discussing every play and re-hashing close calls. For once, Caroline just watches and doesn't butt into the conversation. Maggie thinks she sees a fleeting look of loneliness cross the woman's face as if maybe Caroline is starting to see what she gave up when she left.

"So, Caroline," Tracy asks during a lull in the boys' rapid-fire discussion, "have you found a place to live yet?"

Jack and Maggie wait with bated breath for the answer, hoping for a miracle. They are disappointed, however, when Caroline answers breezily, "No, not yet. I really haven't even had a chance to look."

"You've had all week," Tracy says pointedly. "What have you been doing? I would think having a home would be a priority."

"I'm in mourning," Caroline says, adopting a sad smile. "I just can't seem to find the energy for house hunting. Maybe after Harold is laid to rest I'll feel more like doing something."

The knowledge that Caroline doesn't plan to leave any time soon, added to the fatigue still lingering from her illness, hits Maggie like a ton of bricks. All at once, she can't wait to get home and go to bed. Catching Jack's attention, she signals she is ready to go, and Jack quickly rounds up his sons and gets them moving toward the door. Maggie and Jack hug Dan and Tracy and thank them for their hospitality while Caroline walks out without speaking and follows the boys to the car.

During the ride home, Trent asks his mother when Harold's funeral will be held, and Caroline starts to cry.

"I don't know!" she sobs. "No one will take my calls or call me back. I think they already buried him without telling me. I hate them! I deserve to be there in the front row with everyone shaking my hand afterward, and they are depriving me of that!"

Only Caroline, Maggie thinks, could make a funeral sound like a social event.

Trying to comfort his mom, Trent says, "Well, if he's already buried, then you don't have to leave, and you can start looking for a house."

This makes her cry even harder. "Why is everyone pressuring me about finding a house? I think you don't want me around."

"Okay, that's enough for now," Maggie intervenes. "We'll

talk about this more tomorrow when everyone isn't tired." She turns up the radio, and silence falls in the car for the duration of the trip.

Maggie thinks the novelty of having their mother live with them again has worn off for the boys, and the reality of living with her dramatic, selfish personality is setting in, and she thinks Caroline realizes it and is resentful. The trick is going to be to get Caroline to move out but to think it is her own idea. Right now, living with them is the easy thing to do, and Caroline is all about the easy things.

Caroline goes straight to her room when they arrive home and doesn't come back down or say goodnight to her children, so the four of them go through their bedtime routine unhindered by her presence.

The next day during lunch, a meal for which Caroline barely gets out of bed in time to attend, she apologizes for getting upset the night before.

"I'm just so sad about Harold I can't think straight," she tells the boys. "I really need to be around you right now, but if you want me to leave, I'll start looking for a place on Monday." This is said with such pathetic tone and drooping of her head and body, the boys can't help but feel guilty, and Maggie is furious at Caroline's manipulation of their feelings.

"It's okay, Mom," Trent says kindly. "We don't want you to leave. We just want you to be happy." He gets up and gives his mother a hug while Brad watches, and Jack and Maggie pretend to be somewhere else.

That is the last discussion they have about Caroline finding her own place. After that, they settle into an uneasy routine where she sleeps in, gets up for lunch, watches television all day, and pretends to house-hunt while the boys go to school and practice and Jack and Maggie work. Maggie is uncomfortable leaving Jack and Caroline home together all day, but she has no choice about going to work, so she resolves to trust Jack and not think about it. It is very difficult having a permanent house guest, made even worse by who the house guest is.

Caroline intervenes constantly when Jack and Maggie are trying to talk to each other and to the boys and turns every conversation around to make it about her. Basketball games, which previously were the highlight of the week, become a place for Caroline to show everyone how sad she is and how grateful she is for Jack and Maggie's charity, while she uses the time to connect with old friends and flirt with any man who talks to her. Jack and Maggie are so uncomfortable with her behavior they find it hard to focus on the games and on Brad. Both boys are also starting to show signs of stress—outbursts of anger over nothing, occasional bad grades, snapping at Jack and Maggie when asked to help—and Maggie worries their family is falling apart.

The worst part for Maggie is she and Jack have virtually no time at all to talk or make love. Jack is up every night patrolling the pasture, and Maggie leaves for school as he is going to bed. Every evening, Caroline is there, making her presence felt and stifling personal conversation. Maggie can feel them drifting apart and is helpless to stop it. Even Sunday Mass gives no relief since she spends the entire time praying for patience to deal with Caroline, forgiveness for thinking mean thoughts about Caroline, praying for Caroline to be a better person, or praying for Caroline to move out. The woman has taken over their lives.

# CHAPTER 37

Toward the end of the second week after Caroline's arrival, Jack is walking around the pasture in the early morning hours with his flashlight and gun, deeply tired and yawning despite the crisp, cold air of the mountain in his face, when he comes upon a cow off in the shadows. As he approaches, the animal bellows in fear and pain and tries to move away from him. Shining the light on her hindquarters, Jack can see she is trying to calve and something is wrong. Talking softly and moving slowly, he is able to get close enough to watch a contraction, but all that happens is one tiny hoof emerges slightly from below the cow's tail.

*Damn it!* Jack thinks. *Looks like I'll have to pull this one.* Waving his arms and walking purposefully toward the distressed cow, he is able to start her toward the barn, and once the cow realizes where she is going, she moves right along, only pausing during contractions. Jack thinks sometimes animals know when humans are trying to help them, and this old girl has borne enough calves to be pretty smart about it.

Once he gets the cow to the barn, he is able to maneuver her into a stanchion and secure her head before checking on the position of the unborn calf. Jack turns on the electric heater he had installed in this part of the barn and removes his coat and shirt, shivering in the cold. Standing in front of the heater, he greases his right arm from fingertip to shoulder with petroleum jelly from the jar stored on a shelf above the heater. Easing up behind the cow, Jack waits for a contraction to finish before sliding his greased hand gently inside her. He barely has room to move his fingers, but he can tell the calf has its head turned back into its shoulder and one leg folded, one of the worst possible ways for it to lie during delivery. Jack can get his hand in far enough to feel what is where, but he doesn't have room to make the necessary adjustments to the calf's position. Swearing under his breath, Jack wipes off his slimy arm, puts his shirt and coat back on and goes to get Brad. He is almost as strong as Jack but his hands and arms are still smaller than his father's.

While Jack is walking to the house, he decides against waking Brad. Today is a school day and Brad has a game that night and needs his sleep. Instead, he walks quietly to the bedroom and shakes Maggie awake.

She sits up, startled, staring around the room. "What's wrong?" she asks, realizing Jack is standing by the bed.

"I need your help to pull a calf," Jack tells her, already turning toward her dresser and pulling out drawers. Finding a tank top, he tosses it to her as she is sliding out from under the covers. "Put this on and then layer on top of it."

Maggie does as she is told, trying to clear the fog from her sleep-dazed mind while she dresses. When she is ready, Jack leads her through the house to the utility room and holds her coat for her. She slides her feet into her heavy boots and follows him out the back door toward the barn.

As they walk, she notices Jack is carrying his gun as well as a flashlight, and she wonders if he has run across any wolves tonight. He is walking so quickly ahead of her she has to trot to keep up, so she doesn't have a chance to ask him. Maggie steps into the relative warmth of the barn and sees the cow standing with its head in the stanchion.

Jack pulls her over in front of a small wall heater that is running full blast against the cold and tells her to take off her coat and all her layers of shirts except the tank top. When she is standing, shivering in front of him, he grabs the petroleum jelly and helps her grease her arm, then directs her over behind the cow.

"Just slide your hand inside," he tells her, "and feel for the calf's head."

Completely grossed out but determined to help her husband, Maggie holds her breath and closes her eyes before doing as Jack asks. The first thing she notices is the heat of the birth canal, and then bands of muscle close hard around her arm and hand as the cow experiences a contraction. Maggie feels the calf's turned head press into her arm, but the intense pressure is so painful she can't feel her own hand and is unable to determine anything else. As the contraction eases, Jack asks what she can feel. She tells him she can feel the head, but it seems to be turned.

Satisfied that Maggie is feeling the correct position of the calf, Jack says, "Okay, that's great. Now see if you can slip your hand around its nose and pull its head around."

Maggie does her best, but her hand keeps sliding off the nose.

"I can't hold on to it," she says, breathing hard and straining to grasp the slippery nose.

"Okay," Jack tells her. "Pull your arm out, and we'll try something else."

Maggie does as she is told, feeling a contraction push her hand the rest of the way out. She is grateful not to have to withstand the full strength of another one.

Jack is busy fashioning a slipknot in a short length of soft rope while Maggie stands shivering with one wet, slimy arm held away from her body. When he finishes, he hands it to Maggie and says, "Let's give it another go. Hold this in your hand and once you're in, put it over the calf's nose and try pulling his head around."

Maggie, once again, inserts her hand carefully inside the cow and reaches as far as she can to find the calf's head. Her face is close to the cow's hind end, and the smell is starting to get to her. Fortunately, Jack has tied the cow's tail up somehow so it isn't in Maggie's way. She slowly inches the little noose around the calf's nose and pulls it tight then starts to put gradual pressure on the rope, but just then, another contraction hits. The cow bellows in pain, and Maggie cries out as well, feeling like her arm is being crushed.

Jack steps up and puts his hands on Maggie's shoulders, talking to her softly in a reassuring tone, "You can do this, Maggie. Just hold on and then pull!" As soon as she feels the muscles of the birth canal start to soften, Maggie again pulls on the rope, firmly and steadily, and suddenly the head slides around in line with the rest of its body.

"Got it!" Maggie says in triumph. "It's around. Now what?" She slides the rope off the nose and waits for instructions.

"Now see if you can do the same thing with its other foot."

Straining with effort, Maggie pushes her arm even farther

inside the cow, feeling her way over the calf's knobby knee and down to the hoof. She fishes the noose over it and applies slow, steady pressure. The foot immediately comes around so the calf's head is resting on both legs with the feet pointing out.

"Good job!" Jack says, "Now get out of there."

"With pleasure," Maggie replies, quickly drawing her arm free. Barely has she stepped away when the cow gives a mighty heave, and the calf slides smoothly out and tumbles onto the straw at their feet. Jack steps up and loosens the stanchion so the cow can get free and then, pulling Maggie with him, gives the new family as much room as possible, the two of them standing quietly in the corner and watching as the mama cleans up her baby. Soon, the calf is on its feet, bumping its head impatiently into the cow's full udder as it tries to keep its balance on wobbly legs, and then, miracle of life, the calf is suckling.

Once Jack is sure the calf and cow have bonded, he turns his attention to Maggie, wiping her mucky, greasy arm clean with a piece of rag and helping his shivering wife back into her layers of shirts and her coat. While he is tugging the hem of her fleece sweater down around her slender hips, his hand grazes the soft, warm skin of her waist, and Jack is suddenly consumed with desire for his wife. It has been over a week since the last time they made love, and Jack feels the deprivation keenly. He drags up the sweater again and puts both hands on her waist, sliding them up her rib cage and pulling her into a passionate kiss.

Maggie responds with fervor, arching into his embrace and kissing him back with all her might, her chilly hands clenched around the back of his neck.

Not breaking the kiss, Jack stumbles backward, letting go of her with one hand to search for the door handle and walks Maggie into the next room, closing it behind them.

The small space they are in is a storage room for supplies for the cattle such as salt blocks and various tools and smells faintly of sulfur. It is dark with very little moonlight shining in through the one small window and very cold. Jack and Maggie break off their kiss, staring at each other in the faint light.

All Maggie can really see are Jack's eyes and the fog of their breath in the icy air, but she can feel the trembling tension in his hands on her waist, a tension she also feels coiling through her belly.

"Yes?" Jack asks softly, pulling her even closer.

"Yes. Please," Maggie answers. "I've missed you so much."

Jack's kiss cuts off anything else she might have said, and then everything is sensation instead of thought. Jack's mouth against hers, soft but firm, warm and wet and seeking, the prickle of his stubble burning against her tender skin; Jack's hands on her belly and then sliding up to her breasts before sweeping them down her body again to cup around her bottom, pressing her back into the cold wall of the storage room with the force of their embrace; Jack's scent, so beloved and familiar, and the sweet taste of him filling her with heat.

Suddenly, Maggie can wait no longer. "Now, Jack," she says urgently against his mouth. "Now, sweetheart. Please."

Jack is happy to comply with his wife's request but is having trouble figuring out the logistics due to the extreme cold, the almost complete dark, and the cramped quarters they find themselves in. Letting go of Maggie, he feels quickly around the small area and finally locates several full bags of grain on the floor. He drags them into the center of the room, creating a makeshift mattress, and then strips off his heavy coat and lays it over the rough burlap. "Come here," he commands, reaching for Maggie's hand and pulling her down beside him on their new bed. "You're going to have to take off at least one of your boots and get your jeans down if this is going to happen," he tells her, stroking her soft cheek in the dark and running his thumb over her full bottom lip.

He hears her breath catch at his caress, and the knowledge of her desire only kindles his own. Impatiently, he helps Maggie pull off one boot, and then he quickly tugs her jeans down over her hips, taking her panties with them, and Maggie kicks out of one leg of the confining garments as Jack covers her shivering body with his. He feels Maggie's hands at his belt and reaches between them to help her, and suddenly they are skin to skin. Jack feels like a teenager again, when hidden trysts were the norm, and every chance to make love was a miracle, and he knows that having this amazing woman love him is another miracle.

Jack wants to make love to Maggie slowly and tenderly and show her all she means to him, but the cold of the barn and the heat of her body immediately change his mind. Jack and Maggie quickly find themselves caught up in a storm of passion made even more intense by the forced abstinence of their conflicting schedules. As Maggie's body welcomes him, Jack loses track of all thought and there is only need, pulsing through him and shaking him to the core.

For Maggie, there is only Jack, driving her relentlessly up and up then sending her crashing over the top in wave after wave of glorious ecstasy. As their breathing slows, Maggie opens her eyes and realizes she can see the outline of Jack's head as he leans down to kiss her gently. "It's getting light," she whispers, smoothing his hair back with butterfly caresses of her trembling fingers. She can still feel him inside and above her and wishes briefly they could stay this way longer, but a shiver wracks her body and she can feel the cold biting into her bare skin.

"I can feel you shiver around me and under me, and as good as it is for me, you must be freezing," Jack murmurs. He pulls his knees under him and sits up, fastening his pants and belt before standing to give Maggie room to maneuver.

She reaches to her ankles and fishes her panties up from the foot still wearing a boot but can't seem to do the same with her jeans. Fumbling around in the dark, shaking from cold, she has to laugh. This is just too funny, making love in the barn in the freezing temperature when they have a perfectly good bed in a warm house.

Jack hears her chuckle in the gloom and asks, "What's so funny?"

"We are," Maggie answers cheerily. "Acting like a couple of horny teenagers instead of a middle-aged married couple. I can't get my jeans back on."

"Do you feel like a middle-aged married couple?" he asks, kneeling again to assist his wife. Going by touch alone, Jack can't figure out the tangled knot of denim either and moves to open the door quietly into the main barn where the cow and calf are. Light and warmth spill into the tiny storage room, illuminating the white skin of Maggie's bare legs and hips, and causing a new twist of desire to course through him.

*Will I ever get enough of this woman?* Jack thinks, and he knows the answer is no.

With the meager light helping, Maggie is able to see that one leg of the jeans has gotten turned inside out in her hurry to get them off, so she untangles them and pulls them up, but then she can't find her boot. "Jack, can you help me look for my boot?" she asks, feeling around on the floor.

Jack finally locates it pushed underneath one of the bags of grain. Once Maggie is dressed, she stands up and steps into the other room in front of the heater while Jack returns the grain to its original position before joining her.

The calf is curled in the straw on the floor sound asleep, and the cow is standing protectively over it. She moves restlessly as if to warn them away, so Jack picks up the rags and supplies they used and puts them away, the two lovers turn off the heater and the light and slip out the door into the icy dawn light.

Jack walks Maggie back to the house, not needing the flashlight anymore but keeping the gun at the ready just in case. He hasn't heard any howling for some time, but he hadn't really been thinking about wolves while they were in the barn. He also hasn't seen them this close to the house, but he isn't taking any chances. When they get to the back step, Maggie turns to Jack and says, "Join me in the shower?"

As much as he is tempted, Jack knows he needs to make one more round of the pasture and then do chores before cleaning up and getting some rest. "Sorry, love," he answers regretfully. "Although, that's not a bad idea. At least we'd be alone in there."

Maggie laughs as he wiggles his eyebrows suggestively and raises her face to his for a kiss.

Jack can feel her shivering and knows she needs to get

inside, so he keeps it short and shoos her through the door into the warm house and turns back to finish his vigil.

Maggie kicks off her boots in the mud room, hangs up her heavy coat, then hurries through the sleeping house to the woodstove to stir up the fire and add more wood. Her teeth are chattering and she is so cold her skin hurts, so she heads to the shower, the thought of where her hand and arm have recently been speeding her steps. Once in the bathroom, Maggie turns on the wall heater and quickly strips, dropping everything she was wearing into the laundry hamper in case it has calf gunk on it, and turns the water on as hot as it will go. When steam starts curling out from behind the shower curtain, she turns the hot water down and steps under the spray, reveling in the heat.

Gradually, she stops shivering, so she washes thoroughly, starting with her hand and arm. She has to laugh when she discovers a piece of straw stuck to her lower back, thoughts of making love with Jack in the barn filling her head. A few minutes later, Maggie is out of the shower and dressed. Pulling her wet hair into a quick ponytail, she heads to the kitchen to start coffee and then breakfast.

She doesn't know if it is the early hour, the strenuous task of helping with the calf, or great sex, but she is starving! When the hash browns are crisp and golden on one side, she turns them over, starts the sausage, and goes upstairs to wake the boys. It is only then that she remembers Caroline is there, and it is as if a weight has dropped over her shoulders. Shaking it off, Maggie is determined to hold on to her feeling of happiness and contentment and heads back to the kitchen to finish breakfast.

By the time she has breakfast on the table, the boys are thundering down the stairs like a small herd of buffalo. Just then, the back door opens and Jack comes in, bringing a waft of cold, clean air with him. He quickly washes up and joins them at the table, and again Maggie finds herself forgetting about Caroline as the four of them eat together and talk about the coming day. After breakfast, the boys offer to clear the table so Maggie goes to dry her hair and put on her makeup while Jack takes a shower.

Jack comes into the bedroom in his towel as Maggie is going

out. She stops for a goodbye kiss and then hurries out to get her bag and coat so they won't be late for school, while Jack climbs under the covers for some much-needed rest. Brad started Maggie's car when he started his pickup since he will have to stay late for practice, and it is nice and toasty when Maggie climbs in and follows the boys to town for school.

All day, the feeling of happiness stays with Maggie, and it seems to rub off on her students. The cold is forgotten as the kids eagerly work on the new project she has assigned, and Maggie finds herself humming under her breath as she walks among the children to supervise their work and answer questions. Even knowing Caroline will be up and underfoot when she gets home can't dampen Maggie's good spirits, and she heads to the parking lot after work with a light heart.

She spends the drive home planning dinner and daydreaming about her husband and the early morning's events. As Maggie pulls up in front of the house and gathers her school bag and purse, she mentally braces herself to face Caroline again, vowing to herself she will be nice no matter what.

Maggie steps into the utility room and happens to glance into the kitchen as she slips off her coat. She freezes in disbelief as she sees Jack and Caroline locked in what appears to be a passionate embrace. Caroline's arms are around Jack's neck, Jack's hands are on Caroline's waist, and they are kissing.

Maggie feels as if an iron band is wrapped around her chest, cold and hard and squeezing the breath from her lungs, traveling down her arms and causing her fingers to go numb and drop the bags she is carrying to the floor with a thud. The sound startles Jack and Caroline, and Maggie sees Jack push Caroline away, but the sick, guilty look on his face tells her all she needs to know.

Maggie bends to pick up the things she has just dropped, hot tears filling her eyes and blurring her vision as she gropes on the floor for her bags. Her ears are ringing, her stomach is rolling, and she still feels as if she can't breathe. There is no conscious thought in her mind, just an overwhelming need to get out of there, to get as far away from the two of them as possible. Finally, her questing hands locate the straps to her purse and bag with school papers in it, and she straightens with her coat still draped over one arm.

Jack is almost to her, his beloved face creased with anxious concern, and she wants to just go to him and let him tell her this is all a mistake, but then she sees Caroline still standing in the kitchen with her lips curved in a triumphant smile. Shaking her head in dismay, Maggie turns and bolts out the back door into the freezing cold of the winter evening, the sky already darkening toward another long night.

Her hands are shaking so badly she has trouble opening the door to the car, but she finally gets the handle to release and blindly climbs in, flinging her coat and bags into the passenger seat and slamming it behind her. Through the frosted window, she can see Jack coming off the porch after her and hastens to start the car. She pulls around the drive and onto the road as fast as she can without spinning the tires on the icy surface and leaves Jack standing there, his hands raised in supplication. By now Maggie is sobbing uncontrollably, barely able to see the road through the tears, but she is determined to get away from the pain of this betrayal.

She drives without thinking, letting her familiarity with the road guide her hands while her mind struggles to come to grips with what just happened. The scene keeps flashing before her—Jack with his mouth on Caroline's mouth, his hands on Caroline's waist, his face as he realizes Maggie has seen them. She wants to believe it is a misunderstanding, that she really hasn't seen them kissing, that there is a reasonable explanation for it, but she knows she is just trying to make herself feel better. The reality is she has walked in on her husband with his ex-wife in his arms, and nothing can change it or make it less hurtful.

Maggie realizes at some level she has been waiting for something like this to happen, perhaps as punishment for daring to try to be happy again. After all, what right does she have to be happy when Clark is dead? This question causes even more tears, her shoulders shaking with the force of her crying.

Eventually, Maggie reaches the edge of town, bright lights shining from the houses, families going about their evening routines with no idea her world has just shattered. Until she pulls into Tracy's driveway, Maggie doesn't realize she is planning to go there, but her need for an understanding ear guides her to her big sister's house. She finds a tissue in the door pocket and tries to wipe her eyes and blow her nose before getting out of the car and going to the door, but as soon as Tracy opens it, Maggie starts crying again.

"What happened?" Tracy asks with concern, enfolding her younger sister in her arms. It takes Maggie some time before she can control her sobs enough to answer, and then the whole thing spills out—the strain of having Caroline in the house, the increasing distance between herself and Jack, and the final scene tonight. By this time, Tracy has led her into the warm, bright kitchen, and they are seated at the table, Maggie holding a hot cup of tea in her trembling hands as she tells her sister what happened. It seems ironic to Maggie that it was in this same kitchen where she first met Jack. Finally out of words, Maggie falls silent, sipping her tea and feeling totally exhausted.

"What are you going to do?" Tracy asks gently, lifting her sister's hair from her tear-stained face to look into her eyes.

"I don't know," Maggie answers miserably, twisting her cup and watching the tea slosh from side to side. "I've never had something like this happen before. I feel so sad and angry and humiliated right now. How could he? I believed him when he said he loved me!" Setting the cup down, Maggie springs from the chair and paces the room in agitation.

Tracy watches her, hurting for her sister but unable to think of anything to say that might help. "That bitch!" Maggie continues. "I think she was after him all along. I think as soon as her husband died, she decided she wanted Jack back. Well, now she can have him, because I don't want to ever see him again!" With this proclamation, she sinks back into the chair again and buries her face in her hands. "Oh, Tracy, this hurts so much!" she wails, leaning forward in agony.

"I know it does, sweetie, but you'll be okay. Whatever you decide, I'll help you through it, and you'll be fine," Tracy reassures her, stroking Maggie's hair while her sister huddles in the chair in utter despair. Inwardly, Tracy really isn't sure if Maggie will be okay. Jack's betrayal so soon after Clark's death is bound to deeply affect her, possibly with lasting results. All Tracy can do is offer loving support and hope for the best. She can't believe Jack would hurt Maggie like this. Maybe Maggie has misunderstood what she saw. It is the only ray of hope Tracy can find in the sad tale, and she vows to talk to Jack and get his side of the story.

Finally, Maggie's tears subside and she sits up with a sigh, reaching for tissue to blow her nose.

"I'm sorry to lay all this on you," she says brokenly. "I just didn't know where else to go."

"It's fine. Really. I'm glad you came here. Do you feel like you could eat something?" Tracy asks.

"No, I feel like I could throw up though. Why do I always get nauseous when I'm upset?"

"It's better than being an emotional eater," Tracy responds. "At least you won't be miserable AND fat!"

Maggie manages a laugh at this and reaches over to hug her sister. "Thanks, Tracy. You always make me feel better."

"That's what I'm here for, doll," Tracy says affectionately. "If you don't want food, how about a hot shower and a soft bed?"

"No, thanks, sis. I think I'm going to go home … I mean to my old home. I still have stuff there in case we're ever stuck in town. I need some time to process this."

With this, Maggie rises from her chair and heads to the door. Tracy walks her out and again invites Maggie to stay there, but Maggie is determined to go home.

She drives to the house where she had lived so happily with Clark and the children and pulls into the garage. Gathering her willpower along with her coat and bags, she gets out, shuts the garage door, and walks into the house. It is quiet, cold, and musty-smelling and feels very empty. Maggie flips on the light, hangs up her coat, drops her purse on the counter, and lays her school bag on the kitchen table before turning up the heat. As the furnace kicks on, she walks through the house to use the bathroom, avoiding looking in the mirror because she knows she is a mess. By the time she washes her hands, the house has started to warm up. Maggie wanders into the living room, looking around disconsolately. Very little is left of the cozy home she and Clark shared, and the house looks as lonely as Maggie feels.

Even though it is only about 7:00, to Maggie it feels as if it is midnight. Her mind is still feverishly replaying the awful episode, and she knows it would be useless to try to sleep, but she feels tired to her very core and has no idea what to do with the rest of the evening.

Belatedly, she realizes that Brad and Trent will be coming home to their parents, and she won't be there, and this makes her start crying again. Maybe Jack and Caroline getting back together will be best for the boys, but in her heart, Maggie knows they will just be hurt again, and she won't be around to help. She hopes Jack will be able to come up with a good explanation for her absence in the meantime.

Maggie thinks about calling Maura, but doesn't feel up to going over the whole thing again, and besides, she knows how much Maura has come to like Jack and hates to spoil Maura's night. Maybe when things have time to settle and she has come to some sort of decision, then she will make the call. This train of thought brings back memories of the last time she and Maura saw each other, the weekend of Maggie and Jack's wedding, and causes more heartache.

*How could things have come to this in so short a time?* Maggie wonders. *I was so happy that day.*

As the night wears on, Maggie alternates between despair and anger and is still unresolved as to how to handle the situation. She tries to imagine confronting Jack and telling him they are finished, but can't bring herself to see the end of the scene. She tries to imagine Jack apologizing and begging her to come home, but that doesn't seem possible either. She thinks about calling the house to check on the boys and say goodnight but doesn't know how she will react if Jack answers. She actually goes to get her cell phone from her purse, but it isn't there. After a thorough search of the bag, her school bag, and the car, she realizes the phone must have fallen out when she dropped her purse in the utility room at the ranch earlier.

Finally, in an attempt to distract herself, she gets out her school papers and tries to grade essays. After reading one through several times and still not knowing what it is about, she gives up on the idea and decides to take a shower. Maybe it will help her relax, and she will be able to sleep after all. Surprisingly, it works and Maggie falls immediately into a deep, dreamless sea of rest.

# CHAPTER 38

While Maggie sleeps the deep sleep of emotional exhaustion, Jack is making the rounds checking cows in sub-zero temperatures, while guilt, remorse, and anger eat at his soul. He keeps seeing Maggie's shocked-stricken face and the disgust and condemnation in her expression as she turned to leave. He keeps seeing her getting in her car and driving away and leaving him standing alone in the driveway. *What the hell happened?* Jack asks himself. He remembers waking up late that afternoon, his first thought of Maggie and making love to her in the barn earlier that morning, and feeling relaxed and happier than he has since Caroline came to stay with them. He hummed as he dressed, looking forward to seeing Maggie when she came home from work.

Jack felt a brief moment of exasperation when he went into the bathroom and saw Caroline's clothes and makeup and hair accessories scattered around carelessly in the previously tidy room, but told himself to relax and let it go. He was still in a good mood as he entered the kitchen and managed to reply pleasantly when Caroline said hello and started a conversation. Jack fixed himself a snack and sat at the kitchen table to eat while he listened to her babble on about some television show she had watched that morning.

As he finished eating, Jack saw Maggie's car pulling into the drive and watched her get out and walk toward the house, enjoying the way the setting sun sparkled off her shiny hair, turning it to a coppery halo. He took his plate to the sink as she came in the door, and it was as he stepped away from the sink that disaster struck. Caroline had quietly moved up close behind him and as he turned, he ran right into her, almost knocking her down, so he grabbed her by the waist to keep her from falling. She threw her arms around him to get her balance, or so he assumed, but then as he started to ask her what she thought she was doing, she reached up and kissed him. His mouth was open because he was talking, and her kiss caught him so much by surprise that he simply froze, not really registering what was happening through the shock of her open mouth warmly and wetly pressed to his.

The sound of something falling startled him back to reality, and he jerked away from Caroline, seeing over her shoulder the sight of Maggie's face as she stood in the utility room with her bags at her feet and her coat over one arm. Jack knew he should go to her or at least say something, but he felt as if he were in a nightmare where movement is impossible and speech doesn't exist. It wasn't until Maggie picked up her things and went out the door that he was finally able to break free from his daze and run after her. By then she was in the car, and then she was gone.

Jack was trembling with anger, fear, and remorse when he re-entered the house, and seeing Caroline's smirking face was enough to put him over the edge.

"Well, she didn't seem to like that much, did she?" Caroline said, laughing with triumph. "Oh, the look on her face! Priceless!"

"You bitch!" Jack said bitterly, stalking toward his ex-wife. "You planned that whole thing!"

"Of course," Caroline said archly. "Didn't you like it? It's been a long time since we've kissed."

"Never would be too soon for me! Do you realize what you've done?"

"Yes. I showed that patronizing, self-righteous, mealy-mouthed goody-two-shoes what it's like to watch another woman kiss her husband. I hope she got the message, and I hope she never comes back!"

"I haven't been your husband for years!" Jack shouted, losing what self-control he had left at this criticism of Maggie. "Even when we were married, you didn't want me, so now that I'm finally happy, you come around here and try to ruin it. Well, I've got news for you. I'm not going to let you. Maggie is a big enough person to see through your manipulations, and you'll be the one who never comes back. You're lucky I'm not a violent man or, so help me God, I would make you regret this! Now get out of my sight before I change my mind!"

Caroline seemed to realize that her little scheme wasn't going to have the effect she intended and backed slowly from the kitchen toward the stairs, away from Jack's anger, never taking her eyes off her enraged ex-spouse. When she reached the foot of the stairs, she turned and quickly ran up. Jack could hear her start crying before she was halfway to the top, but he had no sympathy in his heart for her, nor did he believe the tears were anything except an act meant to make him feel bad. He did feel bad, but it was for himself and Maggie, not Caroline.

Blowing out his breath in a huge sigh, Jack's shoulders slumped in defeat. He had no idea what to do next—no idea how to go about getting his wife back home and setting things to rights between them. All he knew was how much he loved Maggie and that he would do anything to make this up to her. He just hoped she would let him.

Now on his third round of the pasture, his feet feeling like blocks of ice, his cheeks and nose numb despite the scarf wrapped around his head and face, Jack is trying to keep his mind from even considering the possibility that Maggie might not come back. After Caroline went upstairs, Jack waited in the kitchen, hoping Maggie would turn around and he would hear her car crunching on the ice as she returned, but the only car that pulled in was Brad's pickup as the boys got home from basketball practice.

They were surprised and concerned to see Jack sitting motionless at the table in the empty kitchen. Jack told them he and Maggie had an argument and she went out for some air, hoping it might be true, and then got up and started dinner. He could tell his sons were confused and upset, but they both politely refrained from asking any questions and simply joined him in preparing the meal, not even asking where their mother was. After dinner, they helped him clear the table and do the dishes without complaint, all of them listening for the sound of Maggie's car, but to no avail.

Finally, Trent said, "Dad, just call her. It's dark and it's late, and she should be home by now. Call her."

Knowing his son was right, Jack dialed Maggie's cell phone, holding his breath as he waited for it to ring, not sure she would answer and not sure of what he would say if she did. What he didn't expect was to hear it ringing in the utility room. He walked toward the sound and saw her phone lying on the floor near the edge of the washer, and he remembered Maggie dropping her purse when she saw Caroline and him kissing. He hung up, cursing under his breath, and stooped to pick it up. Carrying the phone back to the kitchen, he handed it to Trent.

"Take this to Maggie at school tomorrow. I'm sure she's either at Tracy's or at her old house. Things will look better in the morning, and I'm sure she'll call or come back home tomorrow." Jack turned away from his son's troubled eyes and walked back to the utility room to get ready to go check the cows. "You two need to do your homework and get to bed. If you need anything, your mom is upstairs."

This was the last conversation Jack had before going out into the cold for his nightly vigil. Now he is wondering if he should have told the boys the truth about what happened because who knows what story Caroline will spin for them while Jack isn't around to point out the truth.

He is also wondering if he has made a mistake by not going after Maggie when she left. His gut tells him to give her some space and some time to think, but he realizes Maggie doesn't know Caroline the way he does and has no idea the depth of her vindictive, manipulative nature. He is still extremely angry at his former wife, but part of his anger is directed at Maggie as well for not trusting him enough to even question what she thought she saw and for walking away instead of fighting for their relationship.

He is so deep in thought he almost doesn't see the quick flash of movement in the trees to his right, but some instinct brings him around just in time to catch a glimpse of eyes in the beam of his flashlight as a large gray wolf darts out of sight. Jack is instantly on high alert, spinning to pan the edge of the forest for more of the pack, knowing where there is one, there probably are more, but his questing gaze can't detect any other animals, and they definitely aren't making any noise to help him locate them. Jack stands still and listens to the cattle, their lowing and restless stamping a sure sign of a predator in the vicinity, but all is quiet. This makes Jack believe the wolf is alone, probably out scouting for prey, so he resumes his trek around the pasture.

Although the need to be more aware of his surroundings is urgent enough to push the situation with Maggie to the back of his mind, Jack continues to stew over it, alternating between despair, anger, hope, and guilt. The sight of his sons' worried faces at the breakfast table when he finally stumbles in, frozen and exhausted, doesn't do anything to alleviate his pain.

"Do you think Maggie will talk to us?" Trent asks hesitantly. "Was she pretty mad?"

"She was pretty mad, Trent, but she's mad at me, not you. I'm sure she'll treat you the same as she always does. In fact, I'm sure we'll figure this out soon, and everything will be back to normal." As Jack speaks, he finds himself praying that his words are true. Soon the boys are off to school, and he stumbles wearily into the living room to stoke the fire before undressing and crawling into bed. This morning is a far cry from yesterday, when he was enjoying the afterglow from making love to his wife, but Jack is so tired and heartsick, he falls straight to sleep anyway.

Catherine Bridwell

# CHAPTER 39

Maggie wakes in the night with a start, knowing something is wrong, and looks around her in bewilderment. The clock beside the bed says 2:41 a.m., and she knows she is home, but it isn't supposed to be home anymore. Suddenly, the memory of what happened between Jack and Caroline the previous day comes back to her. Her stomach feels as if a hard, hot ball of lead has been dropped into it.

Completely awake now, Maggie turns on her side and curls into a ball, pulling her knees into her for comfort as she tries to come to terms with the painful images rolling through her brain. Looking back on it, Maggie is actually surprised at her own reaction. She is not normally the type of person who gives up without a fight, but this time she fled at the first sign of a battle. What can that mean? Maggie knows she has been feeling increasingly out of place at the ranch ever since Caroline moved in and realizes subconsciously she has been questioning her right to be there, her right to be in Jack's life at all since his ex-wife returned, and most of all her right to be in Brad and Trent's lives now that their real mom is back.

A small voice in the back of her mind whispers, *I told you so. That's what you get for daring to be happy when your husband is dead.* "Shut up!" Maggie says out loud, startling herself in the deep quiet of the empty house.

At that moment, she realizes that ever since she first became attracted to Jack, she has been waiting for some sort of retribution, some higher power to send down punishment because part of her is still so guilty to feel the way she does about him, especially so soon after losing Clark. Even the reassurances of Father Murphy, while comforting, have not really convinced Maggie it is okay to love Jack.

Maggie feels as though a light has come on inside her head,

shining brightly as it illuminates her actions over the past few weeks. From the day Caroline moved in, Maggie has quietly but surely pulled back from everyone, letting Caroline take over in a myriad of ways. From the mess in the bathroom to the dinner conversation, Caroline was in control because Maggie let her be. Jack's nightly patrol of the pasture only added to the situation, turning the family's schedule upside down and taking away any chance for Jack and Maggie to talk privately, to discuss what was happening in their home.

Maggie rolls onto her back and stares at the dark ceiling, letting the revelations sink in. While it isn't Maggie's fault Jack and Caroline kissed, it is Maggie's fault that Caroline felt empowered enough to touch him. When Maggie rolls the scene through her head again, she sees Caroline kissing Jack and Jack pulling away and realizes she has played right into Caroline's hands, letting herself be driven away from her own home. She should have stayed and confronted the situation right then, but Caroline was counting on Maggie jumping to conclusions and running. Maggie feels ashamed for the way she treated Jack, not even letting him explain, and driving away while he tried to stop her. She wants to do something about it right now, but it is after 3:00 a.m. and she doesn't even have a working phone in her possession.

Maggie spends the remainder of the night tossing and turning as sleep eludes her, planning how she is going to rectify the situation, so when her alarm finally goes off at 6:00, she is already awake and quickly jumps out of bed to face the day. When she first gets to school, she thinks about calling Jack from the phone in the teacher's lounge but feels it is too public a place for her to say what she needs to say. She misses her cell phone dearly. The day seems to drag as Maggie watches the clock and thinks about what she wants to tell Jack when she finally talks to him.

She is very surprised to find her cell phone on her desk when she walks back into her classroom after noon recess and can only surmise one of the boys has dropped it off, but since they are already back in class, it is too late for her to contact them. She considers calling Jack right then, but knows she will wake him, and before she can decide whether or not to dial, it is time for her class to resume. A part of her is a little relieved to put off the difficult conversation for a while, but she also longs to put it behind them and go back home where she belongs.

By the time school is out, Maggie has decided to wait and talk to Jack in person rather than over the phone, but her plans are short-lived when the principal, Mrs. Thompson, walks in and reminds Maggie of the PTA meeting that evening. Maggie is tempted to just blow it off and go home, but they are planning the annual Valentine's Day party and Maggie is the chairperson of the planning committee. The hours between the end of school and the start of the meeting drag by. Maggie grades papers and tidies up the house, and then there is nothing else to do. She knows she should eat but can't bring herself to try her nervous stomach with food. She thinks about going over to Tracy's but doesn't feel like talking to her sister about it again.

Finally, at about 6:00, fed up with worrying, Maggie drives to the church, parks, and goes inside. Kneeling in the warm quiet, she bows her head to pray, letting all the hurt, anger, pride, and jealousy spill out into the care of the One who gives unconditional love and forgiveness. Maggie feels herself emptied out and made new again, filled with hope and love. With tears in her eyes, she gives thanks and rises from her kneeling position to sit in the pew. She has left her phone in the car out of habit when entering the church, so she doesn't know how long she has been there, but it is long enough that her knees and back are hurting from kneeling. The PTA meeting seems far away and unimportant, and all she can think of is healing the rift between her and Jack.

Just as Maggie is starting to rise to leave, the door to the church bursts open. She turns in time to see Jack coming across the entry and hurries to meet him.

Jack sweeps her into a hard hug, kissing her up-turned face frantically before pulling away to speak. "The boys didn't come home tonight. Have you seen them?" he asks, his eyes filled with worry.

"No, I haven't seen them at all today. One of them brought me my phone, but I must have been in the teacher's room or something when they came over. When were they supposed to be home?" Maggie asks.

"An hour ago. Trent stayed in town to play video games with his friends, and Brad had an early

short practice. They should have been home by 5:30. I started calling at 6:00, first their cell phones and then their friends. Brad picked Trent up at 5:00, so something happened between there

283

and home. I watched for them all the way to town, but didn't see any sign of Brad's pickup. Where could they be?" Jack lets go of Maggie and paces the small entryway of the church. "Do you think they ran off or something?"

"No, I'm sure there's a logical explanation. Maybe Brad had car trouble and stopped to get something fixed or maybe they stopped to eat," Maggie offers.

"I drove through town and didn't see them anywhere," Jack says. "I just have a bad feeling something is wrong!"

"Well, then we'll just have to find them and make sure they're okay," Maggie replies. "Let's go."

Their recent troubles forgotten in the urgency of worry over the boys, Jack and Maggie leave the church hand in hand to search for the missing teenagers.

# CHAPTER 40

Jack is right, and something is indeed very wrong. Brad's basketball practice finished early because they have a game the next day and half the team is sick. The coach goes over the offense a few times and then sends them home, so Brad picks Trent up at 5:00 and the two head home as usual.

Trent is skipping around on the radio dial trying to find a song he likes and talking to his brother about the game he and his friends are currently involved in, and Brad is trying to keep all the characters straight as he listens when a deer comes down the bank and crosses the road in front of the pickup. Brad instinctively hits the brakes, but the road is so icy they just start sliding right toward the running animal. Brad whips the wheel to the right to avoid hitting the deer, and the pickup slides sideways down the road before hitting the frozen drift on the edge of the upcoming corner and going airborne.

To Brad, it seems as though everything is in slow motion and at the same time happening too fast to comprehend. One second everything is okay and the next, they are sliding, hitting, flying, and then the world goes dark.

When Brad opens his eyes, he thinks at first it must be a school day, because he is awake and it is still dark, but the light is wrong for his bedroom and a feeling of disaster lurks in the back of his mind. The feeling gathers momentum, bursting into the memory of the truck going off the icy road and turning slowly mid-air, falling and falling before crashing into the deep snow below the road.

Brad struggles to sit up, not understanding at first why it is so difficult. After fighting uselessly for several seconds, he realizes the truck is on its side and the seatbelt is holding him, dangling above the driver-side window, which is buried in snow. Brad feels around in the gloom of the cab to locate the seatbelt latch and pushes the release button. He falls onto the window with his hip, shoulder, and head and scrambles to a sitting position, looking frantically around the cab. The engine isn't running but the dashboard lights are still glowing, and in the dim light, Brad reaches up around the steering column and turns the key to the auxiliary position. He doesn't think they are in danger of catching on fire, but he doesn't want to make their situation more difficult. His next thought is his little brother.

"Trent!" Brad says, his voice hoarse with fear. "Hey, buddy. You okay?"

A faint moan is the only answer, and using the light from the dash, Brad is able to locate Trent hanging from his seatbelt above, his eyes closed and his head drooping limply toward the ground. Brad stands up carefully and puts his arms around Trent, supporting his brother's weight as he releases the seatbelt and lowers the smaller boy to the bottom of the cab, maneuvering around the steering wheel. Trent's eyes open, and Brad can see he is trying to figure out where he is.

"Hey, man. We had a little accident," Brad says, squatting beside him and trying to speak calmly and quietly. "How do you feel? Are you hurt anywhere?"

Trent's eyes clear and he mumbles something, and as Brad leans closer to hear what Trent said, he bumps his knee into Trent's shin and the boy lets out a piercing scream.

"Guess you're hurt after all, bro," Brad says, easing down beside Trent and gingerly propping his brother against the seat back of the sideways pickup. "Let's see what's going on."

"No, no, don't touch me!" Trent yells. "It'll hurt! Don't touch me!"

"Okay, take it easy," Brad says. "I won't touch you. Just calm down and tell me where it hurts."

"My leg, between my knee and my ankle. It's on fire."

"Anywhere else? How's your head and neck? What about your arms?"

Trent shakes his head in denial and eventually, Brad determines the only injury either one has sustained is Trent's leg which appears to be broken. Brad doesn't say it out loud, but he can tell by the way Trent's eyes dart away when he looks at it and sees how his foot doesn't quite match the angle of the leg that Trent knows it isn't good.

Brad finds his cell phone in his pocket and tries to call for help, but the stretch of road where they slid off is outside cell service. Looking into his brother's frightened, pain-stricken eyes, Brad feels his own fear bubbling to the surface, replacing the rush of adrenaline he is riding and leaving him feeling shaky and near tears. In an effort to hold back the rising tide of panic that threatens to engulf him, Brad settles carefully onto the driver's window with his back to the roof beside his brother and tries to regain his composure.

*What would Dad do? What would Maggie do?* Brad asks himself, focusing on his breathing and opening his mind to solutions instead of clogging his thoughts with panic. *Trent is hurt and can't walk. We don't have cell service. I can't get the truck back on its wheels or back on the road, so I'll have to go for help.* Brad comes to this conclusion after several minutes of intense concentration, thinking of other solutions and discarding them just as quickly.

"Hey, Trent," Brad finally speaks. "I need to go get someone to help you out of here and get you to the hospital. Do you think you can hang out here until I get back?"

"No! Don't leave me here!" Trent quickly replies. "I don't want to be alone. What if something happens to you and nobody ever finds me? I don't want to die!" His flushed face, trembling lips, and eyes on the verge of tears convince Brad that he won't be able to leave his little brother in the truck alone.

"Okay, okay, calm down," Brad says. "I won't leave you. Let's try to figure out another plan. How's your leg feeling?"

"It hurts," Trent answers, still about to cry. "What's going to happen to us, Brad?"

"Dad will find us," Brad reassures him. "We just have to stay here and wait for him. Let's make sure we stay warm." As he tries to comfort Trent, Brad is aware of the cold quickly creeping into his rear and legs through the glass of the side window and knows he needs to keep his brother warm to avoid shock. Brad stands as carefully as he can, trying not to bump Trent in the process and edges around the now-vertical front seat into the back seat. There is just enough light for Brad to see to pull the back seat forward and reach the extra blankets and coats Jack makes him keep there. Moving into the front again, he kneels down and, taking Trent under the arms, pulls him to a standing position, cautioning his brother to keep his weight off the injured leg. With Trent leaning on him for support, Brad quickly spreads his heaviest coat over the window then lowers the younger boy back down. Brad sits down beside him and covers both of them with several blankets. He is hoping their combined body heat will be enough to keep them from freezing to death while waiting for someone to come.

After a few minutes, Brad feels Trent's tense body start to relax as he leans against his brother, and Brad lets the feeling seep into himself. He lets his eyes rove the cab of the truck as he tries to come up with a better solution to their predicament.

Brad realizes the pickup is buried in the snow at least the height of the windshield since he can see the white wall pressed against the glass. Not even the headlights are shining through, and the radio isn't picking up a station, so the only sounds are the breathing of the two frightened boys. It occurs to him to see if they can even get out of the vehicle, so he eases out from under the blankets, tucking them back around Trent while he explains his plan.

Brad steps up onto the steering column in order to reach the passenger door overhead and tries to open it. At first, nothing happens, and then as he gives an extra hard shove, the door moves just enough to dump a glob of snow right into his upturned face. With a yelp of surprise, Brad lets the door slam shut again and shakes the cold, wet snow out of his eyes before climbing back down to his brother.

"At least we can get out if we have to," he tells Trent. "The bad part is, I think most of the truck is buried, so it will be hard for anyone to see it down here."

"What if they can't find us?" Trent asks in a small voice, not looking at his brother.

"Well, then I'll have to leave you here and go for help whether you like it or not," Brad replies. "I'm not planning on spending the rest of the night here."

"Ok," Trent says, his voice shaking a little. "I think you should go before it gets any later."

"Are you sure?" Brad asks. "I think it's the best thing to do, but I want you to be okay with it too."

"Yes, I'm sure," Trent says more strongly. "See if you can climb out and get up to the road first, and if you can, then come back down and shut the door again and start toward town."

"All right, then," Brad says, glad to have something concrete to do. Once again, he extricates himself from the blankets and wraps them tightly back around his brother.

This time he puts one foot on the steering column and the other against the back of the front seat to get more leverage and then, using both hands, pushes up against the door with all his strength. Slowly, the door opens, dumping more snow on both of them, but this time they are prepared and Brad doesn't stop pushing until the door is standing straight up, and he can see the stars through the opening. Taking a deep breath of the frigid air, he gets a firm grip on the edges of the door frame and carefully pulls himself up through the opening and onto the side of the wrecked pickup. He gingerly finds his footing on the slippery surface and stands up.

Brad's analysis of their situation has been spot-on. They have gone off the road at the one spot where there are no trees to block their flight, and the pickup is buried under about 18 inches of snow dropped onto it by the impact of the landing. He thinks about trying to unbury it with his hands, but it occurs to him it will help insulate the vehicle and keep Trent warmer while he is gone. Leaning down to look back inside, he can see his little brother in the glow of the dash lights with his face tilted up inquiringly.

"Can you see the road?" Trent asks, a tremor of hope in his voice.

Brad straightens and looks back up the steep slope, straining to make out the berm of snow that marks the edge of the road.

"No, man," he stoops back down to reply. "We're a long way down and it's almost completely dark now. I'm going to try to walk up."

"Ok," comes the faint reply as Brad moves across the truck toward the uphill side, feeling with his feet through the snow for the edge. When he is sure of his footing, he gathers himself and then steps off, sinking immediately to his hips in the deep snow. Brad lunges uphill, trying to reach firmer ground, but the snow is too deep, and he slides right back into his own tracks. Snow is going up his pant legs into his boots, melting when it touches his warm skin and leaving an icy dampness all along both legs. He has no gloves, so he pulls his hands up into the sleeves of his coat and buries his face as deep into the collar as he can to keep the freezing air from burning his nose and lungs. Looking up the steep slope above him, Brad feels despair and hopelessness hovering near, and with the resolve of desperation, he begins again. This time he moves slowly, stomping down the snow as best he can to make a sort of trail, sliding back again and again, but very gradually making progress up the hill. He feels quite warm from all his struggles and is just starting to believe he might actually make it to the road eventually when he hears it.

Brad stands stock still and scans the nearby forest, listening intently, but the only sound now is his own ragged breathing. Shaking his head and chastising himself as an idiot, the boy continues his difficult task, all the while trying to watch the forest and listen while he works. A flicker of motion catches his eye off to the left, and he whirls in that direction, but there is nothing there. A branch cracking on the slope above startles him, and he lets out a soft exclamation of surprise, again straining his ears in the snow-muffled silence that surrounds him. Something has made the branch crack, and Brad is afraid he knows what it is. The sweat on his face turns icy with fear as again he senses motion on his left. This time he stands still and very, very slowly turns only his head. At first he doesn't see anything. The gloom under the trees in the starry, snow-glowing night is very deep, but Brad lets his eyes relax and lose focus and then at last he sees it—a low, gray shape, slinking stealthily from one tree to another, barely noticeable unless a person is looking for it. Again, a branch snaps from above and as Brad turns to look up toward the road, an unearthly howl splits the night. Brad's shriek of fright is lost in the answering howl from the boy's left, as the two wolves communicate the location of their prey with their primitive hunting calls.

The whole forest seems to wait with bated breath as the mournful lament fades to silence. Brad stands in his tracks, trembling, trying not to cry, as the realization hits him. He is not going to make it to the road. The wolf pack hanging around the area has found him, and they are hungry. With that thought, Brad turns with a hoarse cry and lunges back down the hard-earned trail he has made toward the pickup.

In his haste, he loses his footing and slides the last few feet, banging into the cab with a painful thud. Stunned for a moment, Brad lies in the snow, his heart beating like a roaring train in his chest. Willing himself to move despite the panic that wants to immobilize him, he digs his frozen hands into the snow and pushes himself to his feet and feels along the truck toward the bed. As soon as he can find purchase for his feet, he scrambles up to the open door and quickly descends back into the gloom of the cab, slamming the door shut over his head. Covered with snow from his fall, wet, cold, and exhausted from breaking trail, the frightened boy still has the presence of mind to try to protect his younger brother. Trent is sitting where Brad left him, shivering in the blankets, his face white from pain and fear.

"Hey, buddy, little change of plans," Brad gasps, as he tries to compose himself. "Let's stay here where it's warm and wolves can't get in. By morning, they'll be gone, and I'll walk out. You okay with that?" His voice is shaking, but he tries to project an air of authority to soothe the younger boy.

"Sure, Brad," Trent says, his eyes even wider. "Whatever you think is best. How many are out there?"

"I don't know," Brad answers, trying to brush the snow off without getting it on the injured boy. "I saw one and heard two, but there could be more. You know they run in packs."

Trying to act casual, Brad fits himself around the steering wheel into the spot next to Trent and pulls the covers up around them both. His heart is still racing and he is still breathing hard, but he doesn't want Trent to know just how scared he is. "How's the leg?" he asks.

"It still hurts, but I'm pretending it doesn't," Trent answers. "Dad's coming, right, Brad?" he asks, his tone begging for reassurance.

"Yes, Trent, Dad's coming," Brad answers, offering the comfort his brother needs and trying to believe it. "Just try to rest."

# CHAPTER 41

Jack is coming just as fast as he can, which is not very fast at all considering how slowly he is driving to make sure they don't miss something along the road that might tell him and Maggie what has happened to his sons. They are in Jack's pickup, lights on bright, creeping up the road from town, eyes glued to the road, sure that the next corner or the one after that will show them what they are seeking—Brad's pickup parked on the side of the road.

Periodically, Maggie calls the boys' cell phones, but both are going straight to voicemail, a sign they are out of service. Frustrated, Maggie slips her cell phone back into her purse, frantic with worry. Suddenly, a connection is made in her brain, a connection so obvious she groans out loud in aggravation.

"What?" Jack asks, turning to her.

"Cell service!" Maggie answers. "Where on the road do we always lose service? That's where we need to start looking, not down here where their phones would work! Why didn't I think of it sooner?" she says, clenching her hands together anxiously.

"It doesn't matter," Jack says, pressing down on the accelerator so the pickup seems to jump forward. "You thought of it now!"

Wordlessly, the two sit tensely in the vehicle, watching the glow of the headlights glare off the icy road and snow-mounded edges ahead of them as the road grows narrower and more winding, climbing upward toward the ranch. In a few minutes, although it seems much longer, they reach the place in the road where their cell phones always lose service and, once again, Jack slows down to a crawl as they search ahead and beside the road for a trace of the boys or the pickup they were driving. They are almost at the end of that section of road, and Maggie is getting a sick feeling in her stomach when they both see it at the same time. Jack stops as quickly as he can on the slick road, and they both sit speechless, not quite daring to say anything.

Finally, Jack turns to Maggie. "Do you see what I see?" he asks quietly, as if afraid she might not affirm his conclusion.

"It looks like someone slid right here, then spun sideways and kept sliding," Maggie answers, looking closely at the road in the headlights. "Go a little further, but slowly," she says.

Jack does as she asks, creeping down the road toward the big sweeping corner ahead of them. The trees are thick here on both sides of the road, casting heavy shadows, except for one spot right in the middle of the corner where, for no reason except the ironies of nature, the foliage parts and in daylight, a person can see out over the valley below. Tonight, however, Jack and Maggie's eyes are drawn to something else—a mark on the three-foot high barrier of snow the plows have pushed up along the edges of the road, a mark that might be from a pickup hitting it before going up and over the top.

Coming to a stop again, Jack puts the truck in park and gets two flashlights out from under the seat beneath him. Handing one to Maggie, he reaches overhead and takes his gun from the gun rack, and the two of them step out into the frozen evening. It is very quiet and gloomy, and if she wasn't so worried, she would say it was beautiful, with the snow reflecting back the starlight against the black shadows of the evergreens. She and Jack make their way to the frozen berm, stepping carefully to avoid slipping on the road, which is covered in ice. Jack kneels down and shines his light on the mark they are both staring at.

"It looks like a tire hit the berm right here," Jack says. Moving his light along the snow, he touches another mark higher up. "I think the side of the truck hit here and maybe they went over," he concludes, standing again. "Come on."

He climbs the bank, reaching back to give Maggie a hand up. They stand on the ridge of snow, shining their flashlights down the steep slope. At first, Maggie can't see anything except trees and snow, but then her eyes catch on a dark patch far below that isn't the right shape. It is square, and in the forest, square isn't normal. "Look, Jack!" she says, frantically waving her light over the area. "What's that?"

Jack turns his beam to join Maggie's, and together they stare downward.

"I think it's them," Jack says, relief making his voice tremble. "I think that's the door of the pickup. It looks like they got it open and started up but didn't get very far," he continues, playing his light over the tracked-up snow next to the dark patch. "Let's get down there. I'll go first and try to tramp it down, so give me a minute and then follow."

Holding his gun in one hand and the flashlight in the other, Jack steps off the berm into the deep snow, keeping his balance with difficulty on the steep hillside. Very carefully, feeling his way as much as seeing it, Jack heads down, tromping a path as best he can for Maggie to tread. Several times he slips and falls in the first few feet, but he manages to keep both weapon and light up out of the snow and soon finds a method that isn't so precarious, leaning back up the hill and using his weight and the inertia of the snow to slow him down.

Maggie stands atop the bank, watching and shining her light ahead of her husband to help guide him. Jack is about a third of the way down the slope when he calls back to Maggie to follow him. She is about to lower herself onto the path when a prickling sensation up the back of her neck makes her stop and turn back toward the road. She feels as though someone or something is watching her, and a sense of a malign presence strikes her almost as though she has been touched. Staring intently into the night, she shines her light around the area. There is nothing, just the road and the pickup, the trees and the snow. Shivering, Maggie turns back to Jack and looks once more over her shoulder, feeling as uneasy as she can ever remember feeling.

Maggie sits on the berm and slides down into Jack's trail. Recalling how he fell, she moves slowly, making sure her footing is solid before transferring her weight on each step. Trying to shake off the impression of being watched, she concentrates on the task before her, shutting out everything except where her feet should go next.

She is so focused on where she is going, she doesn't realize she has arrived at the bottom until she sees Jack's boots in the circle of her flashlight just before she runs right into him.

"Sorry," she says, gasping for breath. "I was looking down."

"It's okay," Jack answers. "If I boost you up, can you open the door?"

"I'll try," Maggie says, stepping into Jack's outstretched hands and holding onto his shoulder as he lifts her up to the vehicle, which she can now see is Brad's truck lying on its side in the snow. She has to move very carefully as her boots want to slide on the slick surface of the pickup. Bending down, she fits her gloved hand into the door handle, opens the latch, and pulls the door open, shining her light into the cab as she leans over the opening. Two pale faces with round, startled eyes look back at her and Maggie's heart fills with joy.

"They're okay!" she cries to Jack, who is climbing up the truck much as Brad had done earlier in the night.

"We're here," she calls down to the waiting teenagers. "Your dad and I are here, and we're going to get you out."

By this time, Jack is on the side of the truck peering down at his sons. "Are you guys okay?" he asks, his voice tight with emotion.

"Yes, Dad," Brad answers, blinking his eyes in the harsh glare of the flashlight his father is shining on them. "Trent's leg is broken, but other than that, we're fine. Are the wolves gone?" he asks, his face tightening with fear.

"Wolves?"

"Yeah, there were at least two of them out there earlier. I saw one and heard them both howling," Brad replies.

"So did I, Dad," Trent speaks up, raising his head up from the blankets he has pulled up around his neck. "They were really close!"

When Maggie hears this, she realizes the meaning of the unsettling sensation she felt before climbing down the bank. Something has been watching her, and it isn't friendly. Shuddering with memories and horror, she swings her light around the crash site, thinking that every shadow will turn out to be a wolf, but nothing moves and no eyes shine green in the beam of her light.

*Maybe they got tired of waiting*, she tries to tell herself, but part of her knows that isn't the case. Wolves are endlessly patient if they think they are going to get a meal. *Probably the lights and us talking scared them away*, she then reasons with herself. This makes her feel better, and she focuses her attention back to the task at hand.

Jack has lowered himself through the open door and is looking at Trent's leg. Maggie can't make out much in the uncertain light, but she can hear the fear in Trent's voice when he asks, "How bad is it, Dad?"

"Well, it's sure broken," Jack answers, "But once we get you to the hospital, the doctors will be able to fix it up just fine," he goes on, reaching out to ruffle his son's hair.

Trent's body sags with relief, and Maggie can see Brad let out a deep breath as well, letting his father take over the care of Trent.

"Let's get you out of here," Jack says, standing again and looking around the cab. "Brad, can you climb out and help Maggie lift from the top while I push from down here?" he asks.

"Sure, Dad," Brad says, quickly scrambling up out of the cab to kneel on the opposite side of the door. There are only a few inches of surface between the top of the door frame and the curve of the roof, but Brad doesn't seem to notice, and Maggie is struck by his physical grace and strength. She watches while Jack carefully raises Trent up to a standing position and then squats down behind the boy, helping Trent to straddle his bent head.

Once Trent is in position, Jack slowly stands up with Trent on his shoulders, using the dash and the back of the seat for support. Seated upon his father's shoulders, Trent is high enough for Brad and Maggie to reach him easily. With Jack supporting him from below and Brad and Maggie lifting from above, they are able to get Trent into a sitting position on the side of the pickup without causing him too much pain. Jack hands up the boys' backpacks so they will have their school books and looks around the cab once more.

He knows how much it is going to hurt Trent to get him up the hill and is racking his brain for a way to do it without making the boy suffer too much. He doesn't think he can carry him, as Trent weighs too much. He also knows the trail is too narrow and steep for them to carry him up it side by side. Seeing the blankets on the window at his feet gives Jack an idea. He hands them up to Maggie and slides around into the back seat. Feeling carefully behind it, he finds what he is looking for—a hatchet and a package of bungee cords. Jack hands these above him as well and then climbs out, being careful not to bump one of the others and knock them off the truck. He shuts the door beneath him, which gives them all more room to maneuver. Handing the hatchet to Brad, he asks, "Son, can you go cut two straight branches about two inches around and a couple of feet long?"

"Okay, Dad," Brad answers, eager to help in any way possible. He jumps down off the cab and moves cautiously up the packed trail to the nearest fir tree, where he quickly cuts the desired branches and hands them to his father along with the hatchet.

Jack strips the smaller branches off leaving two poles that he lays on either side of Trent's injured leg, which Maggie has wrapped gently in a folded blanket per Jack's instructions. He uses the bungee cords to strap the splints in place. Through it all, Trent never makes a peep, although his face is pale and sweating before Jack is finished.

"Good job, son," Jack says gently, placing his hands on Trent's shoulders and gripping them comfortingly. "You okay?"

"I think so," Trent answers, letting the breath he'd been holding out in a whoosh. "Now what?"

Before Jack can reply, a howl rends the still night, echoing off the trees and mountain slopes. It barely fades when others answer, some to the left of them, some below, and some above. The family perched on the cab of the wrecked pickup listens without making a sound, their heads turning toward the din and their eyes darting into the darkness trying to see where their stalkers might be.

It seems to Maggie to last for several minutes, but it is probably much less than that, before finally stopping. Her skin is crawling, her heart is racing, and she is shaking all over with reaction. It is all she can do to not jump down and start running up the hill toward the road.

Sensing her distress, Jack reaches out and squeezes her numb fingers in his warm ones. His touch is enough to calm her and taking a deep breath, she fights to control her nerves. She catches his eyes over Trent's head and can see the concern in them. The reality of their situation hits her and she knows the boys need her to be strong if they are all going to get safely home. Maggie squares her shoulders and repeats Trent's question. "Now what?"

"Well," Jack answers slowly, thinking it through as he speaks, "I think we can put Trent on a blanket and carry him up the trail. Maggie, you take the gun and your flashlight and go up first. You can walk backward and shine the light for us, and if you see a wolf, shoot it."

"I could hold the other flashlight," Trent offers.

"That's pretty brave, buddy," Jack tells his son, his voice once again tight with emotion. Jack motions for Maggie to hand the boy the other flashlight she is holding. Trent takes the flashlight eagerly, happy for something to distract him from his plight. Jack lifts him up and Maggie and Brad spread the heaviest of the blankets under him. Once Trent is seated on the blanket, Jack helps Maggie down onto the trail. She backs several feet up the hill, shouldering the boys' backpacks, holding the gun in one hand and the light steady on the trio still on the pickup with the other.

Jack grabs a corner of the blanket and spins it around so Trent's back is toward the hill and then he climbs down as well, directing Trent to lie flat and Brad to grab the corners of the blanket toward Trent's feet while he takes a firm grip on the corners at the end by Trent's head. Jack backs up the trail until he is level with Brad, who is still perched on the cab of the pickup, holding the blanket taut between them with Trent in its folds.

Brad slides down the cab, doing his best not to jostle his brother or let go of the blanket. When he is safely on the ground, Jack and Brad start up the hill, carrying the injured boy between them on the blanket.

Trent lies still, shining the flashlight around the trees closest to the trail while Maggie shines her light in front of her down the trail. With Jack's back to her, she isn't sure how much good the light is, but it gives her something to do. The gun is comfortingly heavy in the crook of her arm as she backs up the hill, placing every step with care so she doesn't slip and crash down into Jack and Brad with their precious burden. Maggie periodically shines the light around the forest on both sides of the trail, looking for the flash of eyes or the movement of a gray shadow close to the ground. She still has the sensation of being watched, her skin crawling as she imagines the slinking shape growing closer in the dark.

She is expecting the new howls, but still starts uncontrollably, the light jerking into the gloom under the trees. There are the eyes she has been dreading and, for an instant, fear freezes her in her tracks. An instant is all it takes, and the wolf is gone before Maggie has time to swing the gun up. Answering howls from behind her sound so close Maggie is sure the wolf is in the trail at her back, but when she turns the light up the trail, there is nothing there.

"Jack, we need to hurry," Maggie whispers nervously.

"I know, sweetheart," Jack answers, panting with the effort of carrying Trent up the hill. "We're trying. Go up as fast as you can so you're on flat ground. It'll give you a better shot," Jack advises.

Taking him at his word, Maggie turns and struggles up the trail as quickly as she can, her breath coming hard, the cold biting into her face and causing her eyes to tear. It seems to take forever to reach the berm at the edge of the road, and it is all she can do to pull herself up and over the top.

Shaking with fear, Maggie drops the backpacks, turns, and shines the light back down toward her family. They are about halfway up the slope, Jack with his back to her. She can see Brad's face, creased with effort, and can hear the sounds of their heavy breathing as they work their way up the trail. She swings the light below them and side to side. There, blending into the shadows under a big pine, is a wolf. It is black and sits, panting, looking right at her, seeming to grin mockingly as she stares in horror.

Without stopping to think, Maggie whips the gun up and takes aim through the scope, keeping the flashlight trained on the wolf. Centering the crosshairs on the animal and making sure she is clear of her menfolk, Maggie holds her breath and gently squeezes the trigger. The wolf leaps into the air, yelping, and then falls into a jumbled heap under the tree.

In the silence following the shot, Maggie hears both boys yell out in fright, and then behind her on the road comes a shrill human scream. Maggie whirls around, and there, illuminated by the headlights of Jack's pickup and her car, is Caroline. Maggie stares at her, her brain unable to figure out why the woman is there. Caroline continues to scream, turning in circles on the frozen road in panic.

"Caroline!" Maggie shouts.

Caroline stops screaming and whirling and stares at Maggie. "What happened?" she whimpers.

"We're trying to get the boys back to the road," Maggie answers her. "There are some wolves around." Maggie turns back to the downhill slope and sees that Jack and Brad are almost to the last steep pitch below the berm. "Everyone okay?" she calls.

"Fine," Jack's panting voice answers. "I think you got him."

Just then, Caroline starts screaming again.

Maggie faces her once more, exasperated with the woman's hysterics. This time, however, there is a reason for Caroline's screams. Standing between her and Caroline is the biggest wolf Maggie has seen yet. It is facing Caroline, slunk low and growling, as it advances on the terrified woman. Maggie catches a trace of movement to her left and sees another wolf crouched under a tree at the side of the road, ready to help its pack.

"Caroline, shut up!" Maggie yells. Surprisingly, Caroline does. In the silence, the wolf turns toward Maggie. Calmly, trying not to move too quickly, Maggie again raises the gun to her shoulder and takes careful aim. She can see Caroline in the background behind the animal and knows how dangerous a shot it is, but there is no other choice. Maggie blows out a shaky breath, takes a half-one back in and holds it, then as gently as if it is dynamite, pulls the trigger. The wolf goes down without a sound, and Maggie sees the other one turn and run while her ears are once again assaulted with Caroline's shrieks.

"You almost shot me!" she is yelling in between screams. "How dare you!"

Without speaking, Maggie walks up to Caroline and thrusts the gun into the startled woman's hands. "Hold this," she snaps. "I'm going to help Jack. If you see a wolf, shoot it."

Without waiting for a reaction, Maggie hurries back to the berm with her light, reaching it just in time to see the top of Jack's head rise toward the road. Maggie leans over and grabs part of the blanket, helping to pull the injured boy up to rest on the frozen pile of snow. Breathing harshly from his effort, Jack reaches down and hauls Brad the rest of the way up, boosting him over the obstacle into the road, where he lies exhausted. Jack clambers up and pulls Maggie into a rib-crushing hug. They are both shaking and trying to catch their breath.

"It's okay," Jack is murmuring over and over to his wife. "It's okay now."

After a few seconds, Jack releases her and helps Brad up from the ground, hugging his son tightly and rocking him back and forth. "You did great, son," he tells him. "I'm so proud of you."

Meanwhile, Trent is sitting on the frozen snow bank watching everyone. "What about me?" he asks plaintively.

Laughing, they all turn to him and envelope him in a group hug, being careful not to bump his splinted leg. Jack picks him up in his arms and carries him to the waiting pickup while Brad races ahead to open the door. Jack sets Trent down on the back seat then slides him into the sheltering warmth, shutting him safely inside. Drooping with exhaustion, the three look at each other, and Jack reaches to put an arm around both their shoulders, holding them close to him. Maggie snuggles into her husband's warm, strong embrace and gives a silent prayer of thanksgiving. Just then, their pleasant triumph is interrupted by an unhappy voice.

"What about me?" Caroline asks angrily, unconsciously parroting her younger son. "Do you know THAT WOMAN almost shot me?" she screeches. "Trent is *my* son, and you didn't even let me talk to him!" She stomps toward the trio, who watch her advance without replying.

Finally, Jack says, "He's in the truck if you want to talk to him." He still stands with his arms around Brad and Maggie right outside the pickup door.

Caroline looks uncertainly at the three of them and stops her furious march, realizing they will need to move before she can open the door. Rather than ask, she spins on her heel and hurries around the hood of the pickup. They stand and watch her as she walks to the other side and opens the back door to speak to Trent.

After a few seconds, she comes back to face them. "My son is hurt," she announces importantly. "He needs to get to a hospital."

"I know that, Caroline," Jack answers in a solemn tone. "We just packed him out of a car wreck." He waits patiently to see what else she has to say, knowing she isn't yet finished.

"Well," she huffs. "Someone could have told me! When we get back to town, I'm filing charges against you!" Here she pauses and points at Maggie, wagging her finger in Maggie's astonished face. "You tried to kill me!"

Jack is cold, tired, worried about his son, and still trying to wrap his head around having almost been attacked by a wolf pack, and seeing his ex-wife chastising Maggie, who just saved everyone's lives, is too much.

He lets go of Brad and Maggie, reaches out abruptly and grabs Caroline's wagging finger. Holding it in an iron grip, he takes a step toward her

"Don't you ever, ever, point your finger at my wife again," Jack says very softly, leaning over the defiant woman in front of him. "You are causing nothing but more trouble on a night when we have had way too much of it." He pauses, looking around at the scene, the lights of Caroline's car beyond the crumpled wolf, the angle of its dead body, and the ejected cartridge that shows where Maggie was standing when she shot. "It's obvious," he continues, "that Maggie killed that wolf just before it attacked you. She saved your life; she didn't try to take it." Dropping her hand as if it is hot, Jack steps back to Brad and Maggie and says, "Let's get out of here."

"You take the front," Maggie says to Brad. "You need to get warm, and I'll keep Trent's leg from bouncing around." The three of them climb into the warm vehicle, leaving Caroline still standing in the road with her hand in the air and her mouth open. Realizing they are leaving, she rushes to the pickup and pounds on Jack's window.

Giving a huge weary sigh, he rolls it down. "What now?" he asks.

"Trent is my son, and I should be the one to ride with him," she announces. "Just ask him. I'm sure he wants me."

⁓⁓⁓

Trent looks at Maggie with panic in his eyes. "Please, Maggie," he begs. "Don't let her in here. She'll talk all the way, and I'm so tired." As he says this, his eyes fill with tears, and Maggie can see the effort it's costing him to continue to put on a brave front for them.

Maggie leans around and touches Jack's shoulder. "Jack," she says softly. "Trent doesn't want her. Let's go."

Jack looks out the window at Caroline and says, "If you want to see Trent, meet us at the hospital. I wouldn't stand out here too long," he continues. "There are usually more than two wolves in a pack."

Jack rolls up the window, puts the pickup in gear, and quickly turns around in the road, leaving Caroline standing in the snow screaming at them.

As they drive away, Maggie looks back and watches her run to her car and get in, and then all her attention is centered on Trent. "How's the leg?" she asks, keeping her voice casual so as to hide from Trent her extreme concern about his injury. She saw his leg earlier when they wrapped the blanket around it and knows it is a serious break. Considering all he has been through, she is actually surprised Trent hasn't gone into shock.

"It hurts, Maggie," Trent answers, trying to keep from crying. "The truck is bouncing it."

"Here, let me help," Maggie says, sliding closer and very gently lifting Trent's leg onto her lap where she carefully but firmly stabilizes the broken limb. As soon as she does, she can see the boy relax, and soon he drifts into a light doze, which is nature's way of protecting wounded children from pain.

# CHAPTER 42

All the way to the hospital Maggie watches Trent, counting his breaths and occasionally checking to make sure he is warm, but the boy never stirs from his sleep. She is grateful he is spared the worst parts of the trip, for the icy road is wash-boarded in places and feels rough even to her. Maggie is still holding at bay the memory of shooting the wolves. It keeps trying to come through and overwhelm her with fright, and she keeps refusing to let it. *Later*, she tells herself. *Later you can fall apart.*

She does feel sort of bad for Caroline, who trails behind in her car. As a mother, she knows she would want to be in the car with her son, but honestly, Caroline never even asked them what was wrong with him, nor did she seem overly concerned with anything except how it might affect her, so Maggie lets it go, resolving to be nice at the hospital no matter what is said.

This proves more difficult than Maggie anticipates, as the first thing Caroline says as she bursts through the curtain to Trent's cubicle is, "Get that woman out of here!" as she motions to Maggie, who is sitting quietly at Trent's side with Jack on the other. "I'm his mother, and I don't want her here!"

Jack turns a steely gaze on Caroline and says, "This isn't about you. This is about Trent and what is best for him." Maggie starts to get up to leave the room, but Jack motions her to stay as he looks at the doctor who is attending to the injured boy. "What would you prefer, Dr. Jones?" he asks courteously.

The nurse who was checking Trent's blood pressure shows the result to the doctor. Shaking his head, the doctor takes Caroline by the arm and politely escorts her from the cubicle explaining that Trent had responded negatively to her presence. He calls a nurse to

305

show Caroline where the waiting room is.

Maggie can hear her wailing clear down the hall, "But I'm his mother! I have a right to stay!" She then hears the nurse's soothing response as they turn the corner and quiet settles back over the emergency room.

"Hey, buddy," Jack says, ruffling Trent's hair. "How's the pain?" The doctor has given Trent pain medication through an IV that was started when they first arrived, and it seems to be taking effect. Once his mother is out of earshot, Trent relaxes, although his eyes are looking a little glassy. The occasional shiver still shakes his gangly frame, but the doctor says he isn't in danger now of going into shock.

"I'm good, Dad," Trent answers, speaking slowly and grinning a little. "Guess Maggie showed those wolves!"

Jack laughs back as he answers, "She sure did, son. Now you know who to take with you in the mountains!"

The doctor finishes his examination and speaks to all of them. Even Brad, who has been loitering listlessly in the corner, comes close to listen. "It's a clean break with very little tissue damage, and it's fairly straight. I'm going to give you just a little more medication, Trent, and when you're asleep, I'm going to set the bone and put a cast on it. When you wake up, it will be all over."

Trent, whose eyes have become large and concerned during this speech, clings to Jack and Maggie's hands. "Can they stay?" he asks.

"Until you go to sleep," the doctor assures him. "Then we'll take you into a different room to put the cast on. Depending on how you feel when you wake up, you may be able to go home tonight."

"Okay," the drowsy boy replies. While the doctor is talking, the nurse has been quietly administering the additional medication, and in no time at all, Trent is deeply asleep.

Jack and Maggie rise from their chairs as the staff wheels out the bed. They gather Brad between them and head for the waiting room.

The nurse says she will come find them when it is over. As they walk down the hallway, Maggie can feel the tremors running through Brad's body and knows he is close to the breaking point. He pulls away from them as they enter the dimly-lit waiting room and goes to a corner seat with his head in his hands.

Caroline, who has been sitting in a chair nearest the door,

looks over at her oldest son but makes no move to go to him. Maggie tilts her head at Jack, indicating she thinks Brad needs him, and Jack leaves her to sit next to Brad.

Putting his large hand on Brad's back, Jack can feel the effort the boy is putting forth to control his emotions. "Just let it go, son," he offers, rubbing the boy's tense shoulders. "It's all over now. Everything is okay."

Brad says something, but it is muffled by his hands, so Jack leans closer to hear him. "It's my fault," Brad says, beginning to cry into his cupped hands. "Trent got hurt because of me."

Jack lets him cry for a minute and then, as Brad regains his composure, pulls him upright and offers him his handkerchief. Brad blows his nose vigorously and wipes his eyes dry with his coat sleeve. Jack, realizing he is also still wearing his coat, shrugs out of the garment, damp from snow and effort, and Brad does the same.

"Better?" Jack asks. Brad nods, not looking at his father. "Why don't you tell me exactly what happened?"

Jack listens while Brad tells him about the deer crossing the road in front of him and sliding into the bank. He describes how it felt tumbling through the air, and Jack feels a bolt of fear strike his heart anew at the thought of how much worse it might have been. When all the words are out and Brad sits looking at his father with his heart in his eyes, Jack pulls Brad close in a hard hug and tells him, "It wasn't your fault, Brad. It was an accident. You did everything you could to avoid it and once it happened, you did everything you could to take care of your brother. There was nothing different you could have done, so stop blaming yourself. I'm very proud of you and very lucky to have a son who reacted so well in a bad situation." Jack can feel Brad relax in his hold and knows he has found the right thing to say.

They straighten up, and then Maggie is there offering them both hot chocolate she made while they were talking. Jack takes her hand and pulls her down to sit beside him, her smile warming him as much as the drink she brings.

The three wait together for the procedure to be over, talking now and then, but mostly just taking comfort from each other's nearness. Maggie realizes the memory of shooting the wolves is fading now and no longer has the power to dominate her emotions. She is able to think calmly about it and answer Jack and Brad's questions. They didn't see her shoot the second wolf on the road and listen in fascination as she tells the story.

Maggie can see Caroline also listening from her seat by the door, but she doesn't acknowledge their presence in the slightest. Jack tells Brad how he knew to look for them and of his strong feeling something was wrong.

Brad and Maggie shake their heads in wonder, and Maggie again sends a prayer of thanksgiving winging above. She is so grateful everyone is okay. Beneath that is the relief of knowing things are good between her and Jack again. She knows they might need to have a difficult conversation once this crisis is over, but she is confident all will be well.

Finally, the doctor steps into the waiting room and everyone gathers around. "Trent did fine," the doctor says. "I was able to set the leg the first try. His leg is in a cast, and he's resting comfortably. If his vital signs continue as strong as they've been so far, he can go home in an hour."

Jack thanks the doctor and shakes his hand, and the man leaves the room.

Caroline glares at Jack and Maggie. "I'll never forgive you for this, Jack," she hisses. "You let my son get hurt, and then you wouldn't even let me in the room with him." Looking at them through narrowed eyes, she says maliciously, "You know, I may rethink this custody thing. Maybe you aren't a fit parent."

The tension is broken by Maggie's laughter. "Oh, come on, Caroline. You may pretend to want the boys to live with you, but the reality of taking care of them is more than you can handle. I'm sure you love them, but really, how would you take care of them day after day? You don't even have a home."

Angered even more by this, Caroline swells into a fury, fairly bristling with indignation. "How dare you!" she explodes, but then words fail her, and she sits back down abruptly.

Maggie pulls up a chair to face her. "I dare because I love Brad and Trent as much as you do," she says in a quiet voice, looking Caroline in the eye. "The boys live with us and from tonight on, you don't. You are welcome to spend time with them at your home, but that's it. I don't know why I didn't think of it sooner, but I've thought of it now. Here," she says, pulling something from her pocket and enfolding it in Caroline's surprised hand. "Here is the key to my house in town. You can live there for free for a month, which will give you time to get a job and start paying rent or find somewhere else to go. Why don't you go to the ranch and pack your stuff? Maybe Trent will be awake when you get back."

Caroline stares at Maggie with dawning comprehension. Moving stiffly but still without speaking, she rises from her chair, looking at the key in her hand and back at Maggie. "You don't have to be nice to me," she whispers, "not after how I acted."

"I'm not being nice to you," Maggie replies dryly. "I'm saving my family."

Caroline nods, then turns and walks away. Maggie stands up as Jack and Brad step nearer, and the three of them watch Caroline until she turns the corner.

"That's a brilliant idea," Jack says, fairly bubbling over with enthusiasm. "Are you sure you want her in your house, though?" he questions. "She's liable to leave it a mess."

"It's just a house," Maggie answers. "My home is with you and the boys at the ranch. That's the place where I don't want her."

Jack pulls Maggie close, examining her face intently. "I'm sorry, Maggie," he says, "Sorry for allowing Caroline to invade our home and our relationship. I know her well enough to know she was going to cause trouble, and I let her stay anyway."

Taking a deep breath, Maggie says, "There's nothing to be sorry for, Jack. I let her in just as much as you did, and then I didn't trust you when I should have. Please, forgive me."

"Oh, you silly woman," Jack says, holding her even tighter. "I love you so much." He bends to kiss her, the two of them completely forgetting about Brad who makes a gagging sound and thoughtfully turns his back on them.

Maggie responds, letting her kiss tell Jack how much she missed him and loves him and wants to be home with him. At last, Jack draws back, leaving her warm and breathless, and they sit down on the uncomfortable waiting room chairs next to Brad.

A half-hour later, the nurse comes in and tells them Trent is awake and asking for them, so they troop off to his room. He is sitting up in bed, drinking through a straw from a 7-Up can with his broken leg in a cast and propped up on pillows. His face breaks into a grin when he sees them.

"Hey, guys! You wanna sign my cast?" he asks, gesturing at his leg. "The nurse gave me a marker."

"Sure," Brad teases. "I'll just write, 'To the dumbest brother ever'. That ought to do it!" Seeing Trent start to droop, Brad says, "Seriously, man, you were totally brave out there. Way to go." He takes the marker from Trent's outstretched hand and signs the new cast with a flourish.

Jack and Maggie follow suit and stand back to survey their handiwork. "Just wait until I get back to school," Trent says, a blissful look on his face. "All the girls will want to write on it! Hey, can I get something to eat?"

Maggie shakes her head at the twists and turns of a teenage boy's thoughts and answers, "Of course. Jack, maybe you and Brad could go get pizzas before the pizza place closes. It's almost 9:00. Better get two, because I know how much you boys eat!"

Jack agrees, so he and Brad gather their coats and head out to the pizza parlor, leaving Maggie alone with Trent. She sits in the chair beside him while he fusses with the remote control for the television and moves the head of his bed up and down a few times. Finally, the boy puts down the remote and looks straight at Maggie. She knows he has something important to tell her, so she sits quietly, smiling back at him and waiting.

"Maggie, do you know what I kept thinking about out there?" he asks. "I kept thinking that I wanted Dad to come and get me, and I wanted you there to give me a hug and tell me it was going to be okay. And then you both came and it was okay, just like I wanted. I prayed, Maggie. I never did that before today, but I prayed hard that someone would find us. God must have listened because you did. You know what else I prayed about? That you would stay and be my mom forever and not be mad at Dad anymore."

"God does listen," Maggie answers, wiping tears from her eyes. "You and Brad are safe, and I'm going to stay and be your mom forever if that's what you want. I love you, Trent." She stands and gives Trent a hug, feeling his young, strong body in her arms and smelling his special boy smell, trying very hard to stop crying.

When she pulls away, Trent also wipes his eyes while she pretends not to notice. The two sit in companionable silence and watch a basketball game while they wait for the others to return.

"Maggie," Trent asks presently. "Where is my mother?"

"She went back to the ranch to pack her stuff," Maggie tells him. "She's going to be staying at my house in town, so you can stop by and see her after school whenever you want."

"That's a relief," Trent says. "To tell the truth, it was weird having her back at home. Is she going to come see me again tonight?"

"She should be on her way back to town now," Maggie answers.

Sure enough, by the time Jack and Brad return with the pizzas and everyone has a hot, greasy, slice on their plate, Caroline walks in the door of the hospital room.

"Hi, Mom," Trent exclaims. "Want some pizza?"

"If it's not too much trouble," Caroline says, walking toward the bed. Maggie tactfully moves toward the doorway to let Caroline have a spot next to Trent. "How are you, darling?"

"I'm great," Trent says. "I can go home soon, I think. How are you?"

"Hungry," Caroline answers, smiling at her son. Brad hands her a plateful of pizza, and she perches on the side of the bed and eats with the rest of them.

Maggie watches, monitoring the mood of the room and the body language of the two boys. She feels as protective now with Caroline in the room as she had on the mountain earlier when the wolves were threatening and is ready to intervene if Caroline says anything out of line. Fortunately, the woman behaves herself and soon the pizza is gone, the trash thrown away.

Jack is signing discharge papers while Maggie helps Trent put on the oversized sweat pants the hospital provides since his jeans won't go over the bulky cast.

Brad ties Trent's shoe on his good foot before helping his brother stand up to try out his new crutches. Of course, Trent is a natural on the crutches, quickly getting the hang of it and zooming around the room like a maniac. Maggie has been worrying about him going up and down the stairs to his room, but after seeing how well he does, she is able to discard that concern.

Out in the frozen parking lot, the boys give quick hugs to

311

Caroline and get into Jack's pickup, this time with Brad in the back with Trent and Maggie in the front passenger seat. They lead Caroline to Maggie's house and wait outside while Maggie goes in and shows Caroline where the thermostat to the furnace is.

The last stop in town is at the church so Maggie can get her car. Shivering with the cold and trying to see through the small hole thawed on the frosted windshield, Maggie follows the pickup toward home. It is the first time she has been alone since Jack showed up at the church earlier in the evening.

She feels unsettled and uneasy at first, remembering what it was like to travel up this same road, not knowing if the boys were all right, but gradually the feeling gives way to relief and contentment as she thinks about walking in the door and knowing Caroline won't be there. Cranking the radio up, Maggie sings along, losing herself in the music and not noticing her surroundings.

She is startled to see Jack's brake lights come on ahead of her and slows down to park behind him on the side of the road. In the darkness, she hadn't realized they have come upon the same corner where the wreck occurred. She watches from the car as Jack gets out and goes into the road where the dead wolf still lies. Picking up the heavy body, he carries it to the pickup and puts it in the back. Maggie shudders to see its huge head, the teeth permanently fixed in a snarl, hanging limply as her husband lifts it up and over the side. She knows the animal is dead, but she doesn't like seeing it, mostly because it reminds her of what a dangerous spot they were in not that long ago. She is glad when Jack closes the door and starts driving again and even more glad when the four of them walk through the front door.

"Home, sweet home," Jack remarks as he hangs his coat in the utility room and helps Trent take his off while he tries not to drop the crutches.

"You need a bath, young man," Maggie orders. "I'll run it, and then your dad can help you get in without falling down or getting your cast wet." She hurries to the bathroom and turns the water on, laying a folded towel on the side of the tub for Trent to rest his leg on while Jack stirs the coals in the stove and adds wood to get the fire going again.

It is still bitter cold outside, and Maggie knows Jack will have to go back out soon to patrol the cattle. Brad settles in next to the stove with his homework while Trent is taking a bath, yawning periodically as he works. As soon as Trent is done, Brad goes to take a shower, and Jack helps Trent find some pajamas that will work with the cast. As she predicted earlier, Trent has no trouble with the stairs, hopping nimbly up them as if the crutches are part of his body.

Maggie has been puttering around putting things to rights and making sure the house is the way she likes it to be. She feels as though she is reclaiming her territory, and it feels great. Soon, both boys are ready for bed, and she and Jack go up to say goodnight. Maggie is on the verge of tears again with gratitude for having them both safely home, and she can tell by the tightness in Jack's voice that he feels the same way. She squeezes his hand tightly as they walk back downstairs together.

"I could use a shower, too," Jack remarks. "I was sweating something awful hauling Trent up that hill. Want to come wash my back?" Gently, he rubs her lower vertebra, suggesting with his touch what he wants to do in the shower. Smiling, Maggie agrees, and the two lock the rest of the world outside the steamy shower where, lost in each other's eyes, they renew their love for one another in a way as old as time.

Late that night, Jack lies awake with his sleeping wife in his arms, savoring the feel of her soft, warm skin against his and thinking about the events of the evening. He is so glad to have her back home and so grateful the boys are okay. He shivers to think how badly it could have gone.

He remembers looking up over his shoulder at Maggie as the wolf snarled at them from under the tree, hoping she had a clear shot and the courage to take it. He needn't have worried, he thinks now, about Maggie taking care of things. She helped him find the boys, splinted Trent's leg, led them up the bank and covered their ascent, even protected Caroline and found a long-term solution to Caroline's housing issue. *Yes, indeed*, Jack reflects as he drifts off to sleep, *Maggie knew what to do.*

Catherine Bridwell

# EPILOGUE

Maggie sits at her desk, listening with half her attention on the sound of the children getting on the school bus and also trying to focus on grading the papers in front of her. She needs to finish in the next thirty minutes so she will be ready when Jack and Trent pick her up to go to the track meet in New Plymouth to watch Brad compete. Gazing into the distance, she thinks fondly of the boys and of Jack, missing him even though she has only been apart from him since this morning.

The time between the night of the wreck and now seems to have passed in the blink of an eye to Maggie. With two members of its pack dead, the wolves decided to move on and left the valley as swiftly and silently as they arrived, making Jack's nightly patrol unnecessary. He only checked the cows once a night from then until the last calf was born.

The February thaw broke the cold spell that had such a grip on the area, and then there was rain and mud and wind, but in no time at all, spring was here. Jack and Maggie traded their bleacher seats at basketball games for ones trackside as they traveled around to watch Brad and Trent at their respective meets.

Jack spent more time at the other wintering grounds for the cattle, helping prepare to put the cattle back on pasture and back on the mountain after branding. Maggie took a day off work and the boys were allowed to miss school so they could help brand the new calves and vaccinate all the cattle. It was a long day, especially since Maggie was expected to feed the hungry crew at lunch, but she loved every minute of it (although the lingering smell of burnt hair was something she could do without). The next day was even better as they hauled the cattle to the various spring pastures and drove some up into the mountains on horseback from central corrals. Maggie was sore the next day, but getting up into the hills in the fresh spring air with her husband and stepsons was exhilarating.

Now she sits staring into the afternoon sunlight, grading finished, finally letting herself think of what she has been avoiding all day. Today is the anniversary of the day Clark was killed, and Maggie has felt the echo of pain all day, sliding along her bones and reaching into her stomach, making her jumpy and vague. Now she invites the pain in and lets herself feel it again, remembering everything that happened. Tears fill her eyes as she thinks about her children and their anguish at losing their father, but for her, it seems less sharp. *Time does have a way of healing,* she marvels.

She suspects Jack has a great deal to do with it as well. "Thank you, Clark," she whispers. "Thank you for loving me and for helping me to let go so I could love someone else."

A breath of air brushes across Maggie's neck, making her shiver, and she knows Clark is answering, "You're welcome," as he had so many times in their lives together.

Maggie bows her head in a brief prayer for her first husband and resolutely comes to her feet. She has a track meet to go to and a life to live with a man she loves, and she doesn't want to waste a second of it.

# ABOUT THE AUTHOR

Catherine Bridwell was born and raised in the small town of Council, Idaho, and lived there until 2018, raising her family and working as a public school business manager for the past 35 years. She is also a financial consultant, specializing in public school finance. She is a participant of the Idaho Creative Authors Network (ICAN) events and in 2017 was given the ICAN award for best children's short story. She currently lives in Jerome, Idaho. This is her first novel.

Catherine Bridwell

Made in the USA
Middletown, DE
23 March 2021